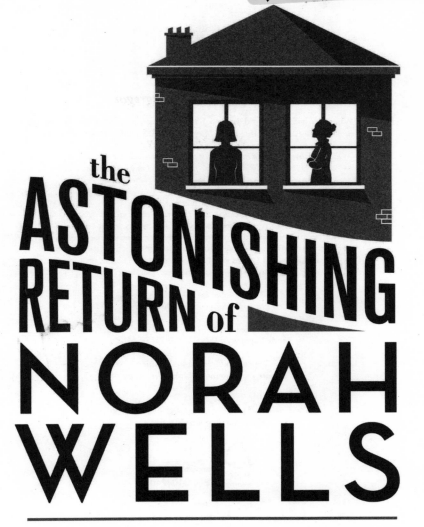

the
ASTONISHING
RETURN of
NORAH
WELLS

VIRGINIA MACGREGOR

sphere

SPHERE

First published in Great Britain in 2016 by Sphere

1 3 5 7 9 10 8 6 4 2

Copyright © Virginia Macgregor 2016

The moral right of the author has been asserted.

Lyrics to 'What a Wonderful World' by Bob Thiele (as George Douglas) and George David
Weiss. © Carlin American Inc. BMG Management US, LLC. Imagen US, LLC.

A CIP catalogue record for this book
is available from the British Library.

Hardback ISBN 978-0-7515-5420-5
Trade Paperback ISBN 978-0-7515-5421-2

Typeset in Granjon by M Rules
Printed and bound in Great Britain by
Clays Ltd, St Ives plc

Papers used by Sphere are from well-managed forests
and other responsible sources.

MIX
Paper from
responsible sources
FSC
www.fsc.org   FSC® C104740

Sphere
An imprint of
Little, Brown Book Group
Carmelite House
50 Victoria Embankment
London EC4Y 0DZ

An Hachette UK Company
www.hachette.co.uk

www.littlebrown.co.uk

To my beloved daughter, Tennessee Skye

ACKNOWLEDGEMENTS

Thank you to my agent, Bryony Woods, for championing my stories. Thank you to Manpreet Grewal, my editor, for helping me polish my novels until they shine. Thank you to the whole team at Little, Brown – Emma, Kirsteen, Thalia, Zoe, Andy, Jack – for bringing *The Astonishing Return of Norah Wells* to the world. Thank you to my writing buddies Helen Dahlke, Jane Cooper, Charlie Penny and Jo Seldon. Thank you, Richard, for making the best coffee and for being one of the loveliest people I know. Thank you Vi and Seb, for being there, like Louis. Thank you to my incredible nanny, Samantha Pittick, for loving my little girl and looking after her so well while I write. Thank you, Mama, for reading my first drafts, for sharing my stories with the world and for believing in me as a writer. Thank you to my late auntie, Marina du Fontenioux, for building me a place to write when I was nine years old and for championing my novels, even in your last days. Thank you Tennessee Skye, my gorgeous little girl, for making me fall in love with the world all over again. And thank you Hugh, my first reader, my best friend and the love of my life.

[From below comes the noise of a door slamming.]

Henrik Ibsen, *A Doll's House*

Dear Adam,

I'm sorry.

I have to go.

I love you. Tell Ella and Willa I love them too. And take care of Louis.

If you need help, ask Fay, she'll know what to do.

Please don't try to find me.

Norah

The world is waking up. Or it's trying to, anyway.

It's waking up in the small town of Holdingwell.

It's waking up on Willoughby Street.

It's waking up in Number 77, the tall red-brick house with scaffolding that stretches up to the roof.

At the top of the house, dawn tugs at a teenage girl. She rubs her eyes, sticky with the soot of make-up. Her bed is littered with A4 paper; strips of neon highlighter smudge the words. At the foot of her bed sit a pair of battered running shoes. The girl sinks deeper under her duvet and prays to the alarm on her phone: *Just give me a few more minutes . . .*

On the landing, a little girl hovers outside her father's bedroom. She spent the night out here, comforted by his sleeping body on the other side of the door. They've made a deal: no more sneaking in in the middle of the night, not unless it gets really bad. *If you don't pander to them, the dreams will go away,* says her father. *You need to train them, like we trained Louis.* But the little girl isn't sure. She's never heard of anyone who could train a ghost.

On the other side of the door, the father reaches out for the woman he loves. Nothing but cool, empty sheets. He rubs his eyes and reaches for his glasses, and listens to the house waking up.

A bark from the kitchen.

His little girl's footsteps on the landing.

His teenage daughter's alarm.

In the tall red-brick house, a big dog lies heavily in his den under the stairs, his fur as curly as an old lady's perm. He drools, his mouth slack with sleep. He smells a shift in the air. He's smelt it all night, weaving between dreams of lampposts and the Chihuahuas from across the street and the bone he's going to get tonight because it's Friday.

Across town, in the Pediatric Ward of Holdingwell General, The Mother Who Stayed washes her hands. She rubs her palms, scrubs under her nails, and laces her fingers under the scalding water. Her raw skin flushes pink and she wonders whether one day she'll rub so many cells off her hands her skin will give way to flesh and bone. She closes her eyes and releases a long breath to ease the nausea. She thinks of the May bank holiday – a whole weekend away from the hospital. Sleep. Peace. Home.

Back on Willoughby Street, two old ladies lift their net curtains and look at the tall red-brick house. On the doorstep, under the full bloom of a cherry tree, they see The Mother Who Left put down her trumpet case and look up at the house she hasn't seen for six years.

FRIDAY MORNING

Willa

Six-year-old Willa presses her nose to her bedroom window. She looks down through the scaffolding at the front garden.

The clatter of the recycling box on the paving stones drew her to the window. Sometimes, the clink of a jam jar tells Willa that a wild animal has come looking for food. There are more wild animals on Willoughby Street than most people realise: crows that swoop down for trays of chips from the kebab van and fat sewer rats with their skinny tails and otters with their old-man heads that duck in and out of the lake in Holdingwell Park. And Willa's favourite: the foxes that stalk through the garden at night – flashes of red like they're on fire.

Mrs Fox will be there for her birthday on Sunday, Willa can feel it. Mrs Fox and her new cubs. And that will make it the best birthday ever.

But on this Friday morning, Willa doesn't see any of the wild animals she loves. Instead, she looks down at the long red hair of a woman who stands a few feet away from the front door. The woman stares up at the windows of the house as though she's looking for someone. Willa catches her eye and smiles; the woman takes a step back and bows her head.

With his big grey muzzle, Louis nudges open the bedroom door and lumbers over to Willa's feet. He knows he's not allowed upstairs, but that's only when Mummy's watching, and Mummy's at work. Willa bends down and kisses his big furry nose. Louis is not a fox or any other wild animal, but Willa still loves him more than anything in the world.

'Willa, we're late!' Ella, Willa's fourteen-year-old sister, crashes into the bedroom in a cloud of sweet perfume.

Willa loves the smell and she loves the big yellow bottle in the shape of a trophy that sits on Ella's bedside table: it's called *Shalimar*, which means strong and beautiful – that's how Willa thinks of Ella.

'Come on, Willa, I've got a maths test this morning.'

Ella never used to care about tests, not until she was made to repeat a year. *She's going through a bad patch*, Daddy said.

Mummy called a family meeting so they could all help Ella, but Ella never showed up.

'Willa?'

Willa doesn't move. There's something about the woman with the leggings, the baggy jumper, the wheelie suitcase and the black music case that makes her want to stare for a bit longer.

Miss Rose Pegg, one of the twins from across the road, steps out of her front door with a watering can. A Chihuahua yaps at her feet.

'Yoo-hoo,' she calls over to the woman on the doorstep.

But the woman on the doorstep doesn't turn round.

Weird.

'What are you looking at?' Ella picks up Willa's school bag and stuffs it with Willa's *Fantastic Mr Fox* lunch box.

She comes over to the window and eases the bag over Willa's shoulders.

'Why's she not ringing the bell?' Willa adjusts the straps of her backpack so that it sits high on her shoulder blades.

Ella leans into the window and sucks in her breath.

Louis puts his paws on the windowsill and growls.

'What is it?' Willa asks.

Ella stands back.

'Ella?'

'It's no one.'

But Ella's face doesn't look like it's no one.

Willa feels a crash in her tummy like when a baddie in a film cuts the cord of a lift and it plummets a hundred floors in one big whoosh.

As she looks back down at the doorstep Willa scratches the star-shaped scar under her eye. It's hot and itchy. She doesn't care what Ella says – the woman definitely doesn't look like a no one.

Ella

@findingmum

Best Day Ever: Mum's Come Home! #dreamcometrue

Willa turns away from the window and says:

'She's got my hair.'

'Who?'

'No One Woman.'

Ella switches off her phone.

'It's red, like mine.' Then Willa peers over Ella's shoulder. 'Who were you texting?'

'I was tweeting.'

'What were you tweeting?'

Ella shoves her phone in the pocket of her school blazer. What's she going to tell Willa? She thought she'd have time to prepare her, to explain who Mum was and where she'd been and why Fay was pretending to be her mum and why Dad and Fay acted like a couple when Dad was still married to Mum.

'Nothing. It's for my project, Willa.'

She glances out of the window again. Mum looks smaller than she remembers. And there are grey bits in her hair.

Ella kneels in front of Willa and zips up her fleece.

Louis has still got his paws on the windowsill. He must remember Mum too. He loved her as much as Ella did and Dad did – and Willa did, even though Willa was too small to remember. Ella pats Louis's paws: 'Get down from there, Louis.'

Louis barks, then slumps down at Willa's feet.

'The Missing Persons Project?' Willa asks.

'Yes.'

'Have you found a missing person?'

'Sort of. Come on, Willa, we've got to go.'

This is what Ella wants to do: tear downstairs, pull open the front door, throw her arms around Mum and tell her how much she's missed her and how much she loves her and how glad she is that she's home and she wants to ask her where she's been and whether she's okay.

Try to be a bit less impulsive. Try to think things through more. Fay's pep talk at their family meeting last Sunday night. Her advice for handling Mr Pain-in-the-Backside Stuckton, Ella's maths teacher. Fay was a pain the backside too. Mainly when she was right. God, Fay – what was she going to do when she found out Mum was home?

Ella had imagined Mum's return a zillion times and it had never been as messy as this. She takes a breath. *Stay calm. Think things through. Christ, be like Fay.*

On the way out, she'll shoot Mum a look to show her she can't talk because of Willa. And then she'll come home as soon as she can. When Ella was little, she and Mum only had to look at each other to know what the other was thinking. That wouldn't have changed, would it?

'Come on.' Ella takes Willa's hand and yanks her down the stairs. Louis follows them.

'Shouldn't we say goodbye to Dad?' Willa asks.

'We're late.'

If they say goodbye to Dad then he'll walk them to the door and he'll see Mum and he'll give everything away and Willa won't understand.

'What about your trumpet?'

Ella's trumpet is in the kitchen. With Dad.

'My lesson's been cancelled.' Another lie.

'Your lesson's never cancelled.'

'Well, it has been.'

'Weird.'

Ella loves Willa more than anyone, but God she can be annoying.

'Come on, Willa.'

Willa kneels down and puts her arms around Louis's big belly. 'See you later, Louis.'

Later. By the time Willa comes home from school, her whole world will have changed. And from the way Louis is looking up at Ella, it's obvious he knows it too.

Norah

Norah stands outside her old home and looks up at the scaffolding that stretches up the front of the house. The roof's covered in a sheet of blue tarpaulin, its corners held down by bricks. So it's still not fixed.

She listens to the sounds coming through the open window.

A squeal of laughter and feet stomping down the stairs and Adam calling from the kitchen:

'Get a move on, girls, or you'll miss the bus.' A stronger voice than she remembers.

The front door flies open and a little girl with a jagged fringe and a copper bob steps out.

Norah holds her breath. *She looks just like me*, she thinks. *The same red hair. The same transparent skin and brown eyes.* When Norah left, Willa still looked like Adam – blue eyes, fine blonde hair. They say that all babies look like their fathers, that it's an evolutionary trick to keep men from abandoning their families: when fathers see themselves reflected in their babies, they swell with the pride of ownership. Maybe one day evolution will catch up and recognise that mothers, too, have to be persuaded to stay.

She wants to reach out and take Willa's hand but Ella pushes her forward. For a second Ella looks up and catches Norah's eye; she gives her a nod, smiles and then looks down again.

Norah feels her eldest daughter's name rising in her throat, but before it reaches her mouth it disappears. She moves out of their way.

When Willa gets to the gate, she looks back at Norah. Norah's chest contracts; there's a scar under her left eye.

'Come on,' Ella says, yanking her away, and the two girls skip through the gate.

Willa runs ahead of Ella and posts something through the Miss Peggs' letter box and then the two of them disappear down Willoughby Street.

Norah lets out a breath. She didn't expect a great reunion; she knew things would be hard when she came back, but just skittering past with no words?

'Ella – you've forgotten your trumpet!' Adam comes out swinging a black case.

He never helped to get Ella ready for school, didn't have a clue about timetables and routines. On the rare occasion when she put him in charge, she would come back to find the house in a mess, Ella forgotten at school. When it was just the two of them their bohemian muddling-through hadn't mattered, but kids changed things – or it should have.

I love you, isn't that enough? Adam used to say when she asked him to help. Some couples fall apart because their children become their world; Adam barely noticed the girls.

Standing on the bottom step, Norah looks up at him. He's taller than she remembers. Straighter too. A navy suit, his blond hair tamed into a side parting, grey creeping in by his temples, his chin clean-shaven. And his glasses have gone.

Would she have recognised him if she'd walked past him on the street?

His eyes dart between Norah and the pavement. 'You saw the girls?'

Norah nods. 'Yes. Briefly. They were in a rush.'

'Did you say anything?'

11

'No.'

His shoulders relax.

Norah looks at the trumpet case in his hands. 'So she plays?'

When Norah left, eight-year-old Ella would follow her around squeaking out tunes on her yellow plastic trumpet, a gift from her godmother, Fay. She'd beg Norah to give her lessons and to take her to concerts. *One day I'll be as good as you, won't I?* she'd asked.

Adam's brow contracts. Has he forgotten what she looks like? Should she introduce herself? Offer to shake his hand? Stretch out her cheek for a kiss?

Hi, I'm your wife.

I walked out on you.

I'm back.

How've you been?

Should she say *sorry*, to get the ball rolling?

As Norah steps forward Adam stumbles back through the doorway. Still clumsy.

He clears his throat. 'She's not a natural.' He looks down at Ella's trumpet case. 'Not like you. But she's trying.'

'And Willa.' Norah touches the skin under her left eye. 'She's got a scar.'

'Yes.'

She waits for him to expand, but he keeps standing in the doorway.

'Can I come in?' Norah asks.

'Come in?' Adam looks over Norah's shoulder, as if he hopes to find the answer coming up the road.

'Yes. Into the house.'

Into the house they bought together.

Adam sways from foot to foot; she remembers this tic.

What if he says no? What if he leaves her standing there? I'd deserve that, she thinks.

'Right. Yes. I suppose so.' He nods and steps aside.

'Thanks.' Every word that comes out of her mouth sounds so *small*.

The house smells of polish and plug-in air-freshener. The threadbare carpet has been replaced with wood flooring – golden and full of light; wallpaper, covered in peonies. *Softer than roses*, someone had once told her. *No thorns*. Covering every bit of wall space in the hall are photographs of the girls. Taking photographs that made them look like a family – the one fatherly duty Adam had lived up to.

She scans the photos taken since she left. Ella on stage with her trumpet; Ella and Willa on the swings in Holdingwell Park, kicking their legs so high it looks as though they're about to take off; Willa hugging Louis in front of a Christmas tree; Ella grinning over a birthday cake with ten candles; Ella holding up a pair of muddy running shoes. There's one picture that makes Norah stop walking: Willa blowing on the filaments of a dandelion clock. The scar's there, larger and redder than the one she saw this morning. It must have happened when she was a baby. Norah feels sick. It's the thing a mother fears most, isn't it? Her child getting hurt.

Norah swallows hard. *My baby got hurt, and I wasn't here.*

Norah blinks the thought away.

'These are good,' she says, scanning the photographs.

He blushes and shoots his fingers through his hair, messing up his side parting.

'They're just snaps.' He keeps walking.

Norah keeps looking around.

Even the dimensions of the rooms have shifted, nudged by new pieces of furniture. There'd been a time when Norah could have walked through her home with her eyes shut. Now she'd need a guide.

'I like what you've done with the place,' she mumbles as she follows Adam into the kitchen.

'It's not me—' he starts.

'Not you?'

'The house—' He doesn't finish the sentence.

No. She didn't think he'd be responsible for the changes.

Adam puts down Ella's trumpet case and picks up his briefcase from a white marble counter.

Norah remembers the peeling paint, the wobbly kitchen table, the damp under the stairs, the stained carpets, the leak in the roof of the attic she used as a studio.

One of the walls of the kitchen is filled with framed crayon drawings: all animals, a wobbly *Willa* signed in the corners. Adam wouldn't have done that – or the old Adam wouldn't. When Ella was little Norah put up her pictures around the house with Blu-Tack and they'd stay there, their edges curling, eventually falling to the floor and leaving a small crater where the Blu-Tack had ripped off the paint.

In the middle of the table sits a photography book, along with a notepad and a sheet of paper with *The Open University* as a header across the top, and next to them an expensive camera plugged into a laptop.

When they'd met, Adam had worked for his father's photography business. It was old-style: manual cameras and dark rooms and prints. He'd loved taking pictures of Norah. *My favourite subject,* he'd say. And then the business went bust and he found himself without qualifications.

My dad's been replaced by a camera phone, he told her on the day his dad closed the shop.

14

But Adam had a good eye. *There's always room for a photographer with real talent*, she'd said to him.

And they'd talked about it, him taking it seriously, doing a course . . . but that too had got lost along the way.

She turns to face Adam. 'So, you've got a new job?'

'Sorry?'

'The suit?'

The man she used to know spent his days in the navy overalls issued to workers at the recycling plant. It didn't matter how many times she washed them, she couldn't get rid of the smell.

Adam pulls at his tie and it draws in close to his throat. She notices the shaving rash by his collar and wants to reach out and touch his skin.

'Oh – not new, no,' he says. 'I've been working as a manager at the plant for four years.'

A manager. She hadn't thought he had it in him. Employees. Pay slips. Spreadsheets. The confidence to stand up in front of people and tell them what to do. No, her Adam wouldn't have wanted that responsibility. *Her Adam.* Did he even exist any more?

Adam checks his watch. 'I have to go to work.'

'Of course.'

She'd hoped for this: a few hours alone in her old home, time to find her bearings.

As she follows Adam into the hall she notices that the door to the den is open. Her heart lurches.

'Louis?'

She steps forward and leans in.

'He's sleeping in Willa's room.'

She lets out a breath. Thank God. And then she notices that where there was once a piece of chip-board, there's now a proper door leading down to the basement.

'You use the basement?'

He nods. 'For my photography.'

'Oh – that's good.'

He looks at his watch again. 'I really have to go.' He positions bicycle clips on the hem of his trousers, threads a fluorescent harness over his suit jacket, presses his hair down with a helmet and fastens the strap under his chin. He used to ride a motorbike, take her out on the back. They'd leave Ella with Fay and go to a field outside Holdingwell and lie in the long grass and make love.

'You cycle?'

He blushes. 'Keeps me fit.' He pats his flat stomach. So that's gone too.

She takes a breath. 'Can I stay?'

A muscle works in his jaw.

'I mean, until you get back. Just for a few hours.' She fiddles with a button on her coat. 'Or I can go and get a coffee somewhere ...'

He still doesn't answer.

'Or I could go—'

'Go?' He rubs his forefinger up the bridge of his nose, like he used to when he had glasses.

'I could come back later, when you've finished work. We could talk – if you want to talk.'

He rifles through the drawer of a cabinet in the hallway, pulls out a set of door keys. 'You can use these.'

She doesn't tell him she still has a set. As he holds out the keys to her she sees it: the ring on his left hand. Like her, he hasn't taken it off.

She reaches out for his hand: 'Adam – you ...'

He puts his hands in his pockets and looks up. 'We've got the roofers in all day – there'll be noise,' he says. 'They said it'd be done in time for the bank holiday.'

Norah wonders how different Adam's reaction might have been had she walked back into the house a few weeks after she left. Would he have shouted at her for leaving him? Would he have taken her in his arms and told her that he missed her?

'I'd better go.' He moves towards the door. 'I'll try to get off work early – to be home before the girls get back. I need to talk to them first.'

'I understand.'

'And—'

'And?'

'Nothing.' He looks at his watch again. 'I'll try not to be long.'

'You'd better go then.'

He nods. 'Bye.'

'Bye.' She raises a hand. And, just like that, he's gone.

Adam

Adam skids round the corner of Willoughby Street, squeezes the brakes and jolts to a stop. He climbs off his bike, lets it clatter to the pavement, slumps onto the ground and presses his back against a brick wall.

He'd talked through the scenario of Norah coming home with Fay. *You'll show her the father you've become. You'll tell her you've moved on.*

Breathe, he says to himself, closing his eyes.

When Norah left, his panic attacks got worse. The tiniest thing acted as a trigger: being alone with Willa in the house, Ella coming out late through the school gates, walking past the pub and feeling the pull to go in. Fay had taught him to breathe, to focus – *identify a safe, happy place,* she'd said. What he hadn't told Fay was that Norah was his safe and happy place, and that as soon as he thought of her he felt the vacuum she'd left behind and the panic attack got worse.

He breathes out.

Faces flash in front of him.

Ella, a smile he hasn't seen in months, her eyes shining. The one who's never stopped hoping that her mum would come home.

Willa. Dear little Willa who won't understand what's happened but who'll go along with it in her usual jolly way – until it sinks in that she's been lied to all this time.

And then the woman he loves. Who taught him to breathe. What's he meant to tell her?

He wipes the sweat from his brow. His hands shake.

Breathe Adam, for Christ's sake, breathe.

You're an amazing father, she said to him the other day.

Who'd have thought that the woman who hated him, who thought he was a waste of space, who wasn't good enough for her best friend, would be the one to bring him back to life?

He should go back and tell Norah to leave.

'Mr Wells?'

A shuffling of feet. A series of high-pitched yaps.

He opens his eyes.

'Are you okay?' Lily Pegg's skinny face an inch from his own. Her brow folded into a thousand lines.

'We saw her come back.' Rose Pegg yanks at one of the three Chihuahuas at her feet.

The old Pegg twins who live opposite the Wellses – in their eighties and they never miss a thing.

Maybe they have X-ray vision like Superman, Willa once said.

'Does the New Mrs Wells know about the Return?' Rose asks.

They insist on calling her that, even though they aren't married.

Adam stands up and brushes down his trousers.

'I'd better get to work.'

'We've been expecting her to come home,' says Lily. 'We thought it would be around now.'

'Yes, any day now,' adds Rose.

A year ago, they'd offered to help Ella with her @findingmum campaign. They'd bought a second-hand laptop and asked Ella to help them set up a Twitter account. Adam hadn't had the heart to tell them that they were only making things worse.

'Is the Old Mrs Wells okay?' Lily asks.

Old Mrs Wells. It made him laugh. Norah would have to grow up before she grew old.

'Yes, she's okay,' he says.

'Has she seen the children?' asks Rose.

'I really have to go.'

Adam props his bike up against the wall.

Lily stoops down, picks up Adam's helmet and hands it to him. 'She's very thin.'

X-ray vision. Or binoculars. Whatever it was, they saw too much.

'And pale,' adds Rose.

Thin and pale. That was Norah's signature style, wasn't it? It's what he'd fallen in love with. That beautiful frailty – everything that Fay wasn't. But the Miss Peggs were right: as he saw her standing on the doorstep, looking up at him, he'd remembered how protective he'd felt of her, how he'd always been worried that, if he wasn't careful, she'd fade away.

He takes the helmet from Lily. 'Thank you.'

'Do you think the New Mrs Wells will mind?' asks Rose.

New Mrs Wells? Old Mrs Wells? God, they were like the chorus in a Greek tragedy.

Adam climbs onto his bike.

'Maybe we can pay her a visit,' Rose calls after him. 'Welcome her home.'

He pretends not to hear. 'Bye,' he calls over his shoulder, raising his hand.

More yapping.

'We've known all along, haven't we, sister?' Lily Pegg says. 'All along.'

'But it's still astonishing, isn't it, sister?'

Adam cycles harder.

Lily Pegg's voice, dissolving behind him:

'Yes, astonishing.'

Ella

Ella sits at the back of the classroom, biting the nail of her little finger. Her arms and legs are so full of electricity she can't sit still.

She sends a tweet from under her desk. Her followers are going to be psyched that Mum's come home.

Ella just needs to get through registration, make Mrs Noble think she's here for the day, and then she can run home. She's wearing Mum's old trainers: they help her run faster. When she fitted into them, just over a year ago, she'd felt it was a sign.

They'd been wrong, Dad and Fay and the police and everyone else who said Mum wasn't coming home. Everyone except the Miss Peggs. They never doubted Ella.

Ella closes her eyes and pictures the woman standing on their doorstep, her red hair brushing her shoulder blades, the same length as Ella's, and nearly the same colour. Ella's hair was lighter, but she washes it with a special shampoo for redheads she found in Superdrug, so that when the light hits it she can see Mum's golden reflections.

When Fay took down the photos of Mum, Ella saved them and put them up in her room. She'd stared at them for so long that she knew Mum's face off by heart: her big smile, her brown eyes, the freckles on her cheeks like Willa.

Ella remembers how Mum's long skirts swept the pavement, the jangling of her bangles on her skinny wrists, the dangly earrings that got caught in her hair. So light on her feet she looked like she floated above the ground. *A walking wind chime*, Fay used to call Mum.

'Ready for your test in period one?' Mrs Noble asks.

Ella looks up. 'My test?'

'Your maths re-sit, Ella.'

Ella bites her lip. 'Oh – yes. I've been revising all week.' If Ella goes home now she'll miss the test, but tests don't matter. Nothing matters now that Mum's home. And Mum won't mind her missing some school. When Ella was little, she'd take

21

her out for special occasions. She'd call up school and put on a serious voice and say, *Yes, poor Ella has a temperature,* and she'd wink at her at the same time and then they'd go and build a snowman in Holdingwell Park or take the train to London to see the dinosaurs at the Natural History Museum. *School's not the only place you get an education,* Mum said. *She's the coolest mum in the world,* Ella's friends chorused.

But they didn't need to say it: Ella knew that Mum was the coolest – and the best – mum in the world.

The bell rings. The class files out. Ella joins the throng of bodies pushing down the corridor and then ducks out through a side door.

Willa

'Willa? Willa?'

Willa picks up her orange pencil and colours in the doorstep woman's hair. It's the same crayon she uses for her own hair and Mrs Fox's fur. Ella's hair is red too, but it's a lighter, blonder red, a bit like someone got a splodge of yellow paint (Dad's hair) and some red paint (Willa's hair) and mixed it all together. Mummy calls Willa's hair copper. She says it's the most beautiful colour in the world, and not to let anyone tell her otherwise.

'Willa? Are you listening?'

Willa hears her name being called but it sounds like it's coming from the end of a long, long tunnel. Plus, it's usually safer not to answer because sometimes the voices don't come from the outside, where everyone else can hear them, but from one of the stories in her head – and if Willa talks back to them the boys and girls in her class roll their eyes and whisper.

A hand with a thick gold wedding ring lands on her picture. Willa looks up.

'It's break time,' says Mr Mann.

Mr Mann is married to a man. He was Ella's teacher too.

Willa looks around the empty classroom.

'You can finish the picture later – I'll keep it safe for you in my drawer.'

Mr Mann knows that sometimes the other girls take Willa's pictures and pin them up on the wall and laugh at them.

You need to defend yourself, says Ella. *You need to say mean things back. Show them that you're not scared.* But Willa can never think of mean things to say back. Plus, Mummy says that, more often than not, mean people are sad people and that we should feel sorry for them. When Willa explained this theory to Ella, Ella said that it was that kind of thinking that made people walk all over Mummy. Willa didn't think it was fair that the only choices available were (a) being mean, or (b) being walked over.

Willa scratches her scar. She'd like to finish the picture now, while she still remembers the doorstep woman's face and her clothes and her trumpet case and her wheelie suitcase. The woman makes her think of the zillions of pictures of Auntie Norah on Ella's bedroom wall. Auntie Norah used to live with Ella and Mummy and Daddy before Willa was born, but now she lives in Australia and can't afford to come and visit because the plane's really expensive. Maybe she's saved up and come over on holiday as a surprise for Ella. Ella's always going on about Auntie Norah and how much she loves her and how much Auntie Norah loves her back and how alike they are. If the doorstep lady is Auntie Norah, Willa could give her the picture as a gift and then maybe she'd love Willa as much as she loves Ella.

There's just one thing that doesn't add up: if the doorstep woman *is* Auntie Norah, why didn't Ella say hello and give her a hug?

Willa keeps colouring. 'Are you going to have an African baby soon?' Willa asks Mr Mann. Sometimes if you can get Mr Mann to talk about things he likes to talk about he gets distracted and forgets about the instructions he gave you. Mr Mann is trying to adopt a baby with his husband because two men can't have babies.

Mr Mann sits on the edge of the desk and sighs. 'I don't think we'll get a baby.'

'Why not?' Willa draws a few grey streaks in No One Woman's hair.

'They don't give babies to people who are too old.'

'You're not very old.'

'I'm afraid I am.' Mr Mann tugs at a bit of his hair 'I have some grey bits, like the woman in your picture.' Then he leans in closer and gasps. 'Who's in the picture, Willa?'

'No One Woman.'

His brow goes wrinkly. Maybe he *is* too old to have a baby.

'She turned up this morning.'

'She did?'

'Yep. Ella wouldn't let me stop to talk to her.'

'Oh.'

Mr Mann frowns a serious frown like when he's explaining something hard in maths or reading a sad bit from a book at story time.

He looks more closely at the picture and blinks. And then he stands up.

'It'll do you good to get some fresh air,' Mr Mann says. 'Why don't you run along? You can finish your picture later.'

Unless it's snowing or there's thunder and lightning, Mr Mann doesn't let them stay in for break. He thinks that fresh air makes their brains work better.

Willa packs up her crayons. She takes an envelope from a pile in her backpack and hands it to Mr Mann along with her picture.

'You can open it later,' she says.

As she skips out into the playground, Willa glances back into the classroom. Mr Mann hasn't even looked at the envelope she gave him: he's too busy staring at her picture of No One Woman.

Norah

At the top of the house, Norah opens the door to the attic, which now has a nameplate: *Ella's Room*. Norah had spent hours up here with Ella: the floor covered with watercolour paints and brushes, manuscript pages with half-written songs, Louis Armstrong singing of clouds and skies and roses. They would paint and dance and spin round the room as though nothing existed beyond this place.

Something soft brushes Norah's legs.

'Louis!' She kneels beside him and folds her arms around his neck.

Like Adam, Louis has got skinnier, and his caramel coat is

turning silver. But he smells just as she remembers: of earth and sun and rain, of the house, of Adam and Ella and Willa.

Louis nudges the attic door and settles on the bed Norah had put in for the nights when she stayed up late composing.

She looks around the room.

On the bookcase lies the yellow plastic trumpet Ella played as a little girl.

Norah's Louis Armstrong CDs stand in the same rack in the same corner, and next to them, her old vinyls and her record player. She closes her eyes and remembers the evenings she spent here playing and writing and listening to music.

Her old music stand is full of Ella's pieces. Scales. Jazz solos. And then the notation for a song called 'Mr Fox in the Fields'.

A bottle of Shalimar stands on the dresser. Norah opens it and breathes in the sweet fug of the perfume she still wears.

The wardrobe is stuffed with Norah's old concert clothes. When she was little, Ella enjoyed trying them on, her skinny limbs drowning in the long silk cuffs and velvet skirts.

There are only a few signs that the room belongs to a teenage girl. Textbooks, highlighters, bits of paper covered with maths problems on the floor by the bed, a stack of running magazines on the windowsill and, on top of those, a poster for the Holding-well 10k in two days' time, the race Norah used to run every year.

Norah picks up a sponsorship sheet stapled to the poster, with words scrawled across the top:

Please Sponsor me: Ella Wells
I'm running for: The British Heart Foundation.

Running, playing the trumpet, keeping Norah's clothes. *She's been waiting for me*, Norah thinks. *She still loves me.*

Then she notices the pinboard filled with Adam's portraits, the ones missing from the stairs – and others too, pulled from their frames, ripped out of photo albums, pinned up, one overlapping the other, dozens of them staring down at Ella's desk.

Norah recognises the one of her and Ella with medals round their necks after the mothers and daughters' race at Holdingwell Primary Sports Day. And there's another photo she remembers too, from Ella's naming ceremony. They'd held it in a field outside Holdingwell; she'd wanted to be outside, under the bright blue sky – no rooms, no walls. Norah scans the faces: Fay, Ella's godmother, stands in the middle of the group wearing a pale pink dress; she's holding baby Ella in her arms, looking at her as though no one else in the world exists. Fay's love for them all – it's why Norah gave her Willa to look after on the day she left. She hopes her best friend has stayed in their lives.

Norah takes the picture off the pinboard. There's something not right with the image. She holds it up closer. A mark, so faint you don't see it at first. Someone has scratched a black cross over Fay's face.

Ella

@findingmum
Nearly home! #bestdayever

Ella's been training so hard for the 10k that the short distance between school and home shouldn't leave her out of breath, but her heart pounds against her ribcage and sweat runs down the back of her school shirt. Waiting for the bus would have taken too long, and it would have been far too slow anyway.

As she runs past Holdingwell Primary she remembers the day she stood at the gates waiting for Mum to come and collect her. How cold it was. How the minutes seemed like hours. And then the days and weeks and months and years that followed. How she kept having nightmares. How she couldn't watch films about people who'd been kidnapped, about psychos who locked women in their basements for twenty years, because they'd flood her head with bad pictures of what might have happened to Mum.

Ella blinks. None of that matters, not now that Mum's home.

She sees Willa walking across the playground to the girls' loos, her head bowed, her jagged red fringe falling into her eyes. How are they going to tell her?

Mum will find a way to explain, she'll have a plan.

When Ella gets to the post office she stops to catch her breath and sends another tweet. There's a stream of messages waiting for her. She scans for her favourite follower: @onmymind showed up on her Twitter account a year ago. She always posts replies.

@findingmum Really excited for you. Keep us posted

There's another one too, from @sunnysideofthestreet. Ella thinks he started following her because she tweets about jazz and he likes Louis Armstrong, like Mum. He replies in weird phrases: some are song lyrics and others just seem random. **We have all the time in the world,** he wrote this time. Which irritates Ella. Who's to say Mum will still be at the house? After six years of waiting Ella's going to get back to Mum as fast as her legs will carry her.

And then @liliesandroses, the Pegg sisters from across the road: **#theastonishingreturn**, they'd written. So they'd seen Mum too.

She looks into the post office window and spots Sai standing behind the counter with his mum. The post office is where Ella and Sai met. She had come in one day, to post some letters to missing persons associations around the world, thinking that maybe whoever had taken Mum had left the country and taken her to one of those foreign places where it's really hard to trace people. Ella wishes she could tell Sai what happened this morning. He's the only one who never stopped believing her about Mum coming back. He knows what it's like to lose someone you love. But Dad's made Ella promise not to see him, not until she improves her marks. And anyway, Ella has to keep going – she has to get home.

She runs down the high street, where they're putting up banners for the Holdingwell 10k. Past Pound Stretcher and the kebab van and the Lotus Flower Indian restaurant and the Three Feathers pub on the corner, where Dad used to hang out. And she keeps running until she turns into Willoughby Street.

The roofers have arrived with their dirty white van and their big ladders and their hard hats. Even though lunchtime's hours away, they're sitting on the scaffolding eating sandwiches and sipping cans of Red Bull. They promised Dad that the roof would be fixed for the bank holiday, but the new tiles are still heaped up in the front garden.

Ella stands on the top step. Even though she's stopped running, her heart's thudding so hard she can hear the rush of blood in her ears.

It's going to be fine, she breathes out.

All the crap of the last few years – having to repeat Year 9, Dad turning into a control freak about Sai, Fay taking over, acting like Mum's never going to come home – none of it matters. Mum's home now. Everything is going to be okay again.

She straightens her uniform, threads her fingers through her hair and wipes her brow. Then she puts her key in the lock and pushes open the front door.

Norah

Norah looks down at her body under the water: the folds in her skin, the softening around the middle, the sinking inwards and downwards. She brushes her fingers over the scar where her left breast used to be. She's able to see the humour in her body now; *like Cyclops*, she whispers to herself as she glances at her lone breast swinging off to the side.

She thought the operation would be the end of it: a clean cut. But it's never that simple, is it?

Spotlights bounce off the white tiles. No cracks. The grout bright as bleached teeth. On a shelf, four plastic baskets packed neatly with creams and shower gels. The girls' baskets named: WILLA. ELLA. Neat black capitals.

Norah slides under the water.

When she took Ella to the pool they'd go under the water and speak to each other, bubbles floating from their mouths and noses, lips opening and closing like fish around their words. They'd stay down there, just the two of them, floating in their secret watery world for as long as their lungs could bear it.

Tell me what I said, Ella would splutter as she came up for air.

And, most of the time, Norah got it right. It was one of the things about motherhood that had blown her away, how you can know another human better than yourself.

How do you always know what I'm thinking? Ella had once asked her as they stood under the changing room showers.

I'm your mum, Norah had answered. Simple as that.

A strange muffled sound reaches Norah under the water. Norah smiles. She pushes herself up, sloshing water over the edge of the bath. Louis stands in the swirling steam, watching her. He barks again, pads closer to the bathtub, hangs his head over the rim and thumps his tail hard against the tiles.

'Lovely Louis,' she says, reaching out a wet hand, stroking the top of his head and then scratching under his chin.

He steps back and continues to thump his tail.

'What is it, buddy?'

He walks to the door.

Norah climbs out of the bath and looks at the wet tiles; who-ever's moved in with Adam won't like the mess she's made. Louis looks worried too.

Norah reaches for the white dressing gown on the back of the door and the white slippers under the sink; both a size too big.

Louis paces between Norah and the door and then he barks again and goes out onto the landing.

'Louis – what is it?' Norah calls after him. And then she hears the front door bang and footsteps across the hall.

'Mum?' A voice echoes up through the house.

Ella

@findingmum

I'm home. And so's Mum! #happy

In the hallway, Ella shoves her phone into her school bag. She got another tweet, this time from @hisloveishome, the religious nut who's been following her: *forgiveness is love*. What does forgiveness have to do with anything? He tells her he's been praying for her and for Mum to come home, which is nice of him, but as far as Ella's concerned, if there was a God, and if he cared, Mum wouldn't have been taken away in the first place.

Ella runs up the stairs.

When she reaches the landing she stops outside the bathroom door and takes a breath.

The door opens.

Mum's wearing Fay's dressing gown and slippers.

Ella blinks. Can it really be Mum, standing there all wet and dripping from the bath?

'Ella – I thought you were at school—'

'I had to come home.' Ella throws her arms around Mum. She shuts her eyes and holds on. Mum squeezes her back, and although Mum's arms feel skinnier than she remembers, it's the best hug in the world. Ella had promised herself that she wouldn't cry: today's a happy day, the happiest day of her life. But her eyes are stinging and she can feel a wet bit on her neck where Mum's face is tucked in.

'I couldn't let on that I knew who you were, not with Willa,' Ella whispers into Mum's hair. 'Willa doesn't know about you. But she will, we'll tell her. And then we'll throw you a party. It's Willa's birthday on Sunday so we can have a big joint party to welcome you home too. And everything will be back to how it's meant to be.'

Ella can't get the words out fast enough. There's so much to catch up on. She squeezes Mum tighter. *I'm never going to let you go*, she thinks. *Now that you've come home, I'm going to keep you safe.*

Mum sits down at the top of the stairs and pats the space beside her. Ella joins her and Louis comes and puts his head on her lap. When Ella was little, the three of them used to sit on the stairs all the time. Mum said that stairs were a good place to talk, much better than chairs or sofas.

She reaches up and touches Ella's hair. 'It's got really long.'

'I wanted it to look like yours.' Ella knows how dorky that sounds, but sometimes dorky is okay, especially when your Mum's just come home.

'Dad tells me that you're learning to play the trumpet.'

'I'm not very good.' Ella looks up Mum. 'Maybe, now that you're back, you can give me some lessons?' That's what she'd dreamt of, that Mum would come back and that they'd play together.

Mum smiles. 'Of course.'

Ella notices how thin Mum's wrists are and how she's got

shadows under her eyes and how she's really pale, even paler than you'd expect from someone with red hair. And her hair's thinner than she remembers. There are bits where you can see through to her scalp. God knows what she's been through. Ella doesn't want to ask, in case it brings back bad memories.

'I'm glad you're home,' Ella says.

'I'm so sorry—' Mum's voice chokes up.

'It's not your fault, Mum.' Ella wishes she could have found Mum herself. Maybe if she'd insisted that Dad and Fay help her look. Maybe if she'd pushed harder with her Twitter campaign. Maybe if she'd camped outside the police station and *made* them listen to her. She'd let Mum down.

'I'm sorry – about everything. That I left, that I haven't been in touch—'

Ella grabs Mum's hand and holds it to her cheek. She feels Mum's fingers shaking. 'You didn't *leave*, Mum. You were taken away from us. They wouldn't let you make contact. You would have done anything to come home – just like I did everything I could to find you. It's okay, Mum, I understand—'

It's what they do, isn't it? Kidnappers. Abductors. Murderers. Whatever you want to call them. They brainwash people, make them think it's their fault. *It's normal that Mum blames herself,* thinks Ella. *She loves us. She couldn't bear to be away from us.*

Mum shakes her head. 'I left, Ella.'

Ella lets go of Mum's hand.

'What?' Ella's muscles seize up. Maybe she hadn't heard right.

'It's not because I didn't love you.'

Of course Mum loves Ella. She's always loved Ella. Even

34

when Willa was born and she came out looking like Mum, whereas Ella looked more like Dad, and even when Willa was a baby and needed lots of attention and people thought Ella would get jealous, Ella didn't mind. She knew that Mum loved her. That maybe she loved her best of all.

'I had to go. I couldn't breathe—'

This wasn't how her reunion with Mum was meant to go. 'What do you mean, you couldn't breathe?'

Louis lifts his head off Ella's lap.

Ella slowly stands up. Louis gets to his feet as well. She doesn't understand. The words that are coming out of Mum's mouth don't make sense.

'You *left*?'

Mum stands up too. Ella notices that she's taller than Mum, that she needs to bow her head slightly to look her in the eye.

'You mean, you weren't kidnapped or anything?'

'No.'

Ella's cheeks burn. A mum wouldn't choose to leave her kids behind. Her eight-year-old daughter and her new baby and her husband. She wouldn't just up and leave.

Mum stares at her feet. 'I chose to go, Ella.'

This time Mum says the words so slowly and deliberately that she must know what she's saying.

'You *chose* to go?'

Mum nods and looks up, her eyes watery.

Ella feels like the ground is cracking under her feet, like in those films when there's an earthquake and everything you thought was solid and rooted – roads and houses and sky-scrapers – starts shaking and splitting open.

There might be another explanation, dear, Miss Rose Pegg had suggested once when Ella told her about her latest theory – that

35

one of Mum's fans had got obsessed with her and abducted her. *It happens all the time,* Ella had said. *Celebrity stalkers.*

The Miss Peggs had joined Ella's campaign. They'd said they'd help her find Mum. But every now and then they'd say something weird, like that maybe Ella shouldn't get her hopes up too much, that maybe it was for the best, that maybe Mum's disappearance was more complicated than any of them thought.

The Miss Peggs had tried to tell her. And so had Dad. And Fay. But she didn't believe them. She thought she knew Mum better than them. Mum wouldn't just take off. She wouldn't leave them. Dad worshipped her. So did Ella. And Willa — Willa was a baby. No one walks out on a baby.

God, Willa. What was she meant to tell her now? That Mum abandoned her when she was a few months old, just because she felt like it? And that she didn't love her enough to come home, to even check whether she was okay?

She looks at Mum for a moment and thinks of that poem they studied in English once, about a statue in the desert, the statue of a really important person like a god or a king or an emperor or something, a statue that people thought would be there for ever and ever, but over time it breaks and crumbles and turns to dust.

She turns and runs down the stairs. Louis thunders down beside her.

'It's complicated, Ella. But I can explain,' Mum calls after her.

Ella stops and turns round. 'It sounds pretty simple to me.'

'Ella—'

'I'm an idiot.'

'What? No, of course you're not.'

Mum, kidnapped? She'd actually let herself believe that?

Ella stands in the middle of the hallway. Everything's spinning.

'I'm a bloody idiot!' she yells over her shoulder.

She feels Mum coming down the stairs behind her. She puts her hand on Ella's shoulder. Ella doesn't move.

'Please Ella – stay. Let me explain.'

Ella straightens her spine, lifts her head and turns round. 'Don't bother. In fact, you shouldn't have bothered coming back at all. We were getting on fine without you.'

She pushes Louis out of the way, runs out of the house, slamming the front door behind her, and runs down the path – and then she stops and turns round and looks back.

Mum being home was meant to make everything better.

Today was meant to be the best day of Ella's life.

Ella kicks at the fence. A bloody white picket fence that Fay put in as part of her renovations. As part of her wipe-any-sign-of-Mum-off-the-face-of-the-planet mission. It turns out Fay had been right. Mum was never meant to come home.

Norah

Norah stands in the hallway, her hair dripping, her eyes red. Louis looks up at her, his head cocked to the side.

'I guess I deserved that, eh, Louis?' she says.

She notices that her hands are shaking.

When Ella left, Louis had stood for a while by the front door, and then he'd come back to join Norah.

She'll understand; she just needs a bit of time.

Norah climbs the stairs to the room she used to share with Adam. Louis pads behind her. In the bedroom, she goes to sit on the bed: it's new too, a big white sleigh bed straight out of a fairy tale. The bed she and Adam had shared was two singles pushed together. Norah had always felt the dip between them: *the rift valley,* she'd joked.

Louis stops outside the door and wags his tail.

'Come on Louis!' She pats the bed beside her.

He doesn't move.

'What's wrong?'

He yelps and shakes his head.

Norah looks at the white carpet and the white bedspread and the white curtains. They remind her of something. A sick feeling settles in her stomach, though she can't work out why.

'Come on, buddy, you look like you could do with a nap.'

Norah and Louis used to take naps together while Willa slept and Ella was at school. Neither of them slept well at night. Norah listening for her girls waking up, needing her, Louis watching Norah to make sure she didn't sleepwalk. It was his job to find her and nudge her back to bed.

She'd missed those nights, the bedroom door left open, Louis sneaking in and settling between them: the biggest, softest hot water bottle in the world, Adam shifting in his sleep and moaning and telling her to kick the dog off the bed.

You're jealous of the dog? She'd laughed. Except it hadn't been far from the truth.

Some nights Ella came in too, and with Willa asleep in the cot beside the bed they were all together, the five of them. At times like that she'd thought that maybe she could bear it, that Adam would wake up and see how amazing it was to have children, to be a family, that he'd fall in love with the girls like she had, but then, in the morning, she'd feel alone again, holding a thousand puppet-strings that yanked so hard she thought she'd split apart.

Had Adam slept here in the months after she left? Had Louis kept him company? And when did he take a new woman into his bed? God, had the girls come in when she was here, like they had with Norah?

She looks at Louis, his paws on the doorframe, his eyes shining.

'Are you happy I'm home, Louis?'

He whines and bows his head.

She remembers the day she left, how Louis hadn't left her side, how he'd followed her around the house as she packed, watched her dig her trumpet out from under the stairs, walked with her to the front door and then, sensing that there was something wrong, he'd dumped his big body on the doormat. She'd kissed the top of his head and whispered *Look after them, Louis*, and then she'd stepped over him and left.

Norah had imagined the draught blowing past Louis as the door shut. As she'd turned round to look at the house one last time she'd seen him standing at the kitchen window, barking behind the glass like in a silent film. He must have seen the Miss Peggs coming out, beckoning Norah in, and then, a while later, when she came out again he was still at the window and he'd watched her walking down Willoughby Street for the last time.

It had taken all her resolve not to turn round and run back to him.

Louis twitches his tail and edges one paw over the threshold.

As he walks over she spots a photograph on Adam's bedside table. It's of him, the girls – and Fay. *If you need help, ask Fay, she'll know what to do*, that's what she'd written in her note. She's relieved to see that Adam had put aside his prejudices and taken the advice. When Norah left she knew that the girls would need Fay: a warm, female influence, the godmother she'd chosen for Ella. The one person she knew she could count on.

Norah lies down on the bed and stretches out her hand: 'Louis?'

He leaps onto the bed, nuzzles in under Norah's arm and falls asleep.

FRIDAY AFTERNOON

Willa

The pocket of Willa's school skirt buzzes. She puts down her recorder, takes out her phone and reads the screen:

Call me. It's urgent. Ella x

Ella gave Willa the mobile for Christmas. She bought it second hand on eBay. *This way we can always be in touch,* Ella told her.

They're not allowed mobiles at school, so the kids have got really good at keeping them hidden. If Willa wants to call Ella back, she'll have to go to the loo.

She puts up her hand and calls out, 'Excuse me, Mr Mann?'

The classroom is full of high-pitched screeches from everyone's recorders, so it takes a while for Mr Mann to notice.

'What is it, Willa?' Mr Mann calls above the noise. When he raises his voice it comes out high-pitched and squeaky like the recorders.

Willa stands up. 'Can I go to the loo, please?'

'To the ladies, Willa.' Mr Mann is big on manners.

'To the ladies.'

'It's nearly home time, can't you wait?'

'I really need to go.' Willa grabs her crotch.

Mr Mann frowns and jerks his head to the door, which Willa takes as a cue to leave.

*

Willa sits on the loo, looks up Ella's number and presses *call*.

Ella answers on the first ring. 'I need you to do something, Willa.'

Willa doesn't like the sound of Ella's voice: it's hard and jerky, like when she's talking to Mummy.

'Okay.'

'I'm not going to pick you up today.'

Willa grabs a straggly bit of her bob that's longer than all the other bits and puts it in her mouth.

'Did you hear what I said, Willa?'

For a second, Willa chews her hair and then takes it out again. 'So who's going to get me then?'

'No one.'

'You want me to walk home alone?' Willa's never done that before.

The loo seat feels cold under Willa's bum. She lets out a small trickle of pee and hopes that Ella doesn't hear because it's kind of gross to listen to someone peeing when you're talking to them on the phone.

'Fay's coming.'

Ella calls Mummy Fay, which is what you do when you're older and want to sound cool. Willa doesn't think she'll ever want to call Mummy anything other than Mummy, even when she's as big as Ella.

'But she'll be late,' Ella goes on. 'And she'll probably come with someone.'

'The No One Woman?'

'The what?'

'The woman we saw this morning, standing on the door-step.' Willa's been thinking about the No One Woman all day. She's even asked Louis about her, but he's not being very

44

talkative today. It was the Miss Peggs who taught Willa how to be psychic. They said it was easier for children and animals because they were closer to the spirit world. Except Louis doesn't always pay attention when she's trying to get in touch.

Willa's thought about how the woman looks just like Auntie Norah in the photos on Ella's wall. And if she's Auntie Norah, she's definitely not No One. She lived with Ella and Daddy before Willa was born and Ella loves her more than anyone in the world. Except for Willa. Ella always says she loves Willa best of all.

'Yes, the No One Woman. Now, you need to concentrate on what I'm going to say next, Willa.'

Everyone's always saying that. *Concentrate, Willa. Listen, Willa. Don't daydream, Willa.*

Willa rips off a bit of loo paper and wonders why it's hard and stiff, more like the tissue paper they use for art than the soft, padded, flowery-smelling loo paper Mummy buys.

'Willa?'

'Yes, I'm listening.'

'When it's home time, I need you to wait outside the school gates – and to stay there, even if it takes ages for Fay to get you.'

'How long's ages?' Willa wanted to get home early to check on Mrs Fox. She'll be giving birth soon, so Willa needs to pre-pare the den under the gooseberry bush.

Ella doesn't answer Willa's question. Instead, she says: 'And when Mr Mann asks where Fay is, you need to make a real fuss.'

Ella's always trying to get Mummy in trouble.

Willa's tried to get Ella to explain why she doesn't like

45

Mummy, but Ella won't say. Willa can't understand why anyone wouldn't love Mummy. Mummy is the warmest, kindest, most thoughtful person she's ever met, and when she's grown up she wants to be just like her.

'But Mr Mann knows that you're the one who picks me up from school,' says Willa.

'Well, tell him that I'm busy so Fay's coming instead.'

'And No One Woman?'

'Yes.' Ella pauses. 'So you've got it, Willa? You need to act really upset. Make sure No One Woman feels guilty.'

'Why would No One Woman feel guilty?'

'It'll remind her of something.'

'I don't understand.'

Ella sighs down the phone. 'Just turn on the tears, okay? I'll explain later.'

When people say they'll explain later it's usually because they don't want to answer your question and hope that, by *later*, you'll have forgotten.

'But I can't.' Willa has never been able to cry.

'Pretend, like when you played Annie last Christmas.'

But playing Annie on stage isn't the same as being Willa at the school gates in front of Mummy and Mr Mann and No One Woman. Anyway, Willa wasn't any good at acting. She'd only been cast because she's got red hair and freckles and because they wanted her to bring Louis in to play the part of Sandy, Annie's dog.

'You can call Fay, but you need to wait a bit, make sure she's really late. And when she turns up,' says Ella, 'I want you to sulk.'

Willa's not very good at sulking either.

'Willa?'

46

'I'll try.'

'Try hard. It's important.'

'Why are you being so mean?'

'I'm not. I just need you to do this. For me.'

Willa doesn't see how any of this is meant to help Ella.

'Why can't you come and collect me?'

The going-home bell rings. It bounces off the tiles in the loo. Mr Mann will be wondering why Willa's taken so long. Mr Mann knows that sometimes Willa needs to be reminded where she's meant to be and what she's meant to be doing.

'I'm going out,' says Ella.

'Out where?'

'Nowhere.'

If it were nowhere, Ella wouldn't be going to all this trouble. And anyway, Willa knows where Ella means. She means she's going to Sai's, which Daddy has *expressly forbidden*.

Willa hears the squeak of Mr Mann's shiny black shoes in the corridor outside. He's not allowed to come into the ladies because he's a man, just like he has to go out of the room when they get changed for gym.

'Willa? Are you in there?' he calls.

'I've got to go, Ella,' Willa whispers.

'Who are you talking to?' asks Mr Mann.

'No one.' Willa puts her mobile away, flushes the loo and comes out.

'What have you been doing all this time?'

Willa thinks this is a bit of a rude question. She's on the loo – it's obvious what she's been doing.

'Nothing. I lost track of time.'

'Willa Wells – away with the fairies again.' Mr Mann shakes

his head but he smiles too. 'Well, you missed the end of music. Come and put your recorder away.'

Willa follows Mr Mann's squeaky shoes back to the classroom.

Ella

@findingmum
Worst Day Ever. #lostcause

Ella takes the bus to the recycling plant.

As soon as she finished her phone call with Willa, she texted Dad: *Call me. It's urgent. Ella.* But he hasn't replied. She has to tell him what happened with Mum and make sure that he gets her to leave before Fay comes home from her shift – and before Willa gets back from school. Up until now, she's hated Fay's family meetings, because most of them were about Ella having done something wrong. She'd suggested, once, that they should rename them *sort out Ella meetings*. No one had found it funny. Anyway, she wants one now. A meeting with just the four of them – Dad, Fay, Ella and Willa (and Louis, he's always at the meetings) – a meeting with only one item on the *agenda*, as Fay calls it: getting Mum to go back to wherever it is she came from.

Ella folds her arms. A fat, ugly crow has settled in her stomach and it's flapping and squawking and pushing against her ribcage.

48

As soon as Ella steps off the bus at the bottom of the hill, she's hit by the smell of rubbish being churned through the plant and the noise from the machines that shred people's thrown-away lives. She remembers coming here with Mum when she was little, how they both held their noses and made faces and rolled their eyes and laughed until their sides hurt. They always laughed at the same things.

At least Dad gets to work in an office now, one of the many changes since Fay turned up and took over. At the time, it used to make Ella feel sick, how Fay tried to rub Mum out of their lives. Now she realises that Fay was right – Ella should have forgotten about Mum and moved on like everyone else.

She takes out her phone. There are more tweets from her followers, the people around the world who've helped her look for Mum.

She's lucky to have you: that's what @onmymind tweeted three hours ago. Before Ella found Mum at home.

There are some responses to the tweet she's just sent about it being her worst day ever.

Ella looks for a message from @blackislight. She's a goth so she's a bit gloomy and cynical, and sometimes writes things which upset Ella – like that Ella should forget about Mum and move on, but this time Ella wants to read her. At least she won't give her any crap about giving Mum a chance.

Hope keeps you a prisoner. Don't hope: be free.

Wow. Don't hope? Ella's been living on nothing but hope. But @blackislight's right, isn't she? From now on Ella will stop expecting good things to happen. She'll live one day at a time. She'll stop hoping.

Ella retweets @blackislight's message and puts away her phone.

Then she walks up to the secretary sitting at the desk outside Dad's office.

'I've come to see Dad.'

After looking Ella up and down, the secretary's eyes settle on the Holdingwell Academy crest on her jumper. 'Shouldn't you be at school?'

'I'm sick.'

The secretary raises her plucked eyebrows.

'I've been sent home.'

As she dials the extension to Dad's office, the secretary swivels her chair away from Ella and makes the call. She cups her hand over the mouthpiece and whispers.

When she turns back, she says, 'I'm afraid he's in a meeting.'

The crow flaps in Ella's stomach.

'Tell him it's his daughter. It's urgent.'

'He's very busy.'

The crow flaps harder.

'You spoke to him?'

'Yes ...'

'So the meeting can't be that important, not if he's answering the phone.'

The secretary looks at Ella and blinks. 'He said he's not to be disturbed.'

Ella ignores the secretary and crashes through the door to his office. 'Dad!'

He's sitting at his desk, looking like death.

'I went home,' says Ella.

Dad stares at Ella, his eyes wide. The vein on his forehead pokes out.

'Oh Ella—'

'She wasn't kidnapped. Or murdered. She *left*, Dad. She walked out on us.'

Dad stares at her.

And then it hits Ella. All those years of trying to get Ella to back down, to move on, to stop her stupid @findingmum campaign.

'You knew, didn't you?'

He doesn't answer.

'Why didn't you tell me?'

'We tried—'

'*We?*'

'Fay and I tried to explain—'

'This has nothing to do with Fay. This is about you, Dad. This is about you lying to me.'

Dad gets up, comes round the desk and pulls out a chair.

'Please sit down, Ella. We can talk about this rationally.'

Ella ignores the chair. 'You lied to me.'

Dad leans against his desk.

'You wouldn't listen.'

'You should have tried harder.'

He reaches a hand out to Ella. She steps back.

'Why did she leave?' Ella hears the wobble in her voice.

Dad drops his hand to his side. Mum's only been home for a few hours and already he looks like the old Dad, shrunken and sad – and weak. Ella blamed Fay for changing him, but now she gets it: Fay helped him. She'd helped them all. After all these years of thinking that if Mum came home everything would be better, it hits Ella as clear as day: Mum leaving was the best thing that ever happened to them.

'She left because I wasn't good enough.'

'Good enough *at what*?'

'It's complicated.'

'That's not an answer.'

'No, I don't suppose it is. I wasn't good enough at being a husband. At being a dad – I never grew up.'

'That's not true, Dad—'

Adam looks right at Ella. 'And you know what the worst bit was? I was too blind to see it. That's why she had to leave.'

Ella wants to hug Dad, to tell him that whatever it is Mum made him think about himself, it's rubbish. That you don't walk out on your family. Not ever. It doesn't matter how bad things get, you stick it out. But she wants to scream at him too. For not forcing her to face the truth, for letting her carry on with this whole ridiculous search.

'I hate her.'

'Please, Ella—'

'What? You going to try to defend her? Explain how there's a single good reason to abandon your kids?'

'I need you to calm down, I need you to understand ... ' he reaches out and touches a strand of her hair. He'd always done that, ever since she was little. She thought it made him think of Mum. It's one of the reasons she'd grown it: she thought it would help Dad remember Mum.

'It's going to be okay, Ella. I'll work it out. We'll work it out together.'

'It's not going to be okay.' Ella clenches her fists. 'Not until you tell her to leave.'

Adam

Adam rubs his eyes. One of his contact lenses flicks out. *Damn.* He scrabbles around for it on his desk and finds the blue disc sitting on the shift key of his keyboard. He throws it in the bin and gets out his old pair of glasses from his desk drawer.

Tell her to leave. Everything was so black and white for Ella.

He dials Fay's mobile, hoping he'll catch her before she finishes her shift, and closes his eyes as he listens to the dialling tone. *A power greater than ourselves can restore us to sanity.* That's what he'd learnt at the AA meetings Fay had taken him to. He believed in that step more than any of the others. Except the power he ascribed to wasn't an abstract God, it was a flesh-and-blood power, a power that had walked into his life the day Norah left.

Fay's mobile goes straight to voicemail.

It's me. Call me when you get this. Whatever happens, call me before you go home.

And then he leaves another message.

Pick up the girls from school. Take them to the Holdingwell Café for a hot chocolate or something. Don't go home until I call you.

He can't tell her in a phone message. They've been through too much together. And what was he meant to say, anyway? *My wife's come home. Your best friend. And I don't know how I feel about her any more. I thought I was over her, but you know what she's like, how she pulls you in . . .*

God, what a mess.

He looks around his office. Fay decorated this too: the painting of a rowing boat on a still lake, the Nespresso machine standing in the corner, the ergonomic chair he's sitting on. Soft yellow walls. *They'll lighten your mood, make you feel good,* she'd said as she stood there with her paint pot and brush and stepladder. A bunch of white peonies from the garden in a vase on his desk, the fresh flowers she brought in for him every week.

Fay's the reason he's sitting here, behind this desk, rather than standing in a pair of blue overalls, sorting bottles from cans. She did the same to Number 77 Willoughby Street. Fixed the broken bits of furniture. Oiled the door hinges. Sifted the clothes and letters and books. Threw things out. And then she redecorated.

It'll be a fresh start, she said as she boxed up the junk of their lives. *It will help the girls.*

Ella had locked herself in the attic and told Fay not to touch her room. It was the only bit of Norah that Ella had left. *And Mum will need her stuff when she gets home,* Ella had said.

Ella and Fay used to be friends. But the day Norah left, all that changed.

She's just been waiting for Mum to get out of the way so she could take over, Ella had yelled in one of her fits of rage. *She's probably fancied you all along. She's probably the reason Mum's disappeared.*

In the blink of an eye, Fay had gone from Fairy Godmother to Evil Stepmother.

What Ella didn't understand was that Fay had done all this for them. She'd never intended to take Norah's place. It had just happened, an unexpected turn in her life – as unexpected as the love Adam found for her.

That was the truth of it, wasn't it?

Adam grabs his jacket, takes the packet of cigarettes he keeps locked in the top drawer of his desk and walks out past his secretary.

'I'll be out for a while,' he says.

He goes to the back of the plant and opens the garage set aside for the manager's car. His old motorbike is in there.

Fay wanted him to throw it out along with the rest of the rubbish from the house. They'd had a fight:

I need it, he'd said.

You like it, there's a difference, she'd answered. And she'd been right. He liked the wind in his hair. The freedom. The way Norah made him feel – at the beginning, at least.

It's not safe, Fay had said, searching for people carriers on the web. *We'll get a car for the girls, something practical. And we'll get you a bicycle. You can cycle to work. That'll give you wind in your hair. And it'll get you fit.* She'd smiled and kissed him and then said: *I want you to live for ever.*

He'd wanted to say it back: *I want you to live for ever too.* He'd wanted to say more; he'd wanted to say *I love you.* But he always held back. Perhaps, deep down, he knew that to say it would be unfair when he still hoped that Norah would come home.

He strokes the saddle of the motorbike. What he'd give to go for a ride, to keep going and going, to forget what he has to deal with back home.

Instead, he puts on his bicycle clips and helmet, and goes around to the front of the plant to collect his bicycle.

As he free-wheels down the hill towards Holdingwell, he tells himself that it's going to be okay. He's not going to let his family fall apart. Not again. This time, he'll hold it together. He'll be the one to take charge. He'll take Norah's return calmly. He'll keep his promise to Ella: he's going to make it okay.

June, the receptionist in the pediatric ward, looks up from her computer screen.

'Adam – hi.'

'Is she free?'

'I'm afraid she's in theatre. I don't think she'll be long, though – you can wait for her if you like.' June points to a line of green plastic chairs.

Adam nods, waits for June to go back to her computer screen, walks past the chairs, and follows the signs to the operating theatre.

Fay stands outside the family room in her blue scrubs. Her mask hangs at her neck and a pink bandana covers her wisps of white-blonde hair. She's talking to a couple, her palms held out as she explains something. The man and the woman stand so close that they seem to be propping each other up. Fay touches the woman's arm. Adam recognises the expression in Fay's eyes – it's the one she had in the days after Norah left, when she hadn't yet worked out how she could fix things.

This is Fay's other life, the one she had when she was nothing more to him than Norah's best friend. The friend with the successful career and letters after her name, a fancy car, a huge salary. The friend who disapproved of Adam, whose job barely paid the bills, who was a distraction to Norah's musical career – who was too blind to see that his wife was unhappy.

Adam turns and walks out of the hospital.

*

He drives past Holdingwell Primary. Willa's face flashes in front of him: her big brown eyes questioning. A little girl who doesn't know that her mother isn't the woman who works at the hospital; a little girl whose birthday is on Sunday. He feels the seams of his life tearing open.

Adam cycles to the house. By the time he gets there he's hot and sweaty and exhausted.

He looks up at the windows and imagines Norah walking around the home they used to share.

I'm going to go in and tell her that she needs to leave, he says to himself. *That I've moved on. That I'm not the same, pathetic guy she left behind.*

Obsessed, that's what he'd been. Would have done anything for her.

He clenches his jaw. *I'm a good dad. And, apart from a marriage certificate, I'm as close to being Fay's husband as I can be. And I don't need you any more.* Ella's right. He should make Norah leave.

His breath grows shallow. It's coming back, the panic.

He looks up at the house again. His hands flutter by his sides.

Damn it. Get a grip.

This morning, driven by the excuse of having to leave for work, he'd been able to push the feelings away. But seeing Norah now? *His* Norah, home again? God knows what it would do to him.

Not now, he thinks. *I can't do this now.*

He gets on his bike and heads back to the recycling plant.

Ella

Ella stops in front of The Great Escape travel agent's and stares at the posters of palm trees and deserts and twinkling New York skyscrapers. Had Mum stopped here and planned her departure?

The window reflects Ella's face. The late-afternoon sun catches her hair and lights it up like it's on fire. In a second, Mum's face replaces her own: her chestnut eyes, her long red hair. The Mum she remembers. It's a trick Ella's been practising for so long that now the switch happens automatically – sometimes Ella doesn't see her own face at all.

Ella presses her palms against her eyes to make the picture go away.

She takes an elastic band off her wrist, yanks her hair back behind her ears and runs to Superdrug.

The checkout lady beeps through the hairdressing scissors and the black hair dye: 'I hope these aren't for you.' She stops mid-scan and looks at Ella. 'You have such beautiful hair – such a lovely natural colour.'

'It's not natural.' Ella stuffs the items into a plastic bag and heads back out onto the high street.

Since Dad had got together with Fay, he'd got braver about stuff. Grown up. It was one of the Fay-changes Ella didn't

58

mind. But now it was like he'd reverted back to the man he was when Mum left: hiding away, too scared to face people. He was probably desperate for a drink.

He'd told her to go back to school, to wait for Fay to finish her shift, and then they'd come and get her. Stuff that – even the great Fay can't fix this one.

She looks at her watch. It was too late anyway. She'd missed her maths test. *I'm not going back to school. Not now, not ever.*

Ella walks to the one place Dad's forbidden her to go. If he doesn't have the balls to talk to her about Mum, he doesn't get to lay down the law.

Ella lets herself in through the back door. Whenever she comes to visit, she avoids Sai's mum, who's Indian and stares and doesn't talk much and probably disapproves of Ella as much as Dad does of Sai. Mrs Moore spends most of her time serving in the post office; as long as Ella sticks to the flat, she'll be fine.

Ella knocks on Sai's door. No answer. She lets herself in and walks across the top landing.

There's only one bathroom in the flat: a small basin, a shower cubicle with a plastic curtain greyed with age, and a loo with a cracked seat. The linoleum curls up in the corners. And the door doesn't lock.

A hum of voices comes up through the floorboards. Ella puts a stool up against the door handle. Then she places the scissors and the box of hair dye on the side of the basin. She reckons it'll be easier to dye her hair when it's short, so she picks up the scissors first.

The crow in Ella's stomach squawks so loud that Ella thinks the customers downstairs in the post office must hear it too. *Shhh*, she wants to say. *I know what I'm doing.*

She stares at herself in the rust-speckled mirror. Once more, her mum's face replaces her own. The crow stamps its feet.

Ella closes her eyes. *I'm not you,* she whispers. And then she takes a first snip, right by her jaw. And then another. And another. The golden strands fall to the floor. She keeps going until her hair is as short as Sai's; soon it will be as dark too. She smiles at her reflection. They can pretend that they're related – which wouldn't be far from the truth: he's more of a family to her than anyone back home.

Ella makes up the dye and shakes the bottle. If only Willa were here; Ella could dye her hair too and then no one would ever guess that they were related to Mum.

She tips the bottle upside down on her head – a glob of dye plops onto the floor. *Shit.* She grabs the hand towel and mops it up, then realises that the dye's more likely to stain the towel than the linoleum. *Shit, shit, shit.* She puts the towel under the tap and rubs it with soap. The effort of scrubbing and lowering her head has made the dye on Ella's hair trickle down onto her forehead. She takes a bit of loo roll and rubs at her skin. *I can't even get this right.*

There's a light knock on the door. Ella drops the cup of dye into the basin. God, it's everywhere now.

'Sai?' How's she going to explain all this to him?

There's a long pause. And then another gentle knock.

'It's Mrs Moore.'

Sai's mum. God, what's she doing up here? Ella looks at the mess in the sink, the stain on the floor, at the towel with its dirty black splotches, at the blobs of dye on her hair.

'Is it Ella?'

Although Mrs Moore married an Englishman, Ella senses that this quiet, traditional Indian woman isn't so keen on an

60

English girl for her son. Mrs Moore knows what it's like to be in a mixed marriage: her community back home rejected her. And now that her husband isn't around, she's found herself alone with no one but Sai for family. Of course she wants more for him.

'Are you okay?' Mrs Moore asks. 'Can I help you?'

Ella's throat tightens. She opens the door.

The sun shines through the window on the landing, lighting up Mrs Moore's green sari. Her hair is tied back, a red stain in her parting. Sai says that his mum's not meant to have that stain any more, not now that she's a widow. *But Mum will always see herself as married*, he says. *Nothing will ever change that*. Ella likes the thought that people can love each other for ever.

She waits for Mrs Moore to notice the mess. Mrs Moore will never let her come back to see Sai, not after this.

Instead, Sai's mum reaches past Ella and picks up the scissors from the side of the basin. She holds them up and inspects them. 'I wish I had the courage to cut my hair.'

'Courage?' If only it were courage that made Ella do it.

Mrs Moore nods and reaches for one of Ella's short tufts of hair and tucks it behind her ear. 'It suits you like this. You have good cheekbones.' Then she looks over Ella's shoulder at the basin. 'I dye my hair too – to cover up the grey.' She points at her roots. 'It takes a bit of practice.'

'I'm sorry I've made such a mess. I thought Sai might be free to help, but I couldn't find him. I didn't know where else to go . . .'

Mrs Moore shrugs. 'Mess can be cleaned. Would you like me to help you? It is easier with an extra pair of hands.'

It would have been easier if Mrs Moore had shouted at her and told her what an idiot she was for making a mess and ordered her to leave. She can't cope with people being nice right now.

'It will be fun,' says Mrs Moore.

Ella nods. 'Okay.'

First, Mrs Moore holds Ella's head over the basin and washes out the dye. Then she takes her into the kitchen at the back of the flat and sits her on a high stool.

'Don't you need to be in the post office?' asks Ella.

'Sai is looking after it.'

'Does he know I'm here?'

She shakes her head and smiles. 'I saw you walking past the window. And I heard you on the stairs.'

So much for sneaking in.

'We will surprise him, yes?' says Mrs Moore.

How many people can Ella get wrong, she thinks. Mum, Fay, Mrs Moore. She can't trust her own judgement any more.

'I use henna on my hair. It is a dark brown colour but has tinges of red – I think it will suit you better than the black dye. And it is good for your hair; it is from the earth.'

Ella nods and watches Mrs Moore empty a packet of browny red powder into a small bowl, add water and make a paste. When she stands close, Ella smells paper and tape and stamps and newsprint and the metal of coins on Mrs Moore's hands. And another, sweet smell, the same smell as Sai.

As Mrs Moore combs the paste into Ella's hair, Ella closes her eyes and lets her mind float on the movement of the comb and the sound of the bracelets tinkling against each other on Mrs Moore's wrists.

'I always dreamt of having a daughter,' says Mrs Moore. 'Of doing her hair.'

I've always dreamt of having a mum, thinks Ella.

She lets the world outside fall away: the thoughts of Mum coming back, of Dad ignoring her, of what Fay will do when she finds Mum in the house or how Ella's going to protect Willa from the truth. Here, in this small kitchen above the post office, Ella can pretend that nothing else exists. That her life hasn't just capsized.

Willa

Willa sits on the bottom step of the entrance to Holdingwell Primary.

Why's Ella being so weird? she asks Louis. *And why's Mummy late?*

But he's not answering. He must be busy sleeping or eating.

A shiny beetle disappears into a crack in the concrete steps. Maybe there's a mummy in there who's prepared seeds and bits of grass for his tea and a soft nest for him to sleep in. *Snug as a bug in a rug,* that's what Mummy says when she puts Willa to bed.

Willa wishes that Ella were coming to pick her up. Having a sister at Holdingwell Academy makes up for being called Gingernut; even the older girls look at Ella like they wish they had her for a big sister.

Willa gets up and walks over to Mr Mann.

'I don't think anyone's coming to get me,' she says.

Mr Mann looks at his watch. 'Where's Ella?'

'It's Mummy's turn. And she's not here.' Ella told Willa to act upset so Willa sniffs and makes her eyes go sad as she looks at the parents' cars parked along the road.

'Well, why don't I give her a call?'

Mr Mann has the parents' numbers stored in his mobile, in case of an emergency.

Willa nods. 'Thank you.'

Then she goes to the gates because no one stands next to their form teacher at going home time, not unless they're in pre-school.

A man wearing a woolly rainbow jumper stands on the pavement holding a music case. A massive rucksack sits at his feet like he's been camping. He gets out his trumpet and starts playing a tune that Willa recognises from Ella's Louis Armstrong CDs. Something about being back home again in a place called Indiana. Mummy says not to give homeless people money, but the rainbow jumper man is really good and if playing's like his job, he should get paid, shouldn't he?

Willa takes her Fantastic Mr Fox purse out of her schoolbag, fishes out a fifty-pence piece and drops it in the yellow cap at Rainbow Man's feet. He nods and smiles at her with his eyes as he plays.

Everyone should have a family and a house to live in, thinks Willa, including beetles and homeless people.

'Willa!' Mr Mann booms from across the playground.

Several of the kids turn round and look at her.

She's been told off for talking to strangers before, on school trips and stuff. Which she thinks is stupid. Strangers are interesting. Anyway, she's not talking to him, she's listening to his music.

Mr Mann strides across the playground and waves at her to come over.

'Your mother isn't answering her mobile,' he says.

His eyes go crinkly with worry. She wishes that Ella hadn't made her lie to him.

And Willa doesn't want Mummy to get in trouble. She thinks about telling Mr Mann about Ella's plan, about Mummy and No One Woman not knowing that they're meant to be collecting her and about her having to call Mummy on her mobile once she's waited a bit, but if Ella found out she'd feel let down.

Willa scratches the scar under her eye. *Make Mummy come soon, Louis,* she whispers in her head.

'Mummy's probably doing an emergency operation,' Willa says. 'She'll be here soon.'

'I tried the hospital. They said she's gone home.'

'Oh.'

'It's getting late, Willa. I'll have to try your dad.'

Willa digs her nails into her palms. If Daddy finds out he'll be cross at Ella for not collecting her.

'Daddy's in meetings all day. Mummy will come soon, Mr Mann – she never forgets.'

'I'll give it another five minutes,' he says, then he walks away to talk to a parent.

Willa checks that Mr Mann isn't watching, takes her mobile out of her pocket and dials home.

Fay

Fay stands in the hallway, swaying with tiredness. She makes a list of all the things she needs to do for Willa's birthday. It has to be perfect.

She closes her eyes and remembers holding Willa as a baby, her skin so soft and warm.

When Fay opens her eyes she sees Louis padding down the stairs. He keeps looking over his shoulder. She makes eye contact with him and says:

'What were you doing up there, Louis?'

Louis lowers his head, drops his tail and walks past her back into the kitchen. Willa must have let him into her bedroom this morning.

Fay rifles through her bag for her phone. Whenever she's on a night shift Adam leaves her a trail messages. *I love you . . . I miss you . . . only a few hours to go . . . sleep well when you get home – I'll wake you with a kiss.* Like the prince in *Sleeping Beauty*, she'd once joked. Some days, Fay feels so overwhelmed by the love she has for Adam that she is scared it is in fact all a fairy tale, that one day it will dissolve with the dawn.

She sits down on the bottom step and tips out her bag. She must have left her phone in her locker. She's too tired to go back for it now. A long night shift and an operation on a little girl's heart that hadn't yielded the results she'd hoped. All Fay wants is to soak in a long, hot bath and go to sleep and to wake up to a house full of Adam and the girls.

As she repacks her handbag she spots a trumpet case standing in the doorway to the kitchen. A case that has been part of Fay's life since she was a medical student at the Royal Free in London, and had shared a room with Norah. She hasn't seen it since Norah left. Ella must have had it hidden in her room somewhere. But what's it doing here?

She turns the case over in her hands and then freezes. There are new stickers, ones she doesn't recognise: Amsterdam, Strasbourg, Sydney, Berlin. God, Berlin . . .

A creak on the stairs.

A rush of footsteps.

And then a pause.

Fay looks up and, for a second she thinks she sees a ghost.

Despite the baggy clothes and the lines around her eyes, Fay recognises the woman who asked her to watch her baby – *just for a few hours* – and never came back.

Fay's worried she's going to throw up.

'Fay – it's you,' Norah says.

It had taken years to get over the disappearance of her best friend. And then more years to make this house, the girls – and Adam – her own.

She looks down at Norah's feet. 'You're wearing my slippers.'

How had she let herself in? God, did she still have a key?

'Sorry.' Norah removes the slippers and places them neatly on the stairs.

The phone in the hallway rings. Fay jumps.

They stare at each other.

'The phone . . . ' says Norah.

67

'I know.'

Fay goes over to the table by the front door and picks up the receiver.

A pause. A sniff.

'Willa?' Her little girl. Fay feels something collapse in her chest.

'You didn't answer your mobile, Mummy.'

'Sorry, darling, I forgot it at work.'

Fay feels Norah hovering in the background.

'Ella hasn't shown up.'

'What do you mean, Ella hasn't shown up?' Ella always shows up.

'I've been waiting for ages.'

Norah brushes past Fay, picks up her trumpet case and heads to the door.

'Is Mr Mann there? Can he watch you until I get to you?'

'Yes, but come quick.'

'Good. I'll be there as soon as I can.'

Another pause. Another sniff. 'Mummy?'

'Yes my darling?'

'Is she there?'

Fay's chest tightens.

'The woman from this morning?'

The surge of nausea comes back. Willa's seen her? Fay grips the edge of the table. Adam. He must have seen Norah too. And he let her stay — then went to work like any old Friday?

God, Norah's been here for hours.

'Ella said she was no one. She said not to talk to her, but—'

Fay takes a breath. 'Yes,' she says. 'She's still here. I can't talk

68

now, Willa. Just stay where you are. I'll be with you in a minute.'

'Can the No One Woman come with you?'

Fay pauses. So it's started. Norah's only been back a few hours and already Willa's slipping away. Her whole life is slipping away.

Norah

It feels like they're sitting in a truck: six seats, two screens for watching DVDs in the back, a boot big enough for a week's worth of luggage – and Louis.

'Is this Adam's car?' Norah asks.

Fay grinds the gears. 'It's the family car.'

'It's big,' Norah says, looking around.

'It's safe,' Fay replies.

'Safe. Right.'

'And it's good for holidays,' says Fay. 'It's easier to drive.'

It's what you choose a godmother for, isn't it? To step in when there's a family crisis. When a mum disappears. Norah had told Adam to let Fay help – she should feel grateful.

'So you help Adam out?'

'What?'

'You help him look after the girls? The school run, that kind of thing?'

'You could say that.'

'Thank you.' Norah feels the hollowness of her words. You

say thank you when someone picks up your shopping, not when they look after your family for six years. 'I'm glad they've had you, Fay.'

'Have.'

'Sorry?'

'They *have* me. I'm still here.'

'Right. Yes.' Was there really a time when they could talk through the night, finishing each other's sentences? Norah feels like she's talking to a stranger.

'It must have been hard,' Norah says. 'For all of you.'

Fay turns the car into Holdingwell High Street. She doesn't answer.

'I've missed you,' Norah says.

Fay shakes her head.

'What?'

'You can't do this.'

'I only said I missed you.'

Fay shifts gear.

Norah has to take it slowly, give them time to adjust. She looks out at the town. Like a time warp, she thinks. A few more shops, maybe: a Costa, a Tesco Express, three mobile phone stores. But otherwise, nothing's changed.

'So how have you been?'

Fay shrugs.

She looks at Fay's ring finger. She'd often wondered whether her best friend had got married. Fay had always insisted she didn't want kids; she said she spent enough of her time looking after other people's children at the hospital. But a nice man to love her, to make her feel like she mattered – that wouldn't be so bad, she'd said. But she'd never found anyone who lasted: they were all too much like her, sensible surgeons, lawyers, accountants all obsessed with their work. On the rare occasion that Fay had brought a date to the house for supper, Norah grilled him, letting him know that she wouldn't let just anybody get into bed with her best friend. Adam would sit there, hunched over his beer, silent, wishing that he was alone with Norah. Later, when Norah told him off for being rude, he'd complain that they looked down on him for having left school at sixteen and for his job at the recycling plant. *I'm not good enough for them,* he'd say. *Just like I'm not good enough for that friend of yours.*

'Any handsome consultants in the picture?' Norah asks.

'What? No, of course not.'

Of course not?

'I've been busy, Norah. Families don't take care of themselves.'

Fay had always been on Norah's side. She'd understood how hard Norah found giving up her concerts, looking after the girls, putting up with Adam's inability to register that he'd brought children into the world. But Norah had walked out on her too.

'I'm sorry,' Norah says. The word hangs between them, too small to fill the space. 'I should have got in touch—'

'Yes.'

'But I couldn't.'

'You *couldn't?*'

'It was complicated.'

Fay shakes her head.

'I wanted to . . .'

Fay stares straight ahead.

Yes, Norah had thought of getting in touch with Fay to let her know that she was okay and that she missed her. But she hadn't trusted herself. Talking to her best friend would have made her want to come back.

'So it looks like Adam's found someone else,' Norah says.

Fay takes a sharp breath. 'Someone else?'

'The house. It's changed, everything's changed. It's not Adam's—'

'Not Adam's what?'

'Not Adam's style. Someone must have moved in with him.'

Fay winds down the window and breathes in the rush of air. 'Yes.'

Ahead of them, the lights at the pedestrian crossing turn red.

'Is it serious?' Norah asks. 'The relationship?'

Fay doesn't slow down.

'Christ Fay – it's red!'

Fay slams her foot on the brake. They're thrown forward and then jolted back into their seats. And then they sit there, silent, as a mother crosses the street pushing a pram.

'Are you okay?' Norah asks.

Fay raises her eyebrows as if Norah's asked the most stupid question in the world.

'You look tired,' Norah adds.

'I've had a long shift. I usually have a sleep when I get home.'

A sleep? What was she doing at the house if she was meant to be having a sleep? None of this made any sense.

'So it's Ella who collects Willa from school?'

'Yes.'

'So why didn't she?

'She's temperamental.'

'Temperamental?' Ella was never temperamental. Norah's little girl had a steady, generous character.

72

'She's a teenager,' Fay adds.

Norah doesn't like Fay's tone. And she doesn't get why she's being critical of the goddaughter she loved like her own child. At times, Norah had been jealous of how natural Fay was with her, how she did all the right things, things a mother should have done. She got Ella measured for her first pair of shoes and took her to the library to get a reader's card and helped her with her homework.

She adores you, Fay had reassured Norah when she shared her anxieties. *You're the best mum in the world, remember?*

Yes, Norah remembers. But that was a lifetime ago.

Fay flicks the indicator.

'I'm sorry,' Norah says again. 'Maybe we can talk, after we've picked Willa up. I can explain—'

Fay pulls up outside Holdingwell Primary, switches off the ignition and stares out through the windscreen.

'I don't think there's anything to say, Norah.'

'Nothing to say?'

'It's been too long.' Fay opens the car door.

Willa stands alone in the playground with her teacher. When she spots Fay she smiles, hitches her school bag onto her shoulders and runs to the car.

'Mummy!'

The word echoes around the playground.

'Mummy!' Willa yells again. And for a second Norah thinks she might be calling her, that even after all this time, that even though she left her when she was a baby, Willa might know who she is.

But when Fay steps out of the car Willa runs up to her and throws her arms around her plump waist and sings the word again. 'Mummy!'

Ella

@findingmum
Happy families? #getreal

Clutching at the tufts of hair tucked behind her ears, Ella leaves the post office and walks to Holdingwell Primary. She leans against the brick wall round the corner from the main gates and looks at her phone.

@sunnysideofthestreet sends her a message, another one of his lyrics: **I can see the gleaming candlelight still burning bright** … It's from that Louis Armstrong song he's obsessed with, 'Back Home Again in Indiana'. It's one of Ella's favourites. She knows what he's saying: don't give up on Mum. It's the opposite of @blackislight's message. Maybe Ella should get all her Twitter followers together and let them have a big old debate about what she should do about Mum.

Every now and then Ella checks that Willa's still there, waiting.

One by one the cars fill up with children, and their mums and dads drive them away. The playground empties. The sun sinks. Eventually Willa is standing there alone with Mr Mann.

On the day Mum left Mr Mann had waited with Ella too. And when it got dark and Mum still hadn't answered her phone and they couldn't find Dad's number, Mr Mann had driven her home.

The crow flaps its long black wings.

Ella hears the engine of Fay's people carrier pull up outside the gates. She'd ordered this model especially from America: *safest family car in the world*, she called it. Mum couldn't even drive.

It's more fun to walk, Mum had always said as they trudged to school through the rain. And Ella had bought it. Her excuses for being different from everyone else. For not being a proper mum.

Even from here, Ella can tell that Fay is upset. Her shoulders hunched, staring at Willa through the windscreen. If this were a normal day Fay would rush out of the car, scoop Willa into her arms, swing her round and kiss her all over.

It was Fay who had Willa on the night Mum disappeared.

Dad had come home from the pub and found Ella and Mr Mann on the doorstep. She remembers how Dad's eyes blurred in and out of focus behind his grimy glasses as he tried to get the key in the lock, and how he'd called Mum's name over and over through the dark house.

That was the day Fay became part of their lives. Even though she's this amazing surgeon who saves people's lives, she took a break from work and came over every day. She went with Dad to meetings so he'd stop drinking. She played with Willa and changed her and fed her mushy, organic food and took her out in her pram. Fay looked after Ella too, but Ella always made it clear that she knew who her real mum was — and Ella knew that, secretly, Fay was relieved. Fay only wanted Willa. Willa was special: she was a baby, and she couldn't remember Mum. It didn't take long for Fay to stop correcting people in the park and in the shops and at school when they said things like *what a cute little girl you have* and *you must be so proud* and *she looks just like you* – which was an outright lie. The only person Willa looked like was Mum.

Fay watches Fay step out of the car. Willa runs up to her and hugs her. She watches Mum's reaction through the windscreen. Ella wants to yell out at her, *She's not yours, she'll never be yours.*

All those years, Ella kept thinking that the police would find Mum. That someone following Ella's @findingmum campaign would spot her and tell Ella and then Ella would tell Dad and Fay and they'd bring Mum home.

She's coming home, she'd say to herself, over and over until she believed it.

Ella pulls out a packet of cigarettes she swiped from Dad's secret stash. Her fingers tremble as she flicks the lighter.

How dare Mum breeze back in, thinking she can just pick up where she'd left off?

Pictures of Mum flash in front of her. Mum the last time she saw her, the morning she dropped her off at school: her tired smile, Willa asleep in the pram. And Mum today, standing on the doorstep and then walking up to Willa at the school gates, kissing her. It's like the last six years haven't happened. All that hoping and waiting and searching.

Well, Ella isn't going to join in. She isn't going to go home and play happy families.

She reaches for her phone, sends a tweet and then scrolls down her contacts.

Who cares what Dad thinks. There's only one person she wants to be with right now. She's going to see Sai and she's going to stay there for as long as it takes for Mum to leave.

Willa

As she parks the car on Willoughby Street, Mummy hits the kerb. The three of them lurch forward.

'Sorry,' Mummy mumbles.

Since they left school, Mummy's stalled, gone through a red light and scraped the underside of the car by going over a sleeping policeman too fast. And Mummy's the one who's always telling Daddy to drive more carefully. Plus, she hasn't said a word to No One Woman, which is weird if No One Woman's meant to be a guest and even weirder if No One Woman is Auntie Norah from Australia, which must make her either Daddy's sister or Mummy's sister – and if she's Mummy's sister surely she'd be really excited about seeing her and have lots and lots to tell her.

Willa looks at the back of No One Woman's head: the sun bounces off her hair and makes it look like it's on fire. Mummy's hair is white blonde. If they were sisters, surely they wouldn't look so different?

'Why's Daddy so late home?' Willa stares out of the car window. Daddy is standing on the doorstep in his suit with his briefcase at his feet. He usually comes home early on a Friday and has a nap with Mummy, and then makes dinner to give her a break.

'He had lots of work to do,' says Mummy.

'And why's he standing outside?' Willa can see that Daddy's brow is all knotted up, that he's worrying about something.

'He's probably inspecting the roof,' says No One Woman. 'It's meant to be fixed already.'

Willa and Mummy stare at No One Woman. Mummy's probably wondering the same thing as Willa, which is how No One Woman knows about the roof and that Daddy's always complaining about how slow the roofers are.

'That's what he said this morning,' No One Woman adds.

'This morning?' Mummy asks.

'We met. Before he went to work. He gave me a key.'

Daddy gave No One Woman a key?

'Oh,' says Mummy.

'Ella saw her too,' Willa says. 'We were just leaving for school. Daddy hadn't gone to work yet.'

'Oh,' Mummy says again.

It's not just Mummy's driving that's been weird. It's her words too. It's like she's too tired to use proper sentences.

Daddy turns round, holds a hand over his eyes and stares at the three of them sitting in Mummy's car.

'Daddy!' Willa yells, waving through the window.

She jumps out and runs up to the house and throws her arms around Daddy. She expects him to give her a bear hug back and then lift her up onto his shoulders, like he usually does, but his hug's all limp and she can tell he's looking past her at Mummy and No One Woman.

Mummy comes up behind Willa and No One Woman follows her.

Beyond Mummy and No One Woman, Willa spots the Miss Peggs in their garden. They think they're being subtle but they're not, mainly because they always wear purple, so they stand out, and also because they stretch out their necks and stare, which makes it obvious that they're spying. Like now: they're watering their flowers but Willa knows they're only pretending because they keep looking up at No One Woman. The Miss Peggs like to keep an eye on what goes on. They're on the Neighbourhood Watch committee, which is where people get together to make sure nothing bad happens on Willoughby Street.

Willa waves at them and calls over, 'Did you get my card?'

'Yes, thank you, dear,' Miss Rose Pegg calls back.

Then they both go back to staring at No One Woman.

The Miss Peggs have lived here their whole lives, so they probably know that she's Auntie Norah.

Daddy reaches out to give Mummy a kiss on the cheek and misses, because Mummy turns away too fast. Usually Mummy and Daddy give each other a proper kiss on the mouth and Ella rolls her eyes and Willa pretends not to look.

'Where's Ella?' Daddy asks.

Willa doesn't know what to say. If he finds out that she's with Sai he'll get cross.

'She didn't show up,' Mummy says.

When they get into the hallway, Louis bounds up to them and Willa tries to give him a cuddle but he walks right past her and jumps up at No One Woman – which he never does to strangers. And No One Woman bends down and cuddles him, like she's known him her whole life. It's another clue that she must be Auntie Norah, who helped Ella and Mummy and Daddy adopt Louis. Dogs remember people for a really long time.

Mummy says, 'Why don't you go up and get changed out of your school clothes?'

'I'm fine.' Willa wants to stay here with Louis and Mummy and Daddy and No One Woman.

'I think it would be a good idea,' says Mummy. Which is

Mummy's way of saying that she wants you to do something and that you shouldn't argue.

'Can I take Louis?'

Mummy looks at Louis sitting next to No One Woman and nods. 'Just this once.'

Willa grabs Louis by the collar and yanks him up the stairs with her. Even if No One Woman is Auntie Norah, she needs to know that Louis belongs more to them than he does to her. You don't get to be away for ages and ages and expect people and dogs to love you again straight away.

When Willa gets up to her room she closes the door, sits on her bed and pats the quilt beside her for Louis to jump up.

'What's going on, Louis?' She rubs him in the spot behind the ears that's guaranteed to make him go all floppy and happy. Except this time he doesn't respond. His tail thumps the bed and he keeps looking at the door, as if he wishes he were still downstairs.

'Fine,' says Willa. *If you're not going to tell me, I'll have to find out for myself.*

She gets out of her school uniform as fast as she can, leaves it on the floor even though Mummy doesn't like that, throws on some leggings and an old jumper, gently opens the door so that it won't creak and tiptoes to the top of the stairs. Louis follows her out and plops down beside her, but his ears are standing up stiff, like when he hears the foxes in the garden.

Willa's been training herself to hear things like animals do: their hearing is a thousand times more sensitive than a human being's, and Willa reckons that's why they always know what's going on, like when a thunder storm is coming or when a burglar's about to break in.

Willa wants to hear all the things animals can hear. And right now she wants to hear what Mummy and Daddy and No One Woman are saying.

Fay

'I need to make a phone call,' Norah says. 'Reception still best in the garden?'

Adam nods. His shoulders are stooped and, behind his glasses, he's rubbed his eyes raw. She can't remember the last time he wore his glasses in the day.

'Everything's going to be okay, Adam,' Fay says. 'You can deal with this.'

His eyes are fixed on Norah; he doesn't seem to hear.

Fay wants him to hold her, to tell *her* that it's going to be okay. That Norah coming back doesn't change what they have.

'Adam?' She puts a hand on his arm. 'We need to tell her.'

'I think she's worked it out, Fay.'

But Fay's not so sure. She knows Norah, that she sees what she wants to see – and Fay being with Adam? That's not something she would ever have expected.

They watch Norah pacing up and down the lawn.

Fay remembers Norah sitting for hours in the garden, her phone clenched between shoulder and ear, a cigarette balanced in her tiny fingers, Willa on a blanket under the tree.

She's calling the people from her new life, Fay wants to tell Adam. *The people she swapped us for.*

Fay looks out at her garden. When Norah lived here, the grass was overgrown and the colour of wheat. Any plants were accidental, seeds blown in by the wind. A bramble bush so overgrown that it took Fay half a day to pull out; she'd had scratches on her arms for weeks.

And now? A green carpet of lawn, flower borders, a peach tree, a greenhouse for her peonies, a herb garden Willa helped her plant, a water feature and a shed filled with a lawn mower and rakes and brooms and secateurs and flower food and weed killer.

The only thing missing are fairies at the bottom of the garden, Adam had said on the day it was finished.

How do you know they're missing? she'd answered.

And he'd smiled and kissed her and whispered the words between her lips: *You're right, my Fay.*

Adam places a hand on the back of her head and smooths down Fay's hair. She feels so relieved she wants to cry.

'Sorry,' he says.

Her mind scans through what it is, exactly, that he's sorry about.

Sorry for not telling you that Norah's back?

Sorry for letting you believe that the life we've built together means anything? For letting you believe that I loved you?

Fay lets out a breath. She's so tired her mind keeps skipping from hope to disaster. She has to get a grip.

Norah sits on the low stone wall by the herb garden, crushing a sprig of rosemary between her fingers.

Adam's eyes drift back to Norah.

Spellbinding. That's the word reviewers used to describe Norah's trumpet performances.

You're like a drug, Fay used to joke.

That's the effect Norah has on people. And that's what drew Fay to Norah when they were students: the best friend who shook up Fay's plodding, sensible days.

Plodding. Sensible. Was that what she was to Adam? He'd called her his anchor once. At the time, she'd liked it. Now she pictures the heavy thud of metal sinking into the bottom of the sea.

'She has to speak to the girls,' Fay says. 'She has to explain.'

Adam doesn't answer. He keeps looking out at Norah.

'Adam?'

He turns round.

'The girls?' she says again.

'Yes. Of course.' He yanks at his tie, his breath jagged.

Just a few hours into Norah's return and he was panicking again. God, they were back at square one.

'She can't just walk back in and expect—' Stay calm, Fay thinks. It's what you're good at. It's what he likes about you. 'Adam, it's not my job to sort this out.'

She's done enough. It's time for Norah to step up and take responsibility for walking out on her family. And it's time for Adam to stand up for Fay.

'I'll deal with it,' Adam says. 'I promise.' But from the way he's looking at her she knows that he longs for her to sweep in and clear up the mess.

Because that's what she does.

When Ella skips school, fails her exams, smokes in her room; when Willa has nightmares and sleepwalks; when Louis is sick because he's eaten too much – it's Fay who straightens everything out. Calls a family meeting, lets everyone talk in turn, even if that means Ella shouting at her. And she encourages Adam to take a lead, lets him sit at the head of the table and tells him to be firm, that this is what being a father looks like – what love looks like.

She takes a breath. 'Why don't you go and start dinner?'

'Dinner?'

'The pizzas. It's Friday.' The night Adam cooks with the girls. It's all Fay can think of: keep going as normal. 'It'll be good for Willa to have a bit of continuity.'

'Right, the pizzas.' He looks relieved. 'Yes. I'll do that.'

'I'll go upstairs and get changed.'

She turns to go.

Adam reaches for her hand and draws her back round. 'I'm sorry.'

Sorry. Again.

It's all anyone seems able to say.

Louis bounds past them, through the glass doors and out into the garden. He leaps up at Norah.

Willa stands in the doorway, looking at Adam. 'What are you sorry for, Daddy?'

FRIDAY NIGHT

Willa

Willa sits at the kitchen table arranging cubes of mozzarella on the pizza bases. She pushes the back of her wobbly tooth with her tongue and makes a list all the things that feel normal about this Friday evening and all the things that feel weird.

Normal things:

Daddy wearing his pinny because he's in charge of dinner, which happens every Friday because Mummy does night shifts on Thursdays and needs to rest.

The table covered in pizza bases and jars of tomato sauce and bowls of toppings because it's make-your-own-pizza night, which also happens every Friday.

Louis gnawing on his Friday bone in the corner under the window, though he doesn't look as excited about it as usual.

Weird things:

The woman with the long red hair keeps staring at Willa and acting like she knows everyone even though no one's introduced her. She definitely looks like Auntie Norah from the pictures on Ella's wall, Auntie Norah who played the trumpet and was a really fast runner. Anyway, it's weird that she's here.

Other things that are weird:

The fact that Daddy hasn't put on his Beach Boys CD. And that he said he was sorry that Auntie Norah had turned up so unexpectedly. Willa didn't understand why it was his fault and why he should be sorry about it.

The fact that Mummy looks even more tired than she usually looks on a Friday.

The fact that the three grown-ups keep shooting glances at each other and whispering. They talk about Ella and say that Ella's teacher called to say that she's staying later to catch up on some work, but Willa knows that Ella can copy anyone's voice and make it sound real, even a grown-up's.

And that was the weirdest thing of all: Ella not being here – and make-your-own-pizza-night is Ella's favourite.

Every Friday she sits next to Willa at the kitchen table and shows her how to make funny faces with pineapple rings and slices of ham and strips of pepper. Willa gets a heavy feeling in her tummy when she thinks about Ella not being here, and about her going to see Sai.

Willa's been keeping Ella's Sai secrets for ages. She's met him a few times and she thinks he's nice and doesn't believe that he could have done all the bad things Daddy goes on about. For starters, Willa hasn't seen him smoke once, but Ella smokes all the time. But the point is that Daddy doesn't like him, and if he finds out that Ella's staying with him he'll hit the roof.

Willa wipes her hands on her jumper, slips off her stool and goes to sit in the den under the stairs. Although there's lots of household stuff in here, and Mummy's DIY box, and although Daddy walks through the den to get to the stairs that lead down to the basement where he does his photos, Willa's still managed to make it cosy for Louis. She's made a bed for him using a pillowcase stuffed with old tights and socks and bits of cotton wool, so that he's got somewhere snug to sleep. She leans against the wall, takes out her mobile and rings Ella's number. It goes straight to the messaging service, which makes the heavy feeling in Willa's tummy get worse. Ella never switches off her phone. So Willa texts her:

Come home. Please. Willa x

Willa stares at the screen, waiting for a message to ping back, but it stays blank. She doesn't want to go back into the kitchen, not with everything feeling so weird. Not with Ella missing.

A soft knock on the door to the den. 'Willa, darling? It's Mummy.' Mummy whispers her name so low that Willa can hardly make it out. 'Are you okay in there?'

Willa smiles. Mummy always knows when something's wrong. *When my little girl's upset, I can feel it in my bones*, Mummy said once. And Mummy knows all about bones because she's a surgeon.

Willa opens the door and Mummy squeezes in, followed by Louis.

'Silly beast,' Mummy says, patting Louis's big, wobbly tummy, but she lets him in anyway.

Ella thinks that Mummy hates Louis because she doesn't let him jump all over the beds, but Willa knows that she loves him really. Mummy's the one who took Louis to the vet to get a chip put inside him in case he ran away and got lost, and she's the one who bought a special crate for the boot of the car so he could come with them on holiday, and she's the one who buys him special good-for-him food because he's got too much sugar in his blood, and who fills up his water bowl and who takes him for walks when everyone else is too tired.

The den is so small that there's hardly enough room for all three of them to breathe.

Louis sits on top of Mummy.

'So, are you going to tell me what's wrong?' Mummy asks.

Louis lets out a harrumph as though he wants to know too.

Willa thinks for a second. Is it worse to betray Ella's trust or not to say anything and risk Ella doing something she shouldn't do with Sai?

'I think Ella might be in trouble,' Willa says.

Mummy rubs her eyes. They're bloodshot and she can't stop yawning. 'What do you mean, Willa?'

'I think she's with Sai.'

Mummy straightens her back. 'She told you that?'

'Sort of. I think so.' Willa's suddenly worried that maybe she's got it all wrong. Ella hadn't actually said his name, had she? 'I don't think she's at school.'

Mummy wrinkles her brow. 'We should tell Daddy.'

Willa knew this was coming. Ella would never forgive her if she told Daddy where she was. 'Do we have to?'

Mummy nods. 'He'll find out anyway, Willa.'

So Willa, Mummy and Louis leave the den and go back into the kitchen and tell Daddy.

'She's where?' He takes off his pinny and throws it into the sink. And then his face goes red and the vein on his forehead pops out.

Willa once asked Mummy why Daddy gets so upset about Ella and Sai, and she said it's because he loves Ella, which is weird because if he loves Ella he should be pleased that she's found someone who makes her happy.

The No One Woman, who's maybe Auntie Norah and who's been hanging around, gets out of her chair.

'Can I come with you?' she asks Daddy.

That's weird too.

Daddy looks at Mummy but Mummy doesn't look back at him; she looks out of the kitchen window and her eyes are sad.

Daddy looks back at No One Woman and nods and they

both go off in the car to look for Ella, leaving Willa, Mummy and Louis behind staring at the soggy pizza bases.

Fay

Fay stands at the kitchen window and watches Adam and Norah drive away. Adam swerves to avoid an oncoming car that's speeding down Willoughby Street. Fay's written to the council to ask for speed bumps: too many people use the road as a cut-through.

Louis sits pressed up against Fay's leg, his body warm and heavy; Willa stands on her other side, staring out into the dark, spring night. Her breath fogs up the window; she draws a picture of a house with her finger: a square box, a triangle on top, a heart in the middle.

When are you coming to collect Willa? Fay had called after her best friend as she disappeared down the road on that dark, snowy afternoon six years ago.

But Norah hadn't answered.

Willa rubs out the picture of the house. 'Ella's going to be cross at me.' She scratches her scar. It's so red she must have been scratching it all day.

Fay takes her little girl's hand away from her face, wraps her fingers around it and squeezes it tight. 'You did the right thing, Willa.'

'I don't think Sai's as bad as Daddy thinks he is.'

'Daddy just cares about Ella, that's all.'

Willa nods. And then she leans into Fay, her head resting

against her waist. Louis shuffles into them like he wants to join in the hug. If only it could stay this simple: the three of them, standing in their home at the beginning of a bank holiday weekend.

On the afternoon Norah left, Fay had taken Willa into her bed and they'd fallen asleep together. She'd wanted to keep her close.

You're lucky, Norah had said once. *No kids. No husband. No ties. Only yourself to worry about.*

Norah didn't understand that only having to worry about yourself was the biggest burden of all.

Willa looks up at Fay. 'Is No One Woman staying?'

No One Woman. God, if only that were true.

'We'll see.'

'Will she live with us for ever?'

How long is for ever for a child? A day? A few months? Six years? And what's the answer? How long will Norah stay? She thinks of Norah sitting next to Adam in the car, parents off to rescue their teenage daughter. How long will it take for Adam to realise he still loves her? How long before Fay has to move out?

'Mummy?'

'I don't know, Willa.'

Willa gives Fay's hand a squeeze. 'Maybe she'll stay for my birthday.'

'Maybe.'

'I think Louis likes her.' Willa kneels down and puts her arms around Louis's tummy.

Louis looks up at Fay. She'd even thought that he was hers.

Willa gets back up and looks back out of the window onto Willoughby Street.

'You and Daddy aren't going to get a divorce, are you?'

'A divorce?'

'Lots of children at school have parents who are divorced.'

'That's not something you should worry about, Willa.' Fay kisses Willa's forehead.

Get a divorce? We'd have to be married for that.

Willa stops stroking Louis and looks up at Fay: 'And you'll always be my Mummy, won't you?'

Fay swallows hard. She looks out at the blossom falling in the soft spring night. Then she turns to Willa, kneels to be at her level.

'Willa, I'd like you to go and pack a few things.'

Willa's eyes light up. 'Pack my *Adventure Suitcase*?'

Fay's cheeks flush. A rush of heat. Is this how Norah had felt?

'Yes, your Adventure Suitcase.'

'Where are we going?'

'It's a surprise.'

Willa's eyes go even wider. 'A surprise?'

'An adventure.'

Willa jumps up and down. 'What shall I pack?'

Fay starts to make a list: *pyjamas, a warm jumper, underwear, a toothbrush*. Then she stops herself. What the hell is she doing?

'Mummy?'

'Anything you like, darling.'

Willa smiles. '*Anything?*'

That's what Norah would say, isn't it? Nothing practical. No thinking ahead. Just acting on impulse.

'Yes, anything.'

'All the animals from my bed?'

'As many as will fit.'

Willa skips off towards the stairs. Then she stops and turns round.

'What are you taking with you, Mummy?'

Fay smiles. 'I don't need anything.'

You're all I need, Fay thinks. Losing the man she loves, her best friend, her goddaughter: maybe one day she would reconcile herself to that. But not Willa. Willa is hers.

'You can borrow my things, then,' says Willa and runs up the stairs.

Ella

@findingmum

Last day of tweets. #wasteoftime

Ella throws her phone onto the chair.

'What did you tweet?' Sai asks. He's lying on his bed studying his *Larousse Gastronomique*. He dreams of going to Paris to train to be a chef, because that's what his dad always wanted to do. Dad thinks Sai's a drop-out, but Sai's the most driven person Ella has ever met.

'I told them I'm ditching the campaign,' Ella says.

Sai closes his book. 'Why don't you give it some time?'

'I don't need any time.'

'They'll be disappointed.'

'*I'm* bloody disappointed.' She looks out of the window at the

94

street. Men are putting up spectator barriers for the Holding-well 10k. 'I hate her,' she says.

Sai sits up on the side of the bed. 'Maybe if you talk to her, listen to her side of things . . . Those feelings, the ones you had for your Mum, they don't just go, Ella.'

'No. They don't *just* go. It takes a lot. It takes what she did me – to all of us.' She looks back at Sai and tries to smile. 'But it's okay. It's kind of a relief, really, not to be hoping any more.'

'It's not okay, Ella. You're in shock. It's still sinking in, her turning up like this.'

'I'm not in shock. I've just woken up, that's all.'

Ella goes over to Sai's bookcase and picks up his sponsorship form. He'd raised over five hundred pounds for the British Heart Foundation. Sai thinks that if there'd been more research on how people's hearts can go wrong, maybe his dad could have been saved.

She holds up the bit of paper. 'This is amazing, Sai.'

'Yeah, but I'm a bit rubbish at the running bit, aren't I?'

'No you're not.'

They'd been training hard, Louis running alongside them.

Ella puts down the piece of paper.

'You know what my first thought was when she turned up this morning? I thought, *she'll see me run. She'll be there at the 10k and I'll be able to show her how hard I've trained and she'll be proud . . .*'

Sai stretches out his hand to her.

Ella sits beside him on the side of the bed and leans her shoulder against his chest.

'She still can be, you know,' Sai says.

'She won't. She's not staying.'

95

'How do you know?'

'She'll get the message that we don't want her here.'

Sai touches Ella's cheek. 'You really are angry, aren't you?'

Ella takes his hand and lies back, pulling him alongside her, and for a moment they both stare at the ceiling. Sai looks round at her and touches a strand of her short hair. 'I like it,' he says.

She meets his eyes. 'It's not too short?'

'If you can pull off a pixie haircut, it means your face is really beautiful. It means you're perfect, Ella.'

She raises her eyebrows. '*Perfect?*'

He nods and kisses the side of her mouth and then her mouth and then they're kissing properly and Ella doesn't want it to stop because it's the only good thing about her life right now, the only thing that makes her forget about her mum. She pulls him in closer. She feels the weight of his body against hers. She's thought about them going further than this. It's what terrifies Dad.

And then what? she asked Dad once. *What would be so bad about me sleeping with Sai?*

This had been at one of Fay's family meetings.

Why can't Ella sleep with Sai? Willa had asked. At which point Fay had taken her out of the room.

Now Ella understood why Dad was scared. He was scared that she'd end up pregnant and that she and Sai would have to get married and that they'd end up like him and Mum: kids with kids. Sure, Mum and Dad had been a few years older when they'd had her, but they weren't ready, were they? Isn't that what Dad had implied earlier today? That he couldn't cope. And Mum couldn't cope with him not being able to cope. That that's why she'd left.

Sai kisses her neck and whispers:

'And another cool thing about your hair?' he says. 'It'll help you run faster on Monday. More aerodynamic.'

Ella takes a cushion and throws it against him.

He coughs and pushes it out of the way. 'But mainly it's that you're beautiful . . .'

'Good.'

Sai takes Ella's hand and they lie back and listen to each other's breathing.

'Maybe if you think of a happy time,' Sai says.

'What?'

'It'll help you remember why you loved her – and why you wanted her home.'

'I don't want to remember.'

'Just try it.'

'It won't work.'

'You trust me, right?'

She gives him a small nod.

'Close your eyes.' His fingers flutter over her face. She drops her eyelids. 'Good.'

'Was that your way of checking they were closed?'

'Kind of.'

Ella laughs.

'So, think about a moment, a single moment when you knew that you loved your Mum more than anyone or anything else in the world.'

'Sai—'

'Go with it.'

Sai was into this stuff. Guided meditations. Visualisations. It was an Indian thing, he said. Ella screws shut her eyes until darkness sweeps through her whole body.

'Thought of a time?'

A light flashes behind her eyelids.

'Sports day. A year and half before she left.'

'You were, what—?'

'Six.'

'And it was Holdingwell Primary Sports Day?'

'Yep.'

Before Sai needs to say anything else, it comes back to her in a big whoosh. Like she's actually there.

'Tell me,' Sai says.

Ella keeps her eyes closed. She sees a big green space marked out into lanes.

'You remember sports day? At Holdingwell Primary?'

'God, yeah. Torture.'

'Not for me. I was good at that stuff.' Ella pauses. 'And so was Mum. She did the mothers and daughters' race every year. We practised for ages. Ran around Holdingwell in the rain. Me, Mum and Louis.'

'Was your Dad there?'

'He usually forgot. Most of the time, it was just the two of us.' Ella realises that by 'just the two of us' she means more than Dad not being there: Willa wasn't born yet. She had Mum to herself. She's never thought that maybe things would have turned out differently if Willa hadn't come along. That the time she was really happy was when it was just her and Mum and Louis. It didn't matter, then, that Dad was rubbish at being a dad. They had each other. And that felt like enough. More than enough: it felt like the best thing in the world.

'What are you seeing?' Sai asks.

Ella lets her mind float back.

'We're at the start line. Mum's kneeling in front of me doing up my laces.'

'What else do you see?'

Ella screws her eyes tighter shut.

Dad's standing on the slope that leads up to the main school buildings, a camera round his neck. Fay's beside him, holding Mum and Ella's water bottles. She was always right there, wasn't she? Holding them together, and they didn't even see it.

'Is your mum saying anything?' Sai asks.

Ella focuses her gaze back on her mum. She's got bare feet. She said it was the most natural way, that the runners from Kenya, the best in the world, ran without shoes.

They'd get on, Mum and Sai. Ella'd had that thought more than once.

'She's giving me a pep talk . . . ' Ella hears her Mum's voice, deeper than most mums', her words full of breath like when she played the trumpet. 'Run, Ella . . . *Run like a song.*'

'Run like a song?'

'You know the saying, *run like the wind*, right? Well, Mum changed wind to song. She thought that if you saw running like a piece of music, like getting into a beat and a rhythm, like following a story, you'd run from the heart.'

'That's cool.'

She sees Mum's hair, lit up and shining like one of those bright copper pots, her skin transparent in the sun, her eyes fixed on Ella as if, at that moment, no one else in the world existed.

Ella's chest hurts. She wants to open her eyes but she can't pull herself from that sunny day in July, a year before Willa was born.

'Ella?' Sai strokes her arm.

Ella opens her eyes and focuses on one of the glow-in-the-dark stars above his bed. 'I worshipped her Sai. Like, really worshipped her. And now? I'm not even sure if all those amazing things I remembered about her, about the times we had together, actually happened or whether they're just what my head's made up for all these years to make her feel close. Maybe she was never that great.'

'She was awesome.'

'What?'

'I remember her. I remember sports day, how you guys won every year. How I wished Dad would run with me like that in the fathers and sons' race, but he was overweight and struggled with his heart. You and your mum? You were *both* awesome. Everyone saw it.'

'Really? You really remember us? You're not just making it up?'

'Have I ever made things up?'

'No.' And he hadn't. Sai was the single most honest person she'd ever met.

'You really miss him, don't you?' she says.

'Every day,' Sai says.

It's one of the things that makes Ella most angry about Dad – that he assumes Sai dropped out of school because he's thick or got into trouble or something. His Dad died of a heart attack and his Mum couldn't manage in the post office on her own. That's why he left school.

'I love you,' she whispers. And then realises it's the first time she's said it out loud – and that saying it feels like the most natural thing in the world.

'I love you too,' he says and then they kiss again, a kiss that goes deeper and further than ever before.

Adam

Norah's perfume fills the car. In the days and weeks after she left, he had felt it rising from the carpets and curtains, from their bed sheets. From his clothes. And then Ella had started wearing it, as though he were never allowed to forget.

He glances at Norah sitting beside him, her delicate limbs, her long fingers resting on her thighs. They used to hold hands. *It's a sign,* a girl who worked at the recycling plant had once told him. *If you keep holding hands when you've married, especially after you've had kids, it means you'll love each other for ever.*

He rubs his eyes and blinks. Through the blur he looks at the blossom drifting off the windscreen, at the markings on the road. He tries to concentrate on his anger at Ella for going against him like this.

'I learnt to drive,' Norah says.

When they started going out he owned a clapped-out Fiesta and he'd spent hours sitting beside her in the passenger seat, teaching her how to change gear, how to get on to a round-about, how to take a slip road. He thinks about how nervous she was. And how, eventually, she'd given up, said she didn't need to drive, that the bus was fine – that she didn't need to go long distances.

'They came back to me. The things you taught me,' Norah says.

He nods silently.

'I don't think I could steer this thing, though.' She looks around at the dimensions of the Chevrolet.

'You'd get used to it,' Adam says.

'I guess so.' She shifts in her seat and then turns to look at him. 'Did you find my note?'

He'd been gearing himself up for this conversation all day, and still he doesn't feel ready for it. Especially not without Fay there beside him.

'Adam?'

'Yeah. I got your note.'

Please don't try to find me. That's what it had said.

'So you weren't worried—'

'Not worried?'

She tugs at her seatbelt. 'You didn't think that something had happened to me, like Ella did?'

'Your note didn't stop me worrying, Norah.'

In his darker moments he'd thought that maybe Ella was right, that they should get the police involved. He'd imagined a car pulling up alongside Norah, a man grabbing her small body off the pavement and bundling her into the boot. She was so easy to lift: as small and light as a sparrow.

'So why didn't you come after me?'

'You told me not to, Norah. I followed your instructions. Why didn't I come after you? Don't you get it, Norah? I was scared. What if I found you? What then? I couldn't face it, standing there while you told me what a loser I was, how you'd fallen out of love with me, that you didn't want me any more. The note was one thing, but to hear it from your lips . . . '

'I never stopped loving you, Adam.'

'Don't—'

'I just want you to know that I didn't leave because I stopped caring—'

'We'll talk about this later.'

He felt like he was talking to Ella. Stamping his authority. *Be firm*, that's what Fay had taught him. *Sound like you mean it and she'll go along with it.*

Except that had never worked, had it? Ella had seen through him, just as Norah sees through him now.

She turns away from him and stares out through the windscreen. 'So Sai's Ella's boyfriend?'

He nods.

'You're not happy about it?'

'She's too young for him.'

Sai was the first guy Ella had ever shown any interest in, and at first he'd been glad. He and Fay wanted her to behave more like a teenage girl, to stop focusing so much on Willa – and on her campaign to find Norah. *It would be good for her to fall in love*, Fay had said as they lay in bed one night. That was before Ella started slipping at school, smoking, getting angry with everyone.

'And he's not right for her.'

'It's normal, to cling on to your daughter.'

He grips the steering wheel harder. How dare she give him advice.

'It's not that. He's bad news.' Adam says.

Norah lets out a small laugh. 'Bad news? That's what Fay used to say about you.'

Fay. Had there really been a time when they couldn't bear to be in the same room? When the only thing they had in common was their love for Norah?

They'd only touched on the subject a few times. Their old

relationship. *I always loved you, stupid,* Fay had said once. He hadn't understood.

'Fay was right,' Adam says.

'You seem to get on better with her – with Fay,' Norah says.

He gulps, his throat dry. So Fay's right, Norah hasn't worked it out yet.

'Yes. We get on better.'

'I'm glad. I mean, I'm grateful that she's been here for you and the girls.'

'Yes.'

'Willa calls her Mummy.'

So she's got that bit of the picture.

'You don't correct her?' Norah goes on, her voice shaky.

'Correct her? Christ, Norah. Willa's a little girl. She got confused.' He pauses. 'We didn't know where you were – or whether you were ever coming back.'

'I didn't think you'd like it.'

'Like Willa calling Fay Mummy?'

'You've never had much time for Fay, that's all.'

'Things change.' Adam pulls up outside the Holdingwell post office, grateful that this will give them a reason to stop the conversation. He needs to work out what to say to her about Fay, something decent. He can't let Fay down.

'Ella's here?' Norah asks.

'It's where Sai works.' Adam jerks his head up to the flat. 'And lives.' His eyes burn as he looks at the small window of Sai's bedroom. He's sat out here before, watching the shadow of his daughter and the boy she says she loves moving behind the curtains. It was pathetic, wasn't it? Spying on his daughter.

You're a good father, Fay had told him. It was like she'd

wished him into being a better person. And sometimes he'd let himself believe her. But in the end, that was all it was: wishful thinking.

Sweat gathers at the base of his spine.

'You okay, Adam?' Norah puts a hand on his shoulder. 'You're shaking.'

He counts in his head to steady his breath: *One ... two ... three ... four ...*

'I'm fine,' he says, but continues to count. He wishes Fay had come with them. What would she tell him to do?

He turns to Norah. 'I'll wait for you in the car.'

Norah's eyes go wide. 'What?'

'I think you should go in. It's a good opportunity.'

'An opportunity for what?'

'To make amends. It'll be a start.'

Norah stares through the windscreen at the door to the post office. She doesn't move.

'Norah?'

She turns and looks at him. People had been deceived by Norah's bohemian confidence, the way that, despite her small stature, she held her head up high, looked strong, filled rooms with her music and her laughter. But Adam knew her better. He'd seen the fear in her eyes in the moments before she got on stage to play her trumpet. The same fear he'd seen in the months before Ella was born. *It'll be okay,* he'd said. Except he'd been scared too – scared to lose her.

Norah looks down at her lap. 'She hates me.'

'For Christ's sake, Norah, she's been waiting for you to come home ever since she was a little girl. She won't listen to me. I'm the one who banned her from seeing Sai.'

'Adam, I don't think I can do this.'

His jaw tightens. 'You have to.'

Norah goes quiet. Then she nods and steps out of the car.

As he watches Norah walk away he catches sight of a girl in the window above the post office. She's speaking to someone, using her hands like Ella does. But it can't be Ella – the girl's hair is short and dark.

Ella

@findingmum
If she can run away, so can I. #ownmedicine

Ella knows she said she wouldn't tweet any more, but she's been doing it for so long that she can't help it. And anyway, her followers need to know the truth about Mum.

As soon as she's sent the tweet, Ella's phone beeps. Willa again, only a few words this time:

I'm sorry. Please forgive me. Willa x

Ella's heart jolts. She wishes she hadn't left Willa to face everything alone, but she couldn't stay in that house, not with Mum there.

She hears Mrs Moore talking to someone at the bottom of the stairs, her voice agitated. The post office is closed, so it can't be a customer. A moment later, two sets of footsteps come up the stairs to Sai's room.

Ella looks up from where she's sitting on the bed to see Mum standing in the doorway, Mrs Moore behind her.

'I told her she couldn't just come up like this,' says Mrs Moore. 'But she insisted.'

At that moment, Ella loves Mrs Moore. She's being kinder to Ella than any of the people who are meant to look after her. Maybe she can be her mum from now on.

Mum stares at Ella. *My hair,* thinks Ella. She tucks a dark tuft behind her ear and smiles. *At least now you know I don't want to look like you.*

Sai climbs off the bed. 'Who are you?'

'She's no one,' says Ella. 'And she shouldn't be here.'

'Oh, *that* no one.' Sai walks over to Mum and holds out his hand. 'Good to meet you, Mrs Wells.'

'Don't talk to her,' says Ella.

Mrs Moore looks from Mum to Ella. 'Sai, you know this woman?'

'I'm—' Mum hesitates. 'I'm Ella's mum.'

'She means she *was* my mum.' Ella picks up Sai's cookery book and flicks through it.

'I'd better finish up downstairs.' Mrs Moore turns to go.

'I'll come with you, Mum.' Sai looks over to Ella. 'Give you guys some space.'

The crow flaps in Ella's stomach.

'Don't go, Sai. *Mrs Wells* isn't staying.'

Mum walks towards the bed. 'Your dad's waiting in the car downstairs. He's worried. I think you should come home.'

Ella laughs. 'You think *I* should come home?' She hitches up her legs onto Sai's bed and pulls a blanket over her. 'I'm not going anywhere.'

'Willa's worried. At least come home for her.'

'You don't get to comment on what Willa needs.' Ella turns to Sai. 'You know, I thought she was dead?' She paints a banner in the air: '*The Tragic Disappearance of Norah Wells – wife – mother of two.*' Ella shakes her head. 'God, she had me sucked in.'

'I never claimed to be dead,' says Mum.

Ella lets out a laugh. 'Of course you didn't. You didn't claim anything, did you? You didn't bother to let us know where you were or what you were doing or whether you were okay – whether you were ever coming back.'

'I thought your dad would—' Norah starts.

'Leave Dad out of this.'

Sai comes over to the bed, sits down and takes Ella's hand. 'Maybe you should go home, Ella. Clear the air.'

Ella notices Mum looking at Sai with eyes as huge as Willa's when something has amazed her. Dad's probably already told her loads of crap about Sai, like he's the one who makes her smoke, that he's a bad influence, that he's taking advantage of her because he's two years older than her. Dad doesn't get that Sai's more sorted than their whole messed-up family put together.

'Have you told the police?' Ella asks Mum.

'What?'

'Have you told them that you're back? Handed yourself in?'

'I don't understand—'

'You're still on file as a missing person. I've been asking them to look for you. You're wasting their resources. In fact, misleading the police, making them think you've been kidnapped or murdered – that's a criminal offence, isn't it?'

'If you come home with me we can talk, Ella. I can explain.'

'It's not your home any more.'

Mum bows her head.

Ella lets go of Sai's hand, clenches her fists and digs her nails into her palms. She refuses to feel sorry for her.

Sai goes over to the window. 'Ella, I really think you should go.' He looks down at the street. 'Your dad's waiting for you. Staying here's only going to make things worse.' He walks to the door. 'I'll call you later.'

Great. So now the one person who's meant to be on her side is abandoning her.

'Thanks for the support, Sai,' she calls after him. Then she jumps off the bed, storms past her mum and Sai, and runs down the stairs.

For a while, they drive in silence through the quiet streets. Dad keeps glancing at Ella in the rear-view mirror, his eyes small and tired behind his glasses. He hasn't said anything about her hair yet, but she can tell he's angry.

Ella leans forward and pokes her head between the front seats.

'So Dad, now that Mum's back and we're playing happy families, what are you going to tell Willa?'

'Not now, Ella,' says Dad.

'And what about Fay?'

'Ella—'

She keeps going. 'So you haven't filled Mum in on our new family?'

Silence.

Ella laughs. 'Good one, Dad.'

'Told me what?' says Mum in a low, steady voice.

'Oh, not much really. Only that Dad's shacked up with your best friend, and Willa thinks she's her mum.'

Dad looks over at Mum. Mum stares ahead. Dad looks back at the road, changes gear and accelerates into Willoughby Street.

Fay

In a few minutes Willa's standing by the door in her favourite red wellies and the blue raincoat she'd inherited from Ella, with her Adventure Suitcase: the perfect Paddington Bear. In her free hand she holds Louis's lead.

'Louis's staying here,' Fay says, her throat tight.

Willa frowns. 'I think Louis would like to come on an adventure.'

'We need him to look after Ella.'

'Because she'll be upset?'

Fay nods. 'She might be a little upset.'

'Will Ella be upset because Daddy's cross with her about Sai?'

'Yes.'

And because the mum she's spent six years idolising has shown up – and revealed herself to be one big disappointment. And because she's going to find her little sister gone.

Willa lets go of the lead and gives Louis a kiss between his ears.

'Tell Ella and Daddy and No One Woman that we're going on a Big Adventure ... ' Willa looks up at Fay. 'Should we leave a note?'

If they don't hurry up and leave Fay's going to lose her nerve.

'No, that won't be necessary, Willa.' Fay opens the front door. 'Come on, let's go.'

'Is it a surprise?'

'A surprise?'

'Where we're going – is that why you're not saying?'

Fay rubs her brow. 'Yes, a surprise.'

She hasn't got a clue where they're going. She hasn't got a clue what the hell she's doing. She just knows that if she sits back and lets it all happen, she's going to lose everything.

Louis goes to the kitchen, his lead trailing after him, and a moment later he's at the window, looking out as Ella and Fay walk down the steps of Number 77 Willoughby Street, down the paving stones that lead through the garden Fay planted, through the iron gates and out onto the pavement.

At that moment the Miss Peggs come out of their front door with their three Chihuahuas.

Before Fay has the chance to stop her, Willa's waving at them and calling out:

'We're going on a big adventure!' She swings her Adventure Suitcase into the air for them to see.

Rose Pegg catches Fay's eye. Fay looks down at the road.

'That sounds fun,' says Lily Pegg.

'Mummy's not saying where we're going – it's a surprise.'

Fay feels Rose Pegg's eyes bore into her. This is the last thing she needs. She clenches her jaw. *I'm not made for these spontaneous acts. I'm not made for running away.*

She takes Willa's hand. 'Come on, darling.'

'Bye Miss Lily Pegg! Bye Miss Rose Pegg!' Willa calls over her shoulder.

Fay feels the Miss Peggs staring after them.

'Why are we walking so fast?' asks Willa.

'We can't be late for the surprise.'

'Mummy, how long will the adventure take?'

'As long as it needs to take, Willa.'

'Will we be back in time to eat our pizzas tonight?'

'I don't think so.'

Had Norah found it easy? Just walking out like that?

'Okay,' says Willa.

Fay's throat tightens. It's too easy, she thinks, lying to a child.

A girl with a long black skirt and a black roll-neck jumper, black hair and black eyeliner walks towards them. Her head's bowed. Her hands, black fingernails, grip her phone. She crashes into Fay.

'Sorry,' she says. Then she looks past Fay and back at her phone, and then straight at Fay. 'Is this Willoughby Street?'

'Yes it is. And we live here. Over there, Number Seventy-seven—'

'Come on, Willa,' says Fay.

'You live at Number Seventy-seven?' says the goth girl.

'Yes. With Daddy and Louis and Ella—'

'Ella?'

'Yes, Ella's my sister. And No One Woman, who might be Auntie Norah.'

'Thank you,' says the girl and then walks on.

'Why did she say thank you?' asks Willa.

'I don't know—'

'And why's she dressed in so much black?' Willa asks.

'It's her style. Like you like red.'

'But black's sad.'

'Some people like being sad.'

Willa stops walking. 'They *like* being sad?'

'Yes. Sometimes it's easier to be sad than to be happy.'

'Weird.'

They sit on the hard, fold-down seats of the bus stop. Willa goes quiet. Then she eases her hand into Fay's. 'Mummy?'

'Yes, darling?'

'Look.' She points at a poster on the wall of the bus shelter. *Missing. Anna Gabriel. 14. Last seen on Holdingwell High Street on the 21st of March 2014.* And then a blurred picture. Curly brown hair. A sideways smile like the photographer's caught her off guard. *We're a lifeline when someone you love disappears . . .*

Fay feels sick.

'We should tell Ella,' says Willa.

'Tell Ella?'

'She could put a picture of Anna Gabriel on her missing persons website.'

'Oh . . . yes.'

'Lots of people follow Ella's campaign.'

'Yes, they do.'

'And her Twitter account too.' Six years old and she understands all these things. 'I wish you'd let me have a Twitter account. Then I could follow Ella and help her find the missing people.'

'When you're a bit older, Willa.'

'Will I be older on Sunday?'

Fay smiles. 'Yes, you'll be older on Sunday. But not quite old enough to use Twitter.'

Willa gets up and walks up to the poster. She brushes her fingers down the plastic cover. 'It looks old. Do you think that maybe they've found her and forgotten to take the poster down?'

'Maybe.'

'I hope so.'

'Yes.'

'Otherwise her parents must be very sad.'

Fay hears the bus turn into Willoughby Street. She looks up and watches it sway towards the shelter.

'It's here!' Willa picks up her case and goes to stand on the edge of the pavement.

Fay doesn't move.

The bus doors open.

Willa looks over her shoulder. 'Mummy? The bus is here.'

Fay doesn't take her eyes off Anna Gabriel's face. *Her parents must be very sad.* Willa's words crash around in her head.

'Mummy?'

The bus driver thumps his horn. Red spider veins on his cheeks.

Fay stands. *We should go back*, that's what she thinks. This isn't what I do. I'm not the one who runs away.

The driver cranes his neck and looks straight at Fay. 'So, you coming or not?'

Ella

'Fay?' Ella bursts through the front door.

Since Mum's come home, Ella's felt like she's been dangling upside down on one of those crazy rides at Alton Towers. Fay, calm, dependable, what-you-see-is-what-you-get Fay. That's what she needs.

'Fay!'

A plan, a timetable, a list, a family meeting. Something to make sense of all this.

All the lights are on. The smell of raw dough and pepperoni and cheese and tomato sauce from the kitchen.

'Fay!' Ella calls out again.

Dad puts the car keys down on the table in the hall. Mum takes off her shoes.

Louis bounds out from under the stairs.

'Hey, Louis.' Ella kneels down, and puts her arms around his thick, shaggy neck. It's the first time she's thought about it but, at this moment, it makes complete sense: they're the same, Louis and Fay. They can be counted on to be there.

Louis thumps his tail.

'Buddy?'

He looks past Ella at the front door. He probably thinks he's dangling off a rollercoaster too.

'Willa!' Ella calls out.

Ella looks under the stairs; Willa spends more time in there with Louis than in her bedroom. She blinks at the dark space. Louis's Friday bone. His water bowl. But no Willa.

'Willa!' Ella calls up the stairs.

Still no answer.

Ella turns to face Mum and Dad.

'Where the hell are they?'

Ella slams the front door behind her, runs down the front steps, down the path, through the gate and across the street.

'Ella?'

A girl stands in front of her, head to toe in black, eyeliner so thick that her eyes shrink into her face.

@darkislight. Was she really here? Standing on Willoughby Street?

The girl steps forward – expecting what? A hug? A handshake? A kiss?

'Hello dear!' Rose Pegg comes out of her house and joins them on the pavement. 'This young lady came to see you.'

Lily follows Rose out and adds:

'She's from our tweet group.'

'Some tea, my dear?' Rose Pegg holds out a mug. @darkislight smiles and takes the mug between her skinny fingers. The mug, covered in yellow roses, looks all wrong against the rest of her.

'You must be delighted that your mum's returned,' says Lily Pegg.

'I've got to go,' says Ella.

'Why don't you stay, dear? For a cup of tea. Get to know Monica.'

Monica? Ella had never thought of @darkislight having a name.

'I'm in a hurry, Miss Lily Pegg.'

Ella starts running.

'She went the other way—' Rose Pegg's voice follows Ella as she runs.

Ella stops.

The other way?

She turns round. Rose Pegg smiles and points at the bus stop.

How do the Peggs always *know*?

Ella turns and runs up the other side of the road.

Where's Fay taken her?

Her head swims. It's happening again. The person who means more to her than anyone in her life, the people who mean more to her than anything, are disappearing.

As Ella runs to the bus stop she says to herself, *You're going to find her.* She says it over and over: *You have to find her.*

Fay

'Are we nearly there?' Willa's looks out of the bus window

Fay strokes her hair. 'Nearly ...'

Willa nods her head and closes her eyes.

Only they're not nearly anywhere. They're on the second loop of the 147 bus, which is lurching up the high street, empty except for Willa and Fay.

Willa's breathing deepens, her sleepy body heavy against Fay.

They'll get off in a minute. Once she's decided what she's going to do.

Fay catches a reflection of her face in the bus window. She doesn't recognise herself.

The bus swerves into the stop outside The Great Escape travel agent's.

A fist thumps on the bus door.

'Hang on, hang on,' says the driver. He shakes his head and presses a button. The doors clatter open.

Ella runs past him.

'Hey!' he yells after her.

Her cheeks red, a line of sweat on her top lip, breathing so heavily the windows steam up beside her.

Ella bends over and holds her hands to her waist, and breathes in. 'What the hell are you doing on a bus?'

The bus driver shakes his head at Ella. 'You have to pay for a ticket.'

'We're getting off in a minute,' Ella throws over her shoulder. Then she turns to face Fay. 'You're really fucked up, you know?'

Willa sits up with a start. 'Ella?' She rubs her eyes and blinks.

'You don't think you'd have got away with this, do you?' Ella says to Fay.

Fay shrugs.

'You don't have the right. Willa's not . . .'

'I'm not what?' Willa asks.

Ella goes over and snatches Willa's hand away from Fay's arm.

'Ow!' Willa yanks her hand away, and her fingers curl around Fay's.

'Come on Willa, we're going home,' says Ella.

Willa shakes her head. 'No. We're going on a Big Adventure.' She leans over and pulls her case out from the footwell. 'Mummy's taking me.' Willa looks at Fay, waiting for her to speak. 'Aren't you, Mummy?'

Fay looses her fingers from Willa's.

'A Big Adventure, hey?' Ella laughs.

'You can come with us if you like,' says Willa. 'Mummy wouldn't mind, would you?'

Taking the girls, leaving Adam and Norah to it – for a second, that doesn't sound so crazy.

'You have to come home, Fay,' says Ella, her voice softer.

'Why?' Willa asks. 'Why does Mummy have to come home? And why are you being weird? And why—'

'Willa, give the questions a rest,' Ella says.

'But I don't understand . . .'

Fay keeps staring out of the window. The nights are getting longer; there's still a hint of light in the sky.

Ella holds out her hand. 'Fay—'

'Are you going to pay for a ticket, or what?' the driver barks from the front of the bus.

'Just give us a minute,' Ella yells back.

'Come on, Fay.' Ella's voice is shaking.

Does she really want her to come back?

'Willa needs to eat. And to go to bed . . . She needs to be with us. All of us,' Ella says. 'And you have to speak to Mum, tell her she can't just come back like this and expect to pick up where she left off. She'll listen to you.'

'Are you talking about No One Woman?' Willa asks.

'What she's done, it's not fair,' Ella goes on. 'Not on any of us.'

'No, it's not.' Fay gets up and brushes down the wrinkles in her raincoat. She lifts Willa into her arms. 'It's time to go back, my darling.'

'What about our Big Adventure?'

Fay feels her little girl's heart hammering in her chest.

'The best adventures take place at home,' Fay says.

'If you're getting off, hurry up,' yells the bus driver.

Fay catches his eye and nods.

Once Ella, Fay and Willa have walked down the aisle and out onto the pavement, the driver thumps a button to shut the doors, yanks the bus into gear and pulls away.

For a second, the three of them stand on the pavement looking out at the empty high street.

Willa stands between Fay and Ella. She takes each of them by the hand.

119

'Ella?' Willa asks. 'Can I ask a question now?'

'Just one,' Ella says, kissing Willa's hand.

'Why did you call No One Woman Mum?'

Adam

Adam stops on the landing and looks into Willa's room. Fay's sitting on the edge of the bed, smoothing down Willa's knotty hair.

She's the only one who can get Willa to sleep when she's wound up.

He looks at Fay. Dark shadows streak the pale skin under her eyes. She hasn't slept for twenty-four hours now. And then taking Willa out for a walk in the dark, an adventure to get her mind off all the chaos. Even now, Fay put everyone else first.

He goes and sits beside Fay and takes her hand in his.

Willa beams.

It's important for her to see that we're close. That we love each other, Fay had told him in the early days. *It's what gives children secure attachment.*

Now he thinks that maybe it's better if children learn not to get too attached.

'Is No One Woman staying, then?' Willa's voice is thick with sleep.

'We'll see, my darling,' Fay says.

'Daddy?'

'Like Mummy said, we'll see. You need to sleep now.'

'Will she still be here for my birthday?'

Fay doesn't answer. Adam holds her hand tighter.

'We don't know yet, Willa,' he says.

'Is she Auntie Norah?'

'You need to sleep, my darling. It's late. We'll talk in the morning.'

Willa sleeps on her tummy, her arms tucked into her sides. Fay rubs her back gently until Willa's eyes drop closed.

'Will Ella be okay ... ?' Willa's voice drifts away.

'She'll be fine,' Fay whispers.

Adam watches Fay lean over and kiss his little girl – *their* little girl.

'I'll stay with her for a bit,' Fay whispers to Adam.

If they leave Willa too soon after she's gone to sleep, she wakes up frightened, so they take it in turns to sit with her. They listen for her breath to deepen, for her head to sink into her pillow, for her eyelids to stop fluttering.

'Of course.' He kisses Fay's forehead and climbs up the stairs to their bedroom.

As he stands by the window, looking out at the dark, spring night, Fay comes in carrying Willa's clothes.

Fay turns the jumper inside out and puts it in the laundry basket.

'Willa okay?' he asks.

Fay nods. 'For now.'

Couldn't Norah have given them a bit of warning? Time to prepare the kids? He wonders why he ever found this unpredictability attractive.

Fay changes into her nightdress, closes the curtains and pulls back the duvet.

Adam catches her hand.

'Stop that for a second.' He takes her palm to his lips and breathes in the smell of soap.

She rests her head against his chest.

It took him a while to get used to Fay's body, softer and fuller than Norah's.

'I'm sorry,' he whispers into her hair.

'It's not your fault.'

He was surprised that Fay, who used to be so critical of Adam when Norah was around, hadn't once blamed him for Norah's departure.

'I'm still sorry,' he says. 'You don't deserve this.'

Fay draws away from him gently. 'I need to get some sleep.'

She climbs into bed and switches off her bedside lamp.

As he watches her head sink into the pillow, her eyes closing, he whispers:

I won't let you down. Not after all these years. Not after everything you've done for us.

The world is trying to go to sleep.

In the main bedroom, the father wakes from a dream. Her name sits on his lips ... *Norah* ... Had he said it out loud? It's been years since he's dreamt about her.

He leans over to The Mother Who Stayed and kisses her brow. *I love you*, he wants to say, but the words get lost in his throat.

He gets up, puts his glasses on, takes a packet of cigarettes from the chest of drawers.

In the lounge, he finds the big dog asleep next to The Mother Who Left. The dog opens his eyes and follows him into the garden.

As he blows smoke at the stars, he looks at the big dog. *You're not afraid to show it, are you? That you're happy she's home. That you want her to stay.*

He hears the glass doors open, her soft tread across the grass; he turns and looks at The Mother Who Left, her pale skin glowing white under the moon.

Can I have one? she asks, nodding at the cigarette in the father's hand.

They sit beside each other on the bench under the peach tree.

She shifts closer to him and her thigh brushes against his. He leans over and kisses her bare shoulder, and then he stubs out his cigarette and gets up.

The big dog wakes and follows him across the garden back to the house.

I missed you, she calls after him, but he keeps walking.

The little girl tiptoes into her parents' bedroom. Her father's missing. She goes to the window and lifts the curtain and sees him sitting on the bench with the strange woman who turned up on their doorstep this morning. Their heads are bowed, both smoking, Louis at their feet.

She goes over to the bed and climbs in beside The Mother Who Stayed. *What about our big adventure,* she thinks as she drifts off to sleep. *The one you said was going to start when we got home.*

The Mother Who Stayed stirs and puts her arm around her little girl. *I'll never let you go*, she thinks.

The big dog climbs to the top of the house and sits outside the attic door and listens to the teenage girl tearing at her old life.

The teenage girl rips posters from the walls, drags the clothes from the wardrobe, yanks the vinyls from their rack, smashes the bottle of perfume on the wooden floor and stuffs the black bin bags until the room is bare.

The little girl hears a bark. She slips out from her mother's arms and walks up to the attic. The teenage girl flings open the door and throws bin bag after bin bag onto the landing. She's crying.

Do you need some help? the little girl asks.

But her sister doesn't answer. She throws out the last bin bag and closes the door.

Down in the bedroom, The Mother Who Stayed feels the rush of cold air under the sheets as the father comes back to her. She smells smoke and perfume.

At the top of the house, outside her sister's room, the little girl lies down beside the big dog. She puts her arms around his neck and leans her head into his fur. *I love you, Louis,* she whispers as she drifts off to sleep.

SATURDAY MORNING

Just before dawn, the world is waking up.

The big dog lies on the landing. He listens to the house tossing and turning and breathing and dreaming.

The little girl, her arms still wrapped around him, dreams that her sister lifts her up and puts her in one of her big black bags and throws her out onto Willoughby Street. She yells for help, but no one comes. And then she hears the light tread of paws on the pavement, and then a claw ripping through the black plastic.

She squeezes the big dog tighter.

I'll find a way to make it all okay. By Sunday, when it's my birthday, everyone will be happy again.

The father listens to The Mother Who Stayed breathing beside him. He wants to shake her awake and tell her that he's going to fix things. But every time he closes his eyes he feels the touch of The Mother Who Left as she sat beside him on the bench last night.

The Mother Who Stayed opens her eyes and looks at the blue-grey light against the white walls. She remembers her little girl's fingers gripping hers last night. And then she feels them melting away.

I'll keep my promise: I won't let you go. I won't let any of you go.

Downstairs, The Mother Who Left looks out at a garden and thinks of all the things that have happened since she's been gone.

She touches the scar under her T-shirt, still numb after so many years.

I had to come home, didn't I? I had no choice.

At the top of the house, the teenage girl climbs out of her window and sits on the scaffolding; her legs dangle over the side. She lights a cigarette. In her other hand she holds a framed photo: her six-year-old self playing her yellow plastic trumpet, Mum playing her real trumpet. They're facing each other, their eyes smiling. They used to do concerts for Dad, up here in the attic, and he'd take photos and make posters as though Ella were a professional trumpeter, like Mum. *My fabulous trumpeting duo,* Dad would say.

She loosens her grip on the frame and lets it fall through her fingers.

I wish you'd never come home, she says as she watches the frame bounce against the steel rods of the scaffolding.

It keeps falling, down ... down ... down ... until it hits the paving stones of the path below.

The frame splits and the glass smashes into a thousand pieces.

Norah

Norah pours cereal into Willa's bowl.

Willa frowns.

'What's wrong?' Norah asks.

'I'm not sure I'm allowed those.'

Norah looks at the box. 'You're not allowed Coco Pops?'

'Only for special.'

'Oh. What do you usually have?'

'Porridge ... or yoghurt ... or fruit ... or a mix ...'

Of course. Fay.

'Porridge it is.' Norah picks up the bowl and starts tipping the Coco Pops back into the box.

Willa puts her hand on Norah's arm. 'You don't need to put them back.'

'But you said—'

'Maybe today *is* special.'

Norah puts the bowl back down.

'Because you're here,' Willa goes on. 'When we have guests, Mummy lets us have special things to eat. And you're a guest, aren't you?'

A chocolate-cake-for-breakfast kind of mum, that's how Fay had described Norah once.

Norah turns away; she can't bear this for much longer. She goes to get the milk from the fridge.

Norah and Willa (and Louis) are the only ones awake, or the only ones downstairs, anyway.

As Willa watches the Coco Pops swirling around in her bowl, she scratches her scar.

'How did it happen?' Norah asks, sitting beside her. She points at the scar.

'Oh, this?' Willa bounces up and down in her seat. 'Didn't Ella tell you?'

Norah shakes her head.

'It's a cool story.'

'A story?'

'Well, I was only six months old, so I don't remember it exactly, but Ella told me what happened. She's the one who saved me – and Louis, he saved me too.'

'They saved you?'

Willa nods and shoves a spoonful of milky Coco Pops into her mouth. She gulps down the cereal and says:

'Well, they *say* they saved me, but I think I would have been fine. She didn't mean to.'

'Who didn't mean to?'

'You ask lots of questions, don't you?' Willa smiles. 'Like me.'

Before she can stop herself, Norah leans over and kisses the top of Willa's head.

Willa goes stiff and frowns. Norah has to remember that, as far as Willa's concerned, she's still a stranger.

'So, who didn't mean to?' Norah asks again.

Willa relaxes. 'The fox.'

'What do you mean, the fox?' Norah can't get her head around this. A fox in Willa's room? That kind of thing only happened in the papers. In other people's families – in other people's homes. Or in a little girl's imagination.

Willa puts down her spoon and sits up.

'Ella and Louis both came into my room at the same time, because they heard something. Ella said that she saw *a flash of red* and she knew, straight away, that something was wrong. Apparently I was standing up in my cot looking at her.'

'Her?'

'She was a girl fox. Ella says she can't be sure, but I know she was a girl fox.'

'What did Ella do?'

'At first, Ella and Louis were frozen to the spot – Ella says they were in shock – and then, when they saw me reach out and stroke the fox's head—'

'You stroked the fox's head?'

Willa goes on. 'I love animals. Foxes especially. So, the fox lowered her ears and moved closer, and that's when Ella and Louis leapt into action. Louis barked and Ella screamed and then they ran forward. And the fox turned her head to face them – her amber eyes shone, or I'm sure they did – and as Ella and Louis came closer she swiped her paw at me. Just here.' Willa strokes the scar. 'She didn't mean to hurt me.'

'She didn't?'

'She was scared.'

Norah thinks of a red paw against Willa's pale skin. The fox's claws out, a tear under her eye. She can't bear to hear much more of this.

'Weren't you scared?'

'I fell backwards in my cot, which must have been quite funny because I was wearing one of those sleeping bag things. But no, I didn't cry. And no, I wasn't scared. I think I'd remember.'

'And then what happened?'

'The fox tried to leap up over the side of the cot – she wanted to see whether I was okay, but Louis didn't take it that way, so he clambered over the bars, which isn't easy because he's so big, but he did, and he grabbed one of the fox's back legs in his mouth and Ella yanked at the fox's tail. Ella's the bravest person I know.'

'They really looked after you, Ella and Louis, didn't they?'

'And Mummy.'

Norah gulps. 'Yes, and Mummy.'

'Well, it's a good story, Willa. You really bring it to life.'

Willa shrugs. 'I've told it lots of times. And when she's not being moody, Ella likes to tell it to me too. We take it turns to fill bits in.'

'And what did the fox do after that?'

Norah imagines the fox spinning round at Louis, yelping in pain.

'Louis chased him all the way outside, and Ella went to get Daddy.'

'Daddy was home?' God, she'd thought Adam must have been out, that it was a night when the girls were being looked after by a babysitter. 'He was downstairs when this happened?'

Willa hesitates, and then blurts out: 'Daddy was sleeping on the couch. Ella couldn't wake him up.' Willa blushes. 'But he would have helped if he could. He hadn't learnt yet.'

'Learnt what?'

'To be brave. I'm teaching him to be more like Foxy Fox – but Daddy's much braver than he was before.'

'Yes, he is.'

'You knew Daddy, in the old days, didn't you?'

'A bit, yes.'

'Anyway, when Ella found Daddy asleep she called Mummy

at work and she came in an ambulance to get me so that they could do my stitches.'

And that's when Fay had moved in, wasn't it? When Adam had realised that the girls needed a mum, a proper mum.

Norah hears footsteps in the hallway.

'For months after the accident, Mummy slept beside me in the camp bed, the one you've been sleeping on, to make sure that the fox didn't come back. And Daddy went to his special meetings so that if it happened again he would wake up.'

And he *had* woken up, hadn't he? Willa was right, he'd learnt to be brave. To be a father. And that would never have happened if Norah had stayed.

'And you still like foxes?'

'Of course. Mrs Fox didn't mean to hurt me, like I said. She just got scared.'

Willa climbs off her chair and walks over to the kitchen window. Louis follows her.

'Did you see the police car?' Willa asks, pointing out of the kitchen window.

By the time Norah joins Willa at the window, two police officers are at the front door.

Fay

Fay steps away from the kitchen door. *A police car ?* What on earth?

Just as the bell goes, she reaches the front door.

Ella comes tearing down the stairs to join her, yelling 'Dad, you'd better come up!' and, a moment later, Adam rushes up from the basement. Norah comes out of the kitchen and stands in the hall.

Adam stares at Ella, who's smiling, and asks her, 'What the hell's going on,?'

'I thought they should know.'

'What are you talking about?' Adam asks. His eyes are bloodshot. He's shattered too.

'The police. They should know that Mum's not dead.'

'Who didn't die? And why are the police outside our front door?' Willa stands at the kitchen door, looking at Fay.

Fay's head spins. What a mess. Willa sharing breakfast with *a guest* who just so happens to be the mother who walked out on her when she was a baby; Ella filling bin bags with every memory she's had of Norah; Adam hiding away all morning in the basement with his photographs; Norah hanging around the house – waiting for what? For everyone to forgive her? For Fay to leave so that she can pick up where she leaves off? And now the police?

Fay closes her eyes again and feels the burn of tiredness behind her eyelids.

She sways and reaches for the edge of the table in the hallway.

'Mummy?' Willa dashes up to her and takes her hand. 'What's wrong? Why are you wobbly?'

When Fay opens her eyes, everyone's staring at her.

'I'm fine, my darling ... I'm fine. Just a bit tired.'

Willa's hand grips on tighter.

I can't lose them, thinks Fay. Not after all this time.

The doorbell goes again.

'I think you should open the door, Dad,' says Ella. 'Can't keep the police waiting.'

'You had no right to do this, Ella,' Adam says.

'No *right*? You're joking, aren't you?'

Fay walks past Adam and goes to the door. Ella was right: two police officers are standing on the doorstep.

A few weeks after Norah left, Fay and Adam had sat Ella down and explained that her mummy wasn't coming home. Ella had listened to them for a good hour, and then she'd looked from one to the other as though they were out of their minds and said:

You're wrong. Mum's coming home. And I'm the one who's going to find her.

Adam storms past Ella. 'I'll handle this,' he says to Fay. And then he turns to the police: 'If you don't mind, we'll discuss this outside.' He slams the door behind him.

'I don't understand what's going on,' Willa says.

As she looks at her little girl with her shiny brown eyes and her straggly, copper bob and the dark smudges under her eyes, Fay's heart tilts. All this is too much for Willa.

Ella looks from Fay to Norah. 'So, what *do* we tell Willa, guys? You're the experts.'

'The experts?' Norah asks.

'The mothers,' Ella says. 'Aren't mothers meant to know what to do?'

Fay feels dizzy again. Ella's right – how are they meant to explain all this to Willa?

I'm not your mummy. Is that what she's meant to say?

Your mummy's the woman who showed up on our doorstep yesterday, a woman you don't remember.

We've been keeping the truth from you. And now Ella's called the police and alerted them to the return of a missing person who isn't even on their books.

137

Fay opens her mouth, ready to comfort Willa, but Norah steps in front of her, crouches down and takes Willa's hand.

'There's nothing to worry about,' Norah says.

You're about to turn this little girl's life upside down and you tell her she's got nothing to worry about? Surely even Norah isn't as naive as that.

Willa stares at Norah's fingers wrapped around her own, and then looks up at Fay.

Fay feels a pinch in her chest.

'Mummy?'

Fay forces a smile. 'Yes, everything's fine, Willa.'

Ella lets out a cold laugh.

Norah continues. 'The police have come to ask me some questions. They're just doing their job.'

So she's still good at bullshitting.

Willa shrugs. 'Okay.' She slips her fingers out of Norah's hand and turns to Fay. 'Mummy, can I take Louis upstairs?' She smiles, her wobbly front tooth wedged at an angle. Another milestone in this little girl's life – one that Fay thought she would share in. 'Please Mummy, just for a treat, because it's the weekend?'

Fay feels Norah flinch.

'Of course, my darling,' says Fay.

Let Willa have the comforts she can. She deserves to have this weekend, to get through her birthday before having to deal with the truth of who Norah is.

Willa beams, grabs Louis's collar and drags him upstairs. 'It's my birthday tomorrow,' she says to Louis. 'And it's going to be the best birthday ever. And that means you'll get lots of treats too.'

Louis's tail thumps the back of Willa's legs.

Adam comes back in.

'Norah, Fay – would you mind coming out here for a second to talk to the police?'

If Norah's good at bullshitting, Adam's hopeless. The nervous sway in his voice, his eyes darting from Ella to Norah. But Ella seems to buy it. She folds her arms across her chest and smiles.

'Ella, look after your sister, I won't be long,' Adam says.

'Sure, Dad.' Ella looks over to Norah and her brown eyes darken. 'I've been looking after my sister since she was born – what's a few more hours?'

'Ella—'

'And you can tell the police that they'd better keep Mum – before she mucks up anyone else's lives.'

Ever since Norah left, Fay's struggled to find common ground with Ella. But right now, as they stand here, with everything falling apart, she's never felt closer to her. She doesn't want Norah here either.

It's clear to her now: Fay wants Norah to leave – for good. This is her home and her family and no matter what happens, she's going to stay.

Adam

Adam stands on Willoughby Street, Fay on one side of him, Norah on the other. They watch the police walk back to their car.

From that first night in London all those years ago, it had always been the three of them.

Fay got there first. Walking home through the park after a

late shift at the hospital, she'd found Norah lying on a play-ground roundabout, spinning and staring up at the stars. Norah had been sleepwalking; she'd twisted her ankle and had sat down on the roundabout for rest.

Adam had turned up a few minutes after Fay, his shirt hanging out, stumbling along the path that skirted the river after a long night at the pub.

Adam and Fay had fallen out within a few minutes of meeting.

I can manage on my own, Fay had said.

I want him to come with us, Norah had burst out.

He'd felt that was a victory: Norah wanted him.

Already on that first night, he and Fay had felt Norah's pull – and had started competing for her affections.

Looks like I'm coming, Adam had said, tucking his shirt in and brushing his fingers through his hair.

They'd each taken one of Norah's arms and carried her weight as she limped between them through the dark streets.

Mummy and Daddy must be loaded, he'd joked as they stood in the marble hallway of Fay's flat.

You can go now, Fay had said.

Norah had touched her arm. *Come on, Fay,* she'd said, her tone already familiar. *We should offer Adam a coffee. It's the least we can do.*

And so he'd stayed.

And six weeks later he'd proposed.

It was a summer's day, Norah's twenty-first birthday. Adam was meant to be working late, helping his dad in the photography shop – that's what he told Norah. But he'd planned it all: the trek up Primrose Hill, the picnic, cheap champagne, the Tesco's Finest chocolates, an old, battery-operated CD player with Louis Armstrong playing 'What a Wonderful World', the song they would have at their wedding. Tourists had clapped and whooped as Adam got down on one knee.

And she'd said yes. Against all the incredible odds, she'd accepted him.

The night of the proposal, Fay and Norah were meant to have a girly evening. When he walked through her front door behind Norah, he saw the disappointment on Fay's face. She'd spent all day preparing: champagne and chocolates and smoked salmon from Harrods, scented candles and a box of cosmetics from Jo Malone. And Norah's birthday present: a late-summer jazz weekend in New York, just the two of them. She'd placed the plane tickets in an envelope, tied a blue ribbon round it and propped it up on Norah's plate.

Norah had rushed in, flushed and out of breath, her hair hanging loose over her skinny shoulder blades, desperate to tell her new best friend about the proposal. *Sorry I'm late . . .* she'd gasped, kicking off her shoes. She collapsed on the sofa and patted the cushion beside her. *I have to tell you something,* she'd said.

He'd stood by the door, watching.

Fay's eyes fell on the pinprick of a diamond glinting on Norah's finger.

Fay had locked on her smile and opened the champagne.

And then Norah had blurted out: *I can't.* She'd looked from Fay to Adam and then she'd smoothed her T-shirt over her stomach. *I mean – I'm not meant to, am I?* She'd smiled shyly.

He'd asked her before he knew about the baby. He was glad of that: that he'd proposed because he loved her – loved her more than anything in the world. Loved her so much that, when Ella came along and Norah's attention was divided, he'd turned in on himself. Started drinking. And, for the next six years, until Willa was born, he'd lurched between obsessive love and childish jealousy, and a complete denial that he was a father. It had taken Fay to wake him up to life.

Later that night, he'd heard Fay and Norah talking on the balcony.

Do you think I'm doing the right thing? Norah had asked Fay.

Fay had paused and then said: *Sure.* And then she'd paused again. *He's crazy about you, Norah. Of course it's the right thing.*

The three of them watch the police car disappear round the corner of Willoughby Street.

Fay turns to Adam. 'What did you tell the officers?'

'I explained that Ella made a mistake.'

Adam notices that Norah's looking across the road. The Miss Peggs are sitting on a white wooden bench in front of their bungalow, drinking Earl Grey out of a Thermos, as they do every morning. *It's our Neighbourhood Watch duty,* they say. *We like to see the world waking up.*

'Anyone for tea?' Rose calls over the street, holding up her plastic beaker.

It's as though there's nothing strange at all about police cars and Ella shouting so loud the whole street must have heard and Norah, a woman they last saw six years ago, standing out here on the doorstep. Maybe the twins are psychic.

'We're fine, thank you,' Adam calls back.

'We're looking forward to tomorrow,' says Lily.

'Yes, can't wait,' adds Rose.

They smile and go back to fussing over their Chihuahuas.

Tomorrow? Adam hasn't got a clue what they twins are going on about, but then that's not unusual.

'Why didn't you just explain to Ella,' Norah says suddenly. 'Why did you let her believe I was missing?' Her voice is cold.

'You *were* missing, Norah,' Adam says. 'You disappeared from our lives. We tried to explain that you'd chosen to walk out on us, but Ella wouldn't buy it.'

Fay moves a few steps closer to Adam; her arm brushes his. *You can stand up to her,* he feels her telling him.

Fay had chosen him. Now he has to do the same.

He takes Fay's hand. For a moment, as Adam feels her fingers resting in his, he thinks that that they're going to get through this, that maybe it's all going to turn out okay.

Norah looks down at Adam and Fay's hands and then lifts her head until her eyes are level with Fay's.

'And what about you, Fay? You didn't think it might be worth telling Ella what happened? You're her godmother, aren't you? You're *meant* to tell her the truth.'

Adam tightens his grip on Fay's hand.

'Ella didn't want to know the truth,' Fay says.

'That's convenient,' Norah snaps back.

She goes on, her cheeks flushed. 'It's too much for Ella to handle all in one go like this. You should have told her, and you should have told Willa too. God, what were you two playing at?'

'Why?' asks Fay.

'What do you mean, *why*?'

'Why should we have told the girls anything?'

'Ella's upset. She thinks I've been lying to her all this time. And Willa's confused. What's she going to do when she works out that I'm her mum? That this little act you've got going—' She waves her hand between Adam and Fay.

An act? She doesn't have a clue, does she? Doesn't she see that he's changed? That they've all changed.

Fay clenches her jaw. 'This is your fault, Norah. We just picked up the pieces.'

'Not very well, from the looks of it—'

'Hey—' Adam starts.

'It's been a long time.' Fay takes a breath to steady her voice. 'We didn't think you were coming back.'

'That's not the point.'

'You know, Norah,' Fay says, 'it really is the point. If you were interested in any of this – in us – you'd have come home.'

'There's no *us*,' shouts Norah. 'You're nothing to do with this.'

A silence hangs between the three of them.

Then Adam steps forward. 'Fay's right, Norah. It's been years; as far as we were concerned, you were never coming back.'

He remembers the first time he told Fay about the note. He'd read it through so many times he knew it by heart. *Please don't try to find me,* he'd recited. And he'd respected her wishes – thought that maybe, if he got this instruction right, she'd come home. He'd spent hours looking up the road, waiting for her to appear, staring at his phone, thinking that maybe she'd call. But it *had* been years – six whole years. Who stays away that long and then just shows up out of the blue?

He notices Fay's fingers fluttering at her side. He'd never noticed this tremor, not until they got close. And then she'd confided how hard she worked to keep it under control, how, when she was training to be a surgeon, she'd had to prove that she could keep it in check, that it wouldn't get in the way of her operating.

He takes her hand and holds it tight.

How do you see me? Fay had asked him once, a few years into their relationship. *Is it just that you're grateful? Because I'm the one who stayed?* He'd waited for her to finish and he'd paused, then looked her in the eye and said: *You're the girls' real mother now. You're my real wife. And I love you.*

And he'd meant it, hadn't he?

'Let's see how it goes, Norah,' Adam says.

Norah shakes her head. 'No, we won't see how it goes.'

Adam looks up at her. Fay's hand starts shaking again.

Norah looks from Adam to Fay.

'I've come home for good.'

Ella

Ella leaves Willa watching *Fantastic Mr Fox* and goes into the kitchen to get a Coke. Through the window, she sees Dad sitting alone in the car.

'I'll be back in a minute, Willa,' she calls through the lounge door as she crosses the hall.

Ella crosses the street and knocks on the windscreen.

'Dad!'

He jumps.

She walks round the car and he leans over and opens the passenger door for her.

'Thanks,' she says as she sits down beside him.

He winds the window right down and hangs his arm over the side to get rid of his cigarette.

'It's okay, Dad, I'm not Fay.'

He blows a curl of smoke out of the window and then lifts the cigarette back into the car.

'Can I have one?'

He laughs. 'No.'

'Fay doesn't want you to smoke and you don't want me to smoke – that makes us even, doesn't it?'

'I'm not giving you one.'

'Didn't you smoke at fourteen?'

'I didn't know any better.'

He means he didn't have parents like Dad and Fay, who give warnings and threaten to cancel mobile phone contracts and impose curfews.

Ella stares at the blossom drifting across the windscreen.

'The blossom always comes out for Willa's birthday, doesn't it?'

Dad looks out of the windscreen and nods.

'Remember my sixth birthday, Dad?'

'The one when we nearly got sued?'

Ella laughs. 'Yeah.'

Mum had taken Ella and her friends sledging with kitchen

trays on the frozen lake in Holdingwell Park. The ice had cracked, and Sarah Keep had fallen in. Her mum was a lawyer. Obviously.

'She wanted you to have the best birthday,' Dad says.

'It was – even with the suing thing.'

'Mum was good at parties. Even if they were a little alternative.'

'One of the girls threw up in the front garden.'

Mum hadn't planned for any sensible savoury stuff so they spent the day eating cake and sweets and drinking Coke and lemonade until their heads felt like they were going to explode from the sugar high.

'I don't remember you being there, Dad.'

'No.' He pauses. 'I was at the pub – couldn't face the mayhem.'

She likes that he's honest about that now. Facing the truth is part of his AA thing.

'It's a shame you weren't there to take photos.'

'There are lots of things I failed to do, Ella.'

Ella takes his hand. She doesn't want him to feel guilty any more; he's spent years trying to make it up to them.

'Fay saved the day – with the suing thing,' Ella says.

'Fay was there? I don't remember that.'

'I called her on the way back from the park.' Ella had borrowed Sarah Keep's mobile because Mum didn't have one.

Calling Fay was something Ella had done instinctively whenever Mum was in over her head.

'Calling the pediatric surgeon – a good way to avoid being sued. Well done, Ella,' Dad says.

'She stayed that night, when all the other girls were gone. The three of us, Mum, Fay and me, sat in Mum's studio opening my presents.'

Ella holds Dad's hand tight. 'Dad, why did Mum leave? I mean, why did she decide, on that particular day, to walk out on us?'

'I think it was what people call the last straw.'

'What was the last straw?'

'I was.'

'I know you were a bit messed up, Dad, but loads of dads are messed up and mums don't just walk out.'

'I was more than messed up, Ella. The night before she left, I was meant to look after you ...'

'And you didn't?'

'I forgot.'

'You forgot about us?'

'Pretty bad, hey?'

Ella leans into Dad's shoulder. 'Tell me about it.'

He smiles, but she can tell that he's still sad about it. 'Do I have to?'

'I need to understand,' Ella says.

'Well, you know how your mum was really good at the trumpet?'

Ella nods her head against Dad's shoulder. Through the windscreen she can see heavy rainclouds gathering in the sky.

Dad goes on: 'She hadn't played in years. I mean properly, professionally. Not since you and Willa were born. There was too much to do – and I didn't help.'

Ella sits up. 'So it was my fault?'

'No, Ella. Nothing was your fault, you were just a kid. But it got her down that she couldn't play. She missed it. It was part of who she was.'

I was part of who she was, thinks Ella. And she left me.

Dad goes on. 'So, Fay sent a recording to one of her musician friends in London. He was looking for someone to play the trumpet in his band.'

'Fay told you this?'

Dad nods.

'I thought Mum was a solo trumpeter.'

'It would have been a start. A way of her getting back into the industry.'

'So, what happened?'

'Your mum asked me to look after you so she could go and do an audition, play a gig with them, just for one night. She asked the Miss Peggs to watch you until I came home from work.'

'And you never came home?'

'Oh, I came home. I waited for the Miss Peggs to leave and then you helped me get Willa ready for bed – you warmed her bottle and you helped me bathe her and change her ...'

'And then?'

'When you were asleep, I left.'

'You went to the pub?'

The vein in Dad's forehead pushes up against his skin. 'Yeah, I went to the pub. I knew you'd get the Miss Peggs if something was wrong. I was angry that she was out doing something she loved without me. Just like when she was with you and Willa.'

'You were jealous?'

'I felt like there wasn't any room left for me. Guys can be like big kids sometimes. You'll learn that.'

She knows he means Sai – except Sai's the most grown-up person she's ever met. She wishes Dad could see that.

'So, you left us home alone and went to the Three Feathers to drown your sorrows?'

'I thought you'd be okay.'

'How long were you out for?'

'I got back after your mum.'

'She found us alone?'

'Yes, she did.'

'What did she say when you came home?'

'Nothing. She wasn't there. Neither were you. She'd taken you and Willa to Fay's.'

'In the middle of the night?'

'Yeah.' Dad looks through the windscreen down Willoughby Street. 'I should have seen it as warning, but I was blind back then. And angry that she didn't understand.'

Ella notices raindrops on the windscreen.

'What did you do?'

'I called Fay. She shouted at me and then hung up.'

'And then next day Mum left?'

'Yes, while I was at work. While you were at school.'

Ella feels a knot tightening in her stomach. She knows that there are kids out there who have it much worse than her, kids who are starving or dying of diseases, who have parents who beat them up. But still, life sure gave her a screwed-up set of parents.

'I don't think it was a reason to leave,' Ella says.

'Like I said, Ella, it was the last straw for your mum.'

'But still, Dad, you can't think that leaving was right?'

'No, I don't think her leaving was right.'

Ella lets go of Dad's hand and for a minute or so they sit in the car in silence. Then Ella turns to him and says,

'What are you doing out here, Dad?'

'Thinking.'

She wonders whether Mum's at the police station and whether Fay opted to stay with her. That would be just like

150

Fay. Thinking about Mum, the mum who's come home, gives Ella that horrible crushing feeling again, the one that started when she found out that Mum left because she wanted to, the one she keeps getting when she realises that none of the things she'd wished for are ever going to come true.

'What are we going to do, Dad?'

He drops his cigarette in an old Coke can on the dashboard. Then he shifts round in his seat and looks right at her.

'I'm going to fix this, Ella, I promise.'

'But Willa—'

Willa's the one Ella can't stop worrying about. The rest of them will cope, they're grown-ups, they expect the world to be screwed up. But Willa's little. And she still believes in happy endings, like in that film she keeps watching.

'We'll work it out,' Dad says.

By *we*, Dad means Fay. Fay will sit him down and they'll talk things through and she'll come up with a plan and they'll have a family meeting. Except, this time, Ella isn't sure that even the great Fay will be able to sort out the mess they're in.

'Do you love her?'

He nods. 'They don't disappear, the feelings you have for someone.'

'I meant Fay.'

He tugs at his collar. His weekend shirt: light blue gingham, bought by Fay, like the rest of his wardrobe.

'Dad?'

He'd never said the words, not out loud. Or not that Ella had heard. She knew that they'd got really close. That without Fay Dad wouldn't be in the sorted place he was now. But love was something different, wasn't it? Love was what she felt for Sai, that unexplainable feeling that surged through her whole body whenever she was in the same room as him, and the hollow ache when he wasn't there. Love was what she'd always thought Dad felt for Mum, no matter how long she was away.

'I owe my life to Fay,' Dad says.

Ella shakes her head. 'This is going to sound kind of corny, Dad, especially coming from me, but I reckon that when you love someone it's not because of the things they do, it's because of who they are in here.' She points to her heart. 'You fall in love with their essence, or their soul, or whatever you want to call it. And you know what the test is, that tells you that you *really* love them? You think about taking away all the stuff they *do*, the stuff that makes you think they're amazing – and even then, the love you have for them, it stays.'

Not in a million years did she think she'd be sitting in a car giving Dad relationship advice.

'The love stays?' he asks.

Ella nods. 'It does.'

'The police never looked for Mum, did they?'

She'd worked it out: it's why the man had acted so weird on the phone and said that there was no reason for the police to come out. That's when Ella had changed her story: *There's an intruder in the house,* she'd told him. *She's refusing to leave.* And when the man asked whether the intruder was posing a threat, Ella had said *yes*.

Ella remembers how the police officers had glanced at each other as they stood in the hallway – a *what-a-weird-fucking-family* look.

Dad shakes his head. 'I'm sorry, Ella.'

'So where are they? Mum and Fay?'

'They're catching up.'

'God, that must be fun.'

Dad doesn't answer.

'You know you're going to have to choose, right? You're going to have to work out who you love – who you want to stay. That's what *fixing it* means.'

Dad stares out at the house.

'Dad?'

'I'm sorry, Ella.'

'You keep saying that, Dad. But being sorry doesn't help, does it? Being sorry's not a decision.'

'It wasn't meant to be like this.'

'You mean . . . Mum coming home?'

He nods.

Ella and Dad hadn't got on for a while now, but she'd always felt that they had a special bond. Weren't they the only ones that remembered what it was like to be with Mum, and how amazing she was? And now he was sad and shocked – and disappointed, just like she was. Maybe he did still love her.

'Why don't you come inside?'

He shakes his head. 'Just give me a few more minutes.'

'Dad?' She hasn't seen him like this since Mum left. Zoned out, his eyes bloodshot, lost-looking. 'Dad?'

Dad takes Ella's head in his hands and kisses her forehead. 'I promise I'll make it okay, Ella.'

It's what he'd said over and over in the months after Mum disappeared. And he'd tried, really hard, but it had taken ages – years – for things to feel a bit normal again. And now it was like they were back at square one. Worse than square one. Square one was Mum being here and Fay being Ella's godmother and Dad knowing who he loved and Willa knowing who her mum was, even if she was only a baby.

All Ella had ever wanted was for Mum to be home again. *Be careful what you wish for,* isn't that what people said? She'd never understood why you had to be careful about wishing for something good, like Mum coming back. But she gets it now: wishes should come with a health warning. Better still, wishes should be banned altogether.

Willa

Ella said she'd be back in a minute but she was away for ages. *Being back in a minute* was code for going out to have a ciga-rette. Only it's started to rain, so she should have come back in.

Willa wanted Ella to come back because she'd got to the really good bit in the film, when Mr Fox has made friends with all the other animals living underground and worked out what their special talents are, and planned to raid Boggis, Bunce and Bean's supplies. But sometimes, when Ella goes away to smoke, she comes back in a better mood, so Willa doesn't say anything.

Willa stares out into the garden, which looks wet and grey. She hopes that the rain clears for her birthday.

Ella's phone buzzes on the blanket. Willa knows you're not meant to look at people's phones, just like you're not meant to read their diaries, but she's sick of not knowing what's going on. And she's kind of curious to know whether Sai's sending Ella love messages.

The buzz was a tweet coming in. Ella tweets all the time. It's for her school project on missing people – she's been doing it for ages and ages, which makes Willa think that homework at Holdingwell Academy must be much harder than homework at Holdingwell Primary, which you can usually finish in under an hour.

Someone called @onmymind has left Ella a message.

'What are you doing, Willa?'

Willa looks up.

And so does Louis.

Ella stands at the door to the lounge.

Willa puts down the phone. 'It buzzed. Sorry.'

'My phone's private.' Ella snatches her mobile from Willa and shoves it in her pocket.

'Sorry,' Willa says again, but she knows her sorry isn't a real sorry because she'd have liked to have read the message from @onmymind.

Willa expects Ella to walk off in a huff like she's been doing lots lately, but instead she flops down on the sofa and says, 'Come on, let's see what happens to Mr Fox.'

Willa smiles and turns up the volume, and tries to nestle into the crook of Ella's arm but Ella feels all stiff. Maybe she's still cross about the phone.

They've got to the bit where the Caterpillar tractors are about to dig up Mr Fox and Mrs Fox's burrow. Willa looks away from the screen. She hates this bit: no one should have their home dug up like that. Her eyes flit across the back garden. A flash of red under the gooseberry bush. Mrs Fox must be preparing her den for tomorrow, when she's going to give birth because she's pregnant, like Mrs Fox.

Louis's lying on the sofa with his head on Willa's lap. He's heavy and drooling, but Willa doesn't want to push him away in case he gets offended. Although Ella said she wanted to see what happens to Mr Fox, she's been staring into space and checking her phone and doing her jiggling-leg thing, which means she's stressed.

'Why did you throw away all the things in your room?' Willa asks.

Ella grabs a handful of popcorn, which they made for their breakfast, and shoves it in her mouth; Willa knows Ella did that so she doesn't have to answer right away.

'I thought you liked the pictures of Auntie Norah.'

She hopes that Ella will confirm that No One Woman is Auntie Norah, but Ella keeps munching and staring at a bit of the ceiling.

Willa flicks her tongue between her wobbly tooth and her gum. She likes to feel the jagged bits. 'Is No One Woman Auntie Norah?'

'Leave it, Willa, it's not important.'

It must be important if Ella's turned her room upside down and if No One Woman's been taken to the police station.

Willa tries a different tack. 'Why did you cut off your hair and dye it so dark?'

Ella shrugs. 'Felt like it.'

Willa doesn't want to hurt Ella's feelings but she doesn't think her new hairstyle suits her. She preferred her when she had long goldeny hair.

Ella's phone buzzes and she scrolls down the screen. It's probably Sai.

Willa looks at the telly. Mr Fox and his family are digging into the ground next to the tree to find a new home.

Willa strokes Louis's ears. *Do you know why everyone's acting so weird?* she asks him.

He looks up at her with his droopy eyes, which say, *You'll find out soon enough, Willa.* Which is nearly as bad as Ella not saying anything and Mummy saying everything's going to be fine when Willa doesn't even know what's meant to be wrong.

She feeds Louis a bit of popcorn and takes a sip of her hot chocolate. If things didn't feel weird, this would be the best Saturday morning they've had in ages, snuggled up on the sofa watching her favourite film and having treat food.

By the time they get to the bit in the film where everyone's having a big meal and dancing and singing, Ella's body has relaxed and she's put her hand on Louis's head and moved up closer to Willa and they're all hugging again and getting sleepy from the hot chocolate and the popcorn and the fleecy blanket and from staring at the telly.

When Willa wakes up, the DVD has flipped to the menu bit and the theme tune's playing over and over. Ella's head is resting on Louis's shoulders and her fingers are tangled up in his fur, like she's trying to hold on to him in case he runs away. They're both fast asleep.

Willa climbs off the sofa and goes to the kitchen to get a glass of water. Through the window she can see Miss Rose Pegg's round face and round marble eyes staring out of her lounge window – she's hitched up the net curtains. Miss Rose Pegg has to give herself injections because she's got too much sugar in her blood, like Louis. Miss Lily Pegg's face appears next to Miss Rose's. Miss Lily is as skinny as a stick man. The twins are identical, which means they've got the same colour hair and eyes and they're the same height, but it's like Miss Rose has been puffed up with Daddy's bicycle pump.

Just as she's about to turn away from the window, Willow notices that Mummy and Daddy's car is parked outside the house, which is weird because if the car's there, where are Mummy and Daddy and No One Woman?

She heads back to the lounge to see whether Ella is awake so that she can ask her about the car, but as she does she notices that the light's on in the den – and then she hears clomping downstairs in the basement.

When she gets to the bottom of the stairs that lead down through the den to the basement, she sees Daddy sitting on the floor of his office, surrounded by pictures of Mummy. Mummy doesn't like photos of her being put up around the house because she's shy about how she looks, which is silly because Willa thinks that she's the prettiest mummy in the world.

Willa knows that she should turn round and go back upstairs because Daddy looks like he's having a private moment and Mummy warns Willa not to disturb Daddy while he's in his zone, but he looks so sad that she can't help herself.

'Daddy, what are you doing?'

Daddy's head shoots up. 'Willa?'

She goes over and sits beside him on the floor.

'Why are you looking at photos of Mummy?'

'I'm just doing a bit of sorting.'

'What kind of sorting?'

'I've got so many photographs . . . I'm running out of space.'

'You're not going to get rid of any, are you Daddy?'

Willa leans in and looks at a photo of Mummy wearing oven gloves and carrying a big golden turkey; she's got a funny paper hat on her head and she's grinning. Mummy loves Christmas. She's says that it's about family and that family's the most important thing in the world, which Willa agrees with – except that she thinks that sometimes you should be able to adopt people into your family, like Mrs Fox and her cubs.

'Can I have the photo of Mummy? Just to keep in my room? I won't put it up or anything.'

Adam hands her the photograph and then leans in and kisses her forehead. Everyone's kissing her much more than usual. Maybe it's because it's her birthday soon.

As Willa goes back up the stairs she turns round and asks Daddy:

'Where are Mummy and No One Woman?'

His eyebrows droop and he looks even sadder than he looked when she came in.

'They've just gone out for a bit,' Daddy says. 'They'll be home soon, Willa.'

Norah

My best friend stole my life: that's the thought that keeps going round in Norah's head as she looks at Fay across the table. How did Ella put it? *Dad's shacked up with your best friend . . .* Except shacked up doesn't cover it. Fay's done such a big renovation job on Norah's old life that, walking back into her home, she'd felt like a stranger.

Norah's sitting in front of Fay in The Holdingwell Café: plastic tables and orange plastic chairs and linoleum floors and greasy, steamed-up windows – and the best coffee in town. Katie, the owner, used to let Norah stay for hours with the girls.

The usual flush in Fay's cheeks has faded, and she won't

stop fiddling. Her spoon, the packet of sweetener, the plastic peeling from the menu. Norah hasn't seen her like this since those early days, when she would panic before her medical exams.

Norah notices Fay staring at her wedding ring. Fay helped Adam pick out the wedding bands. God, it was worse than that, wasn't it? Fay had paid for the rings. She'd covered the cost of the whole wedding. And they'd never paid her back.

'I'm sorry I got so angry,' Norah says.

Fay takes a sip of coffee and stares out of the window.

If Norah's going to make this work, she has to show them that she's sorry – and that she cares. And, from what she can see, getting Fay on side is vital to that.

Except, right now, she finds it hard even to be within a few feet of her.

Norah knows that there aren't any rules about what your best friend is or isn't allowed to do with your husband after you've walked out on him and disappeared for six years – but she still feels betrayed.

'You look pale,' Norah says.

'I didn't get much sleep.' Fay stares down into her coffee cup. 'Willa came in again last night . . .'

Norah shifts in her seat. 'Again?'

'She doesn't sleep well.'

'Bad dreams?' Norah tries not to be pleased that she's uncovered a crack in Fay's picture-perfect family.

'Sort of.'

And when you have bad dreams, you go to your mum, right?

Fay looks up and Norah holds her gaze until she blinks and looks out of the window.

Willa thinks she's her mum . . . Ella had said that too.

160

'She doesn't know who I am, does she?' Norah says. 'No One Woman?' Norah laughs nervously. She'd overheard Willa calling her that.

Fay jumps up from her chair. 'Sorry.' She clamps her hand to her mouth and runs to the ladies.

Norah looks at the raindrops sliding down the window.

They've been here for hours, drinking coffee, staring out at the grey, rain-heavy sky, barely saying a word.

It was Fay's idea for Adam to drop them off here, for them to stay away from the house long enough to make Ella believe that Norah was being questioned by the police. Norah wonders why she agreed to the stupid plan. Wasn't it just delaying the inevitable? They should be at home, thrashing things out, explaining to Ella what really happened and deciding on a way to tell Willa.

Norah pushes away her coffee cup. Was it really that hard to get through to Ella? They'd had six years to persuade her and she wasn't a kid, she could cope with the truth. Fay and Adam had stood by as she set up a bloody missing persons campaign. Letting a little girl chase a lie – that was cruel.

Norah picks up a flyer from the table: *The Holdingwell 10k – free refills all day.*

She looks over to the corner of the room where she used to play for the customers, Willa asleep at her feet, Ella beside her, blowing on her plastic trumpet.

For a second, she allows herself to believe that maybe all this could still work out as she had hoped. That, after a little awkwardness and a few explanations, everything would fall back into place and they'd welcome her home.

She looks to the loo door; Fay's been ages.

I have to win her trust, she thinks again. Except she hasn't got

161

a clue how to do it. Not when she knows that, however this is going to pan out, one of them will lose everything.

She waits another few minutes and then gets up and walks to the ladies.

Fay's in one of the cubicles, the door open, kneeling in front of the toilet bowl. She heaves and then sits back, shaking.

Norah sits beside her, gathers up the strands of Fay's hair and rubs her back.

Fay brushes her off.

'I was trying to help,' Norah says as she stands up and steps away.

'I don't need your help.' Fay goes over to the washbasin, splashes water onto her face and wipes her mouth.

Tiredness doesn't make you throw up, thinks Norah, not like that, but just as she is about to make a comment, Fay bursts out with:

'It wasn't my idea.' Fay grips the basin and looks at herself in the mirror. 'To let Willa believe that I was her mum.'

'No?'

Fay looks at Norah in the mirror, her eyes bloodshot. 'She was so little. She didn't understand who I was – she just assumed . . .'

'I get it.'

Fay turns round, her eyes swimming. 'No, you don't. They were all I had left of you. They made me feel close to you. It's what people do when they lose someone: they come together.'

She's got the tone she used to have when she was at medical school, when she'd come home and tell Norah about a lecture she'd been to or an article she'd found in the stacks: *did you know that neglect affects the mechanics of a child's brain?*

'You moved into my home, Fay. You changed every-thing.'

'What did you want us to do? We waited for you. For ages, the house stayed as it was. But we had to move on. Living in a time warp wasn't helping Adam or the girls. Look what it did to Ella, hanging on to the hope that you might turn up one day.' She pauses. 'We didn't think you were coming back, Norah.'

Norah washes her hands and wipes them on her leggings. 'I didn't think he was your type.' She tries to say this with as little sarcasm as possible. She's genuinely interested in how her best friend, who could barely stand to be in the same room as Adam, found herself in bed with him.

'My *type*?' Fay asks.

'You always said he wasn't good enough for me.'

'That was a long time ago.'

A long time ago? It feels like yesterday that they stood here, in these same loos, Norah telling Fay she was pregnant with Willa, that she didn't know how Adam would cope when he hadn't even got used to Ella being around; Fay telling Norah that Adam had to take responsibility.

'All I mean is that you and Adam never had much time for each other before—'

'*Before* you walked out on us?'

They look at each other, their expressions strained under the strip lights.

A woman pushes through the door and stares at them. Fay and Norah walk back into the café and settle into their places by the window.

For a while, they don't say anything. Then Norah leans forward.

163

'I thought you were happy with the life you had,' Norah says. 'When we talked, you'd always say that you had everything you ever wanted. Money, a career, freedom. You said you didn't want a family. You said that my family was enough for the both of us, that being Ella's godmother was better than being a mum ... I thought you had enough ... '

'*Enough*?' Fay shakes her head and then she stares out at the rain, a million miles away. Then she turns round and focuses her eyes on Norah. 'Don't you see? Through you, they had become my family too. That didn't change because you took up and left. You leaving made them matter even more to me.'

'I married Adam; I gave birth to the girls. Nothing changes that.'

'No, nothing changes that.'

'But?'

'I did what I had to do, Norah.'

Loving them, pulling together in grief – however Fay wants to put it, Norah can get her head around that. But she won't swallow this: Fay dressing it up as her coming to the rescue. She moved into Norah's life because she wanted to.

'Once you did what you had to do, once you'd fixed them, why didn't you just—'

'Leave? Why didn't I just leave?'

Norah bows her head.

Fay spreads her fingers on the table and leans forward. She doesn't look tired any more, or sad. Just angry.

'Adam was a mess, Norah. He couldn't look after himself, let alone the girls. Willa was a baby, Ella a little girl. They were in shock. They didn't know what to do. So yes, Norah, *I did what I had to do*. And then, guess what happened?'

'Don't—'

'Don't what, Norah? Tell you the truth? Tell you that when people help each other out they form an attachment? And that sometimes that attachment turns into love? It's called sticking together when you've gone through a tough time. It's called being a family. A real family.'

'And moving into Adam's bed was just an organic part of the process – that's what you're saying?'

Fay straightens her spine and looks straight at Norah. 'You're right.'

'Right?'

Fay's stopped fidgeting. She's sitting still and tall and she's still staring at Norah.

'I love him. That's why I stayed.'

Norah doesn't recognise her best friend.

Fay leans forward. 'And guess what? I've always loved him. I've loved him from the minute I met him, from the night we found you in the park and brought you home—'

There are times when a shift happens, when one small join in the great scaffolding of life comes loose and nothing ever looks the same again.

'But you seduced him,' Fay goes on, 'like you seduce the whole world. I didn't have a chance.'

'Seduce the whole world? What are you talking about?'

Fay shakes her head. 'Don't pretend you don't know what you do. How you sweep into people's lives and make them fall in love with you, how you draw them in until you're the centre of their world, until no one else matters—'

'I didn't—'

'You *did*.' Fay takes a breath. 'The night we met, Adam didn't even look at me.'

'You're crazy, Fay. He fancied me, that's all.'

'He didn't fancy you, Norah. He *fell* for you. Head over bloody heels. Madly. Blindly.'

'Blindly? You mean because he didn't register that you had a crush on him? What was stopping you? Why the hell didn't you say something?' Norah slumps back in her chair. 'God, this is pathetic.'

'Pathetic? I would have lost you both. You wouldn't have been able to deal with me telling you about my feelings for him—'

'You didn't give me a chance—'

'And I thought he didn't care about me – not like that.'

'*Thought?* And now?'

Norah notices that the café has gone quiet. Customers are looking over at them and whispering. One of the waitresses turns up the radio behind the bar.

'I don't know how he felt about me,' Fay says, her voice calm. 'He seemed to love you ...'

'Seemed?' Norah laughs. 'You think he loved you back then too?'

This is what couples do, isn't it? Rewrite the stories of their love.

'We don't always know what we truly feel. The way he is now, it makes me think that maybe—'

'He loved you all along?'

'I don't expect you to understand.'

'Well, Fay, why don't you explain it to me, your great theory of love and of how someone can be in love with someone without knowing it? Adam couldn't stand you. He ...'

She stops herself. Getting Fay on side? Wasn't that the plan? But how could she, after everything she'd just heard? And after watching Fay throw up like that?

'He didn't realise,' Fay says.

'He didn't realise what?'

'That maybe love is something different.'

'Different from loving me?'

Fay takes a sip of cold coffee, puts down her cup and nods. 'Yes, different from you, Norah. That there's infatuation – and love.'

Norah feels like she's been punched in the stomach. Infatuation?

She never thought the day would come when Fay would lecture her about love. None of Fay's relationships had lasted. The men she dated confided in Norah: *she's too intense . . . too controlling . . . too demanding. She wants everything to be perfect . . . she won't let me breathe.* But maybe that was what Adam needed, someone to expect him to be perfect, to stop making excuses for him.

'I get it,' Norah says. 'He needed someone to take over, right? To make him feel safe. He needed a fucking harbour—'

Fay empties another sachet of sweetener into her coffee. 'Like I said, I don't expect you to understand.'

A long pause hangs between them. Norah knew this would happen, that they would both say too much and that there would be no going back.

'So that's why you never came after me.'

'You didn't want us to come after you. You said to give you time, that you'd come back when you were ready—'

'You read my note?'

Fay takes her purse out of her bag and removes a folded-up piece of paper from the section where the bank notes go. She unfolds it and lies it down on the table. Norah stares at her handwriting and scans the words. They don't seem to have anything to do with her any more.

'Why do you have it?'

'Adam wanted me to get rid of it.'

'And you didn't?'

'I kept it as a reminder.'

'That I'd left?'

Fay shakes her head. 'That you might come home.' She pauses. 'And we did look for you.'

'We?'

'All of us, in our way. Ella thought the police weren't doing enough to find you, so she saved up her pocket money to hire a detective—' Fay pulls a napkin out of the dispenser and tears at it. 'She didn't get very far.'

No, Norah hadn't wanted to be found, or that's what she'd told herself.

'It was Ella who gave me the idea,' Fay says. 'I hired someone myself.'

'You had me traced?'

'I had to make sure you were okay.'

'And you found me?'

Fay nods.

God.

'Why didn't you contact me?'

'I didn't want to interfere – not with what was going on—'

'What was going on?'

Fay looks out of the window. 'Your new life. In Germany.'

And maybe, by then, you didn't want me to come back. Maybe by then you'd already done a makeover on the house and told Willa that you were her mother. Oh, and got into bed with Adam.

'Did you tell anyone?'

Fay shakes her head.

168

'So you lied to Adam?'

'I didn't lie to him.'

'Same thing. You kept it from him – from all of them.'

'Yes. I kept it from them.' Fay's phone buzzes. She looks at the screen. 'Adam's waiting outside.'

The exchange of texts, the making of plans, the life of a couple. He really had replaced her with Fay.

Norah follows Fay out into the damp, spring day. The sun's come out; after the rain everything shines, like the world's been scrubbed clean. Adam leans against the bonnet of the car. He looks the part, Norah thinks. A father. A husband.

Adam goes up to Fay and kisses her cheek.

Norah feels a jolt.

'You okay?' he asks Fay.

She nods.

Norah opens the car door. 'Ella will be disappointed they haven't locked me up for the night.'

Adam smiles, but he looks tired. She wonders what he's been doing with the girls all this time. How he's managed Ella and how he's kept up the pretense with Willa. But he's a good dad now, isn't he? Fay's made sure of that.

Norah climbs into the back seat. She smells smoke, the one habit he hasn't kicked.

Adam gets in behind the steering wheel.

Fay doesn't move from the pavement.

'Are you getting in?' Adam nods at the passenger seat.

Fay shakes her head. 'I'm going to stay at mine tonight. I'll walk.'

'Fay, please—' starts Adam. 'Come home with us.'

'I need to give you all some space. *I* need some space.'

Adam's shoulders fall. Norah wants to yell at him: don't you see what she's doing? She's making you feel guilty. She's making you go after her. By walking out on you like this, she's hitting you where you're weakest.

'What will I tell the girls? What will I tell Willa?' Adam asks, his eyes fixed on Fay.

Norah hears the panic in Adam's voice. Was this how it all began? Unable to cope on his own, he'd found himself begging her to stay?

'I'm sure you'll think of something,' says Fay.

Adam reaches his hand out of the window. 'You're really not coming?' The vein on his forehead pushes up under his skin.

Norah feels a thud in her chest. If Fay's loved Adam this whole time, if she thinks that *he's* loved *her* this whole time, they've been in competition, haven't they? All those years when she'd trusted Fay, when Fay was the one person she knew she could go to, who she could be sure would understand. All those conversations they'd had about Adam, how Fay had agreed, told her she was right to be upset, that Adam should be doing more for the kids, that his love for her didn't count if it didn't translate into concrete actions. God, Fay was probably paving the way for Norah's departure.

He needs to start acting like a proper husband, a proper dad. Fay had said. *You need to do something to make Adam wake up – grow up.* And then the words come back to her, clear as day: *You should threaten to leave him.* She'd actually said those words.

She'd thought she'd left on impulse, when it suddenly dawned on her that things were never going to get any better. But maybe her mind had been planning her departure long before then. And maybe it was Fay who'd first planted the idea in Norah's head.

170

Norah opens her mouth to say something. She thought she wanted Fay to be out of the way, but if she's going to move forward she needs her to come with them: she's the mum, the wife, the one who stayed. And leaving Adam like this is just going to make him want her more. Fay's the only one who can help Norah get through to Adam and the girls.

'Fay—' Norah says. But then she stalls. *Please come home with us?* She can't bring herself to say it.

'I'll be back tomorrow, for Willa's birthday.' She steps away from the kerb and waits for Adam to start the engine.

As they pull away Norah looks through the rear-view mirror at her best friend standing alone on the pavement.

SATURDAY AFTERNOON

Ella

@findingmum

She's not getting anywhere near Willa. #hadyourchance

Ella's followers have gone crazy. @onmymind keeps tweeting: **be patient ... wait ... see what happens ... your mum loves you ...** But Ella's never stopped waiting. Her life froze on the day Mum left her at the school gates and disappeared. It's time to move on now.

@liliesandroses have been at it too. **We knew she'd come home ...** Ella wishes that this time, when the Miss Peggs had their psychic premonition, they'd called on their angels or spirit guides or whatever and told them that it would be best if Mum *didn't* come home. It would have been better if Ella had spent the rest of her life believing in an imaginary mum rather than having to face the woman who showed up yesterday.

And then @hisloveishome, the Jesus freak, harping on about forgiveness: **Don't give up on her. Give her a chance.**

It's easy for you to say, Ella thinks. She's not your mum. Plus you're religious. You believe there's a God who's got this big plan for the world and that *everything's meant to be*. Ella doesn't believe that anyone's in charge – if there were, He should be fired for incompetence.

Give her a chance? Mum's had her chance. She's had years and years to come back and explain and make good. It's too late. Whatever Dad said, things aren't going to be okay, not until she leaves.

Ella switches off her phone, then eases Willa's sleepy head from her lap and covers her with a blanket. She hopes that Willa didn't read the messages. Willa has a sneaky way of working things out.

There was a time when Ella hated Fay, how she walked into their lives trying to take Mum's place, how she let Willa call her Mummy and how Dad went along with it. But now Ella would do anything to protect Willa from the truth. Mum doesn't deserve to be in Willa's life.

With the theme tune of *Fantastic Mr Fox* still playing in the background, Ella goes over and sits on the camp bed Mum slept on last night. She flips open the lid of the wheelie suitcase and looks down at Mum's things: her wash bag, her clothes – leggings and T-shirts and baggy jumpers. She notices a CD and pulls it out. There's a picture of Mum on the front, holding her trumpet to her lips. Ella's cheeks burn. While Dad and Fay have been juggling their jobs, looking after Willa and Ella, Mum's been jamming in cool music studios producing CDs. The things Ella had wished she could share with her.

Ella takes the CD and slips it under her sweatshirt.

Then she notices that Mum's left her wallet behind. She zips open the coin compartment and finds German euros among pound coins and pennies. There are photos under the see-through plastic bits inside. The crow starts flapping again, its wings spread like dark shadows inside her body. The top photo is of Ella on her seventh birthday; Dad took it. A beaming smile, her eyes staring straight into the camera, so sure that life was good. The next picture is of Willa as a baby, her eyes still blue like Dad's; they went brown a few weeks after Mum left. Ella expects the third picture to be of Dad, but it's of a little boy.

The crow stamps its feet; its claws dig into Ella's stomach.

So Mum's got another kid. God, she's probably got a whole new family, people she loves more than Dad and Willa. More than Ella. That's why she stayed away. Well, she should go back to them and forget that she was ever meant to be part of their lives.

Ella takes out the picture of the little boy and shoves it in her pocket.

Then she closes the case, checks that Willa's still asleep and steps out into the hall.

She remembers how, on the day Mum disappeared, Fay had stood on the doorstep cradling Willa in her arms.

Norah hasn't come to collect her, Fay said to Dad, not realising Ella was there, hearing it all.

That's when Ella knew something was really wrong – though, it turned out, she hadn't thought far enough. She hadn't thought of the worst scenario of all: that Mum hadn't been kidnapped. That she'd just walked out on them.

Ella climbs the stairs to the attic landing and grabs the bin bags she's filled with Mum's old things. She stops in the bathroom to empty the pedal bin so that, if someone snoops in the bag, they'll think it's rubbish; no one will save the pictures of Mum and her clothes and books and CDs, the things that have decorated Ella's room since she was a little girl. Ella tips the plastic lining into her black bag, and as the cotton buds and dried-out contact lenses and an old tube of toothpaste tumble out she notices a white plastic stick wrapped up in toilet paper. Using her fingertips in case it turns out to be something gross, she unravels the toilet paper. And that's when she realises what it is. It's a pee stick. A stick that tells you if you're pregnant.

There are two windows. And two blue lines.

She hears Dad's car pull up outside.

Ella shoves the stick in her pocket along with the photo, tips everything back into the pedal bin, places it back under the basin and goes up to her bedroom, taking the bin bag with her.

When she gets to her room, she empties her pockets into the top drawer of her desk.

'What are you doing?'

Ella jumps. She didn't hear Willa come up the stairs.

'You shouldn't spy on people, Willa.'

'I wasn't. I just came up to see you.'

Willa stands at the door, a crease mark across her cheek, Louis beside her like a guard.

'So what's in the drawer?'

'Nothing.'

'It didn't look like nothing.'

'Just tidying up.'

Willa walks over to the window. Louis doesn't leave her side. 'Daddy's back!' Willa says.

Ella joins her and the three of them look down through the scaffolding.

Mum and Dad step out of the car. Dad takes a cigarette stub from Mum and flicks it into a bush at the side of the road.

Cherry blossom drifts across the street and swirls around Mum and Dad's heads.

'It looks like confetti,' says Willa. 'Like they're getting married.'

'It's just blossom, Willa.' But Ella had the same thought.

Ella had imagined the reunion between her parents a thousand times: how they'd hug and cry and kiss and stare into each other's eyes and promise nothing would separate them ever again.

Willa gets up on tiptoe and looks out of the window. She turns to look at Ella and scratches at the scar under her eye.

'Ella?'

'What is it, Willa?'

'Where's Mummy?'

Adam

Adam bangs on the door and presses the doorbell and looks through the kitchen window and bangs on the door again.

'Fay!' He bangs again. 'Fay, it's me!"

He left Norah at home with the girls. Probably a stupid idea, but he had to come after Fay. He'd told Fay a million times that she didn't need to keep her house, that it was a waste to leave it standing empty, that she had a home with them now, but she'd always found excuses for keeping it.

'Fay!'

Six years of living together and he never got a key to her place. Just when he thinks he might be a halfway-decent human being, something like this reminds him that he's way off the mark. And that if there's anything even the slightest bit okay about his messed-up self, it's down to Fay.

He grabs the brass doorknocker and hammers it down yet again.

As he steps back, he looks up. The cottage is dark. Maybe she went to her Mum's. Or maybe she went back to work. That would be Fay all over — to go out of her way to honour her word to Willa.

Damn.

He pulls his bike away from the wall. Then he notices a light flick on behind the curtains. He drops his bike and goes round the side of the cottage, through the gate to the back garden.

The grass is feathered through with weeds. Dry, spindly plants reach out like spears from terracotta pots. The fountain is dried up, its stones slick with moss.

He and Fay went to see a romantic comedy once. Following a blazing row, the woman had stormed off down the street.

He has to go after her, Fay had said. *He has to show her he cares.*

But she told him to leave her alone, Adam had insisted, confused and frustrated, as he'd always been, by what seemed to him like the contrary behaviour of women.

Yes, but she wants him to go after her.

He remembers the pause that followed Fay's words. Their conversation, as so often in those early days, had skated too close to Norah.

Adam yanks at the frame of the lounge window.

Fay had gone on: *If you have to overcome some obstacles, that's even better . . . It shows perseverance. It shows you really care.*

He looks up at her window. He's meant to climb up, isn't he? But, unlike in films, there are no conveniently placed footholds. And it's getting dark. He wouldn't be able to see what he was doing.

'Fay!' he yells up again.

He picks up a stone from the fountain and throws it up to her window, but it bounces off the brick. He grabs a rock and

180

hurls it at the downstairs window. It's the only way he can think of getting inside the house.

He's shocked by the noise of the smash and the spray of splintered glass. He waits for her face to appear at the upstairs window, but the curtains stay closed.

Reaching his hand through the jagged gash in the glass, Adam unlocks the window and climbs into the house.

How long has it been since he's stood in her lounge? Not since before Norah left. And even before that, only a few times: the occasional awkward dinner. Picking Ella up after a weekend with her godmother. This was where Norah had left Willa on the day she walked away. Had Norah ever wondered whether the favour she asked of her best friend might have consequences that reached further than she could ever imagine?

Adam climbs the dark stairs. He's never been up here.

The bathroom door is open. And the door to the spare room. The third must be her bedroom.

'Fay . . . ' He knocks lightly. 'Fay . . . '

Still no answer.

He opens the door.

She's sitting on the side of the bed, staring down at a photo frame on her lap.

'Fay? I've been calling for ages. Why didn't you answer?'

She doesn't look up.

He comes and sits beside her, and looks down at the photograph.

Adam in the second-hand suit Fay had found for him in a charity shop. Norah, eight months pregnant, in the dress Fay had adjusted over and over again as the day drew close.

'I took the photo,' she says.

'I know.'

She shakes her head. 'God I'm an idiot.'

He puts his arm around her shoulders. 'You're the most amazing human being I've ever met,' he says.

She shakes her head. 'An idiot, Adam. Remember how I helped you on the day of the wedding? God.'

They hadn't spoken of this, not once.

'I was a mess, Fay. If it hadn't been for you ... '

Fay laughs. 'Exactly.' She traces the outline of Adam and Norah's figures on the photograph.

'You did the right thing,' he says. 'A good, kind thing. You always do.'

He'd had his first proper panic attack. Standing in a tiny room at the town hall, waiting for Norah to come through the doors – and then his breath had got stuck somewhere in his chest, had refused to come out no matter how hard he strained.

The registrar had tried to calm him down, and when his breathing got worse she'd gone out into the hallway to get Fay.

He'd heard the registrar speaking to Norah, loud and official, used to dealing with these dramas.

He's fine ... he just wants a word with Ms Bridges ...

And he'd heard Norah laugh. *He's probably forgotten the ring. You'd better go and sort him out, Fay.*

By the time Fay had got to him his chest hurt so much he thought he was going to have a heart attack.

Adam lifts one of Fay's hands off the photo frame and laces his fingers with hers.

'You helped me breathe that day,' he says. 'Like you've helped me breathe ever since Norah left.'

She keeps staring at the photograph.

Once she'd got him breathing steadily she'd grabbed his shoulders and looked him in the eye and given him a pep talk:

182

You're going to go out there and you're going to tell her how much you love her and you're going to say 'I do', and it's going to be fine. It's going to be just fine.

And that's what he'd done.

Fay had gone back out to get Norah. Adam had taken his place again at the front of the room. The registrar, used to these dramas, had smiled, clicked play on the stereo and 'What a Wonderful World' had filled the room.

Afterwards, on the steps of the town hall, Fay took the photo she was staring at now.

But something had happened before that, hadn't it? Something they'd never mentioned. Something they'd tried to forget.

Just before Fay went back to get Norah, he'd fallen into Fay's arms. And she'd held him. And they'd stood there, in silence, holding on for a little longer than was allowed.

They wouldn't hold each other like that again until years later.

Fay puts the photograph back on her bedside table. 'You shouldn't be here,' she says.

'This is the only place I should be.'

'You know that's not true.'

'I can't do this without you.'

'You have to. For the girls.'

'Come with me.'

'I told you, I need some time.'

'Sitting here on your own in the dark staring at our wedding photo? Christ, Fay, how's that going to help?' He stands up and holds out his hand. 'Come home with me. We'll deal with it, all together.' When she doesn't move he kneels in front of her. 'It's going to be okay.'

'Don't say that.' She pulls her fingers out of his, her cheeks flushed.

He tucks a strand of hair behind her ear.

'I'll make it okay,' he whispers. He leans forward and kisses her, and then he kisses her harder and pulls her off the bed and onto the carpet and lifts her jumper over her head and kisses her shoulder and her neck and then he feels the weight of her falling into him.

SATURDAY NIGHT

Norah

Norah strokes Louis under the kitchen table. His legs are jittery, just like they were when she was too busy looking after Ella and Willa to take him out for a walk. He'd been forgotten today, poor old man. She'd found him hoovering up bits of popcorn in the lounge, his bowl in the kitchen, empty.

I'm sorry, Louis, she says under her breath.

Norah listens to the scraping of knives and forks. Adam's made Willa beans on toast.

Ella's upstairs, sulking.

No one's spoken for ages.

'So Mummy's not coming home at all tonight?' Willa asks.

'I'm afraid not,' says Adam.

'But she said she didn't have to work this weekend. She said she'd got special permission because it's my birthday.'

Adam puts down his knife and fork. 'It was an emergency. You know how important Fay's—' he coughs. 'How important Mummy's job is, how she's one of the very best surgeons and that sometimes there's a complicated operation and no one else is good enough to do it.' He pauses. 'She's promised she'll be back for your birthday tomorrow.' He glances at Norah. 'You know that Mummy keeps her promises.'

Norah knows he's saying all this for her benefit. *Look how amazing Fay is. The Mother Who Stayed.*

'What if the emergency keeps going? What if she's needed tomorrow too?'

'She'll be here, Willa.'

Willa pushes the beans around on her plate. 'Daddy?'

'What?'

'Where did you go this afternoon?'

'Eat your beans, Willa.'

'Were you getting something for the party?'

'Maybe.'

She'd looked for him too; she'd thought that Fay being out of the way would give them the chance to talk. He'd come back red-faced and flustered, and she'd leant in, expecting to smell beer on his breath. And then she'd felt guilty.

Norah clears her throat. 'Maybe I should take some food up to Ella.'

'I'm not sure—' Adam starts.

'I have to try,' Norah says.

'Try what?' Willa asks.

'She'll be hungry, she needs to eat.'

'But Ella's put her KEEP OUT note on her door: that means she won't come out for anyone.'

'Her KEEP OUT note?'

'It's for when Ella and Mummy have rows. Like when Mummy wants to go in and tidy up – Ella doesn't like anyone touching her things so she tells her to KEEP OUT.'

'Willa—' Adam says, his tone warning her not to continue.

No, do continue, thinks Norah. It's a relief to hear that Fay hasn't got everything right.

Willa shrugs. 'I just thought Auntie Norah should know that Ella's upset and that she won't be hungry.'

Adam kisses Willa's head. 'It's okay, darling. It's all going to be okay.'

*

Norah carries a plate of beans on toast up the stairs. Louis follows her. When they get to the landing, she leans over to give him a stroke between the ears. 'Good dog,' she says.

She knocks on Ella's door.

No answer.

She hears the creak of the bed.

Louis looks at the door and yelps.

'It's okay, Louis,' Norah whispers. She knocks again. 'Ella, it's Mum. I've brought up some food.'

There's a thud, and then footsteps to the door.

'What did you say?' Ella's voice is low and mean.

Louis looks over his shoulder down the stairs and sniffs the air.

Norah puts the plate on the floor and calls through the door: 'Ella, it's Mum—'

The door flies open.

Ella stands over Norah, her eyes on fire.

'You're not my mum.' She spits out the words.

If Ella doesn't like Fay, if she's spent all this time looking for Norah, surely she still loves her. Surely that couldn't disappear in just a day.

'Ella, please.'

'And you're not Willa's mum either.' Ella steps forward and points at Norah. 'You don't deserve to be anyone's mum.' And then she looks down at Louis. 'And he's not your dog. You walked out on him too.'

She slams the door in Norah's face.

Norah steps back, her legs shaking.

You don't deserve to be anyone's mum. Ella's words echo around Norah's head.

'Louis?' She kneels down and holds his head in her hands.

She needs him to look at her, to let her know it's okay, that Ella doesn't mean it. Who else is going to reassure her that she hasn't lost her little girl?

Louis gives out a low whine and licks her hand, then hangs his head and pads down to the next landing.

I need to get her back, Norah thinks. A wave of determination comes over her. *I need to get them all back.*

'Auntie Norah?'

Norah looks down the stairs.

Willa stands there next to Louis, looking up her.

'What did Ella mean?' asks Willa. 'What did she mean when she said you weren't her mum?'

Willa

Willa kicks at her duvet.

Sometimes, you love someone so much, that you see them as your mum. That's what Auntie Norah said. *It just means you're close, that's all.*

Willa hadn't understood. People only have one mummy and Mummy was Ella's mummy. Auntie Norah was an *auntie*, that's why she was called Auntie rather than Mummy.

Willa's head hurts. She kicks the duvet right off and lets it flop to the floor.

The full moon presses so hard against her curtains that even when she shuts her eyes really tight she can't make the glow go away. There are too many things to think about to go to sleep.

Plus, her wobbly tooth hurts – it's hanging on a bit of gum. She wishes it would hurry up and fall out.

Her hands flutter by her side. She tugs at her nightie and scratches the scar under her eye. And then she thinks about how weird things have got in the last few days. Weirder, even, than they were yesterday.

First, it's weird that Mummy went to work even though she promised she'd be here for the whole bank holiday weekend. Mummy never goes back on her promises.

Second, Willa doesn't understand why the police showed up in the first place.

Third, it's weird that Ella's in a bad mood. Well, that bit's not weird – but it's weird that she won't let Willa into her room. Willa and Louis are the two people who Ella always lets in. *Maybe I've done something wrong*, thinks Willa.

Fourth, it's really, *really* weird that Ella went and cut off all her hair and dyed it dark because her long, silky hair was the thing she liked best about herself and she always said that she'd never cut it, not for a million pounds.

Fifth, it's weird that Ella had a shouting match with Auntie Norah, who she's meant to love.

Sixth, it's weird that Ella's hasn't been out to train for her 10k run today. The race is on Monday – Dad doesn't know, but she's been training with Sai and Louis every day for ages.

And seventh, it's weird that Dad disappeared this afternoon without telling them where he went and that he left them alone with Auntie Norah, who's basically a stranger.

At first Willa went down to the basement to see if Daddy was in his photography studio but he wasn't there and then she went to look out of the kitchen window to see if the car was there and it was and then she went to the garage and worked out that Daddy's bike was gone, but why would Daddy go off by bike in the middle of the afternoon without telling anyone? And why did he change the subject when she asked him about it? Maybe he went out to get her a birthday present, but still, he shouldn't have left her with Auntie Norah.

There are other things that are keeping Willa awake too. Like that it's her seventh birthday tomorrow and she's been waiting for that for months. And more exciting even than her birthday is that she's sure Mrs Fox is going to give birth soon. Mummy foxes are pregnant for fifty-three days before they give birth and Willa's counted the days since she first noticed the saggy bit on Mrs Fox's belly and she just knows it has to be tomorrow.

When Willa hears a screamy yowl, a bit like an owl hooting, only deeper, she knows Mrs Fox is calling her.

She climbs out of bed, her hands fluttering even more fiercely by her side, and goes downstairs.

In the lounge, Willa finds Louis asleep on the camp bed with Auntie Norah, his head resting on her thigh. Louis doesn't get that close to strangers, which means she must be Auntie Norah because Auntie Norah lived with Louis too. Ella said that it was Auntie Norah's idea to get him from the Animal Ark.

Willa steps in closer and studies her face. Auntie Norah's hair is like her own, a deep red and knotty and straggly too – though Willa's is shorter. Mummy says it's easier to look after that way. Mummy also says red hair is beautiful and that it makes you special and that she shouldn't listen to the girls at school when they call her Gingernut because they don't understand what true beauty is. Mummy must find Auntie Norah beautiful too.

Looking closer, Willa notices a pattern of golden freckles on Auntie Norah's nose and cheeks. Willa has those too.

If she is Auntie Norah, then they must be related, which means Willa's meant to look a bit like her.

And Auntie Norah makes Willa think of someone else too: the ghost she used to see that made Willa want to go and sleep in Mummy and Daddy's bed. Maybe that's why she didn't have bad dreams tonight and why she isn't scared: because if a ghost turns into a real person, you don't need to be scared any more, do you?

Willa notices a piece of paper poking up out of Auntie Norah's bag. It's wrong to look at people's private things, but how else is she going to find out what's going on when every time she asks a question she's told 'it's nothing', or 'it's no one'. She eases the paper out and opens it up and holds it up to the moonlight coming through the glass doors. It's addressed to Daddy, and it's signed from Norah. And it's creased and yellowy like it's really old. And it says that Auntie Norah is leaving. And that she loves Ella and Willa. And she mentions Mummy too. Weird.

Willa folds the piece of paper, puts it back in Auntie Norah's bag, and walks across the garden to her special place.

It's a dark place and even in spring it smells of autumn leaves and wet soil. Willa looks under the gooseberry bush: there's a flattened patch on the grass. And the ground feels warm under Willa's fingers.

Mrs Fox — she must be close.

Willa purses her lips and lets out a low whistle. A rustle in the undergrowth. *It's okay, Mrs Fox, Louis's inside.*

Willa narrows her eyes and then she sees it – a red tail with a dash of white, a spark darting past.

Mrs Fox . . . she whispers. *It's me, Willa. You can come out.*

'Willa?' A voice from behind.

Willa's hands stop fluttering. She rubs her eyes. The moon looks brighter. The earth feels closer. Her eyes widen. It takes her a second to realise where she is.

'Willa?' The voice again.

Willa notices the gooseberry bush and it comes back to her: she was looking for Mrs Fox.

Auntie Norah stands in the garden, her legs and feet bare under her baggy T-shirt. There's something weird about her boobs, like she's only got one dangling to the side. Mummy definitely has two boobs. And Ella's nearly got two boobs too.

Louis comes bounding up behind her.

'What are you doing out here, Willa?'

Willa remembers what Ella said about not talking to Auntie Norah. But if she doesn't explain, Auntie Norah might tell Daddy that she found Willa out here.

'I couldn't sleep,' Willa says.

Louis comes over and sniffs under the gooseberry bush.

'Neither could I.' Auntie Norah looks up into the starry sky. 'It must be the full moon.'

Willa nods.

'So what are you looking for?' Auntie Norah bends over and gazes in the gap next to where Louis is sitting.

'Foxes. Mrs Fox in particular. She's going to have babies soon and I need to make sure she's okay.'

'That sounds interesting.'

Willa nods again.

'Most people don't believe me when I tell them that I see the foxes. But I do. They come out most nights; you just have to be patient.' Willa takes a breath. She's worried she's said too much.

But Auntie Norah smiles and says, 'Sometimes other people see things differently from how we see them.'

Willa likes this explanation. And she likes that Auntie Norah is a grown-up and yet doesn't try to talk her out of spending time looking for foxes. She wishes Ella were here to see how nice she's being; maybe it would make her love her again. She thinks about asking Auntie Norah about the note but decides against it because she might think that Willa's a snoop.

'So have you seen a fox tonight?' asks Auntie Norah.

Willa nods. 'Sort of. Just a glimpse – under there.' She flattens Louis's ears because his head blocks the view, and points to the black hole behind the gooseberry bush.

Auntie Norah follows the line of her arm.

Once again, Willa notices Auntie Norah's red hair: it shines under the moon.

'Why is Ella so angry at you?'

Auntie Norah sits down next to Willa and Louis on the grass. She winds Louis's fur around her fingers and he closes his eyes. If she were a stranger, Louis wouldn't let her do that.

'I'm afraid that I hurt Ella. I hurt her very badly.'

'But you've only been here for a day.'

'Ella and I have known each other for a long time.'

'Oh.' Willa scratches her scar. 'You *are* Auntie Norah, then. The Auntie Norah who lived with us before I was born and who played the trumpet and who ran marathons.'

'Sort of.'

That's what Ella said. And again, Willa doesn't understand how you can *sort of* be someone. But Willa doesn't care. She must be Auntie Norah.

A scream pierces the night sky.

'That was Mrs Fox,' Willa says, breathless.

'You know their cries?'

'She's calling Mr Fox. He goes off on adventures but he's meant to be at home looking after her because she's pregnant.' Willa looks into Auntie Norah's eyes. In this light they're dark brown, like a conker. 'You won't tell Daddy, will you?'

'About what?'

'About me being out here. He doesn't like it.'

'Why doesn't he like it?'

'Well, there are two main reasons.' Willa takes a breath. 'First, it's because I sleepwalk and Daddy worries that I'll go off somewhere and get lost.'

Auntie Norah smiles.

'Why are you smiling?' asks Willa.

'I sleepwalk too.'

'You do?'

Auntie Norah nods.

'I've never met anyone who sleepwalks before. I mean, I know there are other people who do it, especially children, but you're the first real grown-up person I've met who does it.'

'We're a special breed. And I'm not really a grown-up.' She winks.

'You're not?'

Auntie Norah shakes her head.

'Do you remember what happens when you sleepwalk?'

196

'Most things.'

'So do I. Mummy says that's not normal. She says you're meant to forget everything. But I remember it, like it's a film playing in my head. It was while I was sleepwalking that I first met Mrs Fox.'

'Well, I can understand why your daddy might be worried about you walking out of the house on your own.'

'Was he worried about you too?'

'What do you mean?'

'When you lived with us, before I was born, was he worried when you went sleepwalking?'

'Yes, he was.' Auntie Norah's chest heaves. Willa tries really hard not to look at her boob pushing into her T-shirt.

'And did you used to find the keys?'

'The keys?'

'To the windows and doors? Daddy and Mummy hide them but I always find them.' It's as if, when Willa sleepwalks, she hears a voice, a ghost voice, telling her exactly where to look.

'Yes, I always found them.' Auntie Norah tugs at her T-shirt. 'You said there was a second reason Daddy doesn't like you to come out and look for the foxes.'

'Oh, because of the accident. And because he doesn't want the foxes to come back again.'

'*Again?* They came back after the accident?'

'Mummy thought it was Louis who'd dug up her flowers, but flowers make Louis sneeze so he stays away from them. So I camped out in the lounge overnight and kept watch through the glass doors to see who the flower-killer was.'

'And it was a fox?'

Willa nods. 'I went out to the gooseberry bush and saw Mrs

Fox. And baby foxes, four of them, small as the palm of your hand.' Willa cups her hands to show Auntie Norah.

'I stroked them and they wriggled a bit but they didn't wake up. They were really little and really sleepy. Anyway, I was going to sneak them back up to my bedroom but Louis barked his head off and woke Mummy and Daddy and Ella up, so I didn't get the chance.'

'And you weren't worried Mrs Fox might hurt you – after what happened when you were a baby?'

Willa sighs. People never get it. 'I told you, it wasn't her fault. She was scared.'

'Right.'

'Plus, I loved the little foxes,' Willa said. 'They were so fluffy and curled up and alone looking – and I was worried their mummy wouldn't come back.' Willa takes a breath. 'Mummy let me keep them for twenty-four hours, before Daddy called the RSPCA. Mrs Fox ran away because I'd touched her cubs so Mummy got some tiny bottles from the hospital that they use for babies that are born early, and we filled them with milk and fed the little foxes. I asked Mummy if we could keep them but she said it was best not to, that foxes were meant to live in the wild.'

'Did you ever see the mummy fox again?'

Willa nods. 'That was the worst thing. She kept coming back to the gooseberry bush to look for her babies. I wish I'd never touched them – it was my fault she ran away.'

When Willa told Mummy that they should get the baby foxes and bring them back, Mummy shook her head and said that the mummy fox wouldn't want them any more, because they'd smell wrong. Willa didn't understand what smelling wrong had to do with anything. Mummy explained that when you belong to someone you smell of them, and that because the foxes had been away from their mummy and lived with Willa and Ella and Mummy and Daddy for a while, they'd smell like they belonged to them. Willa hoped she'd always smell of Mummy.

Auntie Norah blinks and her eyes go misty. 'That's quite a story.' And then she tries to smile, one of those strained smiles people use when they're trying not to cry. Willa doesn't understand why she's so upset. She wishes Mummy were here: Mummy's good at making people feel better when they're sad.

'So, it's your birthday tomorrow?' asks Auntie Norah.

Willa nods. 'I'll be seven.'

'You must be excited.'

Willa shrugs. 'I was.'

'Not any more?'

'Mummy promised she'd be here.'

Willa notices a red flush in Auntie Norah's cheeks.

'I'm sure she will be. She wouldn't miss it for the world.'

Willa thinks that if Auntie Norah lived here when Ella was little, she must have been friends with Mummy, because they would have been living in the same house. In fact, Mummy might be Auntie Norah's sister, because that's what Auntie means. Mummy must be so happy to have Auntie Norah to visit too, which makes it doubly weird that she's not here. What happens if Auntie Norah doesn't stay very long and goes back to Australia and they don't see her for ages? Mummy will be sad that she didn't spend more time with her.

'Will you still be here? When Mummy comes back?'

Auntie Norah hesitates. 'Maybe.' Then she looks back at the

house. 'Come on, why don't we go inside and warm up. I'll make you a hot chocolate.'

'What if Mrs Fox has her cubs tonight and I'm not there to help?'

'You know what, Willa? I don't think Mrs Fox will come out now – the sky will be light soon and she won't want to be out here for everyone to see. She'll probably wait until tomorrow night.'

Willa chews her lip. 'You sure?'

Auntie Norah stands up and holds out a hand to Willa. Willa grabs it and springs onto her feet. She likes that Auntie Norah is taking her seriously about Mrs Fox.

As they walk across the grass to the house with Louis lumbering behind them, something catches their eye and they both look up at the same time.

Ella has switched on the light in the attic. She's standing at the window, staring down at them.

Ella

@findingmum
Either she goes or I do. #choose

Ella closes her curtains. She doesn't trust Mum or what she's been talking to Willa about out there. And she doesn't like that it's Mum who found Willa wandering out in the garden.

It should have been Ella who heard Willa getting up. And what happened to Louis? Faithful Louis, who's always the first to pick up on Willa's sleepwalking? But then he seems to be under Mum's spell too. As for Dad, he's such a deep sleeper he wouldn't wake up if the roof blew off. That leaves the one person who's always been there for Willa – Fay. Ella doesn't believe what Dad said about Fay working. Mum's scared her off.

Ella waits until she hears Willa go back to her bedroom. Then she walks out onto the landing and looks down the staircase to Dad's bedroom. She's going to wake him up and get him to explain what's going on and make him work out some kind of plan for getting rid of Mum. And she's going to tell him about what she found in the bathroom bin. That should shake him up a bit.

After going down the first few steps, Ella stops. The crow shakes its feathers and squawks.

Mum stands at Dad's door. She's wearing a big shapeless T-shirt and her skinny legs poke out underneath. She's humming some stupid jazz tune. Mum used to hum all the time. And then she got pregnant with Willa and stopped.

Mum steps forward and knocks on the bedroom door.

A beat of silence.

Don't answer it, Dad, whispers Ella.

Heavy footsteps across the bedroom and then Dad's face at the door, his hair a mess, his dorky glasses lopsided.

'Can we talk?' Mum asks.

No! That's what Dad should say. *We can't talk. You're going to leave. Now.* Stop being such a wimp, Dad, Ella thinks.

Dad lets Mum in and closes the door behind them.

The crow pecks and pecks at Ella's stomach.

201

Mum doesn't have a right to go in there: it's Fay's bedroom now, Fay and Dad's. It's where Willa goes when she needs her parents.

The first time Dad made Ella lie about Fay being Willa's mum was on Christmas Eve, a year and a bit after Mum left. Willa was two.

Ella was sitting at the kitchen table, drawing a missing poster for Mum.

Willa pointed at Mum's red hair, her eyes wide.

Dad had warned Ella not to do her *finding Mum stuff* in front of Willa, but Ella didn't care. Sooner or later she'd have to know the truth.

Ella reckoned that, because it was Christmas, maybe people would notice her posters more, that they'd be thinking about their families and getting together around turkey and stuffing and roast potatoes – and that they'd feel sad that a mum was missing from her family.

Willa went back to playing with her Winnie the Pooh toys. And then, without warning, she pulled Roo out of Kanga's pouch, held him out to Fay and said, *Mu-Mum-Mummy!*

Unlike the other children at nursery, Willa hadn't started talking yet. She didn't make many sounds at all. She never cried, not even when she fell over and scraped skin off her knees. And now she'd said her first word: *Mummy*. And she'd said it to Fay.

Ella walks down the last few stairs and stands beside the closed bedroom door. She leans in and tries to hear what Mum and Dad are saying, but their voices are muffled.

None of this is right.

After getting out her phone and sending a tweet, Ella runs down to the bottom of the stairs. She throws a coat over her pyjamas and looks at the trainers lying by the door. They're the old ones that belong to Mum. Ella doesn't have time to look for another pair of shoes so she pushes her feet into the soft canvas and runs out through the front door.

Already the sky is getting lighter. It's Sunday so the streets are empty: nothing but the sound of pigeons cooing on rooftops.

Ella runs across Holdingwell. It's good to feel the cold on her face; she opens her mouth, lets the night air sweep across her tongue and gulps it down her throat.

When she gets to Fay's house Ella leans against a wall to catch her breath.

Dad tried to persuade Fay to sell the cottage, but Fay always found an excuse to delay. At first Ella was relieved – she thought it meant that Fay knew what Ella knew: that Mum was coming home and that Fay would have to go back to her old life. But now Ella's worried. Worried for Willa and Dad. Maybe even a little worried for herself. She can't picture their lives without Fay.

It's clear: she has to find a way to tell Fay that she belongs with them, back on Willoughby Street. And she has to find a way to make Mum leave.

Fay's is the only house with a light on. She knew Fay wasn't at work.

Standing on the pavement, Ella watches Fay through the kitchen window. She's in an old flannel dressing gown, her hands covered in flour, and she's got some in her hair too. The radio hums around her, one of those cheesy romantic songs that Fay loves. When Fay first moved in Ella hated hearing Fay's music in their home; Ella would blast Mum's Louis Armstrong CDs from the attic to drown it out. Now, Ella feels sorry for doing that. She feels sorry for everything.

She even feels sorry for telling Fay that she wasn't Willa's mum. Fay's the one who stayed, isn't she? If anyone deserves to be Willa's mum, it's her.

Ella closes her eyes and wishes the night would take her away to wherever it goes when the sun comes up.

Don't call her that, Ella had said when Willa first called Fay Mummy. *She's not your mother.*

Ella! Dad had snapped.

Willa frowned.

Fay stepped away from the table.

Well she's not, Ella said.

Come with me, said Dad. *Now.* He stormed out of the kitchen.

Ella followed him into the hall.

They went and sat at the bottom of the stairs.

It's not right, Dad. We can't lie to Willa — she needs to know who her real mum is.

Dad shook his head. *Ella, it's more complicated than that.*

No it's not. Fay's not Willa's mum.

Fay loves Willa like her own child. And all Willa's known is Fay — she's too small to remember Mum. Do you want your little sister to grow up without having a mother?

She's not going to grow up without having a mother. They're going to find Mum—

Ella, please. Dad shook his head. *We've been through this. Your mum's not coming back—*

Ella pressed her hands over her ears. Dad pulled them away.

Whatever you think about what happened to Mum, we have to look after Willa. We have to make sure that she feels safe, that she knows she has a proper family.

We had a proper family, thought Ella. And we'll have one again, as soon as Mum comes home.

Through the open kitchen door, Ella watched Willa stretching out her pudgy arms to Fay. The scar under her eye was still a raw, angry red.

So you're going to marry her, then? Ella asked.

What? No. It's not like that, Ella.

Since the fox attack, Fay had slept in Willa's room, but in the last few weeks, Ella had heard Fay sneaking out into Dad's room late at night. She could tell they were getting closer – and that one day Fay would go into Dad's room and stay and then they'd forget about Mum altogether.

Well I'm never going to call Fay Mum.

Okay—

And just because you've given up looking for Mum, it doesn't mean I have to.

Dad nodded slowly. *I know how much you loved her, Ella.*

I still do.

Dad tugged at his collar. *Yes, of course you do.* He stood up and held out his hand. *Why don't you come back into the kitchen and help with the mince pies? And we should celebrate Willa's first word, don't you think?*

Ella's stomach tightened. She shook her head. *Not now, Dad.* She turned and walked up the stairs. And she'd kept walking until she got right to the top, to Mum's old room.

It takes Ella a second to notice that Fay is staring right at her through the kitchen window. When Ella raises a hand to wave,

Fay disappears from the kitchen. A moment later she's at the front door.

'What are you doing here, Ella?'

'Why aren't you at work?'

Fay opens the door wider. 'You'd better come in.'

The house smells of Fay. At home, Ella no longer notices it because it's blended with all the other smells: the smell of Louis and Willa and Dad, the smell of the new furniture, of the white paint on the walls. It's even mingled with Ella's smell. But here, in a place that belongs only to Fay, the smell hits her again. *A walking Ariel advert*, Ella used to whisper whenever she caught a whiff of Fay's clean clothes and her clean hair and her soap-clean skin. Ella preferred Mum's perfume, the one which, until a few days ago, she wore too – a smell of far-away places that were dark and rich and mysterious. But now Ella hates that smell. That's why she smashed the bottle of Shalimar she'd saved up for, for ages. Ella swears to herself that she'll never wear that perfume again.

On the way to the kitchen, Ella looks through the lounge door.

'Your window's smashed—'

Fay stops walking. 'Yes.'

Ella goes to the lounge door and looks at the shards of glass all over the carpet. 'Did you have a break-in?'

'Not exactly.'

'Have you called the police?'

'Nothing's been taken. It's fine.'

'God. I never think of there being burglars and stuff in Holdingwell.'

'No.'

Ella doesn't get why Fay – *make-sure-all-the-doors-and-windows-are-locked-don't-forget-to-set-the-alarm-Fay* – is being so chilled about this.

She follows her into the kitchen. The surfaces are covered with bags of flour and sugar, packs of butter, tubs of sprinkles, bowls and whisks. There's a bottle of red food dye next to a baking tin in the shape of a fox.

'So you'll be there for Willa's birthday?' Ella asks.

Fay tips the batter into the tin. 'Of course.'

'It's just, I thought, with Mum and everything . . .'

'Want to try some?' Fay holds out the bowl. Ella dips her finger into the leftover batter. Closing her eyes, she tastes the mix of raw eggs and flour and sugar and vanilla and thinks back to how bad Mum was at cooking. She'd burn things and set off the smoke alarm, how Dad would have to order a take-away. *Life's too short*, she'd say and then she'd get out her trumpet and play Ella a tune – as though they could eat music. Fay started cooking three-course meals from the day she moved in. Filled the kitchen with cookery books. Went to classes. Watched TV shows, set up her iPad in the kitchen with YouTube clips on how to make roast dinners.

Just because you can cook, it doesn't make you a mum, Ella had wanted to tell her. 'If Willa wants me to come, I'll be there,' Fay says.

'Of course she wants you to come.' Ella pauses. 'You're her mum.'

Fay blinks. 'Does your Dad know you're here?'

Ella shakes her head.

'Ella—'

'He's busy. I didn't want to disturb him.' Blood rushes to Ella's cheeks. Busy talking to Mum in his bedroom, the mum who abandoned them. 'Can I stay with you?'

'You want to stay here?'

'I can't face going back. Not now.'

Fay nods. 'Okay. But I'll have to call your dad. He'll be worried.'

Ella shrugs.

'And if you stay, you should get some sleep. You look exhausted.'

'What about you, are you going to sleep?' She's never seen Fay look so bad. She's usually one of those bouncy, rosy, irritatingly energetic people. It's like all the life's been zapped out of her.

'When Willa's cake is done,' says Fay.

'Can I help?'

Fay smiles. 'Okay.'

She carries the tin over to the oven. Then she comes back, picks up the icing sugar and the red dye and hands it to Ella. 'We'd better get to work.'

As Fay leans over the cake book, her finger tracing the instructions for icing the fox cake, Ella can't help but look at her stomach. Fay's always been rounder than Mum, with fuller boobs and arms and legs. She probably looked like a grown woman when she was Ella's age. But the small hill of flesh that presses against the belt of her dressing gown, that's new. Ella imagines Fay's stomach growing and growing. She thinks of the small being in there, about how it belongs to Dad. To all of them.

'Fay—?'

Fay turns round. 'Yes?'

Ella keeps staring at Fay's stomach. She thinks of the pregnancy test lying in the top drawer of her desk back home.

She takes a breath to steady her nerves. If she's going to get Mum to leave, she's going to need Fay's help.

'What is it, Ella?'

'Do you hate Mum?'

Adam

Adam watches Norah walk around the bedroom. She hums and with the tips of her fingers, she traces the pieces of furniture Fay bought for the room.

Don't touch them, he wants to say. *They're Fay's. They're ours. They're nothing to do with you.* And he should say those things. For Fay, at least. For the new life they've built together with the girls. And for what he and Fay shared a few hours ago, in the bedroom of her cottage.

But when he looks at Norah there's another voice in his head. A voice that says *I've missed you.*

'I found Willa outside,' Norah says.

His chest tightens. Willa was outside? In the middle of the night? He's losing it again – his grip on his family, his role as a dad. Fay has to come home: he can't do this without her.

'We thought she was getting better.' He pushes his glasses up his nose. 'She hasn't sleepwalked in months. We'll have to be more careful.'

'Like old times, eh?'

He nods. 'Kind of.'

Although Ella had done everything to be like Norah, it was Willa who was most naturally like her mother. She looked like her. She lived impulsively. She invited everyone into her life without questioning who they were or where they came from. And she sleepwalked. And yet Willa hasn't got a clue who Norah is – before she showed up on the doorstep yesterday morning, Willa didn't even know Norah existed.

'Willa's been telling me some fox stories.'

He doesn't answer. He doesn't want to be drawn into Norah's attempt to paste over the past.

'I'm sorry,' she says.

'Sorry?' What a pointless word, he wants to say.

'I'm sorry the accident happened,' she adds. 'I'm sorry I wasn't there for her. For you.'

He turns straightens the bed sheets and closes the curtains. If he does things the way Fay would, maybe this conversation won't feel like so much of a betrayal.

'Amazing how much she loves the foxes. I mean, considering . . . ' Norah says.

'Considering they hurt her?'

For a moment, he holds her gaze.

'She says there are still foxes that come into the garden.'

He can tell by her tone that she's on Willa's side. Norah, always ready to believe in the miraculous.

He shakes his head. 'After the attack, traps were set all over the area. Illegally, of course: we're meant to use humane deterrents. But people were angry at what happened to Willa – it got a lot of press coverage. Anyway, the local foxes were either hunted down or they ran away. There shouldn't be any left.'

'What about the cubs she found?'

'An anomaly. Pest control did another sweep through the neighbourhood. They said it was a one-off.'

210

'So she dreams them up?'

'I suppose they're like her imaginary friends.'

'She seems pretty convinced that there's a Mrs Fox about to give birth.'

'She's a little girl; she likes to tell herself stories.' He hears the impatient tremor in his voice. Norah was always like this: took children at face value. Gave in to Ella's whims. Acted like she was one of them. *Peter Pan*, isn't that what Fay used to call her?

And if Fay had insinuated that Norah was a child, he'd made it worse by treating her like one. He'd bowed to her whims, had given her too much of the wrong kind of love.

What pathetic parents they'd been.

Fay's the real mother in all of this. The woman he loves. He says this to himself over and over. *Fay, the woman I love . . .*

'Which side do you sleep on?'

'Sorry?'

'I'm just interested.'

There's no just to Norah's interest. She's pulling at the layers he's built over his years with Fay.

Adam nods at the right side of the bed.

Norah raises her eyebrows. 'You never liked the right side.'

'Fay needs to be close to the bathroom. Her irregular hours, her night shifts.' He clears his throat. 'And she likes to be near the door for when Willa comes in.'

'Right.'

Norah walks over to Adam's bedside table and picks up a photograph she saw when she first walked into this room, but this time she notices it, how Adam's face is pressed to Fay's,

211

how wide their smiles are. And how the girls are smiling too as they squint into the sun.

Adam takes the frame out of Norah's hands. 'Don't.'

As his fingers brush against hers, a shock runs through his arm.

He clenches his jaw. *Fay, the woman I love . . .*

'Adam?' Norah looks up at him.

Divorce. Death. There are guidelines for those. You get angry and lash out. You mourn. But disappearance? It doesn't allow you to let go, to turn your love from a living thing to a memory.

Norah steps closer.

Tell her to leave. Tell her to turn round and walk out through the door and never come back.

'I missed you,' she says.

He closes his eyes.

It's fifteen years ago. Fay's gone to sleep. They're in her living room. He and Norah had only known each other for a few hours and already he's sure she'll be in his life for ever.

Norah leans in again, her breath warm, her lips, the shape of her mouth, achingly familiar.

Tell her to leave . . . he thinks, but his arms draw her in.

The shape of her feels different. He lifts the hem of her T-shirt but she puts her hands over his and pushes them away.

'Not there,' she says.

He breathes into her hair. 'I've missed you.'

She lets her weight fall into his arms. So small and frail he could wrap her up and make her disappear.

'I never found anyone else,' she whispers. 'You know that, don't you? That I've never loved anyone but you.'

She makes people love her, Fay had said that once about Norah. And he'd tried to disagree, to say that loving someone was a choice, but Fay was right, wasn't she? Norah pulled people in.

He holds her tighter.

And then his phone rings.

They jump apart.

He takes it out of his pocket and turns away.

'Hello?' His hands are shaking.

A pause.

'Adam?'

Christ.

'Adam, it's me.'

Blood rushes to his ears. He watches Norah move to the other side of the room.

'Can you hear me?' asks Fay.

'Yes . . . Sorry . . . Yes, I can hear you.'

'I've got Ella.'

'What?'

He can't think straight. Ella with Fay? That doesn't make any sense.

'She came over. She was upset.'

'She came over to you?'

Another pause.

'Yes, Adam. She came over to me.'

He's offended her. Fay's worked so hard to build a relationship with Ella.

Adam looks at Norah. *God, what have I done?*

'I'm going to let her crash on the sofa for a few hours,' says Fay. 'We'll come round at lunchtime with the cake.'

'You're coming back?'

213

'I'm coming for Willa's birthday. Like I promised.'

'Of course.'

'Adam?' Her voice softer now.

'Yes?'

'Thank you – for coming earlier.'

He looks at Norah. God, he's betrayed them both, hasn't he?

'Adam? Everything okay?' Fay asks.

Adam watches Norah pick his clothes up off the chair. He should have told her to leave. He should tell her to leave now.

'Yes, everything's okay.'

'We'll see you tomorrow, then.'

Something drops out of the pile of Adam's clothes that Norah is holding. *Damn*. He forgot to empty his pockets.

'Adam, are you still there?'

'Yes, yes. Of course.'

'I said we'll see you tomorrow. We'll get a taxi.'

Norah bends down to the floor.

The phone goes dead. Fay was waiting for him to say something, that he was grateful she was looking after Ella, that he was sorry, that he missed her. She was waiting for him to say *I love you*.

He switches off his phone and goes over to Norah.

'I'm sorry,' Norah says, giving him the small velvet box. 'I was trying to find somewhere to sit. This dropped out.'

He'd filled out the divorce petition for missing spouses. Had carried the ring around for weeks. Planned to propose this weekend, on Willa's birthday.

He takes the box and shoves it into the top drawer of the dressing table.

'Was that Fay?'

'What?'

'On the phone?'

He goes over and holds open the door.

'I think you should leave.'

'Adam—'

He looks out into the dark landing and waits for her to move.

'We need to talk,' Norah says.

She comes and joins him at the door, too close. He steps away.

'There's nothing to talk about.'

'Yes there is, Adam. I have to explain. I have to tell you why I came back—'

'Not now,' he says, and closes the door on her.

Norah

Norah can still feel his touch.

She looks up to the attic and thinks about how Ella can't face being in the same house as her – and how the person she has turned to is Fay.

I love you, Norah's last words to Ella on that snowy November day at the school gates.

She goes down to the next landing and pushes open Willa's door. Louis lies asleep at the foot of her bed. Even when Willa was a baby he guarded her, like Ella did too. Willa's two sentinels.

After leaving Ella at school that day, Norah took Willa straight to Fay. She pushed her pram down the high street and kept walking until her face and hands were numb with cold.

It was the busker who had made up her mind. That glowing figure in a rainbow jumper who had stood on the streets of Holdingwell ever since she could remember. Sometimes she thought that he was a ghost who followed her around, someone only she could see. And then she'd invited him to play at Ella's sixth birthday, preferring the idea of paying him rather than an entertainment company. Parents had complained – a man with dirty nails and a ragged rainbow jumper playing strange jazz tunes to their children. But Ella had loved it, and that was all that mattered.

On the day Norah left she stood in front of him, Willa in her arms, her crying turning to gulps and then hiccups and then deep breaths – and then she'd grown quiet, stilled by his playing.

Norah had closed her eyes, feeling the vibration of the instrument on her lips, her fingers on the stops, the melody rising up through her ribcage – and then the lights, the audience, her black velvet dress sweeping the stage.

The man lowered his trumpet. *Are you all right?* he asked.

He knew, didn't he? That she wasn't all right. That soon she'd be gone.

Just keep playing, she'd answered. Because that's what she needed more than anything.

He nodded, put the trumpet to his lips and continued with his tune. *A wonderful world . . .*

Yes, he knew, otherwise he wouldn't have played that song.

She'd believed in those words once, that there was such a

place, and she knew that if she stayed she would never find it again.

How long had she stood there, listening to him? It might have been a minute or an hour or a day. She'd stayed until her body was full of music, until it felt alive again. Until she knew she had no choice but to leave.

Downstairs, on the camp bed, Norah watches the shadows of dawn flit across the room. She slips her hands under her T-shirt and touches the scar next to her right breast. Had she imagined Adam glancing at her chest, his eyebrows coming together as he tried to make sense of the lone breast swinging under her T-shirt?

He hadn't wanted to talk, but she'd have to tell them soon. And then they'd understand – and then they'd want her to stay, wouldn't they?

Norah reaches down for her handbag and rummages around for her phone. She can't help scanning the messages. He always stays in touch: sends her a quick text to check that she's arrived safely, emails photographs of Nat, leaves her a voice-mail on his way home from the surgery. But this is different. She hasn't gone abroad for a concert tour or taken a trip to a European city for a recording. She's gone back to her old life. And she asked him not to get in touch, to give her a few days to sort everything out. She made him promise. But still, she looks to see whether he's contacted her.

Before she switches off her phone, she sends a tweet.

Her agent sent her on a course, *it's important to feed your fans,* she'd said, *to keep them connected.* And then, embarrassingly, Norah got addicted to checking Twitter, to following, to sending messages to strangers. She'd got lonely, and this made her feel connected. It gave her hope that she might see them again.

As she puts back her phone, she notices that her CD isn't there, the one she wanted to give Ella, and that her purse has been flipped open. She turns it over – the photographs are the wrong way round. And the one of Nat is missing.

The world has been up all night and it's only now, at dawn, that it's going to sleep.

It's going to sleep in the small stone cottage on Fisher's Lane, where soft white roses grow over the door.

In the lounge, near the boarded-up window, sleeps the teenage girl, the dust of icing sugar on her lips. She dreams of the day she stood in the Holdingwell Café, playing the trumpet with The Mother Who Left. She's transported by her mother's playing, by the breath of her little sister, fast asleep in her pram, by what feels like a hundred eyes looking at them, by the feeling that life couldn't get any better than this.

And then she hears a cry, and when she looks down she sees that the pram is empty and as she turns round there's no one playing beside her and the café is empty – but there's a figure at the door, she's holding a cake in the shape of fox, lit up with candles. *Make a wish,* she says, *make a wish . . .*

In the upstairs bedroom of the stone cottage, The Mother Who Stayed climbs out of bed, takes her duvet and lies on the floor. She strokes the rug where the father lay only a few hours ago, where they'd made love and fallen asleep together and, when she'd woken, he was gone.

Across town, on Willoughby Street, in the tall red-brick house, a slideshow plays behind the father's closed eyes. All the photos he's ever taken. They're blank. A brilliant white blank.

A floor below him, the little girl's head presses heavily into her pillow. She takes the hand of The Mother Who Left. The little girl points at the fox that darts across the garden and, together, they start running, faster and faster, until their feet no longer touch the ground, until they take off and disappear . . .

And below the little girl, curled up on the camp bed in the lounge, The Mother Who Left holds a hand to her chest and feels the rise and fall of the place he touched.

SUNDAY MORNING

The world is waking up. Or it's trying to, anyway.

In the tall red-brick house the big dog lies curled up on the floor beside the little girl. A tremor runs through his paws. He can't sleep. *There are too many people to keep safe,* he thinks.

Beside him, the little girl stirs. *Today's my birthday.* She smiles and screws shut her eyes. *I wish for everyone to forget about all the things that are making them sad. I wish for them to be really, really happy: Daddy and Ella and the Miss Peggs and Mr Mann and Mr Mann's husband and all the children at school (even the ones who call me Gingernut), and Auntie Norah and Louis and Mrs Fox and her cubs and all the animals in the world. And Mummy. Especially Mummy.*

In the room above the little girl's, the father sits on the end of the bed and rubs his bloodshot eyes. He looks out of the window. *Please come home,* he whispers at the lightening sky. *I need you to come home.*

Downstairs in the lounge, The Mother Who Left stands by the open glass doors and looks out at the garden. *Today, I'll tell them . . .* She hears a rustle at the far end of the garden and then she sees it – a flash of red.

Across town, the teenage girl lies on the couch of the woman

223

who, time and again, she'd pushed away. She's wide awake. She tugs at the dark tufts of hair by her ears. As she stares at the ceiling, her mother's face comes in and out of focus. The most beautiful mum in the world, she used to think. She blinks. *Go away,* she whispers. *Go away . . .*

The Mother Who Stayed makes breakfast for the teenage girl. She brings it to her on a tray, a rose from the front door tucked into the napkin ring. *You need to keep your strength up,* she says. *For the race tomorrow.* And then she leans in and holds her.

I won't let you go, she thinks. *I won't let any of you go.*

Then the teenage girl and The Mother Who Stayed get dressed and take a taxi home.

Willa

Willa's heart beats hard. The palms of her hands and the soles of her feet tingle. Her eyes flutter. She tugs at her nightdress and scratches at the scar under her left eye.

Something's going to happen today, she can feel it.

That's when she remembers. Today Mrs Fox is going to give birth to her cubs, and that means the babies will have the same birthday as Willa and they can all celebrate together.

With Louis trailing behind her, Willa goes from room to room to see if anyone's awake.

Ella's missing, her room turned upside down. Willa knows it's wrong to snoop, especially in your big sister's room, but no one's telling her what's going on. And it can't hurt to look, can it?

Louis stands in the doorway to the attic and refuses to move.

'It's okay, Louis. If we get caught, I'll tell them it was my fault.'

He still doesn't move, which makes Willa feel even worse about being up here. But then she thinks about how upset Mummy is and how tired Daddy looks and how cross Ella is, and that if she doesn't work out what's happening and do something about it, then no one will be happy – and today's her birthday so they *have* to be happy.

She sits at Ella's desk and opens her laptop. Ella uses the same password for everything: *L0uisArmstr0ng*, because Auntie

Norah loves Louis Armstrong and so Ella loves Louis Armstrong and Louis is called Louis after him too. With Ella having gone off Auntie Norah and having torn all the Louis Armstrong posters off her wall, Willa hopes that Ella hasn't changed the password.

She types the letters and numbers into the box and the screen flashes to the desktop of Ella's computer.

Bingo.

She clicks on Ella's Twitter account and watches it load.

She's asked her so many times to tell her more about her school project, but all she says is that it's about researching missing people, especially missing mums, and that she's hoping that her project will help to bring missing mummies and missing children back together again. Willa can't think of anything worse than Mummy going missing.

She scans the tweets.

It's weird, because Ella makes it sound like *her* mummy is missing. Maybe she's pretending so that the other people with their missing mummies will listen to her and give her information. Willa keeps reading. *Mum's come home*. Weird again. And then her heart stops. There's a tweet from @rosesandlilies. That must be the Miss Peggs – and they've tweeted *we knew she'd come home*. Do they mean Auntie Norah? And if so, how did they know? And why was Auntie Norah missing? And why was Ella calling her Mum?

Willa logs off and looks over at Louis, who's still standing in the doorway.

'What's going on, Louis?'

Louis tilts his head to one side. She can tell he knows more than she does and that he's not letting on.

She leans back and looks at Ella's special drawer, the one at the top of her desk, which doesn't have a proper handle. She's always suspected that Ella pulled the handle off so that no one would get into her private things. Willa grabs a paperclip from a tin on the desk and folds it open.

Louis barks.

'*Shhh,* Louis, someone's going to hear.'

Even though Ella's a bit mean to Mummy with her big KEEP OUT sign, Mummy understands. She says that they should respect Ella's privacy. Willa gulps. Mummy would be upset if she found Willa here.

But then there's something else Mummy says, especially when Willa can't make up her mind about something: *Listen to your heart,* Mummy says. *Your heart never lies.* And, right now, her heart's telling her that she has to find out what's going on.

Willa pokes the end of the paperclip into the lock.

Louis barks. She loves Louis, but he can be a nuisance.

She twizzles the paperclip until the lock clicks and then she opens the drawer. There are scrunched-up papers and elastic bands and flyers for concerts and letters from Sai (which Willa wants to read, but knows that would be really bad). Then she spots a weird plastic stick with a purple handle and a window with two blue lines.

Yuck.

It's probably to do with having periods. Periods sound gross; Willa hopes she never gets them.

Before closing the drawer, she flips through a few of the bits of paper and uncovers a photo. It's one of those small passport photos, and it's of a little boy.

Louis barks.

Willa drops the photo.

'*Shhh!*' she hisses at Louis.

But he keeps barking and barking and barking until she's put the photo down and closed the drawer and locked it again with the paperclip and come back out onto the landing.

'Everything's weird, Louis,' she says. 'Weirder than weird.'

Willa walks down to Mummy and Daddy's room. Daddy's sleeping, his arm thrown across Mummy's side of the bed as though he's forgotten she's at work dealing with the emergency.

Downstairs, Auntie Norah's missing from the camp bed.

Willa flicks her tongue against her wobbly tooth. The taste of blood. She pushes again and this time the tooth comes loose. She puts her fingers in her mouth and pulls. A sharp pain as the last bit of gum lets go of the root. She places the tooth on Auntie Norah's pillow.

As she walks past the downstairs loo she hears Auntie Norah brushing her teeth.

She goes into the kitchen and fills up Louis's food bowl and glances out of the window. A guy with floppy brown hair is running down the street carrying a red parcel. It's Sai!

He stops next to three people huddled on the pavement. They talk to him and point to the house, and he nods.

Who are those people? And why are they standing outside the house?

One of them's got dreadlocks and dark skin, darker and shinier than Sai's. He's got a smile that looks like it's going to burst out of his mouth, a big wooden cross on a leather string hangs around his neck and a guitar is strapped to his chest.

Next to him stands the girl she met with Mummy on Friday night when they nearly went on their adventure: black lipstick and black eyeliner and black earrings and her hair is long and straight and black and so are her clothes and her boots. She looks especially black next to the third person, who's wearing a woolly rainbow jumper. He's got a trumpet case, like Auntie Norah's. And a big camping rucksack. It's the busker from outside school. And it's strange, because he's typing something into his phone, and Willa thought that you weren't meant to have a phone when you were poor and homeless. He looks up at her and smiles, and Willa smiles back and it's like they've known each other for ages.

Maybe they're all here for her birthday.

Maybe Mummy or Ella's invited them because they know how much Willa likes meeting new people.

And maybe the man with the guitar and the man with the trumpet are going to play at her party.

Willa can't think what the girl dressed in black's here for, though.

Across the road, the Miss Peggs' lace curtains twitch. Lily holds up one of the Chihuahuas to the window.

Sai leaves the three people behind, jogs up to the house and rings the bell.

Willa runs to open the front door. Louis abandons his bowl in the kitchen and comes to stand beside her.

Sai's wearing a shiny blue suit with a woolly red tie that looks like a sock; his trousers are so short you can see his hairy legs in the gap between the hem and his trainers. His trainers look weird with his suit.

'What are you doing here?' Willa asks. She can't help looking at the red parcel he's carrying.

'I'm here for your birthday.'

He sounds wheezy and out of breath. He must have run all the way from the post office.

'You're really here for me?'

He nods. 'Here.' He hands her the parcel.

Willa hesitates. Daddy wouldn't like her taking a present from Sai.

'If you don't want it . . . ' says Sai.

Willa holds it tighter. 'No, I definitely want it!' She looks up at him. 'Daddy'll kill you if he finds you here.'

'It was your dad who invited me.'

'Daddy invited *you*?'

Sai laughs. 'He called last night.'

'Weird.'

'That's what I thought. But then I'm not one to turn down a good party.' He ruffles her hair, which she finds kind of annoying because it's what people do to little kids, but she doesn't really mind because he's Ella's boyfriend and if he ruffles her hair that must mean that he likes her. 'And if I'm on my best behaviour, maybe he won't be so cross at me.'

Willa thinks Sai is nice and that Daddy should stop being angry with him. Maybe one day Sai will pick her up from school with Ella: then no one would dare call her Gingernut again.

She looks past Sai, out to the street. The man with the wooden cross unfurls a paper banner with big spray-painted words: *Forgiveness Heals!* Weird.

Along the bottom of the banner there's another line of writing, neater than the spray-painted bit:

@findingmum

Finding Mum. That's the name of Ella's website and the Twitter account she set up for her school project. Maybe now that Willa's seven, Mummy will let her be one of Ella's followers. She could ask Rose and Lily Pegg to let her use their laptop.

'Do you know those people?' she asks Sai.

Sai tugs at his woolly tie. 'Not really.'

No one seems to be giving Willa proper answers. Either he knows them or he doesn't.

'What are they doing out there?'

'I think they know Ella.'

'Oh.' Ella doesn't have any friends her age, so maybe Sai's right. But that doesn't explain what they're doing standing outside their house.

Willa closes the door.

'I guess you've had quite a weekend,' Sai says as he takes off his trainers and lines them up on the mat as though he's had direct instructions from Mummy. 'With your mum being back and everything.'

Willa blinks. 'My mum?' Her scar feels like it's on fire.

Louis presses in against her calves.

Before Sai has the chance to answer, Willa hears shouting from the street. It sounds like Mummy, but Mummy never shouts.

She yanks open the front door again.

Ella's standing by the gate, and Mummy's holding her hand! And she's carrying a big cardboard box.

They're surrounded by all the weird people Willa saw out on the street.

'How does it feel to have your mother home?' asks the guy in the rainbow jumper.

'Have you made your mind up yet?' yells the girl dressed in black.

'Have you forgiven her?' asks the guy with the sandals and the big cross around his neck.

'Where's she been all this time?' asks the girl dressed in black.

Mummy places herself between the people and Ella and puts her hand up like a traffic policeman. 'Not now,' she shouts. Her cheeks are flushed and her eyes are really wide. 'Step away!' she orders.

Willa can feel Sai standing beside her on the doorstep.

'They don't mean any harm,' says Miss Lily Pegg.

'They've come to see you, dear,' Miss Rose Pegg says to Ella. 'Like they told us they would.'

Ella runs up the steps to the front door. Mummy follows, carrying the big cardboard box.

'Ella! Mummy!' Willa jumps up and throws her arms around Mummy and then jumps up and kisses Ella. Louis joins in with the jumping. 'What's going on outside?' Willa asks.

Mummy shakes her head and closes the door behind Ella. 'It's nothing, Willa,' she says.

If there's one thing Willa's worked out recently, is that nothing doesn't mean nothing: it means something – a big something.

'Happy birthday, Willa.' Ella lifts Willa off the ground and spins her around. And then Ella puts her down at looks at Sai and smiles. At least she's happy, thinks Willa.

Mummy puts the big cardboard box down on one of the tables in the hall and takes Willa's hand.

Then Auntie Norah comes out of the lounge, rubbing her eyes, and everyone goes quiet for a bit.

'Daddy invited Sai to my birthday, isn't that cool?' Willa grins.

'Dad did what?' asks Ella.

'I thought maybe we should get to know him,' Daddy says, coming down the stairs. 'Isn't that what you keep saying, Ella?'

Sai steps forward. 'We've just been explaining that to your mum—'

Everyone goes quiet.

Sai goes red, which doesn't usually happen to people with tanned skin.

Willa doesn't know why he keeps calling Auntie Norah Ella's mum. Maybe it's because they're really close, but when Sai said *your* mum the first time, he was talking to Willa. She wishes someone would explain, but at the same time she doesn't want Sai to get in trouble, so she decides to change the subject.

'It's going to be the best birthday ever!' Willa claps her hands and jumps up and down. 'Isn't it, Mummy?'

Mummy smiles a tired smile. 'Yes, my darling.'

'And everyone will be here: you and Ella and Daddy and Louis and Sai – and Ella's friends outside, we could invite them to the party too, and—' She turns round and stares at Auntie Norah standing there with her face puffy with sleep in her big, baggy T-shirt with her weird boob sticking out. 'And Auntie Norah.'

Auntie Norah's eyes go misty like last night.

Willa looks round at everyone standing in the hall. 'And all being together – that will make everyone happy, won't it? Really happy!'

Ella

Ella finishes her tweet and bangs shut her bedroom door.

'What the hell did you think you were doing down there, telling everyone who Mum was?' she asks Sai.

'I thought everyone knew.'

'Willa doesn't.'

'She doesn't know who her mum is?'

'She thinks it's Fay.'

Sai shakes his head. 'What happened to the Ella of *tell the truth at all costs and damn the consequences*?'

'This is different.'

'I don't see how—'

'I didn't have a choice. Fay and Dad said it would upset her, that she was too little.'

'And now that your mum's come home?'

'She's not our mum. She walked out on us.'

'She's still your mum, Ella.'

'Give it a rest, Sai,' Ella snaps.

Sai reaches past Ella to open the door.

'Where are you going?'

'I think you need some space, I'm going home.'

Ella puts her hand on his arm. She can't cope with him walking out on her. 'I'm sorry,' she says. 'It's just a bit much, that's all.'

234

He doesn't move.

She prises his fingers off the door handle and kisses his hand. 'I like the suit.' She strokes the shiny blue sheen of the fabric.

His muscles relax under her touch.

'I thought I should make an effort – impress your dad.'

From the way Dad looked at him, Ella wonders whether it might have been better for Sai to wear jeans and a T-shirt, but she doesn't say anything.

Sai looks up at the damp patch on the ceiling. 'So the roof's still not fixed then?'

'I don't think it'll ever be fixed. All the roofers to do is sit in their van and eat sandwiches,' says Ella.

'Maybe the hole will get bigger and you'll be able to see the stars. That would be cool for summer.'

Ella shrugs. 'Maybe.'

Sai, the eternal optimist. But the summer feels ages away. Getting through this bank holiday weekend is all Ella can think about right now.

He walks around the room touching the loose chunks of paint where Ella has ripped off her posters and the photographs of Mum.

'What happened in here?'

Sai has only been in her bedroom once before, a few months ago when Dad took Fay off for a romantic stay in the country for her birthday. They had a babysitter who was too busy watching TV to notice Ella sneaking Sai into the house.

'I decided to redecorate,' Ella says.

He flicks his nail down the empty CD rack. 'And where's all your music?'

'I had a clear-out.'

'You binned your best friend, Louis Armstrong?'

'You're my best friend.'

Sai smiles. 'Your musical best friend.'

'I've grown out of him.'

Ella goes to the window that looks out onto the back garden and watches Willa run across the sunlit grass with Louis.

'It's always been sunny for Willa's birthday. Even on the day she was born.'

Sai comes over and puts his arm around her. 'Do you remember that day?'

She nods.

Ella had waited at the school gates for ages. Mum had turned up pink-faced, out of breath, with small beads of sweat covering her forehead and wet patches under her arms. Louis walked beside her. Every few seconds he looked up at her and made small, growling noises. And he wouldn't leave Mum's side.

'She kept saying *I'm fine, I'm fine*, but I knew something was wrong. It turned out that *fine* meant going into labour.'

'How did you know – I mean, you were pretty young.'

'I went to ante-natal classes with Mum.'

'You did what?'

'Dad was too busy. At work, he said.' Ella rolls her eyes. 'And he said he already knew all that baby stuff from when I was born. We couldn't afford a babysitter so Mum took me along. Some of it really grossed me out – the stuff about birthing positions and breastfeeding.' Ella wrinkles her nose. 'Put me off having kids for life.'

'That's a shame.' Sai kisses Ella's cheek. 'You'd make a good mum.'

She bats him away. 'Yeah, right.'

No one should get to be a mum until they've passed like a million tests, thinks Ella. There are too many mums out there who haven't got a clue what they're doing. It's not fair on the kids.

'So what happened?' Sai asks.

'By the time Mum got home her face was red and sweaty and she was struggling to breathe, and then she told me to call Dad and tell him to come home. That's when I knew it was serious.'

Music and laughter and cheering and the sound of a TV blared through the mobile. Ever since Mum got pregnant with Willa, Dad had spent his evenings at the Three Feathers.

Dad?

No answer.

Dad, it's Mum. She needs you to come home.

Still no answer. He must have answered the call and then got distracted.

Another cheer. And a laugh, which sounded like Dad's laugh. And then the music got louder and after that the phone went dead.

'So he came home and took care of her?' asked Sai.

'Not exactly.'

Ella went back into the bedroom.

Mum propped herself up. *Did you get through to Dad?* Her voice was small and frayed.

'He was at the pub,' Ella tells Sai. 'But I didn't tell Mum; she didn't need to hear that, not with the baby coming.'

So he's on his way? Mum asked.

Ella nodded again.

Mum fell back against the pillows and closed her eyes. She pulled her mouth over her teeth and held on to the big mound of her stomach.

'So what did you do?' asks Sai.

'I told Mum I wanted to call the ambulance. The woman in the antenatal class said that if we couldn't drive to the hospital and if we couldn't afford a taxi, we should call 999. But Mum said she wanted to wait for Dad.'

Mum had tears in her eyes, which made Ella think of all the other times Mum had cried in the last nine months. When Ella asked Dad why Mum was so upset all the time he said it was the hormones, that babies did that to you. When Ella asked whether Mum had cried when she was in her tummy, Dad had scratched his chin and shrugged. *Don't really remember.*

Sometimes, Ella wondered whether Dad would have been happier if she and Willa had never come along. Maybe if had just been the two of them, he'd have been a better husband and Mum wouldn't have left.

'I got out my toy trumpet, stood at the foot of the bed and played a tune, hoping it would make her feel happier. But she covered her ears and shook her head and said, *Not now, Ella.*'

'I guess being in labour's pretty intense,' says Sai.

'Yeah.'

When playing the trumpet didn't work, Ella had gone to the bathroom to get the heart monitor Mum had bought when she was pregnant with Ella. When Ella asked Mum why there were two sets of earphones she said it was so that both she and Dad could listen to Ella's heartbeat, but Dad didn't seem like the kind of person who'd want to sit there listening to a baby's heartbeat and she'd never seen him listening to Willa's.

Ella put the first set of earphones in Mum's ears, the second pair in her own, and placed the probe on Mum's tummy.

Sometimes it took a while to find the heartbeat, which always made Ella a little scared in case the baby's heart had stopped without telling anyone, but this time they heard it straight away – beat, beat, beating like a galloping horse.

Mum closed her eyes and lay back and her limbs relaxed, and Ella felt glad that she'd found something that helped.

'She seemed to calm down and I thought she was okay,' Ella tells Sai. 'But then I realised that her skin had gone grey and when I shook her, she wouldn't wake up. Louis barked at the end of the bed.' Ella remembers the red flower spreading across the white sheets under Mum's thighs. 'So I called the ambulance. And went to get Dad.'

Sai raises his eyebrows. 'You went to the pub?'

'Yep.'

The pub was so full that people spilled out onto the pavement; they stood clutching their beers and smoking in the late afternoon sunshine. It took a while to find Dad. He was sitting at the bar, holding his glass up to the TV screen and cheering a goal. Ella ducked between all the men and women crowding around Dad and then tugged at his blue overalls.

As he looked down at her his eyes glazed over. He pushed his glasses up his nose and laughed, a smelly, beer-breath laugh.

Ella – what are you doing here?

It's Mum. She's having the baby.

He took off his glasses, rubbed his eyes and stood up. The bar stool crashed to the floor. A few people looked over.

Steady on there, Adam. A man with a massive red spider vein on his nose slapped Dad on the back.

Dad stumbled out onto the pavement and blinked as the sunlight shone on his face.

'I found him at the Three Feathers. He took me home on his motorbike; I sat in front of him holding on to the handlebars. He was so pissed he couldn't drive straight.'

'God.'

'Yeah. Responsibleparenting.com. When we got to the house, the ambulance was already there. They let us get in with Mum. And a few minutes later, Willa was born.'

'In the ambulance?'

'Mum passed out. Dad threw up. So the paramedic handed me the baby.' *Looks like you're going to be the first to meet your baby sister*, she said.

Ella took the baby in her arms. 'Look, Dad,' she said, holding Willa to him, but Dad didn't hear her; he was too busy worrying about Mum.

She looked into the baby's big blue eyes and at her small hands and tiny fingernails and at the way she sucked her mouth in and out as if she was trying to smile and, from that moment, she knew that Willa was hers to keep safe.

'Must have been pretty special,' says Sai.

'Kind of. Special and scary.'

'You've done a good job – looking after Willa.'

Through the window, Ella watches her little sister crouching under the gooseberry bush. She isn't so sure about having done the right thing by Willa. By letting her believe that Fay was her Mum, hadn't she lied to her like everyone else?

Sai wraps his arms around Ella. She lets her body fall into his and wishes time would stand still and that she could stay up here with him, away from everyone and everything.

He lets go and points out of the window. 'Willa's really into her fox thing, isn't she?'

'She thinks we've got the entire cast of *Fantastic Mr Fox* living in the back garden.'

'I got her the soundtrack, to go with the piece you're playing later.' He looks over at the music stand.

'I'm not playing any more.'

'But you've been practising for weeks.'

'I'm crap at it.' She'd wanted so badly to be good at the trumpet, but now she was relieved that she was rubbish. One less thing of Mum's to get rid of.

'No you're not—'

'You think I'm going to play my trumpet with Mum listening?'

Ella takes a cigarette from the pack on her bedside table, lights it and goes over to the window.

Sai comes over, takes it out of her hand and stubs it out on the outside windowsill.

'I don't think you should smoke before the race.'

With everything that's happened in the last two days, Ella had put the 10k out of her mind.

Sai draws her in by the waist and holds her close. She presses her ear to his chest and listens to his heartbeat. She forgets, sometimes, how his asthma makes it hard for him to breathe.

'It's okay, Ella,' he says and lifts her chin. 'I get it: families are complicated.'

He kisses her forehead and then the top of her nose and then her mouth. For a second, all the tension floats out of Ella's body. She's glad Sai is here, with his floppy hair, wearing his silly suit, holding her and kissing her.

He takes a breath and looks into her eyes. 'But Willa's going to find out, you know that, right? I mean, it's not the kind of secret you can keep.' He looks down through the scaffolding. 'Especially with your troops gathering down there.'

241

Ella pushes Sai away. 'No, she's not. Not if we find a way to make Mum leave. And the guys down there are loons. I should never have started that stupid campaign.'

'I don't get it, Ella. You've spent so long looking for your mum and now she's here—'

Ella goes over to her desk and picks up the only picture she hasn't thrown out. It's a poster of Mum with MISSING written in big letters across the top. She'd drawn it in thick wax crayon. Mum's long red hair and her big smile and a trumpet in her hand.

'Look!' she says, holding it up to Sai. 'I drew this when I was eight – a year older than Willa. I didn't know about photo-copiers, so I made dozens. Stayed up all night. And I covered Holdingwell in them. I thought Mum had been abducted or that she'd had an accident and was lying in a ditch somewhere. Or that she'd died.' Ella gulps. 'And now it turns out she chose to leave.' The crow pecks and pecks. 'So she doesn't get to come back and to play happy families. She doesn't get to come between Fay and Dad – and Fay and Willa.'

'I didn't think you liked Fay.'

'I didn't. But that's only because I was too stupid to under-stand. I get it now: Fay's Willa's mum, her real mum. And Willa loves her. And I'm not going to let anyone get in the way of that.'

Sai comes over to Ella, takes the poster out of her hands and puts it down on the desk. 'So how do you plan to make her go away?'

Ella goes to her desk, pulls out the pregnancy test stick and holds it up.

Sai goes red. 'Hey, Ella—'

Ella laughs. 'It's not mine, stupid. It's Fay's. I found it in the bathroom. She's pregnant. If Mum finds out, maybe she'll leave them alone.'

'Fay's pregnant?'

'And there's something else.' She takes a photograph out of the drawer. 'I found this in Mum's purse.'

Sai looks at the picture. 'I don't understand.'

'I reckon Mum's got another family stashed away some-where. She's probably run away from them too. Anyway, with this and with Fay being pregnant, I reckon I can make her leave.'

'You're going to blackmail her?'

Ella shrugs. 'She needs to know that she's not welcome here.'

There's a knock on the door. 'Ella?'

'Shit, it's Dad.' Ella snatches the photograph out of Sai's hand, stuffs it in her back pocket and shoves the pregnancy test under her duvet.

Dad walks in.

'Things are ready downstairs—' he says. And then he sniffs the air. 'Is that smoke?'

'Wow Dad, you should be a private investigator.'

Sai leaps forward. 'It's mine. I'm sorry, Mr Wells.'

Ella looks at Sai. He's the only one in her life right now who's on her side. Stuff family and all that blood is thicker than water crap, it's the people you choose to have in your life that matter. Dad doesn't get to criticise him.

'It's not his cigarette, Dad. Sai's got asthma – and a heart con-dition, the one his dad died of. Do you really think he's going to smoke? And in case you're wondering, he doesn't drink either, which is more than can be said for you. Sai isn't the one who gets me in trouble – I do that all by myself. In fact, he's the one who tries to stop me. Take a good look, Dad, this is me: *I*

243

smoke. *I'm* the fuck-up.' Ella draws on the stub and then puts it back down on the windowsill.

Dad stares at her. 'We'll talk about this later. Let's not spoil your sister's birthday.' He turns to go.

Suddenly Ella feels the urge to tell Dad everything. About Fay being pregnant. About the photograph. About how she doesn't want Willa to know about Mum.

'Dad—'

Sai comes over to her and squeezes her hand. 'Not now, Ella,' he whispers.

Dad turns round. 'What is it?'

Through the window, Ella sees Willa come in from the garden.

'Nothing, Dad. It's nothing.'

Fay

Fay locks herself in the kitchen, leans against the door and breathes out.

You can do this, she tells herself.

Ella's in her room with Sai and Louis.

Norah's tidying the lounge.

And she's sent Adam down to the basement to sort out his camera for the birthday party.

She looks around the kitchen. Twenty-four hours and already the untidiness has crept in. Everything that Fay's built is slipping away.

Adjusting the pieces of paper on the fridge, her eyes scan the chores rota, her shifts at the hospital, Adam's busy periods at the recycling plant, the girls' timetables. Time neatly parcelled. She lifts dirty mugs out of the sink and places them in the dishwasher. Then she gets out the bottle of Dettol and sprays the counters, wiping away the smears of butter and the crumbs and the trails of milk. She scrubs and scrubs until the surfaces shine, until her hands are raw and red. And as she scrubs, she repeats the refrain: *they're my family now.*

When she first moved in, she told herself that she was doing it for the girls. They needed her; Adam wasn't coping. As soon as Norah came home, she'd step aside and pick up her old life.

But that had been a lie, hadn't it?

Sure she cared about the girls – really cared – but that's not why she'd moved in. She loved Adam, that's why. She'd always loved him.

A wave of nausea sweeps over her. She grips the counter.

They're the worst lies, aren't they, she thinks, *the lies you tell yourself.*

A tune presses in from outside. And odd tumbling-together of instruments. Fay looks out of the window and sees the man with dreadlocks playing the guitar next to the rainbow-jumper guy with his trumpet. It's Norah's song. 'What a Wonderful World'. A wonderful, messed-up world.

Dear Willa, who wants these people to come to her birthday party. If it were down to Willa, she'd have everyone she'd ever met living with them at Number 77 Willoughby Street: one big happy family. Is that the reason she'd accepted Fay so easily as her mum? Would she have accepted anyone?

Music leaks down through the ceiling from Ella's room. No matter how many changes Fay has made to the house, its bones have stayed the same: brittle and hollow and ready, at any moment, to betray the movements of the people who live here.

She's glad that Adam called Sai; Ella needs him right now.

I'm going to keep hold of them, the words from last night echo in her head. *No matter what happens, no matter what Norah tries to do, I'm going to keep hold of them, and I'm going to stay.*

A knock on the kitchen door.

Fay puts down the cloth she's been using to scrub the counters and goes over to open the door.

Norah walks in.

'Can I help?' Norah asks.

Help? Fay wants to shout at her. *You abandon your baby girl and then waltz back into her life and expect to pick up where you left off? Blow up a few balloons and wait for everything to slot back into place?*

'If you don't mind ... ' Norah adds.

Yes, I mind. I want you to turn round and go back to whatever life you've been living for close to a decade now and let us get back to how things were before.

Fay hands Norah a jute bag containing paper plates and napkins and cups.

Norah empties the contents onto the kitchen table. A cup rolls to the floor.

Fay holds herself back from going to pick it up, turns away and busies herself with the cake.

'Everything's red,' Norah says, peeling off the cellophane wrappers.

Fay nods. 'Red for Willa's foxes.'

'Ah yes, her foxes.' Norah puts down a paper plate in front of each seat.

'Ella loves blue,' Fay blurts out. She can't help herself from sharing the details of the girls' lives. And then she remembers that Norah's favourite colour was also blue, the colour of jazz.

Fay pushes seven candles into the cake. As far as Fay knows, Norah's never baked a cake in her life. But baking a cake doesn't make you a mum, does it? Norah gave birth to them; Fay could never trump that.

Norah comes over and opens her hand. 'I found this.'

Willa's milk tooth sits in Norah's palm. Fay feels light-headed.

'She must have dropped it in the lounge,' says Norah.

Fay turns it over between her fingers. 'It's her first one.'

'I thought you might like to deal with it.' Norah pauses. 'I imagine you've planned something special.'

She's mocking me, thinks Fay, like she used to: *my friend the organiser, the planner, the chart-list-graph-maker. Always marking moments.*

'Something special?' Fay asks.

'I guess you'll get her to put it under her pillow or something.' Norah picks up the tooth and holds it out to Fay. 'Here, take it.'

Of course she'd made plans. She was going to ease the tooth from under Willa's pillow and replace it with a five-pound note tied in a red ribbon, along with a note from the tooth fairy.

'Thank you.' Fay puts the tooth in an eggcup on the counter.

'I need to ask you something, Fay.'

Fay pushes the final candle into the fox's nose, the wax carved into the shape of a number seven.

'Fay?'

Breathe, Fay says to herself. Whatever it is, you can cope.

Fay looks up at Norah and waits for her to speak.

'How much did you find out, when you had me traced?'

Fay had hoped Norah wouldn't come back to this.

'Not much.'

'How much is not much?'

'The appointment in London, that's the first bit of information the detective gave me.' The light-headedness gets worse. Fay holds on to the counter.

'I'd only just had Willa. I couldn't go through with it, not again.' Norah pulls one of the candles out of the cake and scrapes at the wax. 'Adam and I had barely slept together since her birth. I didn't understand how it had happened, how my body could respond so quickly.'

So she wants a biology lesson now? Following pregnancy, the female body is more fertile, is primed to create a new life.

'I didn't go through with it. I couldn't get rid of him.'

'I know.'

'You know?'

'The trail went cold for a while – well, for about nine months. Then I found the record of a birth in Glasgow hospital.'

Norah goes over to the kitchen table and sits down. Fay keeps standing where she is. She's worried that, if she moves, she'll be sick.

'Did you tell Adam?' asks Norah.

'No.' She'd thought about it, of course, but what good would it do? He was starting to get himself together again. And if Norah wanted him to know she'd come back, wouldn't she? That's what Fay had told herself.

'What else did you find out?' Norah asks.

248

'After that? Not much. Only that you moved to Berlin.' Fay wonders whether she's got any better at lying since Norah's been away. She picks up Willa's wooden fox from the windowsill and traces the edges with her fingertips. Then she looks out of the kitchen window. The wind has picked up and, above them, the tarpaulin has worked itself loose and is flapping against the side of the house.

'You knew I was in Berlin?' Norah asks.

It had taken Fay a good ten days to pluck up the courage to return the private investigator's call. It had been so long since she'd heard from him that she thought he'd given up the case. *She's too good at covering her tracks,* he'd said. And then he found Norah's patient records in a Berlin hospital. Willa was four, Ella eleven, and although Fay hadn't forgotten about Norah, life had moved on.

'I came to visit the hospital,' Fay says.

'So you found out.'

'Yes, I found out.'

When Fay didn't return the investigator's voicemail he'd called again: *I have some important information, I think you'll want to know this.* So she'd met him at the Holdingwell Café and they'd sat on the plastic chairs, drinking coffee, and had heard the word cancer drop from his lips.

'Did you see me?' Norah asks.

'I found your room. You'd just had the mastectomy.'

Fay had stood outside the door, watching Norah asleep in the hospital bed. She was hooked up to a drip, her skin transparent, her long red hair spread out on her pillow like that painting of Ophelia floating in the river. A thick bandage pushed up under her hospital gown, along her chest.

Why hadn't she come home when she found out she was

249

sick? Why hadn't she trusted her best friend, a medic, to help?

'You didn't come to speak to me?'

'I was going to.'

But then a blond man holding a little boy by the hand had stepped past Fay and walked into Norah's room. The little boy ran to Norah's bed and jumped up.

Mama! he'd squealed. *Mama!*

Langsam, said the man. Slowly. *Sie sanft.* Be gentle.

The man walked over and took Norah's hand.

Norah had opened her eyes, looked at them and smiled.

Fay moved away from the door.

'But you didn't, you walked away?' Norah asks.

Fay stares at Norah. 'Yes. And the truth is, Norah, when I came to Berlin I didn't want to find you. And when I saw you had a new family I had an excuse to walk away. You had people who loved you, a new life; you were going to be okay. And yes, I had a family to go home to, a family I'd been living with for years. A family that needed me. I loved them – I *love* them.' She takes a breath. 'You'd been gone for years, Norah. What did you expect? For everything to stay the same? For everyone to just wait for you?'

Norah hangs her head and presses her thumb along the folds of a paper napkin.

Fay looks at Norah's chest hanging unevenly under her jumper. It was just like her not to have reconstructive surgery, not to wear a bra. No trace of vanity. Clumsy as a child and no grasp of how beautiful she was, no matter what clothes she wore, no matter how damaged her body was.

'You're clear now, right?' Fay asks.

Norah tugs at her collar and smiles. 'I might live.'

'What the hell does that mean?'

'We have to talk, Fay. Without fighting. I have to tell you why I came home.'

'You *might* live?' Fay yells.

Before Norah has the time to answer Adam strides in, his camera around his neck. He snaps a picture of Fay and then comes over, takes her by the waist and kisses her.

She pulls away. She doesn't like how much of a show he's making of his affection. And she can't do this, not now that Norah's told her she's sick again. Damn Norah. Damn all of them for coming into her life.

'Camera's all set up,' he says, a false jollity in his voice. 'I've come to help.' Whenever his eyes fall on Norah he jerks his head. Norah's not looking at him either. Fay feels a thud in her chest. What did he do when he came home last night? Did they talk? Did she tell him that she *might live*? Did he get drawn in by her, like he always did?

'You can finish making up the party bags,' she says, pointing to a pile of toys and sweets on the counter.

He holds his hand to his head in mock-salute.

Norah goes over to the table and finishes putting out the napkins. Fay comes to stand next to Adam and passes him the tiny model foxes to put in the party bags.

'The cake looks amazing,' Adam says. 'You're a genius.' He tries to take her hand but she pulls it away. 'Thanks for looking after Ella ...' he whispers. 'Thanks for coming home.'

She nods but doesn't look at him.

'Fay?' he whispers. 'What's wrong?'

What's wrong? I'm losing you, just like I always knew I would.

They watch Norah walk across the room to the window and the three of them stare out across the street.

... *red roses too* ... The tune floats in through the open window. Norah's favourite song and she doesn't even like bloody flowers, thinks Fay.

'You look tired. Why don't you have a break before the party,' he says. 'I can do the rest.'

'I'm fine.' Fay takes the cake out of the box and carries it over to the table. She looks at the red stains on her hands from dying the icing. *I'm just fine.*

SUNDAY AFTERNOON

Norah

Norah looks at red paper napkins and the red paper plates and the big, red fox cake on its stand. Adam's brought in a footstool and an armchair from the lounge and an old crate from the garage. They're all sitting at different heights around the table.

'Everyone smile!' Adam says, standing at the head of the table.

They all lean in.

A family portrait. Under different circumstances, Norah might have laughed.

'Fay, you're not in the shot.'

Fay crouches next to Willa. Willa throws her arm around her.

A flash. And everyone breathes out.

Ella sits next to Sai, her shoulders slumped; she hasn't said a word to Norah since she came in. Adam looks at Sai's arm draped across Ella's shoulders. Fay, her rosebud apron tied tightly over her stomach, keeps finding reasons to get up and walk around the kitchen. There's a fork missing, or a paper cup or the dishwasher bleeps and needs to be turned off. Six years of living with perfect Fay – she'd have thought it would have driven Adam crazy. *Fussing Fay*, they used to joke. But it's what he's fallen in love with, isn't it?

Willa sits on the other side of Ella. She glances over at Norah and scrunches up her freckly nose as though she's trying to work something out.

Norah sits on the footstool like a child. She's promised herself that today, after Willa's party, she'll tell them.

The doorbell rings.

Willa claps her hands and wriggles in her seat.

Adam frowns at her. 'Willa?'

'I thought they should be invited.'

Fay goes into the hall.

A moment later Norah hears a series of high-pitched yaps and then Rose and Lily Pegg sweep into the kitchen. They're wearing identical purple chiffon dresses, the same ones they wore to church every Sunday when Norah lived in Holdingwell. And they've brought their three Chihuahuas with them; they have purple bows tied to their collars.

Rose claps her hands together. 'The two Mrs Wells, both in the same room – astonishing!'

Norah stares at her, stunned. Willa scratched her scar.

Louis gets up and thumps his tail.

'So nice of you to include us,' says Rose as she kisses Willa on the top of her copper bob. 'We loved your note with the picture of the fox blowing out the candles on a cake. You're a good artist.'

'I wanted you to be here,' says Willa. 'You're family!'

Ella offers her chair to Rose. Adam does the same for Lily. Louis guides the Chihuahuas under the table; his tail thumps so hard with excitement that the plates rattle.

The doorbell rings again.

'What on earth?' Adam exclaims.

Willa beams and runs to the door.

A moment later Mr Mann, Willa's teacher, stands in the kitchen – with another man, who's carrying a massive parcel. He puts it down on the floor.

'We don't usually accept invitations from pupils,' Mr Mann says, 'but we thought we'd make an exception for Willa.'

Like they always made exceptions for me, thinks Norah. She'll have to warn Willa about that.

Willa walks over to the parcel.

'Can I open this one now, Mummy?'

Fay nods. She'd have imposed rules, thinks Norah: presents after the cake. But she looks too tired to insist on anything.

Willa yanks at the bow but it's tied too tight.

Adam gets a knife and slices it open for her.

She kneels down and tears at the shiny pink paper until she reveals a big white plastic doll's house. Willa frowns. She'd have preferred a den for her foxes, thinks Norah.

Willa blinks, then looks up at Mr Mann and his husband and smiles. 'Thank you.'

'Just don't tell anyone at school,' says Mr Mann. 'I'm not meant to give presents either.' He leans over and points through a small window. 'There's a family in there – with a dog.'

Willa leans in. 'The dog looks like Louis!'

But not two mothers, thinks Norah.

A trumpet tune drifts in from outside. Ella's Twitter followers, that's what Adam said. The men and women who, more likely than not, the Miss Peggs had invited here, messaging them through their Twitter account, just like they'd contacted Norah.

The Twitter followers had kept Ella hoping for Norah's return. Except now that Norah's back Ella hates her. That much is clear from her behaviour – and from her tweets.

What will they do when Norah steps out of the house? Mob her? Yell at her for being the worst mother in the world? But one of them's holding a *Forgiveness Heals!* banner.

257

Was it possible that they might forgive her?

Willa leans over her fox cake. The candles light up her face and her red hair. She takes such a deep breath that her chest and her tummy expand over the table. She fills her cheeks until they're bulging, and then she blows until all seven candles are out and the air is full of smoke.

Norah did come back once. Six years ago today.

She'd stood on Willoughby Street, like those Twitter followers, looking into this kitchen.

It had taken three days to get here from Shuna, the small Scottish island where she was staying with Nat. A ferry, a bus, a train – all of them slow. She didn't sleep, she just thought of this day a year ago, lying semi-conscious in the ambulance, watching Ella cradle Willa in her arms.

She'd wanted to see that they were okay and to work out how she felt, whether she could imagine herself among them, whether Adam had grown up enough to be a dad. And whether she'd grown up too, because it hadn't just been Adam, had it? She'd failed the girls as well.

Someone had tied balloons to the front door. The kitchen glowed. Adam and Ella and Willa sat around the table. Adam's Beach Boys CD spilled out through the open window. Louis ran between them, his tail thumping the backs of their chairs. And Fay – they must have invited her out of habit. Ever since they'd had Ella and asked Fay to be her godmother, she'd tagged along to their family celebrations. *The spinster fairy godmother*, Norah used to joke.

She'd sensed a change in them.

Adam sat a little straighter in his chair, more alert. He got up and kissed the top of Ella's head and went to pick up some matches on the side; he lit the candle on the cake.

Ella switched off the stereo, disappeared from the kitchen and came back carrying her toy trumpet. The notes of 'Happy Birthday' replaced the Beach Boys.

Fay started singing.

Louis barked and looked out at Norah through the kitchen window.

Willa raised her head, but her back was turned to Norah, so Norah hadn't seen the raw scar under her left eye.

If she'd seen it, would she have gone in? Would she have been able to walk away again?

As Louis ran over to the window, Norah had stepped back.

What is it, Louis? She'd heard Ella call.

Come back here, Louis! Adam yelled. *Good dog, come away from the window.*

No, there wasn't room for her.

Go, she'd whispered to Louis. *Go back to them.*

He'd cocked his head to one side, let out another bark and then walked back to his family.

'Why don't you take another photo, Daddy?' Willa picks up Adam's camera. 'Now that everyone's here.'

Adam rubs his forehead, gets up slowly and takes the camera.

'Come on, we all have to fit in,' says Willa, using her small hands to show how she wants everyone to bunch up around the table. She grabs Louis so that he's sitting next to her at the front. 'Mummy, tell us if we're all sitting right.'

Fay smiles at her weakly and nods. 'It's fine, Willa.' And then she goes to stand at the back.

Adam takes a quick picture and puts the camera back down.

Willa frowns at him, perturbed by his half-heartedness. If

Adam's photographic style hadn't changed from those early London days, Willa would have been used to him spending hours getting the angle and the light just right. It used to drive Norah crazy, mainly because she wished he'd be as meticulous about the other things in his life, like being a father.

As everyone shifts back into position, Willa asks:

'Shall I tell you what I wished for?'

Rose Pegg shakes her head. Her double chin wobbles. 'If you tell us your wishes, they won't come true. It's the law.'

'She's right,' adds Lily Pegg.

Fay squeezes Willa's hand. 'Better keep it secret, darling.'

Birthday cakes and tooth fairies and wishes – classic Fay.

'But I want to, Mummy,' Willa says.

Norah wonders when Fay got used to this little girl calling her Mummy. And when she allowed herself to believe it was true.

Before anyone can stop her, Willa blurts out:

'I wish for everyone to start liking each other and getting on. I wish for Ella and Mummy to become friends and for Ella to stop being angry at Auntie Norah and to love her again, like she did when Auntie Norah lived here, and I wish for Daddy and Louis to stop being cross at Mrs Fox and, above all, I wish that we all get to stay here together – Mummy and Daddy and Ella and Louis and Sai and Auntie Norah—'

'She's not Auntie Norah,' says Ella.

'But she brought a trumpet with her.' And then Willa reaches up and points at Norah's head. 'And she's got red hair, like us. And she said she was Auntie Norah. Sort of.'

'And she's not staying,' says Ella.

'The Old Mrs Wells isn't staying?' asks Rose Pegg.

When they'd used their Twitter account to send a message to

260

Norah, to encourage her to come home, they'd said that every-thing would be okay. That the girls would forgive her.

'Why's she not staying?' asks Willa. 'I think she's nice.'

'Because she's got her own family to go back to,' says Ella.

'Oh!' says Lily Pegg and covers her mouth with her hand.

And then the table falls silent.

Mr Mann and his husband look down at their plates.

Rose Pegg's eyes go as round as marbles.

Adam starts swaying where he's standing.

Fay looks at Willa.

Norah sinks back into her chair.

And Ella pulls a photograph out of her pocket and thumps it down on the table.

Everyone leans in.

Nat's smiling face peers up at them. Norah's chest tightens. She hasn't allowed herself to miss him, but seeing him like this, with his straggly blond hair and his sideways grin, makes her long to take him in her arms.

Please can I come with you? he'd begged her.

'Maybe we should leave,' Mr Mann says, but everyone ignores him.

Norah looks away. She hadn't wanted them to find out like this; there were other things she had to explain first. Like why she came back.

'You see,' says Ella. 'She's got a family. She hasn't got a clue how to be a mum, but she's gone and had another kid. She's probably got a whole bunch of them hidden away—'

'Maybe they can come and live here too,' says Willa. She turns to Norah. 'You could ask them to come round – my cake's big enough to feed lots of people.' She glances down at the candles she's just blown out.

261

Ella scrapes back her chair. 'I'm going upstairs.'

Sai gets up too and follows her out.

Fay turns to Adam. 'Go and talk to her.'

He nods and heads to the door, but Norah gets up and reaches for his arm. 'I'll go, Adam. I'm the one who needs to explain.'

Willa

This isn't like the party at the end of *Fantastic Mr Fox*. No one's dancing or singing or laughing or eating. Mr Mann said he had to go and do some work for school, even though it's a bank holiday tomorrow, and Miss Rose and Miss Lily Pegg said the Chihuahuas needed to get home because they were tired, which was also an excuse because the Chihuahuas are never tired – they're always jumping and yapping and running around in circles. Willa had never seen them sleepy, not once.

No, this wasn't how Willa had imagined her birthday.

As Ella and Sai and Auntie Norah go through the kitchen door, Willa hears Mrs Fox cry out from the garden.

Willa pats Louis's head. *Did you hear her?*

Louis stares up at her as if to say *Yes, of course I heard Mrs Fox. I always hear her.* Although Louis doesn't like Mrs Fox, at least he believes that she exists – which is more than can be said for most people.

Willa's been itching to go out and check again but Mummy

went to so much trouble with the cake and everything that she thought she should wait a bit. Though now that Ella's stormed out, and Sai and Auntie Norah have followed her, Willa wonders whether that means it's the end of the party – in which case, maybe she could sneak out and have a look.

At the end of the table, Mummy and Daddy whisper things. Mummy stares down at the photograph.

'Who do you think he is?' Daddy asks Mummy.

Mummy's skin is usually rosy in the winter and really tanned in the summer, but right now it's pale, paler than Ella and Auntie Norah's, and her eyes are squinty like when she's had a long shift at the hospital.

Willa picks up the photograph from the table and stares at the little boy. He makes her think of someone, but she's not sure who.

Daddy clutches his hair as if it might let the stress out through his head.

Willa's been desperate to ask Mummy why the Miss Peggs keep calling Auntie Norah the Old Mrs Wells. Maybe she is Mummy's sister and she's her older sister, but Wells is Daddy's name and Mummy and Daddy aren't married. Weird.

Louis puts his paws on the table and stares at the cake. Willa waits for Mummy to tell him off but she's so busy looking at the photograph that she doesn't notice.

'No Louis—' Willa says, tapping his paws.

Louis makes his eyes go sad and droopy.

Mummy goes over to fuss with things in the sink.

'Okay, just a little piece.' Willa cuts off a bit of the red tail because it makes her think of when Foxy Fox had his tail shot off by those horrible farmers, Boggis, Bunce and Bean. She places the bit of cake in her palm and holds it out to Louis, who swallows it in one big gulp, leaving slobber in her hand. Mummy's tried really hard to teach Louis table manners but he prefers to eat things in his own way.

Daddy goes over to Mummy. 'Are you okay?' he asks.

Mummy clutches her stomach. Then she puts her hand in front of her mouth and runs out into the hallway.

'Fay!' Daddy goes after her.

Willa hears Mummy opening the door to the downstairs loo and being sick, and then telling Daddy to go away. Mummy's been sick quite a few times in the last week. Maybe she picked up a bug at the hospital.

She looks around the table at the empty seats and at the party poppers no one's popped. No, this definitely wasn't like the feast in *Fantastic Mr Fox*.

She doesn't understand why everyone got so upset about her sharing her wish. How is anyone meant to know what she wished for unless she tells them? And it's a good wish too, about them all staying as one big family, even if that means including people who aren't proper family, like Sai and Auntie Norah and the little boy on the photo, because he's Auntie Norah's son, which means he should be with them too.

Willa looks at her birthday cake. *Maybe we should take some cake to the people outside*, she says to Louis.

She cuts three slices of cake and wraps them in red napkins. Then, when she thinks Louis isn't looking, she wraps a fourth one for Mrs Fox. She'll need some energy if she's just given birth.

Come on Louis, let's check the coast is clear.

Louis gets onto his feet and walks to the door.

Willa stands in the hallway listening to Mummy and Daddy talking in the loo.

'You should see a doctor,' Daddy says. Which is a bit odd because Mummy's a surgeon, so she should know what's wrong with her.

Willa walks up the stairs to the first landing and hears Ella yelling:

'Leave me alone! You're not my mum.' Which is what she said the other day too – and it still doesn't make any sense.

And then Sai says, 'Give her a chance, Ella.' Willa definitely likes Sai.

Ella yells back, 'Stay out of this.' Which Willa doesn't think is very fair because Sai loves Ella and he was only trying to help.

The next thing Willa hears is Ella slamming her door. And that makes Daddy come out of the loo.

'I'd better go and check on things,' Daddy says to Mummy through the loo door. Mummy must be really sick if she has to stay in there for so long.

Mummy doesn't answer Daddy. And, a moment later, she makes being-sick noises again.

As Willa watches Daddy clomping up the stairs, she feels like calling after him and telling him that she doesn't think him going up to check on things is such a good idea; when Ella's in a mood, it's best to leave her alone for a bit or you just make it worse. But then when Daddy's on a mission he doesn't like other people to interfere, so Willa stays quiet. Even though she said it out loud, she hopes that her wish does come true and that everyone manages to get on for a change.

Two more people have joined the group outside. A little boy with squinty eyes and a woman in a wheelchair with a poodle on her lap. Louis goes up to sniff the poodle but he doesn't look impressed. Maybe it's because Louis has got a bit of poodle in him, so he can't fancy something that looks like himself. When he notices that Rose and Lily Pegg have come out with their Chihuahuas he thumps his tail and bounds over and starts slobbering. *Don't embarrass yourself, Louis*, Willa says. But it's a bit too late.

The people outside are wearing blue ribbons on their clothes; blue is Ella's favourite colour. She has a blue ribbon on her Twitter banner.

Willa goes up to the little boy. 'Why are you here?'

The little boy squints harder. 'I'm here for Ella. I've been following her campaign.'

'Her school project?'

The boy furrows his brow and squints harder.

'You mean her campaign?'

'What campaign?'

'To find her mum.'

There it was again. This stuff about Ella having a mum who wasn't Fay. Willa rubs her scar. Maybe Ella was adopted when she was a baby, like the babies Mr Mann and Mr Mann want to adopt. Maybe Ella's red hair and freckles are a fluke. Maybe she isn't related to any of them – not to Daddy or Mummy or even Auntie Norah. Willa's class learnt about people who got adopted and how, when they get older, they want to find their real mummies and daddies.

'We're here to support Ella,' says the little boy.

Willa's head hurts. There's been too much to take in today. 'I've got something to do,' she says, handing the little boy the pieces of cake. 'Will you hand these out to the others? I'll ask Mummy if you can come in.'

'Mummy?'

'Yes, Mummy. She's called Fay.'

He narrows his eyes again but he nods.

On the way in, Willa asks Louis about what the boy meant about Ella looking for her mum but he's not listening. *Too busy thinking about the Chihuahuas, aren't you?* Willa whispers into his floppy brown ears.

On the way past the stairs, Louis looks up towards Ella's room. Willa can tell that he doesn't know whether he should go outside with her to look for Mrs Fox or whether he should make sure that Ella is okay. Along with Willa, Louis is the only one Ella doesn't mind having around when she's upset. Ella's known Louis her whole life, which sometimes makes Willa jealous because she'll never be able to catch up and know Louis for as long because Ella will always be older, but at other times, like now, she doesn't really mind because she knows that Ella needs him.

It's okay, Louis. You can join me later. She gives him a push up the stairs.

The sun casts a warm haze over the garden. Willa loves that her birthday is in the spring, when everything's coming back to life.

'Mrs Fox . . . ' Willa whispers as she walks to the end of the garden. 'Mrs Fox . . . '

She glances back at the house to make sure that no one is watching from any of the windows, and then she goes over to the gooseberry bush, gets down on her knees, closes her eyes and listens. She hears it all. Worms deep in the ground, turning the dark soil. Centipedes crawling under damp rocks. A butterfly pressing its new wings against the walls of its chrysalis.

Buds unfurling on the trees. Blades of grass reaching up to the sun. And just beyond the hedge that leads into the next-door neighbour's garden, the sound of paws padding the earth.

Willa opens her eyes. Right in front of her, a ball of fire against the sun, stands Mrs Fox. She stares into Willa's eyes, and though it's hard to tell with a fox, she looks like she's smiling. As Mrs Fox lowers herself under the gooseberry bush her saggy tummy sweeps the ground. Willa lets out a breath. She hasn't given birth to her cubs yet; she's waited for Willa.

Willa unwraps the piece of birthday cake, places it in the palm of her hand and holds it out to Mrs Fox. Just as Mrs Fox stretches out her muzzle to sniff at the cake, Willa feels a big shove from behind, and then a bark.

She spins round.

'Louis!'

He nudges her again and barks and barks, baring his teeth as though some mean and dangerous beast has taken hold of him.

'Louis! Stop it!'

And then she turns back round to the bush and Mrs Fox has disappeared.

Louis keeps looking through the hole under the gooseberry bush, his ears stiff, his eyes set. A low growl rumbles from his throat.

Willa pushes Louis out of the way. 'You silly dog,' she says. 'You silly, *silly* dog.' She gets up and walks back down the garden. 'You've spoilt my birthday, Louis,' she shouts over her shoulder. 'You've spoilt everything.'

Louis lies down where he is, lowers his head and sets his eyes on the place where Mrs Fox disappeared.

'She's not coming back, you know. You scared her off.'

Willa kicks at a clod of earth and walks to the lounge doors. Then she hears a clatter from the front of the house. It can't be the recycling people or the dustbin men because it's Sunday. And they aren't expecting any more visitors – there are enough of those in the house already. Maybe it's someone who's come to support Ella's campaign. Her heart beats faster. Or maybe Mrs Fox went round to the front.

Willa pokes her head around the side of the house. All the people who came to see Ella have gone home, except the man with the rainbow jumper, who's sitting on the kerb, playing his trumpet. Willa feels sorry that the boy with the squinty eyes didn't stick around. She liked him.

Willa looks around for Mrs Fox, but she's nowhere to be seen. Then she notices a man and a boy walking along the pavement. They stop in front of the rusty gate of Number 77 Willoughby Street. Blossom falls around them and catches in their hair. The little boy lifts his face to the tree and laughs. Then he looks back to the house and mumbles something in a language that Willa doesn't understand.

The man nods, takes the little boy's hand, kisses it and they walk past the pile of tiles that make Daddy cross whenever he sees them because it means the roof still isn't fixed, and climb up the front steps.

As the man reaches up for the doorbell, the boy turns round.

Willa steps out from where she's been hiding at the side of the house.

The boy looks straight at Willa, just as Mrs Fox did a few minutes ago. And that's when Willa recognises him: he's the little boy from the photo. The blond boy with the wonky grin –

269

and now he's grinning at Willa like he knows who she is and has been waiting to meet her.

Adam

'She's not coming out,' says Norah.

Adam sits down beside her at the top of the stairs. Louis slumps down next to Adam and rests his head on his lap.

'She'll come round,' says Norah. 'She needs time, that's all.'

As he strokes Louis's curly hair, he thinks of the picture of the little boy and something collapses inside him. Did Norah make a new family so easily? Did she love the boy more than she loved their two girls?

Music blares out through the door. The radio. Cheap pop.

Adam knows that Ella's doing it on purpose, to upset Norah. She hates that stuff, refuses to listen to anything but jazz.

'It was good of you to invite him. You're a good dad.' She strokes his arm. 'And the girls are doing really well.'

You're a good dad? He wants to laugh. She hasn't got a clue how badly he'd screwed things up in that first year, before Fay moved in.

'I let Willa get attacked by a wild animal, Norah.'

Louis licks Adam's hand.

He remembers that night, standing outside the family room at Holdingwell General. Willa was in the operating theatre because the gash under her eye was so big that it needed special treatment. Ella hung back, looking at Adam as though some-one had swapped her dad for a stranger.

Fay had leant in and whispered: *You're no good to her like this, Adam. Go home and sober up.*

He'd hated her. Hated that she was right. That she'd always been right about him: a loser, a poor excuse for a man, let alone a dad.

And yes, he was drunk. On the night their little girl got hurt, he was blind drunk.

'These things happen, Adam.'

'No they don't. Not if you're a halfway decent parent.'

As he took the bus home on the night of the attack, he looked at his reflection in the window, his face blurred behind his smudged glasses, hair dishevelled, dark shadows under his eyes. No wonder Norah left me, he thought.

And now he was doing it again: messing up, falling short, letting down everyone who mattered to him.

Sober up, that's what Fay had said. He remembers thinking how pointless that instruction was. At least when he was drinking he could forget – that he hadn't been able to hold on to his wife, that he'd allowed his little girl to get attacked by a wild animal in his own home. And that a woman who wasn't even related to them seemed to be raising his children.

He got off at the next stop and walked along the high street until he found an off-licence, where he bought a bottle of vodka and six-pack of beer. Enough to get him through another night. And then he stumbled home, the bottles clink-ing at his side.

He and Norah had been too tolerant of each other's short-comings; they made each other worse, not better.

If it wasn't for Fay, God knows where he'd be now.

271

'But it turned out okay, didn't it?' Norah asks. 'Willa's fine. They're all fine.'

When he got home that night he'd scanned the lounge. On the floor, a white sheet stained with cigarette ash. The couch pressed out of shape from months serving as his bed. Empty bottles on the floor. The smell of sweat and sleep and stale beer.

'I saw it,' he mumbles. 'A flash of red darted across the lawn. I wanted to kill it.'

'The fox?'

He nods.

He remembers picking up one of the empty bottles, stumbling out through the door and hurling it at the fox. The bottle landed in the middle of the lawn, nowhere near her. The fox didn't move: she stood by the hedge, staring at Adam with her amber eyes.

He thought of Willa lying in the operating theatre and felt a burning in his chest. *You monster*, he yelled as he picked up the bottle and ran after the fox. Then he threw the bottle again. It hit a rock and smashed; broken glass showered the hedge next to the fox. But still the fox didn't move.

Adam stared at the shards of glass glinting in the dark grass. A man who can't even scare away an animal, who can't protect his family.

'It was Louis who got rid of it. He bounded past me in the garden, barking like a maniac.'

The fox had stared at him for a moment, then flicked her tail and skittered away.

'It must have been hard, to wait at home for news of Willa.'

She felt sorry for him? Was she so detached from her family

that she didn't care that her daughter had been attacked? She should be telling him how irresponsible he was. That he was a terrible dad. That this was the reason she left.

'Yes, it was hard.'

While he'd waited to hear from Fay he'd sat at the kitchen table with the bottle of vodka, waiting for the numbness to come back. And then he heard voices at the front door. Fay and Ella.

They came into the hall.

He heard Ella yelling. *Get off me! You're not my mum!*

Adam had heard those words so often in the last few months that they no longer shocked him.

The sound of Ella tearing up the stairs. *Dad! Dad!* she called. *Are you there?*

Adam took the bottle of vodka to the sink and tipped it away. Then he came out into the hallway.

I'm here, Ella, he said. *I'm here.*

Norah touches his arm. 'I should have been with you.'

He stays silent. He doesn't need her forgiveness or her apologies or her acceptance or whatever the hell she's trying to communicate. He doesn't need anything from her.

'Things happen to the best parents,' she says.

He shakes her off. 'I didn't think you were into that self-help crap.'

When Fay moved in, took over looking after the girls, she'd bought piles of books about parenting, about adoption, about helping children to eat well and sleep well. How to raise them to be happy. How to help a little girl overcome the trauma of losing her mother. Norah didn't believe in reading about life. *I rely on my intuition,* she'd always said.

Walking out on her family – was that part of her intuition?

'I just meant that you can't protect the people you love from everything. There are some things that are outside our control.'

He stands up. 'Leaving – was that out of your control?'

Why had he never seen it before, this inability of Norah's to face the truth of who she was and what she did and how it affected people? The blindness that allowed him to fail as a father.

And he's failing again. He's letting them all down – and most of all Fay. Fay was pushing him away. He was losing her, just like he'd lost Norah.

His eyes burn with tiredness.

Louis gets up and walks over to the window on the landing. He lets out a low whine and pads down the stairs.

'We need to talk, Adam,' Norah says. 'I need to tell you something.'

'Not now.'

He needs to go and find Willa and help her understand about Fay, about this whole godforsaken mess of a family.

He runs down the stairs.

'Do you love her?' Norah calls after him.

Adam turns round and looks at Norah. There's a pink flush behind her freckles.

He thinks about the ring box that Norah saw fall out of his trouser pocket.

Below him, he hears footsteps across the hall. And then a pause. Norah looks past him. He turns round.

Fay stands there, looking from Adam to Norah.

Do you love her? The words hang between the three of them.

Norah looks at Fay, frozen halfway up the stairs. She's always looked so strong, so firmly rooted, but at this moment, as she grips the banister, he realises that she's just as vulnerable as Norah, just as weak as he is. Was that why the three of them were thrown together that night in a London park? Because they needed each other? That Fay needed them as much as they needed her?

Fay turns to go.

'Fay—' he calls, but she doesn't stop.

Norah

Norah walks down the stairs. She stops and watches Fay walk into the kitchen and close the door behind her. Adam stands in the hallway, shifting from one foot to the other.

When she looks up she sees Ella higher up on the stairs, looking down at her.

She has to speak to her and mend things between them, explain to her why she really came home.

'Ella—' Norah climbs back up the stairs.

Ella stands with her hands on her hips, her eyes dark.

'We need to talk,' Norah says.

Ella shakes her head.

'You think you can turn up here after all this time and act like it's not a big deal? Have a good old heart-to-heart with Dad, catch up on the gossip?'

'It's not like that, Ella.'

Ella looks past Norah. 'You don't have the right to come between then.'

She must have seen Fay, and Adam running after her.

'That's not what I'm trying to do.'

'Really?' Ella shifts her gaze to Norah. 'So why are you here?'

Norah drops her shoulders. She can't tell her, not like this, not when she's so angry.

'We have to take it one step at a time—'

'But one of those steps is getting Dad back, right? Don't you think I've seen it? How you look at him. How you're trying to make him fall in love with you again.'

Never, in all the scenarios that had played through Norah's mind, had she thought she would be having a conversation like this with her daughter.

'I wanted to see you all again. I wanted to see if maybe we could—'

'Kiss and make up?'

'I know it will take more than that.'

Ella tugs at the short bits of hair at the nape of her neck. 'So, suppose for a second that it's not about Dad. Why are you here?'

'I guess I just want us to be a family – whatever that family looks like.'

'It's too late.'

Ella grabs something from her pocket.

'It's never too late, Ella. I know that I've let you all down, that I need to explain, but if you'll just give me some time—'

Ella holds up the pregnancy test. 'Fay's pregnant.'

Norah stares at the pregnancy test. 'I know.'

Ella lowers her arm. 'What do you mean, you *know*?'

Too tired to keep standing, Norah sits down on one of the steps.

'I guessed.'

Fay's mood swings, her nausea, her tiredness. Maybe Norah hadn't wanted to face it – or what it would mean for her and Adam and the girls – but she knew: Fay was pregnant with Adam's child. And that was meant to change everything. A sign, if ever she needed one, that coming back was a bad idea, that it was time to turn round and leave. Except she can't let go, not yet.

'So what's Dad meant to do now, then? Marry her? Walk her down the aisle in a white dress and pretend you never came back? You've ruined it for them.'

Her daughter telling her that her father should marry another woman. Another item on the long list of things she hadn't prepared herself for.

The doorbell rings.

Norah and Ella look down the long staircase. They watch Fay coming out of the kitchen, stopping for a moment when she sees Adam and then opening the front door. Norah hears a voice that makes her heart stop.

She walks down the stairs, Ella following close behind.

When she gets to the bottom step she puts her hand to her mouth.

The sun is so bright that it lights up the two figures standing on the doorstep: the smaller of the two, a little boy of about five, runs into the hall.

Norah walks towards him and he throws his arms around her. 'Mama!' he says over and over. 'Mama!'

'Great,' laughs Ella. 'Fucking great.'

As Fay steps aside a man walks in, short and skinny with blond hair and brown eyes. He and Adam stare at each other.

Willa bursts out of the lounge.

'The boy from the photo!' she cries. 'He's standing on our doorstep – and there's a man with him too!'

Then Willa notices that the man and the boy are already inside.

'You see?' she says.

Norah tries to smile at Willa. None of this is her fault.

Willa runs up to the boy and tugs at his coat. 'Would you like some fox cake?' She beams at him.

But the little boy buries his head deeper into Norah's waist.

'Mama?' he asks, his voice lost as he presses himself against her. *'Warum bist du hier?'* Why are you here?

Willa

All the grown-ups stand in the hallway, staring at their feet.

No one's talking.

Willa pokes her tongue into the raw hollow left by her tooth. Later, she'll ask Mummy to give her some Calpol to make her feel better. She wonders whether Auntie Norah found the tooth. And then she wonders whether Auntie Norah's little boy has lost any of his teeth yet.

Ella and Sai and Louis come downstairs to see what's going on.

The little boy starts crying. Maybe he doesn't like cake, thinks Willa. He's got bags under his eyes and looks pale and scared, and now his face goes red and wet and puffy too.

'*Nat ist mude,*' says the man who came in with the little boy. '*Und er hat Hunger.*'

When Daddy stares at the man, the man translates in a funny accent: 'Nat's very tired and he's hungry too. We've been travelling for hours.'

'I told you to wait, Walter . . . ' Auntie Norah whispers. She doesn't know the rule, that when you whisper it's louder than shouting because it makes everyone want to listen more.

'I told you on the phone. He missed you, Norah.'

This makes Ella stare at Auntie Norah likes she hates her even more, which Willa didn't think was possible.

Mummy looks at Nat; her eyes are sad. Willa can tell that she wants to pick him up and give him a hug and tell him it's okay, like she does when Willa's upset. But instead she just stands there, looking lost.

Auntie Norah lifts Nat up and presses him against her, which makes Nat look a bit happier, but not much.

Mummy stares at the floor.

'He needs to get some sleep,' Auntie Norah says, kissing the top of Nat's head. And then she whispers something to him in another language. 'Through there,' Auntie Norah says to the little boy's daddy, nodding at the lounge door. 'He can sleep on my bed.'

Nat shakes his head really hard and more tears plop down his cheeks. '*Ich bin nicht mude,*' says Nat. '*Ich will nicht schlafen.*' He buries his face in Auntie Norah's chest.

'You have to sleep, little Nat,' says Auntie Norah. And then she smooths his blond sticky-uppy hair , a bit like Daddy when he's just woken up, and she rocks him a bit, which makes Willa think of how Mummy does the same thing when Willa doesn't want to sleep.

Nat wriggles in Auntie Norah's arms and shakes his head. *'Nein. Ich will nicht schlafen.'* His voice is small and tired. *'Ich will mit Dir sein.'* Willa's surprised because she didn't think he understood any English, but he responded to what Auntie Norah said. Maybe he can understand English but not speak it. He wriggles so much that Auntie Norah has to put him down on the floor, and then he clings onto her leg.

Willa knows what it's like to be made to sleep when you don't want to, so she takes Nat's hand and says, 'Would you like to come and see my room?'

Nat stares up at his daddy, who gives him a nod and then Nat looks at Willa, wipes his snotty nose on the back of his sleeve and says, *'Ja.'* After that he turns and points to Louis, who's standing by the kitchen door. *'Kann er auch kommen?'* he asks Willa.

Willa isn't sure what he said, but from the little boy's smile he seems to like Louis, so she goes over and puts her fingers under Louis's collar and walks him over to Nat. Nat kneels down and wraps his arms around Louis's big tummy, which makes Louis close his eyes like he does when he's happy, except once Nat's finished giving him a hug he goes over to the door, where Auntie Norah is putting on her coat.

'Where are you going?' Daddy asks Auntie Norah. The bulgy vein pokes out of his forehead.

'I need some air,' she says.

'Norah—' says Nat's daddy.

Ella shakes her head like she's heard the most incredible thing in the whole world.

Mummy holds onto the banister. She's been holding on to lots of things recently.

And Louis thumps his tail hard against the wooden floor of the hallway.

'I'll pick up some food for dinner,' says Auntie Norah, and then she goes out through the door.

Upstairs, Willa guides Nat around the room. She shows him her crayon drawings of Mrs Fox and the other foxes.

'She's going to have babies soon.' Willa points at the little cubs she's drawn in one picture. 'When she comes into the garden, I'll show you. You can help me name them.'

Louis stands with his paws on the windowsill. Nat goes over to him and Willa follows and looks down through the scaffolding at the front garden.

It's weird, because Auntie Norah was meant to go shopping but she's still standing on the doorstep.

Louis barks and then he turns round and paces a bit and then he leaves the room; Willa hears him charging down the stairs and then, when he gets to the hallway, he starts barking again.

'I think Louis wants to go with Auntie Norah,' Willa says to Nat.

She thinks that this might upset Nat, because he wanted Louis to stay with him, but instead, he smiles and nods.

Willa goes to dig a box out from under her bed, where she keeps a supply of chocolate and sweets from birthdays and Christmases and Easters. Some of them are really old because she loses track of which ones she should eat first, but they still taste okay. She hands Nat a Cadbury's Creme Egg. 'These are really good. Better than real eggs.'

He sits on the bed and peels off the foil wrapper.

'You have to lick out the inside first.' Willa takes the egg and mimes licking it. 'And then you eat the chocolate coating.' She pretends she's munching around the egg.

Nat nibbles the top off the egg. By the time he's finished, his lips are covered in white fondant and smears of chocolate and his sticky smile takes over his face.

'*Danke,*' he says.

'Where is your language from?'

He licks his lips. '*Deutschland.*'

'You're lucky. I wish I could speak two languages.'

Nat licks his lips and points at the crayons on Willa's desk.

'*Darf ich zeichnen*' he asks.

She's not sure what he's asked, but he points to the crayons like he pointed to Louis, so he must like them too.

'You want to draw?'

He nods.

She gets out a piece of plain paper and picks up her pot of crayons and takes them over to the bed. Then she gives Nat her big hardback book, *Wild Animals of the British Isles*, to lean on. He takes them and rests his back against the wall.

For the next ten minutes, Nat sits on the bed, the book on his knees, his head bowed, his blond hair falling into his eyes. He draws and draws as if he hasn't been allowed to draw anything in ages.

When he's finished, he holds up the piece of paper. There are three people on it, and a dog, but the dog's much smaller than Louis. Maybe Nat and Auntie Norah got him from an Animal Ark like the one in Holdingwell. One of the people in the picture is Auntie Norah, because she has the same long red hair, and he's put freckles on her face and she's holding a trumpet. The other grown-up person is Walter, Nat's daddy, and he's got a white coat on, and there's a puppy in his arms that looks like it's got a bleeding paw. And between them stands Nat.

Willa hears Mrs Fox cry out in the garden, like she did earlier, only louder. 'Did you hear that?'

Nat nods but doesn't look up. He's taken a black crayon from the pot and he's labelling the parts of his picture.

Over the dog he writes: Dizzy.

Over Norah he writes: Mama.

And over Walter he writes: Onkel Walter.

SUNDAY NIGHT

Norah

When Norah gets to the pavement outside Number 77 Willoughby Street, she closes her eyes and takes a breath.

I'll get some food, she'd insisted when Fay had a meltdown about not having anything for supper. Norah was glad of the excuse to get out of the house.

She hears the front door open behind her and turns to see Fay clipping on Louis's lead as he strains to get out.

'He's been scratching at the door,' Fay says. 'He wants to come with you. He's not good at staying off the road,' she adds. 'You need to watch him.'

Louis escapes Fay's grasp, runs down the front steps and comes to sit at Norah's feet.

Ella pushes past Fay and Sai follows.

'Ella!' Adam's standing on the doorstep now. 'I need you to stay at home.'

'I'm just walking Sai back,' Ella throws over her shoulder. 'I need some space.'

Space, thinks Norah. *We're more alike than you think.*

As Ella and Sai disappear down the road, Norah watches Fay puts her hand on Adam's shoulder, all the while looking at Norah. And then she closes the front door.

Norah kneels down and puts her arms around Louis's neck. 'You didn't ask for any of this, did you?' She closes her eyes, leans her head against his chest and listens to the hard, thud of his heartbeat.

As they walk past the bungalow belonging to the Miss Peggs,

Louis stops for a moment and looks at the lounge window. Figures move behind the curtains like there's a party going on. The curtains twitch open and Rose looks out – and then they close again.

The Twitter followers are nowhere to be seen and the tent the man in the rainbow jumper put up flaps open and empty.

'Come on, Louis.' She pulls on the lead.

As they walk down Willoughby Street the air cools, the wind picks up and clouds gather in the darkening sky. Once again, Norah's stepping away from the home she left six years ago.

She throws words at the pavement:

What the hell was Walter thinking? I told him I had to deal with this alone, that I needed some time to talk to Adam and the girls, that I wanted to keep things separate – that I'd be home in a few days and then we'd decide what to do.

He missed you, Walter said.

And that, it would seem, was reason enough for them to travel hundreds of miles to come and find her.

Norah turns into the forecourt of the petrol station, the only place open this late on a Sunday.

The wind sweeps the petrol fumes off the tarmac. Her head spins and, for a second, she needs to stop to get her balance.

She's not ready for this. She had to get to know Adam and the girls – and Fay – again. To get their trust back and maybe, with time, for them to forgive her. Walter being here with Nat just confuses things.

She ties Louis up outside, goes into the shop and pulls some macaroni cheese and a pizza from the freezer section.

'And some Marlboro Lights,' she says when she gets to the counter.

The handles of the plastic bags dig into her palm; the scar in the place of her left breast throbs. She didn't want reconstructive surgery, to paste over the reality of what the disease had done to her; she'd done enough pretending in her life. But she misses the easy balance of her old body. She wonders how long it will be before her body gives up on her altogether.

You need the people you love, the consultant had said. *They'll give you something to fight for.* And she owed it to them, didn't she? If she doesn't make it, at least they'll have had a few months together. Long enough to say goodbye.

That's why she came home. But the consultant was wrong. Being around the people you love only made it worse. Being alone, that was what she needed. And as for Adam and the girls and Fay and Walter and Nat, they'd be better off without her.

On the way out of the shop, Norah stops at a display of leaflets arranged in a wooden rack by the door. She picks up a flyer for the Holdingwell 10k. She'd hoped to watch Ella run, that it would be part of them getting close again.

Norah puts back the flyer and picks up a bus timetable. She turns to the Sunday section and is relieved to see that they still leave on the hour. She looks at her watch: the next one goes in twenty-five minutes. And after that, fifteen minutes to the railway station. And then another wait, perhaps, for a slow weekend train to London. From there, she could go anywhere.

'Norah?'

A hand on her arm. Dirty fingernails. Creased skin. Red knuckles. And rainbow sleeve.

She looks up at the busker.

'Remember me?' He smiles.

She nods. He was there six years ago, on the morning she left.

Louis pulls on his lead and pads at the door. Norah goes out and unties him.

'Want to share a cigarette?' she asks the busker.

He nods.

They sit in the dark, smoking, Louis beside them, the bag of frozen food thawing at Norah's feet.

After a while he unzips his backpack and pulls out a CD. 'Here, thought you might like it.'

Norah holds it up to the light. *Home Again*, and a picture of a sky with clouds.

'I believe we're both fans . . . '

'Louis Armstrong?'

Louis looks up when he hears his name.

'Sort of. They're my covers.'

Norah traces the words on the CD case. 'Ironic title,' she says, before drawing on her cigarette. 'For a homeless guy.'

He shrugs. 'I'm not homeless.'

'What are you then?'

'Free.' He smiles. 'A little cold sometimes. But mostly free.'

Norah had often thought of how she'd like to move around the world with nothing but a rucksack, a tent, a temporary home that she could put up and take down anywhere she pleased. Maybe he was right – no matter how hard his life was, it was worth it to be free. And yet he'd stayed in Holdingwell, hadn't he? He'd been here the whole time while she was away. And years before that too. Perhaps there was a freedom in staying, too.

'They're waiting for you at home.' He rubs Louis behind the ear.

She exhales a stream of smoke into the night air.

'I don't think so.'

'I do.'

'How did you know I was here?'

He laughs. 'The twins – they saw you trying to make a run for it.'

Norah remembers Rose Pegg's face at the window, the empty tent in their front garden.

'I wasn't making a run for it.'

'I can take that from you, then.' He looks at the bus timetable in her hand.

'This wasn't . . . I wasn't . . .'

'It's okay. It's human – the desire to run.'

What did that even mean: *it's human*? Fay was human, and she'd never run away from the people she loved.

She hands him the timetable.

As if he knows that a decision's been made, Louis gets up. And he's right, isn't he? Him and the busker. Norah should go home. Home, despite it all. Home for good.

'Thanks for the music,' she says, holding up the CD.

He smiles. 'Any time.'

When she reaches the house, Norah sees Ella standing on the doorstep looking up through the scaffolding to the light in Willa's room.

As Norah looks up, she notices the outline of Nat's face at the window, his nose pressed against the glass: he's looking at Ella. Norah had told him stories about his two sisters who lived in England, but he hadn't understood.

Ella turns round, locks her eyes on Norah and then disappears through the front door.

Norah puts the shopping down in the hallway and goes up to Willa's room. The door is open just wide enough for Norah to look in. Louis walks past her and climbs onto the bed. Willa throws her arms around him.

'Louis,' she whispers as she strokes him behind his ear.

He licks the side of her face.

Nat comes and joins Willa and pats Louis's side.

Willa stares into the dog's eyes and then leans forward and kisses the top of his head. 'We were wondering where'd you'd got to, Louis.' She picks up a piece of paper off the floor. 'Look, Louis, Nat drew a picture.' She turns to Nat. 'Here, why don't you take it and show it to your mummy – it's really good.'

Nat shakes his head and pushes it back to her.

'*Geschenk,*' he says. A present. '*Für deinem Geburtstag.*'

She gives him a kiss on the cheek and then folds up the picture and puts it in her pocket.

'I'll show Auntie Norah myself then,' she says. 'She'll like it.'

Norah turns away from the door and heads downstairs. *Auntie Norah,* she whispers to herself . . . It's time to tell Willa the truth.

Ella

@findingmum
Messed Up Family of the Year Award #whatajoke

They stand outside the front door of the post office and Sai takes her hands.

'I'm glad you came over for Willa's birthday. That you weren't scared away.'

'Wait until my mum tells you her stories about my aunts and uncles back in India.' He smiles. 'Now they're really scary.'

Ella reaches up and kisses him.

'Can I stay tonight?' she asks.

He touches her cheek. 'You need to go back and sort things out. I'll come and get you tomorrow for the race.'

She looks down at the trainers they are both wearing; the ones she helped him choose in TK Maxx when they started training, and her own, inherited from Mum.

'The race? We're still doing that?'

He kisses her and whispers through his lips, 'Of course we are. You're the champion, remember?'

And then he stands there, watching her, waving, until she disappears around the corner.

How long will he love me, she wonders. Will his love run out one day, like Mum's did for us?

They're all squeezed in around the kitchen table, like for Willa's birthday party. Fay leans against the counter. Pale. Not eating.

The wind rattles the windows. The sky's heavy with clouds.

Ella sends the tweet and slips her phone into her pocket. She wishes Sai were here, or at least that he'd let her stay with him at the post office.

Dad keeps stealing glances at Walter, as though he's checking out his competition. Walter's chewing a slice of pizza; he doesn't seem to mind that he's sitting at the same table as his girlfriend's husband and children. Mum's clamped to Nat's side. She keeps reaching up and stroking his hair and taking his fork and pushing bits of gloopy macaroni into his mouth. A brother – something else for Ella to get her head around. Nat closes his eyes and his head drops forward. Louis sits next to Willa; his head rests on her feet like he's worried that she's going to be swept away. He thumps his tail against the tiles; something's rattling him too. Only Willa seems normal, wittering away to Nat about how tomorrow they're going to look for Mrs Fox and her cubs.

Mum clears her throat. 'You ready for the race tomorrow, Ella?'

Everyone looks up at her.

'I'd like to sponsor you,' she says.

And that will make up for you having disappeared for six years, will it?

'I'm not running.'

Willa's head snaps up. 'You're not running? But you have to run. You've been training for ages and ages – and what about Sai and the charity that will help people with poorly hearts, like Sai's dad?

Ella shrugs. 'I don't feel like it.'

She's lying. Of course she's going to go through with it. She wouldn't let Sai down. But she wants it to be just the two of them. She doesn't want them all standing there with banners, Dad taking photos, Mum pretending to be a mum – she's had enough of playing happy families.

'My pizza's still frozen.' Ella throws the slice down on her plate. 'Why are we eating this crap?'

'Ella!' Dad glares at her.

'Well Fay wouldn't serve us this stuff.'

Ella remembers those first years after Mum left, when she refused to eat anything that Fay had made because it wasn't the kind of food Mum used to cook: processed, packaged food, fish fingers, frozen peas, oven chips. Fay's food looked so good that, sometimes, she'd came back down in the middle of the night to open the fridge and sneak it back to her room.

'Walter's got the same job as Mummy, except he looks after animals instead of people,' pipes up Willa. 'I think he should come and live here and work at the Animal Ark.'

Everyone turns to face Willa.

'What are you going on about?' asks Ella.

Willa digs out a piece of paper from her pocket, unfolds it and holds it up for everyone to see: 'Onkel Walter's wearing a white coat – look.' She points at the crayon drawing of Walter. 'He's Auntie Norah's brother.'

The table falls silent. A gust of wind. The branches of the cherry tree tap the window. A tearing sound at the top of the house. The crash of a roof tile on the pavement.

'Mum's *brother*?' asks Ella.

Nat claps his pudgy hands together: 'Onkel Walter! Onkel Walter!'

God, if Nat isn't Walter's kid, then he must be Dad's. Wow, nice one, Mum. First you abandon Dad with two small kids, and then you keep another kid from knowing he exists. Great parenting.

Ella imagines her Twitter followers perking up and looking across the road, the kitchen window a portal to the soap opera of their lives.

Fay stares at Walter, shell-shocked.

Dad looks at Nat. You can see it sinking in, the realisation that he's had a kid all this time, a son who Mum didn't even bother to tell him about.

'You don't have a brother,' Dad says to Mum.

'We found each other – a few years ago,' Mum says, as if going out and finding a brother is the most normal thing in the world.

Maybe Mum enjoys dropping bombs on their family, thinks Ella. Maybe it gives her some kind of sadistic kick to upset everyone like this. Ella looks at Walter and at the freckles across his cheeks and at his brown eyes. Of course he's not Mum's boyfriend.

Dad keeps staring at Nat; the blood's drained from his face.

Fay walks to the kitchen door. Everyone turns to look at her.

'Please excuse me,' she says and walks out.

Ella gets up too.

'Ella, sit down,' says Dad.

But Ella ignores him.

As she follows Fay, Ella remembers how many times Fay's run after her and tried to talk to her and how many times she's slammed the door in her face. *You're not my mum!* she'd yell at her, over and over, hoping that, like a spell, it would make Fay disappear and Mum come back.

Outside the loo door, Ella hears that raw heaving sound when someone's stomach is being yanked up into their throat. It makes Ella feel sick too. Sick that she hasn't realised until now how badly she's treated Fay. Sick at how she never understood how much Fay meant to Dad and to Willa – and to her. And sick at the gross food Mum brought back from the petrol station.

'Fay?' Ella knocks on the door. 'Can I come in?'

Fay unlocks the door and Ella comes in and kneels beside her.

A sour smell rises up from the toilet bowl. Fay sits on the tiles, leaning against the wall and staring up at the ceiling.

They sit in silence for a bit, listening to the wind tearing at the tarpaulin on the roof.

Ella rips off a bit of loo paper, dampens it with warm water, takes Fay's hands and cleans her palms, then the tops of her hands, then her fingers. After that, she dampens the hand towel and holds it to Fay's forehead.

'I'm sorry,' Ella says.

Fay looks at her and smiles weakly. 'You don't have anything to be sorry about.'

'I'm sorry that I was so mean to you. That I kept wanting Mum to come home.'

'It was normal, Ella—'

Ella shakes her head. 'It was stupid. I get it now: you're the one who belongs here – you're the one who Willa needs. Who we all need.'

Fay closes her eyes. 'Things have changed. Your mum's come back. She's going to look after you now.'

'No, she's not. Not properly. And Dad doesn't love her, he loves you. And you're pregnant, and Willa loves you and I – I—' Ella gulps. 'I need you.'

For a moment, Fay looks at Ella and her face softens and Ella feels like maybe things could turn out okay. Maybe Fay can get them out of this mess again. But then Fay gets up off the tiles.

Fay strokes her stomach. 'So you know.' She looks up at Ella. 'And you don't mind?'

Ella smiles. 'I think it's cool. You've spent so long looking after us, you deserve to have your own baby with Dad. And I know you're scared, with Mum having come home and everything, but it's going to be okay. You just have to fight to stay. And I'll help you. We'll make Mum leave—'

'I have to go home, Ella. I need some space – and so do you, all of you.'

'But I don't want you to go.' Ella stands up, throws her arms around Fay and for the first time since Fay moved in, they hug.

Fay's always looked so solid. She's the strong one. The surgeon. The perfect mum and wife, the one who stuck it out with them. But right now, Ella feels like she's hugging a little girl.

'When were you going to tell us,' Ella asks. 'About the baby.'

'On Friday night.'

'Why—?' Oh God. Fay probably had it all planned. Their pizza supper. A family meeting. An announcement that Willa's dream was going to come true, something even better than having fox cubs to look after: a baby brother or sister, someone she could pour all her love and care and imagination into. 'Mum's timing has always been crap,' Ella says.

Somewhere upstairs, a door slams. A gust of wind howls through the bathroom fan. Overhead, the light bulb flickers.

Fay pulls away. 'I've got to go.' She lets herself out of the loo.

Ella follows her and watches her walk to the stairs.

She hears the clink of knives and forks coming from the kitchen. If Fay isn't going to stay and do something about Mum, then Ella will have to take it in hand.

When Ella comes back into the kitchen Willa's sitting up, her brown eyes wide as she stares from Nat to Dad to Mum.

'I don't understand,' she says, all the excitement drained from her voice. 'Why would Daddy be Nat's daddy too?'

Dad's eyes fixed on his plate, the vein on his forehead pushed out. There should be a law against keeping a kid from his dad. Mum should get locked up for this.

Ella walks round the table, kneels beside Willa and takes her hand.

'Because Norah's our mum, Willa. The mum who walked out on us when you were a baby.'

Fay

She pulls her suitcase out of the wardrobe.

How stupid, she thinks, to have allowed herself to believe that everything was going to be okay: that Norah would go home with her new family and leave them all to pick up their old lives.

That's what she'd thought when she saw the man and the boy in Norah's hospital room in Berlin: that if Norah had someone to love her, if she'd moved on, found a better life, then maybe she and Adam could be together.

Fay hardens her jaw. *Stop living in a bloody fairytale*, she tells herself. Norah's got cancer. That changes everything. It's why she came home and it's why she's going to stay. And it's why Fay needs to go home.

She looks at her stomach. *It looks like it might just be the two of us,* she whispers. And as she says the words, she feels a cold gust sweep through the window open. Goosebumps rise on her forearms.

She stares at Adam's side of the bed, the sheets tossed to one side. And then she remembers his shocked face as he sat at the kitchen table, looking at the son he didn't know he had. The

299

child that Norah decided to keep. More than anything, she wants to go downstairs and hold Adam and tell him that she loves him and that they'll work it out, like they have ever since Norah left. They were a team – the best team in the world.

But Adam was no longer hers to look after, was he?

She smells Norah's perfume in the room. Nothing in the house, not the walls she painted or the furniture she bought, feel like hers any more.

How had she left herself believe that this was her home? Her family? The place where she belonged?

Fight for it, like Ella said? But what was the good in that? Downstairs was a little boy who deserved to have a real family, a real dad, real sisters. Especially now that Norah was ill; they should spend every second together. And maybe it would make Norah better, them all being together. Maybe it would all work out for her.

Do you love her? she'd asked Adam. And his silence had said it all.

Outside, another tile crashes onto the path in front of the house. Six years to fix a roof, the only thing she'd ever asked Adam to contribute to the renovation of the house.

Fay stuffs clothes into her suitcase. Her old life is still out there: she just has to wipe away the cobwebs, pull off the dust-sheets and make it her own again.

'Mummy!' Willa bursts through the door, crying.

She throws her arms around Fay's waist.

For a moment, as Fay holds on to Willa and lowers her head into her little girl's thick, tangled hair, time stops and she forgets that she's just lost everything.

'It's okay, my darling,' she whispers. 'Everything's going to be okay.'

300

Willa thrashes her head from side to side. 'Ella said you're not my mummy.'

So, the last piece of the puzzle has fallen into place.

Willa stands back and stares at Fay's suitcase. Her eyes are bloodshot and she's rubbed the scar on her cheek to a fiery red.

'Why are you packing?' Willa asks.

Fay kneels down and takes Willa's hand. 'You need to spend some time getting to know your real mummy, the mummy who gave birth to you.' The words stick in Fay's throat but there's nothing else she can say. Not if she wants to protect Willa.

Footsteps on the landing. And then a voice at the door: 'You have two mummies, Willa.'

Willa and Fay turn round. Norah stands in the doorway.

'You have two mummies,' Norah says again as she walks in. She kneels next to Fay and takes Willa's other hand.

What is Norah playing at? Two mummies? Willa needs clarity. She needs to understand that there's only one real mother: Norah.

Willa shakes her head. 'No one has two mummies.'

'Actually, lots of people do,' says Norah. 'Do you know what it means to be adopted, Willa?'

Willa looked up at Norah: 'Adopted?' Then she looks at Fay.

'Yes,' Norah says.

'Like the girl in Year Five who was adopted from Vietnam and doesn't look anything like her parents?'

'Yes, like that,' says Norah. 'When I was a baby I was adopted, like that girl.'

Fay couldn't get her head around it. Adopted? Since when?

301

And what about Walter? Was he her real brother, then? And did all this mean that Norah had some grand excuse for doing what she did? An abandoned child goes on to desert her own children? It was all too easy.

'My mother couldn't look after me,' Norah continues.

So walking out on your children runs in the family, thinks Fay.

'And so she left me to be cared for by another mummy. That mummy was the mummy I grew up with, the one who picked me up from school and helped me with my homework, who put plasters on my knee – and made me birthday cakes, though none of them were as amazing as the one you had today.'

'Like Mummy—?' Willa looks at Fay.

'Yes, like Mummy.'

Fay's breath catches in her throat.

Willa goes silent and looks down at her feet. When she looks up she asks Norah, 'Why couldn't you look after me? Me and Ella and Daddy?'

Norah blinks.

Fay squeezes Willa's hand.

This was why they'd lied to Willa. Because they couldn't find a way to explain why Norah had left.

'I wasn't well.'

'You were sick?'

'Yes, I was sick.'

'And did you ever get to meet the mummy who carried you in her tummy?'

Norah shakes her head. 'But it doesn't matter. I still know that I've always had two mummies. And now you have two mummies too: you have Mummy Fay, and you have me, Mummy Norah.'

Fay can't bear to hear any more of this.

Willa shakes her head and points at Fay's suitcase. 'But Mummy's packing – she's going away.'

'I think that maybe, if we tell her that we'd like her to stay, she might change her mind.'

Willa straightens her spine, clears her throat and looks straight at Fay. 'Will you stay and be my mummy?'

Fay doesn't know whether to be furious at Norah for having put her in this position or grateful that she isn't cutting her out of Willa's life. But how can she stay here, pretending that she doesn't love Adam, standing on the sidelines of this family, eating her supper propped up against a kitchen counter like an au pair?

'I don't know, Willa,' Fay says.

'But I want you to stay,' says Willa.

'Willa's right.'

Fay looks up. It's Adam.

'We want you to stay,' Adam says, looking right at Fay. The vein on his forehead pushes through his skin. It takes all the willpower she has not to go over and hold him.

Fay realises they're all waiting for her to answer. She suddenly feels achingly tired.

'I'll stay for tonight.'

Willa throws her arms around both Fay and Norah and pulls them into her. Fay feels Norah's breath on her face, smells her scent. She pulls away, leaving Willa with one arm slung around Norah's neck.

Fay hears footsteps on the landing. She looks out through the bedroom door and sees Ella, watching them.

Ella shakes her head and runs up to the attic.

Fay

'Ella?' Fay calls out.

She smells smoke curling out through Ella's open bedroom window.

'Ella?'

No answer.

Fay climbs out of the window, onto the scaffolding.

She looks up and sees Ella's skinny legs dangling off the side of the roof. Fay climbs up to join her.

'Hi,' Fay says.

Ella puts her cigarette behind her back.

'It's okay.'

'Really?' Ella's eyes shine in the dark.

Fay nods. 'Really.'

Ella stares at her. 'What are you doing up here?'

'Can I sit down?'

Ella shifts over.

'I know it's hard – that this weekend has been—'

'Hell?' Ella says.

'Yes, that would be an accurate description,' Fay says. 'But we'll work it out. We have to help Willa get her head around all this, that's all that matters now.'

'She won't. And she shouldn't have to. You're her mum, that's all there is to it.'

Fay puts her hand on Ella's arm. 'She'll listen to you – if you explain it to her, she'll find it easier.'

'Explain what? That I thought I knew who my mum was – that I thought I loved her, that I thought she was the best mum in the world – and then I woke up to the fact that I've been chasing a lie this whole time?' Ella shakes her head. 'And anyway, a kid doesn't get used to having two mums. It's not natural. In fact, it's downright mean. She thinks *you're* her mum. You shouldn't mess with that.'

'It's not my choice.'

'That's lame.'

'Maybe, but it's true.'

'You should fight for her – for all of us.'

Fay hears the wobble in Ella's voice. She wants to hold her but she's afraid she'll push her away.

They sit in silence, and eventually Fay says:

'You haven't come out here in a while.'

Ella looks up. 'You knew I came out here? And you didn't tell Dad?'

'You like being on the roof – and I like being in the garden. I see you, sometimes. And no, I didn't tell Dad.'

'He said it was dangerous. He tried to lock the window and to hide the key. I thought you agreed. *Family rules* and all that.'

'We all need our secrets, Ella?'

Ella taps the end of her cigarette on a roof tile. 'You haven't said that in ages.' Fay watches the ash fall between them. 'I mean,' Ella goes on, 'you used to say it all the time, when I was little ... before ...'

'Yes, I used to say it all the time.' Fay looks down through the scaffolding at the bags of rubbish standing on the doorstep, at her hanging baskets, at the cherry tree. The

305

roofers have stamped thick rubber-soled prints through her flowerbeds. She thinks of the sign hammered into the ground: *Holdingwell in Bloom*. Willoughby Street won the competition last year. Fay's garden was the centrepiece. She'd been so proud.

'But you always did the right thing, didn't you? You didn't pretend to be my friend, like Mum.' Ella stares ahead. 'I'm such an idiot. I actually fell for it: ice-cream in the middle of winter, bunking off school, chocolate whenever I felt like it, never forcing me to do anything that I didn't want to do ... She did it because being your daughter's friend is easier than being her mum, didn't she?'

'There are different ways of being a mum, Ella.'

'Remember when you took me to have my feet measured for my first pair of school shoes?'

'I've still got the photo and the certificate.'

'You do?'

Fay nods. Even when Norah was here, looked after the practical things. It made her feel like she had a role to play in the family, like she mattered.

Ella kicks at a bit of scaffolding. 'What other stuff did you keep?'

'Your first letter to Father Christmas.'

'You kept that?'

'Of course.'

It was early December and Ella was four, when Fay had collected her from nursery and they'd gone to the Holdingwell Café for cake and hot chocolate, and they'd written a letter together, Fay holding Ella's small hand, helping her form the letters. And then they'd walked hand in hand to the post office.

'Do you remember Sai from that time?' Fay asks.

Fay remembers him, a little boy with a centre parting who followed his dad around the shop, franking letters, stacking shelves, holding the door open for customers.

'I don't know. I guess I must have, because it feels like I've always known him. But I don't have an actual memory.' Ella shakes her head. 'He says he remembers me, though.'

'That's nice.'

'Maybe he *thinks* he remembers, but really he's kidding himself – his brain's just made it up because it's what he wants to believe ... like I did with Mum. Or maybe he just says it to make me happy.'

'Wanting to make someone happy is not so bad. But I think he remembers.' Fay thinks back to the little boy whose dark eyes followed them around the shop. 'He was cute.'

Ella raises her eyebrows: 'Cute?'

'Baby cute. A cute little boy – just like you were a cute little girl.'

'I was?'

Fay nods. 'The cutest.'

Even though it's dark, Fay can see the flush in Ella's cheeks.

'Like Willa?' Ella asks.

'Cuter,' Fay whispers.

'*Cuter?*'

'Classically cute—'

'Rather than bonkers cute?'

Fay smiles. 'Exactly.'

'It was fun, wasn't it? Before Mum left, I mean. The stuff we did. Proper fun, the kind of fun a kid should have.'

Fay puts her arm around Ella. 'It was the best.'

Ella leans her head on Fay's shoulder and looks up at the sky as though the stars remind her of that time.

'Remember,' she says, 'remember the day I put Mum's trumpet in the bath and you took it to hospital to put it in a special drier thing?' Ella catches her breath. Fay watches her stare into the distance. 'I wanted to clean it for Mum as a surprise and I nearly ruined it – and you didn't say anything. You helped me fix it ... ' Ella brings the cigarette up to her mouth; her fingers are shaking. 'We always wanted to please her, didn't we?'

'Yes.'

They stare out at the rooftops of Holdingwell.

Fay nods at the cigarette. 'Can I have one?'

'Seriously?'

'Seriously.'

Ella pulls a packet out of her jacket pocket. They're Marlboros, Adam's.

'I just borrowed them,' Ella says. 'For an emergency.'

Fay laughs. 'I guess this counts as an emergency.' She pulls a cigarette out of the packet, waits for Ella to flick the lighter, puts the cigarette between her lips and leans forward. They look at each other through the flame.

For a moment, Fay feels the closeness they used to have when Ella was little. Perhaps, after all these years, after everything they've shared, and despite all the rows – even closer.

And then Fay breathes in.

The rush of smoke. The warmth in her throat, behind her eyes, in her head. The sharp pull at her lungs. The lightness. The feeling that if she breathed in enough smoke she might lift off the roof tiles and float away into the night sky.

She coughs. And then inhales again.

Ella laughs and shakes her head. 'I never thought I'd see you—'

'Letting my hair down?'

'Doing something that wasn't completely good.'

Fay looks down at the Miss Peggs' bungalow. The television in their lounge flashes blue through the open curtains. The busker sits in front of his tent, strumming his guitar. Monica sits crossed legged on the pavement, smoking.

Sometimes, it's easier to be sad – wasn't that what she'd said to Willa?

Ella stubs out her cigarette. 'Thank you, Fay. For all the things you've done for us. For looking after us and keeping us together.' She pauses. 'For being our mum.'

There's a hollow feeling in Fay's chest. How had she let things get so bad between them?

'So, as you've found out about me coming out here to smoke, tell me one of your secrets.' Ella looks up at Fay through her eyelashes, ghostly fair against her dark-dyed hair.

Fay sees the little girl she used to know, the Ella who loved her, the Ella who wanted to be a surgeon. Who'd asked her once whether she could live with her, and whether she could call her Mummy.

Fay takes a breath. 'You know one of my secrets.'

'I do?'

'Friday night. Willa.'

'Oh, Operation Kidnap?' Ella laughs.

'You weren't laughing at the time.'

'No.' Ella pokes Fay in the ribs. 'But you have to admit, you were pretty rubbish.'

'At kidnapping?'

'Yeah. I mean, sitting on an empty bus with a bonkers-cute-gets-everyone's-attention kid like Willa, going round and round Holdingwell, where everyone knows everyone.'

'Pretty lame.'

'Pathetic.'

'Hey!'

'Well it was.'

Ella digs Fay in the ribs again and laughs. Then she turns to look at her; her eyes go dark and she says:

'You should have run away with her. It would have been better for her.'

'I would have come home anyway, even if you hadn't leapt onto the bus.'

Ella looks up. 'Why?'

'You know why.'

Ella blinks. 'Really?'

'You're my little girl too. My less bonkers but just as infuriating little girl.'

'And Dad,' Ella whispers. 'You came back for Dad too?'

'Yes, and Dad. But it's complicated—'

'You love him, right? I mean, not just *we're together and we've got used to it* love him. You're *in love* with him?'

'Yes, I'm in love with him.'

'So it's not complicated.'

'Your mum's come home. It's complicated.'

'Have you ever told him?' Ella asks.

'He knows.'

'But have you ever *told* him? Not just a *love you* at the end of the phone conversation or when you leave the house for a shift at the hospital. A proper, sit down and look into each other's eyes *I love you*.'

310

'I don't know. I can't remember.'

'Well you should.'

'Have you said it to Sai?'

Ella shrugs and looks down through the scaffolding.

Fay nudges Ella. 'You asked me; don't I get to ask you?'

'I'm waiting for him to say it first.'

Fay draws Ella in close again. 'Good plan.'

Ella leans her head on Fay's shoulder. 'I want to stay up here for ever,' she whispers.

'Me too.'

'Down there doesn't feel like home.'

'It'll always be your home.'

Ella lifts her head. 'And yours?'

'We'll see.'

'Don't do that.'

'Do what?'

'Go into sensible mode. Act like any of this is fair. Act like you don't hate every minute of it. That what she's done to all of us, that her fucking family turning up on the doorstep hasn't made you feel like smashing things and standing in the middle of Willoughby Street and yelling your lungs out.'

Fay looks at Ella and pauses. Then she puts her hands over hers.

'She loves you.' Fay says. 'And she needs you – now more than ever.'

Above them, the sky rumbles. The clouds pack together. Fay feels drops of rain on her face.

'She wasn't there when I needed her. You were. You stayed. And you should stay now.' Ella's voice is strong and hard, the same tone Ella had used time and again to push Fay away. 'If you love us, if we're yours, fight to stay.'

Willa

Willa stands by the window in her nightie, her nose pressed against the glass. The world is wet and windy and full of white lights that look like dancing ghosts.

Please let Mrs Fox be okay, she thinks. She doesn't want her to give birth to her cubs in a thunderstorm.

'Willa?'

Daddy comes in, carrying a parcel with a red bow that looks like it's been wrapped by Mummy.

'I've been saving up this present for bedtime,' he says.

Willa runs over to her bed, jumps onto the mattress, yanks up the duvet and pats the space beside her. Daddy comes over and sits on the edge of the bed. He's wearing his glasses, which make him look scruffy and tired.

Lightning blinks through the room like when Daddy takes a photo with his big flash.

'Will the man be okay?' Willa asks.

'What man?'

'Rainbow Man, in the tent. The one who came to help with Ella's project.'

'I'm sure he'll be fine.'

Willa isn't so sure. 'Maybe we should invite him to come in for the night.'

'I think the house is full enough, don't you Willa?'

She nods but she doesn't agree: you can always find more room. She could sleep with Louis in the den and Rainbow Man could have her room.

'Was Ella's project about finding Mummy Norah?'

'Sort of.'

'Do you love Mummy Norah as much as you love Mummy?'

Daddy rubs his eyes behind his glasses. 'I love them differently.'

'So it's okay if I don't love Mummy Norah in the same way that I love Mummy?'

What Willa wants to say is that she's not sure she loves Mummy Norah at all, not like she loves Mummy and Daddy and Ella and Louis and Mrs Fox. But she's worried that might sound mean, especially if Mummy Norah's the mummy who came first.

Daddy's eyes go watery.

'Yes, that's okay Willa.'

'Did she leave because of me? Because I was a naughty baby? Did I make her sick?'

'Sick?' Daddy looks confused. 'Of course not.' He wraps his hand around Willa's. There are rough bits on his palms from when he used to work in the main bit of the recycling plant rather than in the office bit. She likes how his hand covers hers so that it disappears, like when she threads her fingers in Louis's thick fur.

Now Daddy's eyes go so watery that Willa's worried that tears are going to come out, like the raindrops on the window.

He sniffs and looks up at the ceiling.

'I'm sorry, Willa.'

'What are you sorry for?'

'It was my fault that Norah – Mummy Norah – left.'

'Why was it your fault?'

'I wasn't a very good daddy. Or a very good husband. I needed to learn how to be better. Mummy taught me that.'

313

'Will you make sure that Mummy stays?' asks Willa.

She can't help thinking about the suitcase lying in the middle of Mummy and Daddy's bedroom and how, if Mummy Norah left because she was upset, then maybe Mummy might leave too.

'I'll try, Willa.' Daddy gives her a tired smile.

'And Nat.'

He doesn't answer.

'Aren't you sad that you didn't have Nat when he was a baby?'

Daddy nods. 'Of course I'm sad.' He looks up at Willa. 'But Nat had Onkel Walter. Onkel Walter loves him very much.'

'Do you love Nat? I mean, as much as you love me and Ella and Mummy?'

Daddy tilts his head to one side. 'I think I do, Willa. I know I do. But I have to get to know him a little bit.'

'So he's staying?'

'We'll see.' Daddy looks at the package in Willa's hands. 'Are you going to open your present?'

Willa tears open the tissue paper and pulls out a book.

'*Fantastic Mr Fox*!'

'It came before the film,' says Daddy. 'It was written by a very clever man called Roald Dahl.'

Willa can't believe that no one's told her there's a book of her favourite story. She flips through the pages. The pictures are pointy and sketchy and funny – even funnier than the pictures of the characters in the film.

'I thought we could read it together,' says Daddy.

Willa nods and keeps flipping and flipping. She stops at the picture of the big Caterpillar tractors that are about to crash into Mr and Mrs Fox's house.

'Start here,' she says. This is the bit where Mr Fox has to be really brave, which might help you to be brave too and to find a way to get Mummy to stay.'

'You want to start in the middle?'

Willa nods and points at the words.

Daddy swings his legs up onto the bed, draws Willa in under his arm and starts reading: 'The murderous, brutal-looking monsters . . . '

There's a shuffle at the door. '*Vater?*'

They look up. Nat's standing at the door in his pyjamas.

Poor Nat, thinks Willa. He didn't know about Daddy either, just like Willa didn't know about Mummy Norah.

Daddy gets off the bed, walks to the door and lifts Nat off the ground. 'Time for bed, young man.'

Nat doesn't answer. He just stares at Daddy and then touches the bulging vein on Daddy's forehead.

'I don't mind if you put him to bed,' says Willa. 'I'll read my book.'

Willa does mind. She was cosy with Daddy and reading with him made her forget her worries about Mrs Fox and the man in the tent and the fact that Mummy might leave in the morning. But Nat's littler than her, so it's only fair that he should get Daddy.

'You're quite something,' Daddy says and gives Willa a smile, a real, non-tired one this time.

Willa hopes that *quite something* is a good thing.

Daddy blows Willa a kiss and carries Nat out onto the landing.

Willa turns to the where Mr Fox is digging tunnels, even though he's tired and hungry. She mouths the words: *They kept at it with great courage* . . .

315

Ella

@findingmum
I'm not falling for it. #knowthetruth

Ella stares at the tweet from @sunnysideofthestreet. **Gold dust at your feet.** She recognises the line from one of Louis Armstrong's songs. Gold dust at my feet? More like crap, she thinks. Piles and piles of crap like the bin bags full of Mum's old stuff standing on the doorstep. She scrolls down. At last, there's a message from @onmymind. **You have the freedom to choose.** Ella laughs. As if she's ever got to choose anything in her life.

She sends a tweet, pulls her duvet in tight, stares up at the ceiling and listens to the rain. She loves how close it sounds, as though her room is part of the sky. Maybe Sai's right and the roof won't ever get fixed and the damp patch will get bigger and then crumble and leave a massive hole and she'll get to lie here and look up at the stars.

The house creaks as the wind throws itself against the roof.

Maybe, if she stays up here, she'll be swept away. Then she won't ever have to go back downstairs to all those strange people living in her home. Seven of them now: a crazy, cobbled-together family. Weird to think that, after everything, the only one who understands her is Fay.

She can't get the picture of Willa hugging Mum out of her head. *Mummy Fay and Mummy Norah* – more crap. And Willa being sucked in by her just like Dad was, like everyone, even Louis. And Fay, Fay who was meant to be the intelligent, grounded one, telling her that Mum needed her – *now more than ever*? What did that mean?

Louis shuffles in closer against Ella's body.

'What do you see in her, hey Louis?'

He looks at her with droopy eyes. Maybe he only remembers the good times, like Ella used to.

There's a loud tearing overhead. And then a crash. And a moment later, the ceiling starts dripping onto her duvet. Maybe the house will split open and leave them all standing in the rain.

She switches her phone back on and texts Sai:

I'm coming over x

She packs a bag with everything she needs for tomorrow's race, puts on her trainers and kisses the top of Louis's head.

'Don't tell anyone,' she whispers, and then pads quietly down the stairs.

As Ella steps on to Willoughby Street she looks back at the house. The wind has beaten the cherry tree so hard only a few pink petals cling to its branches. The tarpaulin flaps loosely against the side of the house. A flash of red disappears under a hedge.

The tent's dark, so the busker must have gone to sleep. Ella wonders whether he's got two Twitter accounts, whether he's @onmymind.

She breaks into a run. The cold air pushes in and out of her lungs. She breathes in the smell of wet earth, the sweetness of spring, feels the rain on her bare arms and the wind against her face. She can't remember the last time she felt so free.

The rain gets stronger. And although her hair is drenched and her clothes soaked through, Ella keeps running.

She runs past the steel barriers that the police have put up for tomorrow's 10k, the banners stretched across the high street, the water stations.

She runs past Willa's school. And the Animal Ark. Willa keeps saying that she wants to adopt all the animals and bring them home. She'd be better off checking herself into the Ark, they'd be a better family for her.

She runs past The Great Escape, with its posters of planes and palm trees and deserts. Here she takes off Mum's trainers and throws them in the bin on the side of the road.

She wants to strip it all away, every bit of her that's connected to Mum.

As she leans over the bin she hears a squawk overhead. A crow sits on a telephone wire, a shadow bleeding into the stormy sky.

'Go!' Ella yells. 'Just go!'

It lifts off the wire, flaps its wings, squawks one last time and flies into the dark clouds.

Ella starts to run again. The rain falls harder. Her wet socks slap the pavement.

She runs past the Three Feathers, where she went to look for Dad on the day Willa was born.

And she runs past houses, their orange glow spilling out onto the pavement like the windows of an advent calendar: families watching television, laughing, getting ready to sleep. Normal families with mums and dads and siblings who all know each other.

A gust of wind. The electricity wires crackle overhead. Then a snap. The street lamps blink off and then the windows of the houses go black.

When Ella reaches the post office she checks her phone. Still no answer from Sai. She thinks that maybe he's gone to sleep early to prepare for the race, but as she looks up at his bedroom she sees a candle glowing in the window. The electricity must have gone off all over Holdingwell.

Perhaps he doesn't want to see her. She swallows hard and chases away the thought. He probably hasn't looked at his phone.

She grips the drainpipe and lifts herself onto the first windowsill. It's an old house with lots of footholds, so climbing up is easy. And she's done this before, though in daylight and without the wind and rain.

Come on, you can do it, she says to herself. One last windowsill and you'll be outside Sai's room.

Her wet socks make it hard to get a footing, but she knows she can make it. She lifts herself up and looks through Sai's window. He's lying on his bed reading a book, his earphones in. She knocks on the glass but he doesn't hear.

'Sai,' she yells and knocks again.

As she leans forward to knock for a third time, her foot skids on a patch of moss. She sways to the side. Her fingers slip off the windowsill. She falls, grabbing at any surface she can on her way down. The brick scrapes her hands. The pavement speeds towards her.

'Ella?' Someone is shaking her. 'Ella?'

Ella looks up and sees a blur of different colours. A big, white smile, a yellow cap, a rainbow jumper.

She closes her eyes. She feels like she's floating in a big, starless sky.

'Ella?'

She opens her eyes again.

Sai's mum looks down at her; the red stain in her parting glows in the candlelight.

Ella looks around: she's in the kitchen above the post office. Someone must have carried her up. She's sitting on a chair, wrapped in a towel. Her ankle feels like it's on fire.

Mrs Moore kneels beside her. 'Where does it hurt?'

Ella wants to say *everywhere*. And she wants to point, not at her scraped hands and knees or even her ankle, but at her stomach and her chest – at the crow that's been flapping there ever since Mum turned up, squawking and pecking so hard she can't breathe.

'I'm fine,' she says.

Mrs Moore nods, but takes Ella's feet in her hands and eases off her wet socks. She rubs Ella's feet dry with a towel and then presses her fingers along Ella's ankles and the bones at the top of her feet.

'Does this hurt?'

Ella winces. 'It's okay.'

'I think you were lucky. That the man found you, and that you have not done too much damage to yourself.'

'What man?'

'He did not give his name. He brought you to the door.'

Ella tries to remember what happened, but her mind's a blur.

Mrs Moore massages Ella's foot. 'Maybe it would be wise not to run tomorrow.'

Ella takes her socks out of Mrs Moore's hands. 'I'm going to run.'

Mrs Moore nods, like she understands that the race is not just about running ten kilometres through Holdingwell. That it's the only thing that feels normal – that feels good – in Ella's screwed-up life at the moment.

'Would you like me to drive you home?'

Ella shakes her head.

Mrs Moore looks up, still cradling Ella's ankle in her hands. 'May I say something?'

Back home, no one ever asks permission to say something. Perhaps if they did, they wouldn't end up saying stuff that made everything worse. Ella nods.

'Maybe you should try to get to know who your mother is.'

Ella seizes up. Her ankle throbs harder. She wishes she'd told Mrs Moore to stay quiet. The last thing she needs is more advice on how to handle Mum.

'I know who she is.'

Mrs Moore puts down Ella's ankle.

'May I say say a few more words?'

Despite herself, Ella nods again. She knows she's not going to like what Mrs Moore has to say, but there's something about Sai's mum that makes her want to listen.

'Thank you.' Mrs Moore bows her head. 'I think the mother you are holding on to is the mother in your head – in your memory.' She points to her forehead, and then she lowers her hand to her heart. 'And the mother in here, too.' She takes a breath. 'Sai does the same, with his father. Memories can be good, Ella. Sometimes. But sometimes they can trick us. Then can stop us from living today.'

A clatter of footsteps in the corridor. Sai bursts in.

'Ella, what happened?'

His mum stands up, takes Ella's socks and slips out through the kitchen door.

'I don't want to stay at home,' says Ella. The candlelight flickers across Sai's face. 'Why didn't you answer my text?'

'Did you talk to your mum?'

So that was it. He thought that his silence would force her into patching things up with Mum.

'It's not going to work. Her kid's turned up. And her brother.'

'Her *what*?'

'It's all a mess, Sai. Apparently she was adopted and Walter's her long-lost brother, and she's claiming Nat is Dad's. And now Willa knows who Mum really is—'

'Slow down.' He kneels in front of her. 'How did Willa find out?'

'I told her. I had to. And guess what? She's excited to have two mums!' Ella shakes her head. 'I can't understand how Fay is letting all this happen. She's the one who's been there for us—'

'That's not what you used to think.'

'I know.' Ella pauses and looks down at her bare feet. 'I got things wrong. I built up this stupid idea of Mum in my head. God, I'm an idiot.' The burning in her ankle has turned into a series of sharp stabs. She looks up at Sai. 'Can I stay?'

Sai looks down at Ella's bare feet. 'What did you do with your trainers?'

'I threw them away.'

'Where?'

'In a bin.'

'What bin?'

Ella shrugs. 'Somewhere on the high street.'

Sai's dark eyebrows shoot up. 'You loved those trainers.'

Ella shakes her head. 'I don't want to have anything to do with her any more.'

Sai's mum comes back into the kitchen and hands Ella a set of clean pyjamas and another towel. 'You should have a hot shower before you go to bed, to warm up. I've put candles in the bathroom. Sai will change the sheets on his bed; he'll sleep on his couch.'

So this woman, who's meant to have all these strict principles about boys and girls and sex, is letting Ella sleep over – and in Sai's room, with Sai right there beside her?

Ella takes the pyjamas and the towels. 'Thank you.'

'Leave your wet clothes outside the bathroom door. I'll put them over the heaters to dry.' She kisses Ella lightly on the cheek.

Ella feels the crow flapping in her ribcage. This is the sort of thing a mum's meant to do, isn't it? It's what Fay tried to do for Ella, but Ella pushed her away. It's what Mum failed to do.

Norah

'Mummy?' Willa's voice spills out onto the landing.

Norah stands at the bathroom door. She hears Fay banging cupboards in the kitchen downstairs. Walter's tucking Nat in. Adam's on the roof, trying to secure the tarpaulin; he hasn't spoken to her since he found out about his son. Adam looked scared, like he looked when she told him she was pregnant with Willa, but then it was because he knew that a second child would take her even further from him – now, it meant he'd lose Fay. And he looked angry too, at having missed out on his little boy, at the unfairness of it, that he'd learnt to be a father and that his child has been kept from him.

'Mummy?'

Norah finds Willa sitting up in bed, clutching a toy fox. When she sees Norah her eyes go wide:

'Oh. I thought you were—'

'Mummy Fay is downstairs in the kitchen,' Norah says.

Willa nods.

They say that the first months in a child's life are the most important, the time when the bond with its mother is formed. So Willa should remember Norah, shouldn't she? Even if only instinctively. Her smell, the feel of her skin, the sound of her voice, her heartbeat. What they don't tell you is that this initial bond depends on what follows, on those early memories being consolidated by the ones that follow. Willa's memories were cut off and Fay picked up the thread – and now, Fay's all Willa knows.

'Night-night, Willa.' Norah turns to go.

'Could you tuck me in?' Willa calls after her.

Norah hesitates.

'I'd like you to.'

Norah comes and sits on the edge of Willa's bed. It's crowded with soft toys: monkeys and bears and lions – and foxes.

'Ella hasn't come to say goodnight.' Willa nudges in close to Norah.

'I think she's having an early night. She needs to be rested for the big race.'

When Adam went to the attic to check the leak, he found the room empty. He'd wanted to go after her but Norah had heard Fay persuade him to leave it. *When she's ready, she'll find her way home,* Fay had said.

'Is Daddy really Nat's daddy?'

'Yes. Yes he is.'

'So that means Nat's my brother?'

Norah nods.

'Will you all stay and live with us, then? You and Nat and Onkel Walter?'

That had been the plan. First Norah would come home, and then, when the girls and Adam were ready, Nat and Walter would join them. How naive she'd been. They'd made a new life together, Adam, Fay and the girls: a clear, simple two parents, two kids life. A life without her. And now she's come back and Adam no longer knows who he loves, and Ella, who's built a picture of a different mother, a better mother, hates her for leaving – and for coming back. And Fay's pregnant. And even Willa, who would welcome anyone into her home, even wild foxes, doesn't understand how she can have two mummies and a new brother and an uncle.

And it was all her fault.

Remember why you came back, she says to herself.

No matter how hard it is, it *has* to work. She'll talk to them, start from the beginning, make it good.

Rain crashes against the window, so hard it sounds like hail. Willa and Norah look out at the scaffolding.

'Is Daddy still fixing the roof?'

'Yes.'

'He's very brave, isn't he?'

'Yes, he is.' Brave and stupid. Adam may have changed in a thousand ways over the last few years, but he hasn't got a clue what he's doing up there.

'Like Mr Fox.'

'Mr Fox?'

'In the story.' Willa holds up a small hardback book. 'He's brave and adventurous.'

'Yes, it sounds like Daddy is a bit like Mr Fox.'

'Is Onkel Walter brave?'

'Yes, very.'

'And is he good at fixing things?'

'Yes, he is. That's why he's a vet – he knows how to fix animals that are poorly.'

'Daddy isn't very good at fixing things, is he?'

'Well, he's not a vet.' Norah smiles.

'Onkel Walter sounds a bit like Mummy.'

Norah's breath catches in her throat. 'Yes, I suppose they are a bit alike.'

She expected her brother to be like her – a musician or an artist, not someone who got called out in the middle of the night to deliver calves. The perfect man for Fay – that's the first thought she'd had on meeting him.

A flash of lightning streaks through the room.

'Will Daddy be okay up there on his own?'

'He'll be fine.' Norah kisses Willa. And she believes it. Willa's right: Adam might not be able to fix the roof, but he's brave, braver than she's ever seen him. And so, no matter what happens, he'll be okay.

'I like Onkel Walter,' Willa says. 'When I'm older, I want to be a vet. But for all animals – wild ones too.'

Norah thinks of her adoptive father, a zoologist who

taught her to love the natural world. Maybe, in that short time she had with Willa, that was the one thing she'd passed on.

'You're like your grandpa,' Norah says.

Willa sits up. 'I thought my grandpas were in heaven?'

'Heaven?' Christ. Fay had told Willa there was a heaven?

'I never met them, but that's where Mummy says they live. It's a hard-to-get-to place, so I can't see them. Not for the moment, anyway.'

Not for the moment? God. Lying to children – it never turns out well, does it?

'Can I meet my other grandpa, the one you know?'

Norah shakes her head. 'I'm afraid not—'

'Is he in heaven too?' Willa blurts out. 'Most grandpas are.'

'Sort of.' Norah takes a breath. 'You met him once, when you were a baby.'

'I *did*?' Those wide eyes again.

'Yes. He loved animals, like you.'

After she left Adam and the girls it took Norah three years to visit her father.

When she walked into his room he looked up at her with his grey, rheumy eyes, their lids hooded like an owl's, small crusts of sleep buried in the folds of his skin. He stretched out his arms to Nat and she placed her little boy on his lap.

She waited for him to ask her questions about why she hadn't got in touch and where she'd been and why this was the first time he'd met his grandson, but he just sat there, stroking Nat's hair and looking out to sea.

And then he put his hand in front of his mouth and

coughed. His chest heaved. He sounded as though he'd swallowed the sea. She could see that he didn't have long.

Willa scratches her scar.

'Why didn't Mummy and Daddy take me to see him? Before he went to heaven?'

'It would have confused you, Willa. And it might have upset him.'

Willa frowns. 'He would have been upset to see me?'

'Oh no ... no.' Norah takes Willa's hand. 'He would have been upset not to have seen *more* of you. But he lived far away, so it would have been hard. Sometimes it makes people sadder when they realise what they're missing – so it's easier not to make them see it.'

Willa's brow contracts. 'Like with the foxes. It makes me sad that I know they're out there but I can't see them.'

'Yes, like the foxes.'

'But I'm still glad I know they're there.'

Has Adam been to see you? Norah had asked her father when she visited him that day.

He'd blinked. Then nodded. *Adam. Yes.* He held her gaze. *He's changed. He came with a woman.*

A woman?

He nodded again. *Your friend.*

My friend?

The surgeon.

Typical Fay – coming to see Norah's father would have been her idea.

Norah took her father's hand. *If Adam gets in touch again, don't tell him I came.*

'Did you love Grandpa as much as I love Daddy?'

'Yes. Yes, I did. He was the one who wanted to adopt me.'

There's something I have to tell you, Norah. Something impor-tant, her father said in those last hours they spent together.

He'd let go of her hand, levered himself up from the arm-chair, shuffled over to his chest of drawers, yanked open the top drawer and pulled out a box. He'd brought it back to Norah and placed it on her lap.

Willa props up her animals along the wall side of her bed. 'Did you always know you were adopted?'

'I found out early enough.'

Norah lifted the lid off the box her father had handed her. On top lay the photograph of a young woman in her early twenties. Even though the photograph was in black and white, Norah could tell that the young woman's long, straight hair was red.

That's your mother, her father said.

She hadn't felt the shock that was meant to come at times like this. Was it because she'd always known that she didn't belong to the mother and father she grew up with? That she looked too different?

Why didn't you tell me earlier? she had asked her father.

He'd stared out at the sea. *I was scared of losing you. I was self-ish.*

'Have you met your real mummy and daddy, then?' Willa asks.

'Grandpa was my real daddy.'

Willa nods. 'Like Ella and I are Louis's real mummies, even though he didn't come out of our tummy? Like I'll be mummy to the foxes?' She looks at her line of animals. 'Like the nurses and vets at the Animal Ark?'

Norah nods.

So why tell me now, Papa? Norah had asked.

I don't want you to be alone. When I'm gone. Her father had coughed, as if waves were filling his lungs, as if he was drowning. *I did some research. No one knows about your father. But your mother – your biological mother – is living in Berlin. Or she was a few years ago.*

'Were you left in a shelter for babies, like the Animal Ark?' asks Willa.

'My mummy – the one who gave birth to me – left me in a park.' Like in a fairytale, Norah had thought when her father told her the story. Or maybe her mother had been a sleep-walker, like Norah and Willa. Maybe she'd taken her baby girl from her crib in the middle of the night and strolled through the streets and stopped for a rest on the bench and put her down – and walked away.

'In a park?'

'Yes.' In a park. In the same way that Fay and Adam had found her. 'My adoptive father walked there every day. He liked to look at the animals.'

'And one day your daddy spotted you?' Willa's words are breathless. 'And what about Onkel Walter? Was he left in the park too?'

Her father had reached over to the box on Norah's lap and pulled out a photograph. A little boy, the same smile, the same brown eyes.

'Onkel Walter is younger than me. My mother kept him.'

'She kept him and she didn't keep you?' Willa's eyes are wider than wide.

'She was a bit older by the time she had him. She was better able to look after him.'

That's your brother, Walter, Papa had said.

My brother?

He's the only one we know for sure is still around.

Willa rubs at her scar. One more layer of skin and it will start bleeding. It's too much for her, all these references to people abandoning each other and dying.

As Norah kissed her father goodbye he'd whispered in her ear, *Will you go home?*

For her father, family was more important than anything: to know that she'd walked out on Adam and Ella and Willa . . . He must have been so disappointed.

She'd kissed the top of his white head. *I'd better go, Papa. We've got a train to catch.*

He'd nodded and held out his hand and stroked Nat's cheek.

We'll come back soon, she'd said.

But they never did come back.

'So did you go and live with Onkel Walter and your first mummy and daddy?'

'My parents had already gone.'

'Gone where?'

'They'd already died.'

Willa bites her lip. 'So you never got to see them?'

'No, I never got to see them.'

Norah remembers how bereft she'd felt when she found out that her birth mother had passed away, and how guilty that it hurt her more than when her own mother died. No, Norah didn't get to say goodbye. And that's why she'd come home to Adam and the girls. She had to see her children before it was too late, give them the time she had left. And, when the moment was right, introduce them to Nat and Walter.

'Didn't that make you sad?'

'I was loved, that's all that matters.'

'By Grandpa?'

'Yes, by Grandpa.'

Willa pushes her small tongue into the gap left by her front tooth. When she notices Norah looking at her, she lifts up her pillow, takes out her small milk tooth and holds it out. 'You found my tooth.'

So Willa had left it for her. 'Yes, I found it.'

'Mummy gave it to me and said I should put it under my pillow and that the tooth fairy will bring something for my piggy bank.'

'That's right.'

'I don't want any money,' says Willa. 'I want a wish. Do you think the tooth fairy will mind?'

'I guess not,' says Norah. She's not good at these childhood games.

And before she has the time to stop her, Willa's spilling out her wish, like she did when she blew out the candles on her fox cake.

'I want you to stay.'

Fay

From behind the kitchen door, Fay hears Norah's light tread on the stairs, across the hall and into the lounge.

She catches a glimpse of herself in the kitchen window. *You don't belong here,* her reflection says. *You never did.* And Norah's cancer, that put an end to any right she had to fight for Adam and the girls.

She sits down and leans against the door. Louis comes out from under the table, sits beside her and hangs his head in her lap. He's been traipsing after her all night.

A knock on the door. The thump vibrates through her spine.

'Fay?'

It's Norah.

She can't face her right now.

Louis looks up at her and then cocks his head to the door. *I can't Louis. I can't.*

Another knock. 'Fay? Can I come in?' Norah pushes the door and stumbles in.

Louis licks Fay's hand and eases his warm bulk against her calves, as if to pin her down.

'You okay?' Norah asks.

Fay doesn't answer. She goes over and sits at the table. Norah sits opposite her. Louis follows them, eases himself under the table and sits between their feet.

The table's cluttered with dirty plates and cutlery from dinner. Fay should have been clearing up, but she'd lost the energy for tidying up after the Wells family.

Pellets of hail pound the kitchen window.

Norah puts her hand over Fay's. Fay pulls her fingers away.

'I want to stay,' Norah says.

Of course she wants to stay. And, as always, Norah gets what she wants.

'Fay?'

'What?' Fay gets up, grabs some plates from the table and

333

scrapes the uneaten pizza crusts into the bin. Then she dumps the plates in the sink and comes over to grab some more.

'I want us to talk – like we used to. I need you to tell me, I need you to—'

Fay spins round. 'To rubber-stamp your decision to come home? To tell you that everything's going to be just fine? I thought you'd grown up while you were away, Norah.'

This was what it had always been like, even when they were students: Norah sitting in Fay's flat with *tell me I've done the right thing* written all over her face. Like on the day she decided to marry Adam.

'You've got cancer, Norah. You need to be with your family. And they need to be with you. There's nothing to talk about.'

Norah doesn't say anything.

Louis comes out from under the table, stares at Fay and thumps his tail against the tiles.

'You could stay,' Norah says. 'We could make it work. All live here together.'

Fay laughs. Just like Willa: invite the whole world to come together and damn the consequences.

A crash of thunder splits the sky.

'For goodness sake, Norah – don't you get it? They don't want me. I'm the stopgap: I helped them keep going until you got home.'

'They *need* you.'

Fay bows her head and looks into her hands. Yes, that's how it had always been. Fay had earned her place in Norah's life – in the life of her husband and children – because she was needed. But need wasn't love.

'Remember the night we met?' Norah asks. 'The night you and Adam found me?'

Fay looks up. Of course she remembers. It was four in the morning. Fay walking home from a late shift at the Royal Free, where she was doing her training.

Norah had fallen asleep on the bus on her way home from a concert and had sleepwalked her way to the playground.

'I don't know what would have happened if you hadn't found me that night.'

Fay looks at her best friend. If only she had the courage to tell her what really happened that night – that it was Norah who rescued her. Norah and Adam. That they were the ones who made Fay feel connected to the world.

'You'd have been fine,' says Fay.

Adam would have come along anyway, been charmed by her delicate figure, the smile that took over her face, and carried her home. Alone. Maybe that would have been better for all of them.

'No, I wouldn't. It was meant to be – meeting you.'

Wisps of white-blonde hair have come loose around Fay's face. She notices that Norah's looking at her stomach.

'I know,' she says.

Fay's legs buckle. She drops into one of the kitchen chairs.

'It's okay,' Norah says.

Fay shakes her head. *No, it's not okay. Nothing's okay. Not since you came home.*

'I'll go,' Norah says.

'No, you don't—' Fay shakes her head. 'You don't get to come crashing back into our lives and then take off again and expect everything to keep going as though nothing's happened.' Fay turns on the tap and watches the water crash down on the plates. She turns round and points at Norah. 'You know that Adam loves you. He's always loved you. And Willa wants you to stay. And Ella will come round. It's all going to work out for you, Norah.'

'And you?'

Walter comes into the kitchen.

'I think Nat's asleep,' he says to Norah.

The sky above them rumbles. Walter looks up and says, 'Adam's still up there?' He shakes his head. 'You should sue those roofers. Let's hope it holds for tonight.'

Fay walks to the door.

'Excuse me. I think I'll turn in for the night.'

Norah stands up: 'Fay—'

'Goodnight.' Fay slips through the door.

Fay

Later, Fay goes downstairs, walks past Nat sleeping curled up on the camp bed with Norah, and out through the glass doors into the garden.

Fay takes off her shoes and walks barefoot across the wet lawn. For months she battled the weeds and moss. And then she spread new grass seed, covering it with nets so that the birds wouldn't eat it, watering the earth twice a day until new shoots came up.

Tilting her face to the sky, she lets the rain strike her face. For the first time since she got back from the hospital on Friday afternoon, she feels that she can breathe: the wet earth, the grass, the rain-heavy air.

It's become a ritual, coming out here after long hours spent locked up in the windowless operating theatre at Holdingwell General.

The rain falls harder, but she doesn't care. She wants to be on her own, in her garden – just one last time.

She goes over to the flowerbeds and kneels in front of the white peonies she planted when she first moved in. Her knees sink into the soil. She takes off the brown flower heads, scattering the dead petals around her on the lawn. Then she pauses and looks up at the house. Everyone is in there except me, she thinks. She's overcome by the loneliness she used to feel when she visited Norah and Adam and the girls, knowing that she'd never be more than a guest. The same loneliness she felt in her London flat after Norah moved in. She'd given Norah her room because there was more space for her to do her music practice and had moved into the box room. Sometimes Adam stayed over. She'd hear them talking late into the night. Watched them fall in love. Loneliness isn't about being without people, it's about being with people who make you feel alone.

When Fay's finished with the dead flowers, she doesn't stop. She tears at the dense white heads in mid-bloom and yanks them off their stems. And then she goes faster, ripping off more heads, scattering them among the dead petals.

'Mummy?'

And then a bark.

Fay looks up. Louis and Willa stand on the lawn, looking down at her. Willa in her white nightdress and bare feet, a small, perfect version of Norah.

Willa

'What are you doing, Mummy?'

Willa stands in the rain, staring at all the dead petals on the lawn and at all the flower heads that look like they're alive, only they've been pulled off their stems. Mummy's always telling Louis off for digging up her plants.

'Mummy?' Willa kneels down beside her on the wet grass. 'What's wrong?'

Mummy stares at the flowerbed she's torn up, blinking raindrops out of her eyes. Willa's never seen Mummy cry. First Ella, now Mummy: it's like someone's turned the taps on and made everyone cry.

'Is it because of Ella?'

Still Mummy doesn't answer.

'I think she'll come round,' Willa says. 'She's just a bit upset about Auntie Norah.' Even though she likes her, Willa still can't bring herself to call Auntie Norah Mummy.

Or maybe she's upset because Willa's out of bed and it's really late.

'I couldn't sleep,' Willa says. 'The storm's really noisy.'

She wishes Mummy would come in. It's cold and windy out here and Mummy's lips are blue.

Mummy gets up and pulls a packet of Daddy's cigarettes out of her pocket. Mummy's not meant to know that Daddy still smokes sometimes – and now she's lighting one of his cigarettes?

Louis gives Mummy a nudge with the side of his head, like he wants to knock the cigarette out of her hand. But Mummy doesn't move. Willa feels a fluttering in her palms. Mummy's never been like this before. Mummy's always the one who makes everything okay.

'Do you want me to get Daddy?'

Daddy's the best person in the world for cheering Mummy up, like when Ella's been mean to her or when she's seen too many sick children at the hospital.

'It's okay,' Mummy says, her voice sniffly. She gets up and brushes the earth off her knees. Raindrops skid off her face and her bare arms; Willa feels the rain soaking her nightdress too.

'It's not okay!' Willa says, and in a moment she's halfway across the lawn and heading back indoors. 'Come on Louis!' She pats her thigh to make Louis come with her because he's getting wet too, and when he gets wet his bones hurt because he's got arthritis – Mummy should know that, she's the one who explained it to Willa. But Louis bows his head and settles down next to Mummy.

Willa's decided that whatever it is that's wrong with everyone, she's going to fix things, just like Mummy always fixes things for all of them. And she'll start by getting Daddy. Daddy will know how to make Mummy feel better. Next to Ella and Willa and Louis, Daddy loves Mummy more than anyone in the world.

Adam

'Daddy! Daddy!' Willa tugs at the duvet. 'It's Mummy.'

He sits up, still cold from trying to fix the roof in the rain.

Willa's hair and nightdress are dripping, her feet covered in bits of grass and soil.

'Mummy's in the garden and she's tearing up all her flowers and she's smoking.'

'You're not making any sense, Willa.' He gets out of bed and lifts her off the ground and holds her to him. 'It's okay. You've just been dreaming.'

She kicks her legs and wriggles out of his arms.

'No, I haven't been dreaming.'

'Let's get you dry.' He takes her hand and guides her to the door.

'Only if you promise to go and find Mummy.'

'Okay, I promise to go and find Mummy.'

He takes her to the bathroom, towels her dry and helps her into a clean nightie, and then carries her back to her room. Dear Willa, she shouldn't have to be dealing with all this.

'You promise you'll go and get Mummy?' Willa looks up at Adam from her bed, eyes heavy with sleep. 'Mummy's really sad about something. I tried to make her happy again but she won't listen to me. So you have to go out and make things better.'

'I'll go and get Mummy, but you have to promise me you'll get some sleep,' says Adam as he tucks Willa's duvet around her.

'Mummy needs sleep too,' says Willa. 'And she needs to get

dry. She'll catch a cold if she stays out in the rain any longer. Plus, she's poorly, she's been sick ...'

'I'll look after Mummy.' Adam kisses Willa's forehead. 'I promise.'

Adam stands on the lawn, swaying with exhaustion. His eyes are so raw with tiredness he can't focus.

Fay sits on the bench under the peach tree, sheltering from the rain. She's torn up her peonies. And she's smoking, a white cigarette between her soil-stained fingers. Every time she inhales she coughs, but she keeps going, drawing hard on the cigarette until it's burnt down to a stump.

It turns out Willa hasn't been dreaming.

As he walks closer he notices Louis at her feet. The rain has flattened his fur; he looks small and frail.

Adam comes to sit beside her under the tree. Rain falls around them, but here, under the tree, they're sheltered.

She draws on the cigarette again.

'Stop it,' he says to her.

She looks up at him. 'Stop what?'

'This isn't like you, Fay.'

'It isn't?' She flicks a cigarette onto the lawn and takes another out of the packet on her lap. 'Who is it then, if it isn't me?' She strikes a match and lights the cigarette. 'Want to know who I got these from? Ella. It's funny, don't you think, how we've suddenly become friends again? I mean, after everything.' She laughs. 'You know what's even funnier? Ella stole these cigarettes from you!'

Louis looks at Adam. He wants him to do something, to make things how they were. How Adam wishes he could do that. Turn back time. Stop Norah from coming home.

'Fay—'

Fay holds up her cigarette. 'Am I being like Norah?'

'Come on—'

'Isn't this what you love about her? Impulsive Norah. Make-your-pulse-race Norah. All these years of living with safe, predictable Fay. God, you must have been bored out of your mind.' She blows smoke out at the sky. 'Well, now you can have her. No more Fussing Fay getting in the way. I'll just finish this –' she holds up the cigarette – 'and I'll be out of your hair.'

'That's not how I see you, Fay.'

She lowers her cigarette.

'Willa's worried about you,' he adds.

Fay shrugs.

'Don't pretend you don't care.'

'Is there any point in caring?'

'Of course there's a point. You're everything to her.'

'I'm all she knows.'

'You're her mother.'

Fay looks up through the branches of the tree. 'I'm the one who stayed. That doesn't make me her mother.'

'And Ella,' he goes on. 'She realises now, how blind she's been. You said it yourself. She gets how much you did for her, for all of us. She needs you. We all do.'

'You keep saying that.'

'Saying what?'

'That you *need* me.' She yanks at a tuft of wet grass. He's never seen her damage anything. She went through life fixing things, not pulling them apart.

'We do . . . we all do.'

She lifts her head and stares at him. 'I don't want to be

needed. Don't you get that, Adam? If I'm just the fixer, the person who helps you get through the day, who makes things okay, I'm replaceable. Thousands of women could do that. Millions. You should have hired someone from an agency: a live-in au pair would have done the trick.'

'I don't know what you want me to say.'

'I guess that's the problem, Adam. You shouldn't have to work it out. You should just know.'

'You mean everything to me too. I can't do this without you. I can't live without you.' Adam rubs his eyes. Is there anything he can say, anything at all that will make things better?

'I've got it. You needed me – and now you don't need me any longer. I'm glad I was of service. Send me a thank-you card and move on.' Her hands are shaking.

'You're incredible, Fay. You—'

'Don't, Adam.'

'Don't what?'

'Don't try to make me feel better out of some sort of obligation or guilt – or gratitude. God, please, please don't tell me you're grateful.' She draws Louis in towards her. He rests his head on her lap.

How does Louis do it, thinks Adam? How does he love them both?

Fay hugs her legs to her chest and closes her eyes.

He sits down beside her. He wants to put his arm around her and draw her in but he's scared that she'll push him away.

'You used to hate me,' Adam says.

They'd never talked about this. Not once in the whole six years they'd lived together: how it used to be between them before Norah left.

She stubs out the cigarette on the side of the bench. 'I never hated you.'

'You hated me being part of Norah's life.'

'And why do you think that was?'

A stillness settles between them.

He looks up at her.

'Because I loved you, Adam. I loved you every bit as much as Norah did.'

He feels an opening-up in his chest. All those years when he felt inadequate in front of Fay, the perfect best friend, the woman who saw right through to his weaknesses – who reminded him, over and over again, that he wasn't good enough for Norah.

Fay goes on, her voice quiet, 'I didn't hate you. I hated that you had each other – I *hated* that I'd never come first.'

He knows that Fay's waiting for him to tell her that it's not true. That he loves her more than Norah, that Norah coming back hasn't made a difference to what they've had all these years. That it's more than gratitude that he feels. But he can't find the words.

He looks at the petals strewn across the lawn.

'We'll plant some new ones,' he says. 'We'll do it together.'

She doesn't answer.

He thinks of Norah behind the glass doors to the lounge, sleeping on the camp bed with Nat.

Turning back to Fay, he eases the cigarette out from between her fingers and kisses her forehead, like he did Willa's a few moments ago. 'It's cold out here,' he says. 'Please come in, Fay.'

She doesn't answer.

'I promised Willa I'd make sure you got some sleep. And she's right – you're exhausted.'

Fay looks up at the house. 'Is she okay ... ?' she whispers. There's a tremor in her voice. 'Is Willa okay?'

He takes her head between his hands, draws her in and kisses her. For a second, as he feels the warmth of her breath between his lips, he lets himself think that this is going to be okay. That they'll find a way forward.

She pulls away and looks at him, waiting.

Why can't he just say it? Why can't he tell her what she wants to hear?

She shakes her head. 'Go back in.'

'Fay—'

'Just go!'

As he walks back through the rain he feels an emptiness that reminds him of the day Norah left. It's happening again.

It's midnight. The moon shines high. The world is falling asleep.

In the tall red-brick house the big dog lies on the carpet next to The Mother Who Stayed. He persuaded her to come back inside and then he waited on the landing while she had a bath and warmed up. When she came out, she dried him off with her white towel and, for the first time, invited him into her room.

When he closes his eyes he sees the tight bud of life stirring inside her.

Across town, the teenage girl sleeps in the boyfriend's bed. He puts his arms around her and cups his body into hers. As her limbs go heavy, she prays, *may this moment never end*.

Outside, on the patch of grass outside the old ladies' bungalow, the man in the rainbow jumper takes off his boots and slips back into his tent, singing a jazz tune: *The bright blessed day . . . the dark sacred night . . .* He hopes that she hears it, the teenage girl who slipped from the windowsill.

In the room on the first floor of the tall, red-brick house, the little girl listens to the night: Mrs Fox's cries, the singing outside. She gets up and walks to the bedroom on the second floor. The door's open. Her mummy and daddy lie in bed, a big gap between them. Her dog lies by the bed on her mummy's side. She goes over and strokes the tangle of curls on his head. He stirs and opens his eyes.

It's okay, says the little girl. *Stay with Mummy, she needs you tonight.*

She pushes open the door to the lounge. The little blond boy is curled up with his mama on the camp bed and Onkel Walter is asleep on the sofa. She goes up to the mummy who was there first but who went away. The little girl wants to be nice to Mummy Norah, but she's not sure she needs another mummy, not when her real mummy loves her so much.

She walks up to the glass doors and looks out into the empty garden. And then she hears someone move behind her. The little boy has woken up. He joins her at the glass door and she takes his hand.

Tomorrow, I will introduce you to Mrs Fox, says the little girl. *Mrs Fox is going to have lots of little babies and we will look after them together.*

The little boy smiles and stares into the moonlit garden, and then goes back to lie next to his mama.

Upstairs, in the main bedroom, the father listens to the steady breathing of The Mother Who Stayed lying beside him. Even now, after everything, she's here.

I have to get it right this time, he thinks. *I have to get right.*

He hears the dog's paws knock against the feet of the bed – he's running in his sleep, trying to catch someone.

Outside, thunder rumbles through the clouds. The wind picks up again. Someone's singing 'What a Wonderful World'. His words soar through the night sky.

MONDAY MORNING

Willa

Willa rubs her eyes, not sure whether she dreamt the cry of Mrs Fox or whether it was real.

A scream rips through the dawn. It wasn't her dream. Mrs Fox is calling her.

Willa hopes that when the cubs are born they'll be warm and cosy and snug and looked after. She wonders whether fox cubs can have two mummies like she does. Maybe Willa could be an adoptive mummy to the cubs, like Mrs Fox is a second mummy to Kristoffersen.

She heads downstairs.

'Nat,' she whispers, tugging at his T-shirt.

Willa has to be careful not to wake Mummy Norah because they're snuggled in so close.

She leans in to his ear. 'Nat, it's Mrs Fox – she needs us.'

Nat opens his eyes, blinks and then smiles.

'Will you come with me?' She motions her hand for him to join her.

He nods and eases his small body out from under his mummy's arm. Mummy Norah makes some muttering sounds and turns to face the wall.

Willa takes his hand and together they walk out into the back garden; their bare feet leave small prints in the long wet grass.

They crouch by the gap under the gooseberry bush and wait. But Mrs Fox isn't there.

Then there's a cry from the road.

'Maybe she's chosen a new place to give birth,' says Willa.

The children run round the house and on to Willoughby Street. The man in the rainbow jumper stops singing and smiles at them.

'Look!' Willa points to the end of the road.

Nat gives a little skip of delight. She knew he'd see the foxes too.

'We're going to help her! Come on!'

She pulls Nat up the road. There's another rumble overhead and it starts raining.

In the boyfriend's bed in the flat above the post office, the teenage girl wakes up with a start to the roar of an engine. A van driving too fast. And then a clap of thunder.

She gets up and goes to the window. Headlights tear down the street.

Idiot, she thinks.

Under the rain, a mist rises from the pavement, like it does before a beautiful day. Today she's going to race alongside the boy she loves – nothing's going to spoil that. And after the race she'll come back here and she'll stay here until The Mother Who Left and her brother and her little boy have gone. The teenage girl knows who her family is, and it doesn't include them.

On Willoughby Street the little boy and the little girl break into a run.

Over there! the little girl cries. *Mrs Fox – I knew she'd come back!*

It's a little late, but her birthday present has arrived: Mrs Fox and her babies. Soon they'll all be together. Even the dog she loves will get used to them – she'll teach him to love them and look after them and make him his own.

In the tall red-brick house, the big dog's mind rises up from the fog of sleep. He's had an interrupted night: the dreams, the storm, the singing outside. All he wants to do is to sink back into sleep. But his paws tingle. There are people missing from the house. And then he hears a cry, followed by small footsteps on the pavement.

His heart beats faster.

How did they disappear without him waking up?

He runs through the open front door and presses his paws into the tarmac and feels the vibrations of small footsteps. They're moving away.

He sees the man with the rainbow jumper.

Over there, the man whispers and jerks his head towards the end of the street.

The old ladies stand at the fence, looking up the road, their brows wrinkled up.

Two small dots skipping away up the road.

A clap of thunder.

The sky lights up and dims.

The rain falls harder.

There was a storm on the night he was separated from his mother. She'd got his siblings to the shelter, but he was left behind. As the biggest and the strongest, she'd thought he'd make his own way to safety. Only he never found them.

A fox stands on the edge of the pavement, ahead of Willa and Nat; a growl rises in Louis's throat. He's not going to let her get hurt again.

He lurches into a run.

In the bedroom of the tall red-brick house, the father rolls over and falls into a deeper sleep.

Downstairs, The Mother Who Left stirs. She's going to find

a way to win them all back. Even the teenage girl. She's made a mess of the last few days but today's going to be different. Everyone's here now. And she's going to tell them the truth, and then they'll start again.

She reaches out to hug the little boy but there's a cool space beside her. Her heart jolts. Where is he? She leaps out of bed.

At the end of Willoughby Street the little girl and the little boy, their fingers entwined, reach the spot where the fox stands on the pavement. They hold their breath and watch as the fox walks towards them.

In the main bedroom of the tall red-brick house, The Mother Who Stayed hears a loud bark and pulls away from the father.

Willa!

She jumps out of bed.

Outside, the big dog runs towards the children, panting heavily, the rain blurring his eyes.

Fay

Fay feels a flutter in her womb. Not sick, for once. She strokes her stomach and imagines the small life growing inside her. It should make her feel whole, shouldn't it, something that belongs to her, that no one can take away? Except she's never felt so alone.

The electricity went off in the storm last night, so she has to feel her way down the stairs. She pushes open the door to Willa's room; her bed's empty.

'Louis!' she calls. When Fay woke up and didn't find him lying at the foot of her bed, she was sure he'd come down to sleep next to her little girl. 'Louis!' she cries again.

Times of stress . . . changes from the routine . . . those are the times to watch for, the sleep specialist had told her. She should have guessed that, with all this going on, Willa's sleep would be disturbed.

In the hallway, Fay bumps into Norah. Fay pushes past her and calls out:

'Willa!'

Norah catches her arm.

'I can't find Nat either,' Norah says.

A bark from the road.

'Louis!' Fay runs out of the house, Norah following.

Through a curtain of rain, they see the busker, his big rucksack hitched on his shoulders, his trumpet case swinging from his hand. He holds up his hand to wave and then disappears down the road.

At the other end of the street a little boy and a little girl crouch over the kerb; they're staring at something. And running towards the children is Louis, his bulk swaying from side to side, his tongue hanging out.

A tile falls from the roof. Fay grabs Norah and pulls her out of the way.

Mist rises off the pavement.

Fay's chest burns.

'Willa!' she yells as a white van, its headlights on full beam, swerves into the road.

Adam

Adam dreams that the house is caught in a tornado. The wind spins and spins and lifts off the roof. The roof rises into the clouds and floats above Holdingwell. The staircase falls away. He grabs at the walls but they crumble in his hands. Dust rises from the crumbling bricks, clogging his eyes and nose and mouth. He can't breathe. The world goes dark.

When his eyes clear, he's standing alone on an empty patch of land. No roof or walls, no staircase, just a big open sky.

He calls their names:

Fay!

Willa!

Ella!

... *Nat!* He doesn't want to lose him.

357

Nat! he calls again.

But none of them answer.

Adam wakes to the slam of the front door. He reaches out for Fay, but her side of the bed is empty. He sits up.

Has she left me already? I needed time to find the words ... today I was going to tell her ...

He scans the room. Her suitcase is still there.

Six years ago, Fay had stood on their doorstep and handed Willa to him.

Norah didn't come to collect her, she'd said.

As Adam held Willa, her small limbs tucked in to his arms, she'd looked from him to Fay, her mouth a perfect O. They'd waited for her to unleash one of her long, mournful wails, but it never came.

She hasn't cried since Norah dropped her off this morning, Fay said.

Adam had looked back into Willa's face, her brown eyes wide, and had felt certain that she knew it all: that Norah had left, that she was too far away, now, to hear her little girl's cry, and that it was his fault. Maybe Willa already knew, then, that she had a new mother.

On the landing, Adam calls out for Ella, but she doesn't answer. He climbs up the stairs to the attic: her room is still empty.

Willa isn't in her room either.

He checks the bathroom. Looks at the corner where the changing table used to be.

He closes his eyes and thinks again about the night Fay brought Willa back.

Fay was downstairs, making up a bottle of formula as though she'd done such things her whole life. He was angry at her for knowing what to do, for being here instead of Norah.

Willa stared up at him from her changing table, silent. He'd pulled open the press studs of her Babygro, eased her small limbs out of her vest. A warm, rancid smell rose from her nappy.

I don't know how to do this, he whispered to her.

A knock on the door.

I'm dealing with it, Fay. We'll be down in a minute.

Dad? Ella pushed open the door, Louis at her side. She stood there in her pyjamas, her long hair shining under the bathroom lights.

Do you need some help, Dad?

She came over to the changing table, reached up on tiptoes and stroked Willa's cheek.

He kissed the top of Ella's head. *Yes Ella, I could do with some help.*

Ella found the wet wipes, the talcum powder, the fresh nappies, a clean vest and Babygro. And then she gave Adam instructions:

That way round ... no, that way ... The tapes go over the sides ... you need to pull them a bit ... tighter, Dad, or it will fall off.

Eight-year-old Ella was teaching him to be a father.

She kissed Willa's feet and tickled her tummy. *You need to distract her, Dad,* she said and then she looked up at him. *Have you called the police yet, about Mum?*

He crouched down to be at Ella's height and took her hands.

Mum's just gone for a little holiday, Ella. You don't need to
worry. She'll be back soon.
But she wouldn't leave without telling us—
She didn't want you to be upset.
Ella blinked. *So she just left? Without saying goodbye?*
He nodded, unable to look her in the eye.

Adam remembers how, that whole night, he'd waited for Fay
to blame him for Norah having left. But she never did.

Downstairs, there's no Louis lying in the den, or on the
kitchen tiles.

He thinks of the note, propped up on the kitchen table.
Black marks scribbled on the back of a quotation from a roof-
ing firm. *Tell Ella and Willa that I love them.* But how could he
tell them that she loved them and, in the same breath, explain
that she'd left?

He'd given Fay the note and told her to get rid of it. *Burn it,*
he'd said. *I never want to see it again.*

He looks around the lounge. Norah is missing, and so is Nat.
Only Walter remains, breathing heavily in his sleep.

The house is still here, and the roof has held – but they've all
gone.

Adam's eyes fall on the drinks cabinet in the corner, and then
he turns away, takes a breath and clenches his jaw. He won't let
this happen again. He won't let his family fall apart. Today,
he'll take charge: he'll be the man Fay's been training him to be
these past six years. He'll make her proud.

A clap of thunder reminds him of the front door slamming
a few minutes ago. He goes out and stands under the cherry
tree. The wind has stripped it bare; its dark branches reach up
into the grey sky.

I'll take charge . . . he whispers to himself again. *I'll look after my family. I'll tell her . . .*

He knows it now, more than ever, how he feels about her. He's made his decision.

The rain is so heavy that he can't see more than a few feet in front of him. He runs out along the pavement and keeps running until he sees Norah and Fay ahead of him, and a little further on Louis, barking, and beyond him Nat and Willa in their pyjamas. Headlights beam down the street. An engine roars. *Too fast,* he thinks, *it's going too fast.*

A fox steps into the road.

Christ!

Willa releases her hand from Nat's and runs after the fox.

'Willa! Stop!' cries Adam. But the wind and the rain swallow his words.

The van gets closer.

The fox freezes.

The van doesn't slow down.

Willa runs after the fox, her arms outstretched. Nat stands on the kerb, his small body frozen.

The fox makes it to the other side; she tumbles onto the grass verge and disappears under a hedge.

Willa stands in the middle of the road.

The van hurtles towards her.

She holds her hand up to her eyes, blinded by the headlights.

'Willa!' he cries.

But she doesn't move.

Louis bounds in front of her.

Adam runs after him, every muscle in his body strains.

'Willa!'

The van swerves. It throws Louis's bulk up into the air, where he floats for a moment, as if carried by the wind, before falling with a thud onto the tarmac.

Willa rushes to Louis.

Adam keeps running, but he's too far away.

'Willa – no!'

The van slows and swerves again, but it can't avoid her. A sheet of metal crashes against the body of a small girl. She falls beside Louis.

Louis opens his eyes and lets out a low whine.

And then silence.

Ella

@findingmum
I'm never going back #newfamily

Sai strokes Ella's arm. 'You've been tossing and turning all night.'

After seeing the van outside, Ella came back to bed. She doesn't remember when Sai moved from the sofa in the corner of his room to the bed she's sharing with him now, but she knows that he held her for most of the night. If only her father understood how good Sai was to her; that if someone was trouble, she was. Sai was the one who should be protected from her.

She kisses his shoulder, his skin a golden brown.

'Just too many thoughts crashing round in my head.' She

smiles. 'You ready for our big race?' She feels a dull pain in her ankle but she doesn't care. Nothing's going to stop her from running.

'You're sure you're up to it?' He passes his fingers over the raw skin on the palms of her hands.

'I wouldn't miss it for the world. And we've raised all that money for the British Heart Foundation. I have to go ahead with it.'

He nods. 'Stubborn as ever.'

She punches him on the arm.

There's a knock on the door.

Ella pushes him out of the bed. 'Quick! Get back to the couch!'

Sai laughs and rolls onto the floor.

'She likes you, you know.' He pulls on a T-shirt and tries the light switch, but the power's still out. Then he opens the door.

His mum stands with a tray and two steaming glass tumblers. A shaft of light falls through the window and bounces off the gold sequins on her sari. She's beautiful, thinks Ella. She glows, like Sai.

'It's stopped raining at last.' She places the tray on the bedside table. 'And the wind's died down. But there is a lot of damage out there.'

'Will it be okay for the race?' asks Ella.

'When I went out this morning, they were already clearing up the streets. I think it should be fine.' She hands Ella a tumbler.

'Sweet Indian tea,' Sai says. 'It cures everything.'

Ella blows into the tumbler and then takes a sip. It's bitter and rich and sweet. She takes another sip and looks up at Mrs Moore. 'It's delicious, thank you.'

Her mobile phone buzzes from across the room. She left it in the pocket of her jeans. Sai brings it over and she looks down at the screen: five missed calls from Dad, but no voicemail.

Then the landline rings in the house and Sai's mum gives a small bow and disappears through the door and down the stairs.

'Everything okay?' Sai asks, looking at the phone.

Ella nods. 'Just Dad. He probably found out I was missing from upstairs and flipped out. I don't need him lecturing me right now.'

Ella swipes to her Twitter account. She knows she told her followers that she was going to shut down the account, that there was no point in keeping in touch now that the search for Mum was over, but tweeting, having this group of strangers rooting for her, has become such a part of her life that she can't let go, not yet.

There's a message from @onmymind sent late last night: **Run like a song.**

How does @onmymind know about Mum's special saying? Had Ella mentioned it in one of her tweets?

'Don't you think you should call your dad back? He'll be worried,' says Sai. 'Or I could walk your home, so you can talk to him. And your mum.'

But Ella doesn't want to go home. She wants to stay here with Sai and Mrs Moore and her sweet Indian tea. If Mum could just up and leave and find a new family, why couldn't Ella? Sai and his Mum, they can be Ella's family. This can be her home. She composes a tweet and presses send.

She hears Mrs Moore's slippered tread on the stairs.

'Ella,' Mrs Moore calls in her gentle voice. 'Ella.' She comes into the room. Her brown eyes have clouded over like the stormy sky the night before. 'It was your father. He's been trying to call you—'

The light bulb overhead blinks back on.

Ella stares into the warm, amber liquid of her tumbler. 'I don't want to speak to him.'

'It's your sister. There's been an accident.'

In the street outside the tall red-brick house, the little boy stands on the pavement. He can't move. The fox ... the van ... the dog ... and now the little girl lying there ... It's all a muddle. And he doesn't understand what anyone's saying. All the grown-ups are standing in the middle of the road, looking at the little girl. No one seems to notice that he's here on his own. Even his mama has forgotten about him.

We didn't hear it coming, he wants to tell them. *We were following the fox. I didn't mean for my sister to get hurt ...*

A hand presses down on his shoulder. An old lady dressed in purple, and another one beside her.

It's going to be okay, my dear, says the round one.

He doesn't understand their words but their warm faces and the light in their eyes still the thudding in his chest.

Across town, the teenage girl calls her father again and again, but he doesn't pick up.

She throws on her clothes and hobbles down the stairs.

Where are you going? the boy calls after her.

Home. I'm going home.

They're at the hospital, the boy's mother says.

The teenage girl clenches her fists. *This is my fault,* she thinks. *It was my job to look after Willa; I should never have left.*

367

The boy runs after the teenage girl and catches her hand. *Let me come with you*, he says.

At the end of Willoughby Street, The Mother Who Stayed kneels next to the little girl. The grit of the tarmac presses into her knees. *Why didn't she lock the front door? Why didn't she let the little girl sleep with her last night?*

As she strokes the little girl's head she whispers, *It's going to be okay, my darling.* And then she closes her eyes and, for the first time, she prays.

Beside her stands The Mother Who Left, a hand pressed to her throat. *I shouldn't have come back,* she thinks. *I shouldn't have come home.*

And the father, his breathing unsteady, his legs weak, comes over and kneels next to The Mother Who Stayed.

He puts an arm around her. *I'm sorry,* he says.

He wants to tell her that he loves her. That at this moment, as they sit here, looking down on their little girl, he knows for sure. But it's too late, isn't it? He's found the words too late.

Above them, the big dog looks down on Willoughby Street. He's often wondered what it would be like to fly, to be a bird, to see the world from above. He likes it up here. How weightless his body feels. Likes how his senses are no longer overwhelmed by the smells and the sounds of the earth.

As he looks down past the tall red-brick house to the end of the street, he sees the little girl lying on the road. His heart jumps. And then he's falling.

He lands with a thump on the tarmac.

He hears the crunch of bone.

And a tear by his ear.

Warm blood seeps across his tongue and flows out of his mouth.

He wants to get up and walk over to the little girl to make sure she's okay, but his legs won't move.

He closes his eyes and sees the little girl's face; she's smiling at him.

It's okay, Louis, you don't need to look after me any more.

Under his body, the road tremors. The spin of tyres. Blue lights. Sirens.

At the end of Willoughby Street men in green uniforms lift the little girl off the ground and put her in the back of their van with flashing blue lights.

The Mother Who Stayed and The Mother Who Left climb into the back of the van with the father. The uncle says he'll join them later. *I'll take him to the vet,* he says as he lifts the big dog from the road.

Inside the ambulance the little girl's eyes flit open. She looks at her father. At her two mothers. How they're all here with her, and she feels a warmth rising in her chest. Then she blinks and looks past them. *Where's Louis? Where's Ella? And Mrs Fox?* She tries to talk but her lips won't move. Her head pounds. Her right arm feels heavy and numb. Her eyelids drop shut.

Outside the tall red-brick house the uncle carries the big dog to the family car; the father gave him the keys, said to take care of the big dog. He lays the injured animal on the front passenger seat. And then, as he starts the engine, he turns round, reaches out and strokes the big dog's head.

Lieber Hund, he says. *Lieber Hund.*

The car bumps along the road.

The big dog wants to sink into sleep, to float away, like when he was floating above the road. But what about the little girl? He's meant to be looking after her.

Her face appears again, her big brown eyes. *It's okay, you can sleep.*

His heart slows.

There's a bright light, like the headlights of the van coming towards him, but this time it's the sun.

He's standing outside a barn; the place feels familiar. The door to the barn opens. His nose twitches. His paws tingle. His mum comes out. She looks at him and wrinkles her brow. *You'd better stop running off*, she says. *Or one of these days you'll get lost and we won't find you.*

He thought that she was the one who left.

She carries him into the barn and places him in the warm hay. His siblings are all there. He tumbles over them. When his mum lies down, he snuggles in close.

I'm home, he thinks.

Willa

Willa's eyelids flicker. She hears voices but she doesn't want to wake up, not yet. She wants to stay here, in her dream.

Everyone's sitting on picnic blankets in the garden: Mummy and Mummy Norah and Daddy and Ella and Sai and Onkel Walter and Nat. They make room for Mrs Fox and her cubs. Mummy puts out bowls of milk for them.

The only one who's missing is Louis.

'Louis!' calls Willa. 'Come out and join us!' She picks up a piece of chicken breast. 'I've got a treat for you!'

She runs into the house and searches all the rooms but she can't find him.

When she comes back out she asks everyone 'Where's Louis?' But they don't answer, they just keep talking and eating.

Then she hears a screech of brakes from the street. And a whine.

She runs round to the front of the house, and in the distance she sees a thick pelt, the colour of caramel, lying in the middle of the road.

A white van roars past her. Behind the steering wheel sits a man with a red face and a bottle in his hand.

'Louis!' She runs up to him and presses her ear to his chest.

His heart is beating, but it's very faint. Clasping her hands together, she massages his chest like she's seen people do on TV. He whines again. His eyelids open and he stares at her with his big brown eyes; he seems to smile at her too, and then he lets out a breath and slumps further into himself and closes his eyes.

'Someone help!' she calls out. 'Someone come and help!'

She presses her ear back to his chest and listens, but this time there's no heartbeat, just a long, empty silence.

Willa looks around for Mummy or Daddy and Ella. But the street is empty. And then she notices a little girl lying in the road, her body curled up like she's asleep.

Norah

White walls and sterile instruments and screens and drips. A room disinfected of the colour and chaos of living. She's given too much of her life to places like this.

Willa's hair glows red against the white pillow, her face pale. Her arm's in a plaster cast. They're waiting for her to wake up.

Nat sits on her hip, his arms tight around her neck. He hasn't let go of her since the accident.

'There are anomalies on the ECG.' The doctor's voice threads between them. 'We're still trying to work out what's going on.'

'But it's a coma, right?' Norah asks.

He shakes his head.

'She's showing more responses than we'd expect from some-one in a coma. We believe she's in a minimally conscious state.'

Like sleepwalking, thinks Norah, that semi-conscious state that no one really understands. A living dream.

Walter's gone to the vet with Louis. Louis won't wake up either. Maybe he's taken Willa with him, thinks Norah. Willa would like that.

Ella sits on Willa's bed, clutching Willa's good hand.

Sai stands next to Ella, his fingers laced in hers.

Fay's in a chair next to Willa's bed, her eyes fixed on the heart monitor. Adam stands beside her, his hand on her shoulder. The vein in his forehead pushes up against his skin as he looks down at Willa. He hasn't said a word to Norah since they got into the ambulance.

'*Wir liefen nach Frau Fox.*' We were running after Mrs Fox, Nat whispers into Norah's ear.

'*Ich weiss.*' Norah kisses Nat's brow, hitches him up higher on her hip and walks to the door. She needs to get some air. She feels there's no room for her here. That Willa has everyone she needs around her, as does Ella, and Adam.

Ella lifts her head. 'Where are you going?'

Nat's body tenses up.

'Running away again?' Ella asks.

'Ella—' Fay starts.

Ella ignores her. 'If you're going to up and leave the moment things get tough, why did you bother to come back at all?'

Nat leans his head against Norah's chest and holds her tighter. She should have protected him from all this.

Ella stands up. 'Even when you're here, you can't take care of us. Look at what happened to Willa – and Nat: he could have got hurt too.' She gulps her words. 'You're not fit to be a mother.'

Everyone in the room seems to stop breathing for a second. The only sound comes from the steady beat of the heart monitor.

'Ella, not now.' Sai whispers. He rubs her back. 'You're upset. We're all upset—'

She shrugs him off. 'I'm not upset. I just want her to see how pathetic she is – walking out, coming back, leaving again . . . I want her out of our life. For good.'

Norah puts Nat down. '*Geh zu Vater,*' she says, and nudges him towards Adam. Then she turns to Ella. 'Will you come with me for a moment, Ella? So we can talk?'

'You're joking, right?'

Norah goes over to the door and waits. If there's someone who deserves an explanation, it's Ella, the one who never gave up hope that she'd come home.

Sai whispers into her hair: 'Go, Ella. Give her a chance.'

'You'd better make this quick. I need to be with Willa.'

A nurse walks past, pushing a little girl in a wheelchair. She's bald, her skin grey, and there's a drip attached to her arm.

Norah notices a sign above the door that says *The Sanctuary.* 'Let's go in here.' She doesn't want to have this conversation in a corridor.

The little girl and the nurse disappear into a lift.

Norah holds open the door and lets Ella walk in ahead of her. Dim lights, a thick green carpet, the ceiling sky blue with clouds and birds painted on the plaster. The walls have been painted too, with trees and flowers and animals. Willa would love it in here. Dear, dear Willa. Ella's right: none of this would have happened if Norah hadn't come home.

Waves of meditation music come from a set of speakers in the corner.

Ella looks around, her hands on her hips. 'And this crap's meant to make us feel better?'

Norah breathes in, feels the rise and fall of her chest, and then says, 'Do you know why I left, Ella?'

374

Ella shrugs and then she tilts her head up and stares at one of the birds on the ceiling.

Norah's legs feel weak. She sits down on one of the beanbags and stretches out her hand to encourage Ella to sit beside her. Ella doesn't move.

'You know how it feels when you run?' Norah says. 'I mean *really* run? When you forget you're in your body, when your mind switches off, when all you can feel is the breath going in and out of your lungs – when you feel like you could keep going for ever?'

Ella nods slowly.

'It feels like you're flying, right? Like you could do anything?'

Ella grabs a beanbag and slumps down.

'I guess so.'

'I needed to get that feeling back. And not just for one run – I needed to feel it in my life. I needed to find the room to grow again.'

Ella picks at a loose thread on the beanbag.

'So you felt trapped? Big deal. We all feel trapped. It doesn't mean we take off whenever we feel like it – it doesn't mean we leave behind the people we love.'

'You left last night.'

Ella's eyes shine. 'I went to Sai's. For *one* night.'

'We didn't know that.'

'It's different.'

'But you felt you had to get away.'

'You're serious? You're actually comparing us? I'm a teenager – I'm meant to run off to see my boyfriend. I don't have a husband. I'm not a mum.'

Even in this dim light, Norah can see the flush in Ella's cheeks.

375

'I knew Dad would look after you,' says Norah.

'Dad was crap. You knew he was crap. That's why you left.'

'No, that's not why I left. And your father wasn't crap. He just wasn't ready; he needed some time.'

Ella waits for Norah to continue.

'Your dad loved me—'

'Of course he loved you. We all loved you—'

'He loved me too much.'

Ella widens her eyes. 'Oh, he loved you *too* much? So that's the reason you left?' She shakes her head.

'It wasn't healthy. I needed room to breathe. And I needed him to realise he was a dad, to love—' She stops herself.

'You wanted him to love *who*?'

'All of us,' says Norah. 'That when you have a family, you have to love them all, together.'

They look at each other for a moment, and Norah sees that although Ella won't acknowledge it for a while, that maybe she won't ever say it out loud, she understands.

'I knew that, once he understood, he'd be an amazing dad.'

'A bit of a gamble, wouldn't you say?'

'And I knew that you'd look after Willa too.'

'I was a kid, Mum. I couldn't even look after myself. If it hadn't been for Fay we'd have fallen apart.' Ella stares at her. 'I bet you didn't bank on that, did you? That your best friend would move in with your husband and adopt your kids.'

Norah holds Ella's gaze. No, she hadn't banked on that.

'Do you remember Willa's crying?' Norah asks.

Ella nods.

'How, when she'd start, it felt like she'd never stop?' She'd wail for hours, wail until her throat was raw, until she'd held her fists for so long and so tight that there were nail marks in her palms, until her skin was damp and red. 'Your dad couldn't take it. He'd walk out, go to the pub, and he'd only come home when she was asleep. I couldn't take it any more either.'

Ella yanks the thread out of the beanbag and then looks up at Norah, her eyes hard now. 'You left because you got sick of your baby's crying? Crying's what babies do, Mum. Putting up with that stuff is part of the deal when you have a kid.'

'It was more complicated than that.'

'You think that makes it okay? Because it was *complicated*? Welcome to the world, Mum: everything's fucking complicated.'

Norah takes a breath. 'It was what the crying represented: the noise, the dependency. I wasn't a proper mum – or wife. I wasn't a whole person yet, not whole enough for those responsibilities. I was too young and I needed more help, from your dad—'

'Too young? You weren't exactly a sixteen-year-old pushing a buggy around a council estate, were you?'

'No. But I felt too young. Too young to cope with it all. I felt that my life was being drained of anything I loved or enjoyed. I was scared, Ella. It was all slipping away. And I felt stifled. And alone.'

'You had me.' Ella says it so quietly that her words dissolve in the meditation music.

'I know. I know, my darling—' Norah holds out her hand but Ella doesn't move.

'Didn't you like the things we did together? Didn't you like being with me?'

Norah doesn't answer.

'I guess not.' Ella gets up and walks to the door.

'It's like you said, Ella, you don't need me. You have a family, you have Dad and Willa and Fay – Fay loves you all very much.'

Ella spins round. 'Yeah, and she's more of a mum to us than you'll ever be.'

'I never forgot you,' Norah says quietly.

'No? Sure looks like you did.'

'I followed you. I mean—'

'You *followed* me?'

Norah hadn't meant to let this slip, not yet.

'Your campaign, on Twitter.'

Ella blinks. 'You were one of my followers?'

Norah nods.

'God I'm stupid. @onmymind – of course.' Ella kicks the wall.

It was Lily Pegg who'd worked out who Norah was. Not so well disguised after all. *It's the name of one of your songs – on your CD,* she'd written to her in a private message. *We found it on the internet.* They'd started a correspondence. It had made Norah feel closer to Adam and the girls. And when Norah told the Miss Peggs she was ill, they convinced her to come home. *They need to know, dear.*

They hadn't told her about Fay, though: the New Mrs Wells. But then Norah hadn't told them about Nat and Walter either.

Ella tugs at a tuft of her short dark hair and turns away. Norah watches her press the pads of her thumbs to the corners of her eyes. 'All this time . . . ' she mumbles.

'Yes.'

'And even after that, after following me, after seeing how much I wanted you to come home, you still stayed away?'

378

Norah feels that stabbing pain again, by the scar where her left breast used to be. She knew this conversation wouldn't be easy, but all this suddenly feels too much. This room, Willa lying unconscious in a hospital bed down the corridor. Norah has to get this over and done with.

She gets up and takes Ella's hand in both of hers.

'I'm sick, Ella.'

Ella yanks her hand away and opens the door. 'You don't say.'

Norah takes a breath. 'I've got cancer. I had cancer three years ago and I thought I'd dealt with it – I had an operation, I went through all the treatments—'

Ella freezes.

'But it's come back. And it's going to get worse.'

Ella turns round and stares at Norah, her eyes as wide as Willa's. 'I don't understand . . .'

'I came back because I wanted to see you before – I wanted to spend time with you . . . with all of you . . .' her voice trails off.

'You mean you came back because you're going to *die*?'

'It's not like that.'

'If you weren't sick, you would never have come back? Is that what you're saying? Wow, this just gets better and better.'

'No, that's not what I'm saying.'

'Well it sounds like it. It sounds like you would have been more than happy never to let us know where you were or what happened to you or whether you were even alive if you hadn't got ill and scared and decided to come creeping back to us, expecting us to forgive you, to welcome you home, to say that it's okay—'

'Ella, let me explain.'

Ella shakes her head and pushes through the door. Norah

follows and, for a moment they stand together under the bright hospital lights, blinking.

'You can't do this,' says Ella. 'You can't abandon us and then come back and upset everything and make Willa think you're her mum and then reveal that you're going to die. That you're going to leave us for good.' Ella's voice breaks. 'You should have come back before.' She pauses and looks at Norah, her eyes swimming. 'You should never have left, Mum.'

Ella's crying now, big fat drops roll down her cheeks, her skin pale against her dark hair.

Norah grabs Ella's hand and holds it against her chest. For a moment, they stand in silence in the corridor.

'Ella?'

They both look up.

Adam stands at the end of the corridor, staring at them both.

He's holding Nat by the hand. How long has he been there? How much has he heard? And what about Nat? Nat doesn't understand much English, but he picks up on things, like Willa.

Nat runs to Norah and throws his arms around her legs.

'Mama?' He looks up at her, his eyes heavy with tiredness. This has all been too much for him. She lifts him up and holds him against her chest. *'Es ist alles okay,'* she says, kissing him in the folds of his soft neck.

'I think you should leave now, Norah,' Adam says.

'Sorry?'

'We need some time as a family.'

His voice is hard. Something's changed.

Ella stares at him.

He walks up to Ella and puts his arm around her.

'And you're upsetting Ella. You're upsetting all of us by being here.'

The accident. Willa. It's what made up his mind.

'Dad—' Ella starts but he won't listen.

'It's okay, Ella, you were right. None of this would have happened if she'd stayed away.'

Norah has been waiting for this, for Adam to snap out of his indecision, his incessant swaying from side to side. Fay was right: he's changed, grown up, but more than that, he's grown out of Norah. And that's the gamble you take, isn't it? When you want someone to change, that change might mean there's no room left for you.

Ella buries her head in Adam's shoulder, her chest heaving with sobs.

'*Mama, warum weint Ella?*' Why is Ella crying? Nat asks.

'You shouldn't have come back,' Adam blurts out. 'We were happy without you.'

'I have to make sure Willa's okay—'

He clenches his jaw. 'We'll keep you posted.'

'She's my daughter, Adam—'

'You walked out on her,' he says, his voice strong and steady.

'I want to be there for her.'

Adam stares at her. 'You're too late.'

'And Nat, he's you're little boy too.'

Ella turns to look at Norah. She's gone pale, stunned and silent at Adam's authority.

Norah has to tell him too, then he'll understand. 'Ella and I were talking – I was explaining—'

Ella holds up a hand, her eyes glassy, rimmed red, and interrupts: 'Dad's right. You should go.'

'Ella's right,' Adam says. 'You should go, Norah. There's

nothing left to say.' And then he takes his arm from around Ella, yanks his wedding band off his finger, walks over to Norah and holds it out to her.

Norah looks at the gold band and blinks. She can't move.

He drops it on the floor.

Norah watches the ring bounce and spin and settle in a groove between the floor and the wall.

Norah's legs are shaking. She doesn't know if she can make it to the door, let alone out of the hospital.

Ella picks up the ring and hands it to her. 'Take this and go.'

So this is it.

Hadn't she always known that it was foolish to come back? That she'd done too much damage to expect to be forgiven? She wraps her arms tight around Nat's small body, walks past them and disappears down the white corridor.

MONDAY AFTERNOON

Willa

Louis licks Willa's face.

She opens her eyes. They're snuggled up together in the den. He tugs at her jumper and wags his tail. She gets up and it feels the same as when she's sleepwalking, except her legs ache and she can't move one of her arms and there's a thumping in her head.

They walk out into the hall. Everything's white, whiter than usual, like in summer when you stare at the sun.

Willa threads her fingers through Louis's collar and tugs him out onto the street. *Let's go to see the animals at the Ark.* She wants to make sure they're okay after the storm.

Louis nods his head and walks beside her, and then she notices that their feet aren't touching the ground: they're floating above the pavement, above Holdingwell – they're flying!

Empty streets. Empty shops. No one at school, not even a cleaner or the security man.

In a moment, they're standing outside the Ark.

Willa looks in through the windows. Everything's dark. No animals. No nurses or vets.

Where is everyone, Louis?

She hears the sound of a trumpet floating through the morning air. It's that song that Ella loves, 'What a Wonderful World', and the man with the rainbow jumper appears in front of the door to the Ark. He looks at her and his lips smile as he plays. Louis sits at his feet.

Something pulls Willa off the ground.

Louis – I can't go without Louis.

She looks down at the ground, which is speeding away from her. The song keeps playing … *Fields of green … red roses too …* Rainbow Man and Louis are tiny dots on the earth.

Louis!

Shadows stand over her like tall, skinny trees, and then disappear.

Voices rise and fall.

Someone strokes her head.

She blinks and looks up. White walls and strip lights, like the place where Mummy works.

They're looking down at her: Mummy and Daddy and Ella and Sai. But Nat's missing, and Onkel Walter – and so's Mummy Norah.

Ella

@findingmum
Wish she'd never come home. #justgo

Ella slumps into a chair on the other side of the room, gets out her phone and sends a tweet. She tries to convince herself that she and Dad are right about everything being Mum's fault: the accident, Willa lying in a hospital bed, Louis fighting for his life at the vet's. If Mum hadn't come home they'd all be fine. But whenever she closes her eyes she feels Mum holding her hand to her chest and she hears her words: *I wanted to see you before . . .* And then Mrs Moore's voice comes in too: *You have to get to know your mother . . .*

Finding out she was sick? That she was probably going to die? Was that getting to know her?

Ella forces her eyes open. It's not fair, her coming back just because she's sick. She wishes Mum had never come home.

'She's waking up!' Fay cries out. She grabs Willa's hand and holds it to her cheek.

Dad rushes over to the bed, his face softening for the first time since the accident: 'Willa? My darling Willa!'

Ella gets to her feet and runs over to Willa's bed. Willa's eyelids flit open and closed. Her small fingers flutter against the white sheets.

The machines bleep. Nurses rush in. A doctor.

'Willa!' Ella strokes her sister's hair. 'Willa.'

The doctor asks them to leave the room while he checks her over. The nurse says Fay has to leave too, even though she works at the hospital. *You're too close,* she tells her.

It takes an hour for the doctors and nurses to stop fussing and to let them back in to Willa's room.

Although there are black smudges under Willa's eyes, and although her skin's so pale Ella thinks she might be able to see through to her bones, Willa's sitting up in bed, her eyes full of light. And she's smiling. Ella promises herself that she'll never leave Willa again. In all the crap she's spouted, there's one thing Mum was right about: it was Ella's job to look after Willa.

'You're sure Willa's going to be okay?' Dad asks the doctor.

387

'Yes, once we've done a few more checks.' He scratches his forehead. 'But she's been through a lot – she's taken quite a battering. It will take time for her to recover.'

A waking sleep, Ella thinks. *A minimally conscious state* – that's what the doctor said when they brought her in. When she responded to his touch, his instructions, without waking up. Trust Willa to have gone to some limbo that no one understands.

'The arm will take a while to heal,' says the doctor. 'And . . . it would be a good idea for her to stay in bed, at least for a few days.' He smiles. 'Not too much excitement.'

Fay kisses Willa's forehead and closes her eyes. She loves her, thinks Ella. She really loves her.

With the hand that's not in a cast, Willa strokes Fay's hair. 'I'll be fine, Mummy.' Then she frowns. 'Where's Mummy Norah?'

Dad steps forward. 'She's just had to go out for a while.'

Ella's proud of Dad. How at last he's stood up to Mum.

Willa blinks. 'Mummy Norah didn't want to stay?'

'It's okay,' says Fay.

Before Willa woke up, Fay had taken Dad aside and asked him what happened, and he'd kissed her forehead and pulled her into his arms and held her and whispered that it was okay, that he'd sorted everything out. But Fay hadn't looked relieved. She knew, didn't she, about Mum's cancer? That nothing was sorted out. That they were in more of a mess than ever. Mum was dying – they couldn't ignore that, could they?

'What about Nat?' Willa asks.

'Nat's with Mum,' Ella says.

'When are they coming to see me?'

'You need to focus on getting some rest,' says Dad. 'That's all that matters now.'

Willa puts her arms under her and tries to sit up but she collapses against the pillows. 'What about Louis? Is he allowed to see me?'

'Willa ... ' Dad starts, but he's interrupted by a loud knock.

Lily and Rose Pegg's faces appear in the glass bit of the door. Ella's relieved; they'll help distract Willa. She goes to let them in.

The twins dash through the door. It's the first time Ella's seen them without their Chihuahuas.

'We heard—' Lily starts.

'We saw the ambulance,' Rose adds. 'And Walter explained.'

'We've been phoning and phoning the hospital but they kept saying no visitors.'

'We were so worried.'

'So worried.'

They come up to Willa's bed. 'Are you okay, little one?' Rose asks.

Willa smiles. 'Do you want to sign my cast?' She holds up her arm.

'We'll have to get a purple pen from home,' says Lily. 'Do it properly.'

'Where are the Chihuahuas?' asks Willa, looking past them, at the floor.

'They're at home. I don't think they're allowed here.'

'How did you get to the hospital?' Ella asks. The twins don't own a car.

The twins glance at each other. 'Onkel Walter.' They turn to Dad. 'He brought us in the people carrier, and left it in the car park for your dad to drive you all home. He said he'd take the bus back.'

'Was he with Mummy Norah?' Willa asks.

Lily frowns.

Rose shakes her head. 'No. We thought the Old Mrs Wells was here—'

Dad leaps in: 'She had to go out.'

God, how long are they going to keep up this pretence? If Willa wasn't in hospital recovering, Ella would just tell her that Mum had left and that they were never going to see her again. Willa's been fed enough crap; she deserves to hear the truth.

'Is Louis at home?' Willa smiles. 'Maybe he could go and stay with the Chihuahuas for a bit. He'd like that.'

The sisters glance at each other again. Rose's eyes cloud over.

God, no. Please, no, thinks Ella.

Rose sits on the bed beside Willa and takes her hand. 'Willa, dear.' A tear plops down Rose's chubby face.

Willa reaches out and touches Rose's cheek. 'Why are you crying?'

Lily comes to stand behind Rose. 'The thing is, your Onkel Walter had to take Louis to the vet. He wasn't very well after the accident.'

Ella feels like she's been punched in the stomach. Louis. No, not Louis.

Willa looks at Fay. 'He was in the accident?'

Fay nods. 'He tried to save you, Willa.'

Ella can't bear much more of this.

'His heart was weak. He's an old dog—' says Lily.

Willa shakes her head. 'Not *that* old. There are dogs that have got much, much older.'

'I'm afraid that the vet had to put him to sleep.'

The crow shifts in Ella's stomach. She hasn't felt it in a while. Not even when Mum was talking to her earlier. When she was with Sai last night, she thought that maybe it had gone.

'I don't understand . . .' says Willa.

The crow flaps and claws at Ella's ribcage. Its squawk rises up in her throat. She tries to gulp it down but it pushes up, higher and higher. For Christ's sake, just for once say it how it is, thinks Ella. She takes a breath. 'They mean he died, Willa. They mean that Louis is gone.'

For a second, Willa frowns. Then she blinks. And then she smiles. 'No he's not.'

Ella feels herself welling up, like Rose. She can't deal with Willa's crazy optimism. Not with Mum just having walked out. Not with Louis being dead.

'I can feel him,' Willa says. 'He's been looking after me while I've been in hospital. He's fine. Louis is fine.'

Dad clears his throat. 'I think you should rest, Willa. We can explain everything later.'

Willa pulls her hands away from Fay and Ella. 'I want you to explain now.'

'You were knocked over by a van. And so was Louis,' says Ella. 'Louis got poorly. Really poorly He's not with us any more.'

Willa sits up straighter. 'Yes he is.'

And then there's a long silence.

Fay comes over and sits on the bed and sweeps Willa's fringe out of her eyes. 'Willa . . .'

'It's okay, Mummy. He was with me.'

Rose is properly sobbing now. There's a wet patch all the way down the purple flowers on her dress.

'Willa . . . ' Ella starts.

'He was. He was with me just now. And he speaks to me all the time. He doesn't speak to everyone, but he speaks to me. And he can't be gone because otherwise I'd know.' Willa looks past Ella and Mummy and Daddy and Fay. 'Sai?'

Sai steps forward. He smiles at Willa, but Ella can tell that he's forcing himself. He knows how much Louis meant to all of them. 'Isn't your race today?' She turns to Ella. 'Why aren't you warming up?'

Everyone stares at her.

'That's not important right now.' Dad rubs Willa's skinny shoulder blades.

'It is important.' Willa coughs and rubs her eyes.

She needs to rest. She doesn't need to be worrying about some stupid race. But Willa keeps going:

'Ella's trained really hard. And so has Sai. And Louis told me that he thought you'd got really good, Sai, despite your asthma, and that he couldn't wait to see you running over the finishing line.'

Sai turns away and wipes his eyes.

Black feathers clog Ella's lungs.

'And you've raised all that money for the heart charity.' Willa reaches her hand out to Ella. Her fingers are trembling. 'You *have* to do the race.'

Everyone waits for Ella to answer. Ella looks into Willa's eyes; her pale skin makes them brighter than ever.

Ella gulps, takes a breath and then nods. 'Okay.'

The room breathes out. People start shifting again.

'We have to hurry, then,' says Sai. 'The race starts soon.'

'We'll go and make a banner,' says Lily. 'We've got some paint left over from the fence.'

Rose sniffs. 'Yes, a banner.'

'I'll go and get your trainers,' says Sai.

'My trainers?' Ella looks down at the Green Flash plimsolls she has borrowed from Sai.

'Mum went out and rescued them from the bin,' says Sai. 'They're at home.'

The trainers that made Mum feel so close it was like she was running alongside her. Ella told everyone she was doing the race for Sai and his dad, but it was for Mum that she really wanted to run – to make her proud. And now Mum's told her that she's got cancer and Dad's kicked her out and Louis has died and they can't get through to Willa. Ella doesn't know what to think any more.

Willa swings her legs out of bed. 'I'm coming,' she announces.

Fay puts a hand on her shoulder: 'Darling—'

The doctor looks up from his clipboard. He'd been so quiet Ella has forgotten he's there.

'You need to stay in for the night,' he says. 'You might have concussion.'

Willa blinks. 'What's concussion?'

'It means you banged your head when you fell, Willa, and that your brain might have got a bit shaken up, and that it needs time to recover. Quiet time with you lying down here in the hospital,' says Fay.

'My brain didn't get shaken up and it doesn't need time to recover – I don't have concussion, I promise I don't—'

'You don't know if you've got it,' Ella says.

'Yes I do. And I don't. I'm coming.'

'I'm afraid that's not going to be possible,' says the doctor.

Willa sits up straighter. 'But Mummy works here. If she says

393

it's okay, then it's okay. She's a proper surgeon. She saves children all the time.'

The doctor smiles. 'I know. But I don't think she'd want you up and about yet either.'

'Mummy?' Willa looks at Fay, her eyes beaming with hope.

'He's right, Willa.'

Willa's face glows red. She's stubborn; it's something they have in common.

'Why don't we forget the race?' Ella says. 'It's not important.'

'It *is* important.' Willa clenches her fists against the sheets.

Ella's worried that if she doesn't calm down she's going to pass out again.

'You've got to rest, Willa . . . '

'I've got an idea,' says Sai. He walks over to Fay's bag. 'Is this yours, Mrs . . . ?' He looks around. Always so polite, he wouldn't dream of calling a grown-up by their first name. 'Mrs . . . ' He stumbles.

'It's Miss. Miss Bridges. And yes, this is my bag. And you can call me Fay.'

'May I take this out?' He reaches for Fay's iPad.

Fay nods.

He comes over and holds the iPad out to Willa. 'You can watch the whole thing on FaceTime. We'll have our phones on, and it'll be like you're there.'

Ella wants to hug Sai and never let him go.

Willa takes the iPad, flips it open and stares at the screen. 'I don't think it'll be the same—'

'As soon as we finish, we'll come back and tell you all about it,' says Sai.

Willa looks up. 'Promise?'

Sai nods. 'Promise.' Then he heads towards Ella and kisses

her on the cheek. 'I'll go and get your trainers. I'll meet you at the start line.' She leans in to kiss him back but he's already charging through the door. She couldn't have got through this without him.

Willa grabs Fay's hand. 'And will you stay with me, Mummy?'

'Of course,' says Fay. 'We'll watch the race together.'

Ella watches Dad staring at Fay as she gets on to the bed next to Willa and draws her in under her arm, his eyes watery.

As she snuggles into Fay, her eyes falling closed with tiredness, Willa says, 'Go, Ella, hurry – and make sure you win!'

Adam

To avoid bumping into Norah, Adam walks through the garage to the basement stairs.

Go home and get the camera, Fay whispered in his ear as he left the hospital.

It was always like this. No matter how busy or rushed or tired or stressed they were, Fay refused to let go of the details. It's the sort of thing that used to drive him crazy. It's what makes him love her now.

You'll regret not capturing Ella's special moment, she added.

And that was another thing. No matter how bad things got between them, Fay had never given up on Ella, had never showed less love or care for her than she had for Willa. Adam loved Fay for that too.

When you love someone, Dad, it's not because of the things they do . . . It's because of who they are in here. He can see Ella pointing to her heart. *You fall in love with their essence or their soul . . .* Ella's words had danced around in his head all weekend. He'd been scared that, if she was right, it meant that he didn't love Fay, not properly. But watching Fay holding Willa in the hospital bed, he realised that Ella had only been half right. That when you really love someone you love them for who they are *and* for what they do. All those things Fay had done for them since Norah left, they were her. The fact that she'd stayed — that was her too. They made up the woman he loves.

He'd left Ella at the start line of the race to get ready, and said he'd be back in a few minutes. He had to hurry. Grab his camera and drive back.

As he walks down to his basement studio, he hears the shuffling of papers. A moment later, he sees her.

'What are you doing?' He goes up to her and takes the photographs out of her hands.

She looks up at him. 'How's Willa?'

'I asked you to leave.'

He looks around the studio and then walks over to his desk, picks up his camera case and slings it over his shoulder.

'Adam?'

'She's going to be okay.'

'Thank God.' She holds her hands to her chest; her fingers are shaking.

'So you can go with a clear conscience,' he adds.

He stares down at the pile of photos in his hands. Fay in the swimming pool with two-year-old Willa; Fay dressed up in her scrubs for a fancy dress party they'd been to one

Halloween; Fay holding on to Ella's handlebars, teaching her to ride a bike; Fay in a red dress on her thirty-fifth birthday. He'd wanted to propose to her then but, as always, he'd been too scared. *What if she leaves me?* he'd thought. *What if I find myself alone again?*

He steps back from Norah. 'I've got to go. Make sure you've left before I'm back.'

'Why didn't you put the photographs up?' Norah walks towards him and touches the pictures in his hands.

He pulls away. 'She told me not to.'

'Because she didn't like them—?'

'For Christ's sake, Norah, don't you get it? She didn't want me to put them up because she knew you'd come home. She didn't want to let herself believe that the life she had with us was for ever.' He looks down at a photo of Fay and Ella painting in the kitchen, coloured brushstrokes on their cheeks, the warmest smiles in the world.

'I know you're angry – it's normal, after everything. I get it, Adam. Ella's right, and so are you: it was my fault that all this happened, that Willa got hurt. I shouldn't have come home. God . . . I'm sorry, Adam . . . I'm so sorry.' She's staring at the photos of Fay, shaking her head, her lips trembling. 'I'm so sorry.'

He wants to leave here there, to let it sink in until it hurts, like it hurts him every time he thinks about how much he let her down, that he was the reason she left, that all their lives – Ella's, Willa's, Fay's, Norah's – would have turned out differently if only he'd got things right. But he can't. He pulls her towards him and puts his arm around her shoulders and draws her into his chest.

'I'm glad you came home,' he whispers into her hair. 'We

397

needed you to come home.' He kisses her forehead, then lets go of her and steps back. 'But now we need some time to sort all this out.'

She nods and walks to the stairs. Then she turns round.

'Why are you here?' she asks. 'I mean, why aren't you still at the hospital?'

'Ella's doing the race. Fay told me to get the camera.'

'Wow, she's good,' Norah says.

'I don't understand.'

'Fay sent you back to collect the camera because she knew I'd be here. That I'd be here packing with Walter and Nat.' Norah pauses. 'She wanted us to talk.'

Adam thinks of Fay, sitting on the hospital bed with Willa, and he realises that there's nowhere in the world he'd rather be than there with her, holding her and their little girl.

'Can I say something?' Norah asks.

Adam waits for her to continue.

'You don't need her,' Norah says.

Adam looks up. 'What the hell—?'

Norah holds up a hand. 'I don't mean it like that. I'm not saying you shouldn't be together . . . '

'I don't think we should talk about this.'

Norah holds his gaze. 'I don't think there's anything we should talk about *but* this.'

There's a pause.

'There's something I learnt, Adam, while I was away. About us.'

'That you married the wrong man?'

'No. I'll never think that.' She folds her arms over her chest. 'I learnt that we have to be able to be alone first.'

'First?'

She nods. 'Before we love someone else.'

'I'm glad you found enlightenment.' He doesn't have time for this journey of discovery crap. Not with Willa in hospital, not with Ella waiting for him.

'Fay gets it,' Norah goes on. 'She got it way before we did.' She looks over at the photos. 'Maybe she always understood.'

Adam clenches his jaw. 'What did she understand?'

'That needing someone, that being with someone because you're scared of being alone – or because you can't function without them – isn't love.'

'That's not how it is between us.'

For a moment, Adam realises that he isn't sure who us means.

'Yes it was, Adam. You know it was.' Norah smiles lightly. 'There was more, of course, but that was at the root of it.'

'I don't see what that has to do with me and—'

'Don't make the same mistake.'

Norah waits for Adam to respond, and when he doesn't she turns away and walks towards the stairs that lead back up into the house. And then she stops and turns round again.

'Adam?'

He looks up at her.

'There's something you should know.'

He feels something sinking in his chest.

'What is it?'

But then she shakes her head.

'Just tell them I love them ... When they're ready to hear it. Tell all of them that I love them.' She takes a breath. 'And that I'm sorry.' She pulls the keys he gave her three days ago from her pocket, walks over to him, places them in the palm of his hand, kisses his cheek and leaves.

Willa

Mummy's got her arm around Willa; they're lying together on the hospital bed, snuggled in close, like in Mummy and Daddy's big bed at home. Mummy's holding her iPad so they can both watch the race and Daddy's doing a really good job of holding his phone up properly so they can see. Daddy's turning out to be really brave and clever, like Foxy Fox. She'll have to remember to tell him when he comes back after the race.

Willa tries to concentrate on the screen but her eyelids are heavy. The picture of Ella warming up blurs in and out of focus. *Don't sleep* . . . Willa orders herself, but she can feel her eyes dropping shut.

Louis. She smiles. He puts his head on her lap and she rubs him between the ears. *Why's Sai not there yet, Louis? All he had to do was to run home and get Ella's trainers and come straight to the start line.*

Mummy gets up off the bed. 'I've just got to speak to the doctor,' she says. 'I'll be back in a second.'

But as Mummy goes through the door Willa sees her taking her phone out of her bag and looking up a number. She wonders who she's calling, especially as everyone is at the race.

Willa climbs out of bed. Her legs feel wobbly and everything aches, much more than it ached earlier. She's got a headache too: it's thump, thump, thumping away like a palm bashing into the back of her skull. She breathes in and wills her legs to carry her to the door.

She stands by the door and sees Mummy standing in the corridor talking on her phone.

It's me, Ella hears Mummy says.

You only say *it's me* when someone knows your voice really well. It's what Mummy says to Daddy, except it can't be Daddy because he's got his phone linked to the iPad. And it can't be Ella because she's getting ready for the race.

Go and watch her ... Mummy says. She's whispering so it's hard to make out, and Willa's scared that she'll rush back in and find her out of bed and get cross – mainly because she's out of bed, but also because she shouldn't be eavesdropping on a private conversation. But she'll risk staying for a little bit longer: Mummy's only just started the conversation.

Ella needs you.

Why's she talking about Ella?

After the race, you can leave, if that's what you want to do ...

After the race? And what does she mean by *go*? Go where? Willa scratches her scar. It burns.

This isn't about us ... Mummy goes on. *I don't want to talk about what happened, not now* ... Mummy's voice gets louder. *Yes, she'll be okay. Physically, anyway ... Am I angry? Of course I'm bloody angry* ...

Mummy doesn't swear. Not unless there's a really good reason.

And why's she angry?

What do you expect? She nearly died.

Willa's legs feel wobblier than wobbly. And her tummy's achy. She hasn't eaten for ages, so maybe it's that she's hungry – except she doesn't feel hungry. She feels sick. Willa scratches her scar again. It's coming back to her ... Louis bounding up the road towards them ... and the van ...

401

She needs to get back to bed or she'll crumple in a big heap right here by the door and then the doctor will fuss and she'll have to stay in for even longer.

Yes, I sent him to get the camera . . . Mummy says.

Willa knew it. Dad wouldn't want Ella to cross the finishing line without him taking a picture.

For Christ's sake. Mummy's voice is high-pitched and agitated, like when she's talking about the government and the hospital and there not being enough money. Or when she's been upset by Ella, except they're friends now, which is one of the best things to have happened all weekend.

For once in your life think about what you're doing. It will break her heart if you're not there. Mummy's shouting now. Properly shouting. Shouting so much that, as Willa leans into the crack of the door, she can see the doctors and nurses looking at her weirdly. They probably haven't heard her shout before. Or swear. *I'm going to hang up now.*

Mummy jabs at her phone and shoves it into her bag.

Willa staggers back onto the bed and picks up the iPad.

Mummy comes back in and sits beside her. 'You look flushed, Willa.' She leans in and kisses her. And then she scrunches up her brow. 'And you're all hot.'

'Am I?'

'Are you feeling okay?'

Willa nods. 'I'm just excited about the race.' Which isn't a lie, is it? Not a proper one.

Willa holds up the iPad for both of them to see.

On the screen, Ella takes off her plimsolls and rubs one of her ankles; it's twice as big as the other one.

'ELLA – WHAT HAPPENED TO YOUR ANKLE?' Willa yells into the iPad.

402

Daddy repeats the question to Ella, then hands her his phone. Yes, Daddy's definitely being brave and clever.

Ella's face fills the screen.

'It's nothing,' says Ella. But Willa knows what Ella's nothings mean. And she can tell it hurts because every time Ella touches it her mouth goes tight.

Daddy adjusts the camera that's hanging around his neck and then swings his phone over the line of spectators behind the metal barriers.

Willa whispers to Louis in her head: *Look, the Miss Peggs with their Chihuahuas!*

They've made a banner, like they said they would. It's got *Go Ella!* written in the purple paint they've been using for their fence.

Willa feels the thump of Louis's tail.

A man in a yellow quilted jacket yells through a megaphone: 'Please could all runners make their way to the start line.'

Ella cranes her neck – she's looking for Sai, Willa can tell. Then she drops her shoulders and walks slowly to the start line.

Please, Willa prays. *Please make Sai get there on time.* She looks down at Louis. *You'll make sure he comes, won't you, Louis?*

In front of the runners, the big digital clock that's been fixed to the front of Superdrug blinks down the seconds.

The runners get into a long line. Some of them are stretching and others are bobbing up and down on the spot and others are closing their eyes and praying or wishing. Willa uses the opportunity to wish too: *I wish that Ella and Sai win the race and get lots of money for the heart charity and that when the race is over everyone is happy again.*

Willa yawns and rubs her eyes.

Mummy squeezes her hand. 'You can sleep for a bit – I'll wake you when the race gets going. The beginning won't be that interesting.'

Willa shakes her head. 'No. I want to see the whole thing.' Willa's so tired that if she lets her eyes drop shut she won't be able to get them open again, and she's worried that if she drifts off and stops wishing Ella might not win and Ella *has* to win.

'Sai!' Daddy's voice booms through the iPad. He actually sounds like he's pleased to see him, which makes Willa feel happy. Daddy liking Sai is another reason she thinks he's like Foxy Fox at the end of the film: he's understood what's important, like Ella loving Sai, and that it's silly to stop them.

Daddy changes the angle of the phone and Willa spots Sai in his hoodie: a red dot bobbing up and down as he runs towards the start line.

'He's coming! Sai's coming!' Willa wants to get out of her bed and jump up and down but Mummy gives her a *calm down* look.

Sai's got Mummy Norah's old trainers dangling from his hand. Which makes Willa remember that no one's told her where Mummy Norah is, and Nat and Onkel Walter; they'd want to see the race.

'Sai's nearly there!' Willa says. 'They have to let him run.'

'I think he'll make it,' Mummy says.

The phone goes wobbly as Daddy follows Sai weaving through the crowd. Megaphone Man yells, 'On your marks ...'

The runners get onto their toes, their bodies lean forward. 'Set!'

'They're not waiting for Sai,' Willa says. 'They're not.' Sai *has* to run with Ella – that was the plan. Otherwise he won't get the money for the charity that helps people's hearts.

'Willa—' Mummy puts a hand on Willa's shoulder to calm her down, but Willa's kneeling up on the bed, her cheeks flushed, her eyes dancing with excitement.

Daddy must be running because the screen goes shaky and then they hear him yelling at Megaphone Man: 'Graham – stop!'

The man lowers his megaphone and spins round.

'You tell him, Daddy!' Willa yells into the iPad.

Megaphone Man's brow folds into a big crease, and then his eyes go wide and he smiles.

Willa wonders where Mummy Norah is. Ella used to tell Willa how, every year, they'd all go and support Auntie Norah – who's Mummy Norah – running the 10k and how, most years, she won. *She's amazing at everything,* Ella would say. Except, from what Ella said yesterday, Mummy Norah wasn't good at staying with them and being a mummy. But she seems to be a good mummy to Nat, so she can't be that bad at it. And she came back, didn't she?

'Is Ella good at running because she caught it from Mummy Norah?' Willa asks Mummy.

'Caught it?'

Willa nods. 'Mr Mann told us that you catch things from your parents and it makes you be like them.'

Mummy blushes. 'Inherit – not catch.'

'So did Ella inherit her running from Mummy Norah?'

Mummy doesn't answer. Every time Willa mentions Mummy Norah, Mummy goes quiet.

Willa wonders whether she's inherited anything from Mummy Norah or whether, because Mummy Norah left when Willa was so little, she didn't have time to pass things on to her like she did to Ella.

They both turn back to the screen. Ella's standing on tiptoes, staring at Megaphone Man and Daddy, and Sai, who's joined in their conversation.

Some of the runners look cross that they're being made to wait.

Come on Louis, Willa whispers. *Make the man say yes. Do it for Ella.*

Then Megaphone Man nods and juts his chin to the start line and Sai goes and joins Ella.

Willa claps her hands and bounces up and down on the bed. She closes her eyes and sees Louis's droopy brown eyes. *I knew you'd get Sai here.*

When Willa looks back at the iPad she spots Sai handing Ella the trainers and, for a second Ella hesitates, but then she whips off the plimsolls that are far too big for her and laces up the old, worn trainers that she used for her training runs with Sai and Louis. Sai's face is as red as his hoodie and sweaty and bends over to catch his breath. He pulls an inhaler out of his pocket and presses the pump bit and breathes in. He'll have run further than anyone in the race, that's for sure.

'Is Sai okay?' Willa asks.

Mummy says 'yes', but frowns at the same time.

Ella grabs Sai's hand and gives him a kiss, right on the lips, in front of everyone. Willa wishes she were there in person so that she could see Daddy's face, because even if he's brave and clever and understanding like Foxy Fox, he's still Daddy and Daddy wouldn't have liked that.

'Set!' the man yells.

The picture disappears.

'DAD! WE'RE MISSING IT!' Willa yells.

'He's probably taking a photo,' Mummy says. 'Give him a minute.'

Willa hadn't thought about how hard it would be to hold the phone and take photos with his camera. He could take photos with his phone, but he says it's not the same. Real photographers use real cameras.

The picture wobbles back to the start line.

The runners press in to each other.

The man raises his starting gun in the air.

'Go!' He fires the gun and it's so loud that it makes Willa jump and think she should start running too.

On the floor next to Willa's bed, Louis jumps in the air and wags his tail. Willa can tell that he wishes he were doing the race with Ella and Sai.

Maybe next year, says Willa. *When you've trained some more.*

'What did you say, Willa?' Mummy asks.

'Oh, nothing.' Willa's head feels heavy and her broken arm is sore, but she doesn't want to tell Mummy in case she worries and makes her stop watching the race.

For a while they don't see anything because Daddy says they should go and get the car and drive to the halfway point to see Ella and Sai run past.

Louis's not in the hospital room, he's sitting on the front seat of the car next to Daddy and his breath is steaming up the windscreen.

She hopes that Mummy Norah and Nat and Onkel Walter will join them soon. She likes that her family has got this big — how more people keep joining, like the different animals in the den from *Fantastic Mr Fox*. And she's getting used to the idea of having two mummies. And having a little brother could be fun too. And an *Onkel*. They're going to be the best family in the entire world.

Fay

Fay pulls Willa in to her arms and closes her eyes. The warmth of her, the soft smell of her skin, reminds Fay of the hours she spent holding Willa when she was a baby. She would lie beside her all night, listening to her breathing, scared then, too, that she might lose her.

I told Norah to leave, Adam said to Fay.

Which meant Norah hadn't told him about the cancer.

So Fay had sent him back to the house. Norah couldn't leave like this, in the middle of a row. It would be like the first time, all of them left hanging, unable to get on with their lives. It would be worse: Norah was sick, she might not make it.

No, she can't let Norah leave. Fay knows that she's the one who has to go home.

She looks back at the screen.

Because of the traffic around Holdingwell, it takes a while for Adam to reach the halfway point of the race, but they get there just in time to see the first few runners go past.

Willa squirms under Fay's arm, grabs the iPad and looks closer. 'It's only grown-ups going past, Mummy. That means Ella's still in with a chance of winning the junior category.' Willa points at the screen. 'Hold it up more, Daddy!'

The screen shifts.

'By the Animal Ark – look!' Willa yells. 'She's there!'

The screen stops. It's Norah. She's standing there, in the middle of all the other spectators.

So she listened to Fay: she came.

'Back to the runners, Daddy!' says Willa. 'We don't want to miss Ella!'

For a moment the screen doesn't move off Norah, but then it shifts again.

Ella pushes her way through the runners.

'Look! It's Ella!'

'Try to stay calm,' Fay says again. She can feel Willa's tiredness, how much she's straining to stay awake.

Ella's putting most of her weight on her good foot so her run is a bit lopsided, but she's still going fast.

'Ella! Ella! Ella!' yells Willa

'Go Ella! Show them what you're made of!' Adam's voice booms over the crowd.

Fay claps her hands – she can't help being excited. Over this weekend, Ella's come back to her – she's got that, at least.

Ella glances at the crowd and slows down. She must have spotted Norah because she frowns, then looks back round to the front and starts running even faster.

'Mummy? What's happening?'

Willa scratches her scar. Fay pulls her hand away.

Willa looks up at her. 'Ella must have known all along that Auntie Norah wasn't Auntie Norah but Mummy Norah. All those pictures in her room and the fact that she learned the trumpet and kept her trainers and wore them all the time – it means that she really missed Mummy Norah, that she loves her. Doesn't it?'

'Yes, my darling, Ella loves Mummy Norah.'

'But why's Ella so angry with her then – just like she used to be angry with you, Mummy?'

'Ella hasn't seen Mummy Norah in a long time. She has to get used to her again.'

'I think Mummy Norah's nice.'

Fay's chest tightens. 'Yes, she's nice.'

'Maybe Ella doesn't like mummies.'

'Maybe.'

'When the race is over and we're all living together back at the house – because Mummy Norah and Onkel Walter and Nat have to stay now, they're part of the family – once everything is back to normal and we're all used to each other, maybe Ella will see that Mummy Norah is okay – not as nice as you, Mummy' – Willa tucks her head into Fay's shoulder – 'but nice enough for her to like her again, like she used to before she left.'

Fay gulps. What's she meant to say? *Your wish will never come true – it can't . . . happy families, really happy families, only exist in stories.*

Children get used to anything, don't they? They love intensely, and then forget. In a few months, she'll wonder why she ever called Fay Mummy.

Willa looks back at the screen. 'Why isn't Sai running with Ella?'

They look over the heads of the runners.

'Maybe he ran past before Daddy got to the 5k mark.'

Willa shakes her head. 'Ella wanted them to run together – and anyway, she's faster than him.' Willa takes a breath and yells at the iPad: 'DADDY – WHERE'S SAI?'

Adam's face appears on the screen.

'I'll walk back along the route to see if we can spot him,' says Adam. 'Don't worry, Willa, I'll find him.'

For a while, the screen goes fuzzy.

'Why's Daddy wearing his glasses?' Willa asks.

Adam hasn't worn his glasses in the day for a long time.

'His eyes are tired, and when your eyes are tired they're too sore for contact lenses.'

'I quite like Daddy with glasses.'

'You do?'

Willa smiles. 'They're like a disguise.'

'What's he meant to be disguising?'

'You know, like Superman. In real life he has glasses because they make him look kind of ordinary and geeky, so that no one knows who he really is—'

'A superhero?'

Adam the superhero. She wishes he could hear Willa.

'Exactly!' Willa tilts her head to one side. 'I've always thought Foxy Fox should have glasses. It would make him look cleverer.'

'Daddy used to wear glasses all the time,' Fay says.

'When Mummy Norah was here?'

Fay nods.

Fay had persuaded him to wear contacts, had said that glasses masked his kind eyes. Bit by bit, she'd fixed him. But maybe Willa was right, maybe the glasses worked – maybe she'd gone too far.

The screen goes blank for a good five minutes. Then it blinks back to life. A paramedic bends over a guy in a red T-shirt. It's Sai and he's sitting on the pavement, his head between his knees, his inhaler in his hand. An Indian woman sits next to him; the hem of her sari sweeps the road. She rubs his back and whispers in his ear.

'SAI, ARE YOU OKAY?' Willa yells at the screen.

'Quietly,' Fay says.

'I want him to hear me.'

'Look, Louis is there, sitting at Sai's feet.'

'Oh darling.' Fay strokes Willa's hair.

Adam holds his phone to Sai's mouth. All they can hear is his wheezy breath, but he's smiling. He coughs. 'I'm fine, Willa. Just fine.'

'No you're not!' says Willa. 'You've been training with Ella and Louis all winter and you've raised all that money for the heart charity—' Willa turns round to Fay. 'Mummy, all those people won't pay their money if Sai doesn't finish his race.'

'I'm sure they'll understand,' says Fay. 'And if they don't, Daddy and I will give him the money. Sai's part of our family now.' And then she feels a jolt. It's no longer *her* family, is it? Why can't she get used to that?

Sai's voice comes back through the screen. 'Don't ... ' He takes a breath. 'Don't tell Ella.'

But Fay knows that the minute Ella realises Sai isn't following her, she'll turn back.

'She'll work it out, Sai.' Norah's voice.

Sai takes a puff of his inhaler. Then he starts coughing again.

The woman puts her arm around his shoulders and whispers 'Shush ... shush now ... ' She has the same almond-shaped eyes as Sai, brown and filled with light. Fay looks at Willa and wishes that she had something of her, some small mark to account for six years of being her mother.

Sai's voice again. 'Then tell her I want her to keep running – for both of us.'

How were they meant to do that? It would take ages to get back to the car, especially with so many people in the way, and even if one of them started running now there's no way they'd catch up with her.

Willa tugs at Fay's sleeve. 'Can I speak to Mummy Norah?'

412

'Mummy Norah?'

Willa nods. 'I've got an idea. And she's the only one who can help.'

'MUMMY NORAH?' Willa shouts at the iPad. 'DADDY – GIVE MUMMY NORAH THE PHONE!'

'You don't need to shout,' says Fay.

'Sorry. *Mummy Norah*,' she whispers.

Adam hands Norah the phone. Her face appears on the screen, lines fanning out from the sides of her eyes. Fay never thought her best friend would grow old. Peter Pan, that's who she was meant to be.

'Can you still run?' Willa asks Norah.

'Sorry?'

'Can you still run, like you used to?'

Norah shrugs. 'Not quite as fast, but yes, I can run.'

'You need to catch up with Ella and tell her that Sai is okay and that she has to keep going – that he doesn't want her to turn back. Ella's got a bad ankle, so she's not as fast as usual. You'll be able to catch her up—'

Maybe this is what Willa's inherited from me, thinks Fay. She smiles to herself: *caught* from me. The need to fix everything.

'She won't listen to me, Willa,' says Norah.

'She will. I promise. And then she'll finish the race.'

Willa's refusal to believe in anything but the best outcome – Fay will miss that.

'I'm not sure . . . ' Norah looks at Adam.

'Go, Norah,' he says. 'Go.'

'But you said—'

'Go.'

Adam holds up the phone so that they can watch Norah

climbing over the barrier onto the course, to join the runners. In a few seconds, she's gone.

Willa grabs Fay's hand. 'Louis will make sure that Ella listens to Mummy Norah,' Willa says. 'I've asked him.'

Fay kisses Willa's small, pudgy hand. She loves that dog so much she's wished him back to life.

Norah

Ella needs you, that's what Fay had said on the phone.

So she left Walter and Nat at the house. She'll do this one last thing and then they'll go.

As Norah runs along the route she's taken so many times, she feels like a stranger. The sun pierces through the clouds, sharp and bright after the rain; it lights up the Great Escape, the Holdingwell Café, the post office, the Three Feathers, the bus stop, the park, Holdingwell Primary, the Animal Ark. They're just as she remembered.

She'd thought that when you chose to leave a place, a door slammed shut and life went on without you. But perhaps Holdingwell had never let her go.

Norah splashes through the puddles from last night's rain and kicks away twigs and branches from the storm.

She's glad she didn't tell Adam the truth. It wouldn't have been fair; he'd have felt obligated, and that wasn't love.

As she runs past the park she thinks about how she lay spinning in the dark on the night Fay and Adam found her. A thought

414

hits her: was she the one who brought Adam and Fay together, her sleeping body the prop that drew them to each other?

Yells and whistles and claps fill Norah's ears. She keeps running, her eyes set ahead of her, lost in the slap, slap, slap of her pumps against the tarmac. She knows that she's the last person Ella will want to see, but she couldn't say no to Willa. There's too much to make up for already.

The taste of blood fills her mouth. She hasn't eaten anything today, and she can't remember the last time she's run this fast. But she keeps going.

Ahead of her, the wall of runners fractures. Someone knocks into her from behind and kicks her heels.

'Why are you slowing down?' he snaps.

'Sorry . . . I don't know – something's happening ahead.'

A few yards in front of them a man's voice rises above the runners, hoarse and loud: 'What do you think you're doing?'

'Get out of my way!' A voice Norah would recognise anywhere.

A moment later she sees Ella's short dark hair, her head bobbing up down as she runs towards her. Ella elbows people out of the way as she tears back through the runners.

An official steps forward, reaching for Ella's arm, but she ducks away from him.

'Hey!' The official lurches after Ella but he's not built to run. He shakes his head and steps back to the side.

'Ella!' Norah calls. 'Ella!'

Ella looks Norah up and down and then pushes past her.

Norah runs after her. 'Stop!' she calls.

Ella turns back slowly. Her brown eyes cloud over. She registers that it's Norah and then she says, '*Stop what*, Mum? Stop running?' She laughs. 'That's rich—'

Norah catches Ella up. 'I have something to tell you – from Willa. From Sai.'

Ella's face falls. 'Sai – what's wrong with Sai?'

'He wants you to finish the race. He wants you to keep going.'

'What's happened to him?'

'I think it's his asthma – but it's okay, his mum's there.' She gasps for breath. 'He's going to be fine.'

'We were meant to do this together. That was the deal.'

Ella starts running again. Norah lurches after her and catches the hem of her T-shirt. There's a rip as Ella pulls away.

'What the hell?' Ella says.

A picture flashes across Norah's eyes: Ella, five years old, running beside her at the mothers and daughters' race, her skinny legs, her knees hitched up as she tries to keep up. Ella always wanted to come with Norah. Even then, Ella hated being left behind.

Norah pauses and looks Ella in the eye. 'If you turn round and keep going to the finish line, I'll run with you.'

Ella

@findingmum
Leave me alone. #running

That's the tweet Ella would have sent if she hadn't been running.

Mum's arm brushes Ella's. Ella feels a jolt of electricity.

'Go away!' she says. 'I can do this on my own.' She hates the mean things coming out of her mouth, but she can't help it. A raw anger burns in her stomach, pushing up all those horrible words. Mum thinks she can make up for walking out on them by running for a few stupid miles?

'Pretend I'm not here,' says Mum.

Sai wants her to finish the race; that's the only reason she's not going back for him. She wants to make him happy. And to raise the money for the British Heart Foundation. Ella used to think she and Sai had something in common: Mum disappearing, his dad dying. They'd both lost the people they loved most in the world. But now she realises that their situations aren't a bit the same. Sai's dad was a good person – he didn't want to leave Sai. He loved him.

Ella runs faster, hoping she'll lose Mum.

Except Mum doesn't go away. She keeps up with Ella, breathing hard, her face red and sweaty. Someone who's got cancer probably shouldn't be running this hard, but Ella doesn't want to feel sorry for Mum. This isn't about her.

Ella focuses on her breath, the smell of the wet tarmac, the sun breaking through the clouds. And on Sai's face: his dark hair and dark eyebrows and dark skin. So permanent. So unlike Mum, who looked as though she might dissolve into the air at any moment. Maybe that's why Ella loved Sai so much: because she knew he'd never disappear.

'You really care for him, don't you?' Mum says, gasping for breaths between her words.

Ella ignores her and pushes herself to run faster.

She scans the spectators lining the streets. The Miss Peggs have moved from the start and a found a new place to wave their purple *Go Ella!* banner. They gave Ella more sponsorship money than anyone else. Rose holds up one of the Chihuahuas and makes him wave at Ella as she goes past.

They knew about Mum all along, didn't they? God, they'd probably watched her walk out.

Ella thinks that Mum will start lagging soon, but it's like some force is propelling her forward.

She listens to the beat of their feet on the road and the sound of their breathing and notices that they're in sync. For a second she forgets that she's angry. This is what she always wanted, wasn't it? To run with Mum? To be together again?

And then a teenage guy in headphones bashes into the back of Mum. His music's on so loud she can hear it ring out around him.

Mum stumbles.

Before she can stop the words coming out, Ella yells: 'Hey! Watch where you're going! Idiot!' Ella grabs Mum's elbow. 'You okay?'

Mum nods but she's gone pale, and Ella can tell that she's tired and struggling. The force that drove her on came not from her legs or her breath but from the fact that she wanted to be with Ella. She was running to show her that she was sorry. And at that moment, Ella wants to hug her really tight, to tell her how much she's missed her and that she's glad she's home and persuade her to stay, tell her that Dad will come round, that Fay must have some contacts at the hospital, that she'll find a really good doctor for her and that they'll all look after her and make her better.

But then she gets scared. What if Mum gets bored with them? What if she realises that she doesn't love them after all?

That she doesn't like who Ella's become? What if, just when they've got used to her, she dies?

Ella moves away from Mum and starts jogging again, though when Mum joins her she doesn't say anything mean and she doesn't speed up.

Willa

Willa's arm is sore and her head's fuzzy and she wants to sleep, but she has to wait for the end of the race.

She wishes she were there, sitting on Daddy's shoulders, rather than stuck in this stupid hospital bed. But then she looks at Mummy holding the iPad and feels guilty: she should be grateful that Mummy's here, looking after her.

She wonders where Onkel Walter and Nat have got to, and why they're not with Mummy Norah.

It'll be nice to have a little brother to take care of, to be the older sister for a change. She'll teach him to speak English properly and she'll look out for him at school.

When Dad holds his phone to the road, waiting for the runners to come through, Willa looks for Louis but she can't find him; he must have gone off somewhere to get a better view of the race.

'Look Willa, they're coming!' says Mummy.

Willa spots them too, running side by side at exactly the same pace, their arms moving backwards and forwards like they've been programmed to match each other. It doesn't matter that

Ella's chopped off her hair, they still have the same white skin and the same freckles – like sisters.

Louis hasn't shown up yet.

As they reach the finishing line Mummy Norah seems to slow down a bit but Ella motors ahead.

She's made it! She's the first junior to cross the line. She even gets there ahead of some of the grown-ups.

Daddy jumps up and down and Willa wants to hug him – she wants to hug all of them.

'Adam – take a photo!' Mummy says at the screen.

The screen goes the wobbliest it's been all race. And then it freezes on the tarmac while Daddy fiddles with his camera.

Mummy's got the best ideas for when to take photos, and Daddy's brilliant at taking the pictures themselves: they're the perfect team.

Willa's legs twitch. She wants to leap out of bed and skip around and around and around the bed.

The screen goes shaky again, and it's really annoying because Willa wants to see Ella and how she must be smiling her head off at having won.

'HOLD IT STEADY, DADDY!' Willa yells.

A bit more of a wobble and then a steadier hand and the picture comes back into focus.

Willa sees Mummy Norah reach out for Ella to give her a hug, but Ella brushes her off and turns round and starts running back.

'Ella! What are you doing?' cries Daddy.

Mummy Norah stands at the finish line, catching her breath. She's smiling as she watches Ella, like she understands why she's behaving so weirdly. She shouts something, but she's too far away for the iPad to pick it up.

'What did she say?' Willa asks Mummy.

Mummy's eyes have gone all glassy. 'Run like a song. It's what she used to say when Ella was little.'

Willa keeps forgetting that Mummy was around before Willa was born.

She's not sure she knows what *run like a song* means, but it sounds like the kind of thing Ella would like.

Willa looks back at the screen.

'Ella! Over here!' Daddy cries out again. But Ella doesn't seem to hear him, or to see any of them. She just keeps running, as though the race isn't finished yet.

And then it clicks.

Willa turns round to Mummy. 'She's gone back to get Sai, hasn't she? She wouldn't leave him behind.'

And maybe Louis's gone back to do the same.

Ella wouldn't leave behind anyone that she loves. And that's when Willa understands about Mummy Norah and why Ella is so cross with her.

Willa

'Willa ... Willa ... ' Mummy's voice comes through the fog.

Willa sits up in bed. She feels dizzy.

'I didn't want to fall asleep!'

'It's okay, you haven't missed anything.'

Willa looks up at the hospital clock. It's been twenty-seven minutes since Ella turned round to look for Sai. On the screen she can see that most of the spectators have left. The officials are clearing up the water bottles and the orange quarters and the banners.

She hears a funny voice she doesn't recognise saying, 'They should be coming through soon.'

'Who's that?'

'It's Sai's mummy, Mrs Moore.' Mummy lifts the iPad screen to her mouth and says, 'Is Sai okay?' Mummy's always worrying because she's a surgeon and she sees lots of really poorly children.

'I couldn't stop him,' Mrs Moore says. 'He wanted to finish the race, even if it meant walking all the way. I could not change his mind. And then Ella turned up and he was so happy it was as if he had forgotten his asthma attack and how worn out he was, and they set off together.'

'Over there!' Daddy's voice.

The screen scans the bit of road leading up to the finish line.

'Hold this, please,' Daddy says, giving Mrs Moore the phone. On the screen Willa can see Daddy holding his camera to his eyes.

'You need to hold the phone up to the finish line, Mrs Moore!' Willa yells into the phone.

The picture sweeps across the spectators.

And then, in the distance, Willa sees them: they're holding hands, Sai huffing and puffing and Ella running slower than Willa's ever seen her run – but they're not walking, they're definitely jogging. And Louis is running beside them!

The three of them run across the finish line. Ella and Sai give each other a big hug and start kissing. Willa wishes that they'd give Louis a hug too but they're so wrapped up in each other that they don't seem to notice him.

For a moment, everything's a blur and Daddy says that his phone battery's about to run out so he'd better switch it off. Just before he does, though, he holds it up to Sai and Ella again, who are still holding hands and looking at each other with soppy eyes.

'Louis, where's Louis?' Willa asks Mummy. She wants to tell him how proud she is of him for running with Sai and Ella.

'Come on, my darling, you're tired.' Mummy looks at Willa with the same sad eyes she sometimes has when she comes back from a bad day at the hospital.

'Louis was there. I saw him.'

Willa grabs the iPad. 'LOUIS!' she yells into the screen. 'LOUIS!'

As her eyes drop closed, Willa sees Louis standing at the end of the road near the Animal Ark.

Louis! she murmurs. *Over here!*

She feels Mummy stroking her hair but she's too tired to open her eyes.

Louis looks over at Willa. His brown eyes sparkle and he wags his tail.

Louis! Willa calls out again.

But he turns away and runs down the road, his caramel fur blurring into the late afternoon sunshine.

Willa's eyes fly open. It feels like someone's playing the drums inside her head.

'Willa, it's okay.' Mummy runs her fingers through Willa's fringe. 'It's okay.'

But it's not okay. Louis's bounded off and now Willa can't

even hear him in her head any more. She screws shut her eyes. The scar under her eye burns.

Please come back, Louis, she says.

But the words bounce emptily around her head, banging away along with those stupid drums.

MONDAY NIGHT

Ella

Ella can't breathe. She looks around the small hospital room: Walter and Fay and Dad and Sai and Mrs Moore – and Mum – all sitting around Willa. Sai's mum has got them an Indian takeaway to celebrate. Too much noise and too many people and not enough air.

She wonders why Dad didn't tell Mum to get lost again, but it would probably upset Willa and she's been through enough today.

Just on cue, Mum gives Willa a kiss on her forehead, which makes Ella wince.

'Louis will always be with you,' Mum whispers. 'You just have to let go of the Louis you're used to – the big, smelly, noisy Louis who bounces around us and licks our hands and—'

'But I don't want to let go of Louis,' says Willa. Her eyes go watery. Ella's never seen her cry before. Not since the day Mum left.

'I know,' says Mum. 'I know. But if you do, he'll come back.'

Ella wishes Mum would shut up. It's not her job to comfort Willa.

'He will?' asks Willa.

'Don't listen to her,' Ella mumbles.

Mum looks up.

'*You* didn't come back, did you?' Ella says to Mum. 'You

made us wait for years and years. You let us believe you were dead.'

'You thought Mummy Norah was dead?' Willa asks.

Everyone goes really quiet. Even Nat stops scraping at his foil tray.

'I just went away for a little while and your sister wasn't sure where I was.'

'Don't listen to her, Willa,' Ella says. 'She doesn't know anything.' Ella pushes past Mum and storms out the room.

'Long loo break,' says Sai as he comes out through the hospital doors to join Ella in the car park.

It's dark and the stars have come out. Ella sits on a low wall. She's been watching the ambulances come and go.

Although Fay has strapped it up, Ella's ankle throbs.

'I needed some air.'

Sai nods at the cigarette in her hand. 'Strange kind of air.' He takes the cigarette, stubs it out on the wall and flicks it into the bin. Then he leans over and kisses her. His warm breath mingles with the smoke and he's so close that she can feel his heart – the breath and the heart that let him down today.

He pulls away and looks at her. 'My champion,' he says.

'Ditto.' She smiles.

'Why don't you come back in?'

'Not yet.'

She can't cope with it all. Willa lying there, her eyes tired and sad, missing Louis. Nat sitting on Mum's lap, sleeping, making Ella feel guilty for wanting Mum to leave, because it means that he'll miss out on having a family. Dad still angry with Mum, not knowing that she's sick. And Fay, not eating a thing, pregnant with Dad's kid – something else he doesn't know about, that he's messing things up again and that he doesn't even have the chance to make it right.

Ella's head spins. Too many secrets and too many lies.

'So, are you and your mum going to make up, then?' asks Sai.

'Give it a rest, Sai.'

'*Give it a rest?* Christ Ella, you don't know how lucky you are.'

Ella moves away from him. 'Lucky? To have your mum walk out on you when you're a kid? Not to hear from her for years and years – and then to have her turn up out of the blue and give you a crappy excuse for leaving? And for coming back? Anyway, Dad's told her to get lost. By tomorrow she'll be heading back to wherever it is she's come from.'

'You should fight for her to stay.'

'Haven't you listened to a word I've said? I don't want her to stay. She's not my mum any more.'

Sai jumps off the wall and turns away from Ella.

'Don't tell me you're on her side,' she throws at him.

He shakes his head. 'Whatever she's done, she's still your mum. And she *did* come back. And she's been trying to get through to you.'

The crow's flapping again. Flap, flap, flapping so hard Ella wants to scream.

'Mum's ill. And she's not getting better.' Ella takes another cigarette out of her jacket pocket, places it between her fingers and lights it. 'It's the only reason she came back. Not because she loves us or missed us.'

'How ill?'

Ella pauses to draw on her cigarette. 'She's got cancer.'

'What?'

Ella blows a ribbon of smoke into the starry sky. 'She came back to say goodbye.'

'Then you've got an even bigger reason to fight for her, Ella.' His chest wheezes.

Ella shakes her head. 'You don't get it.'

'Don't get it?' He takes out his inhaler and sucks in a few sharp breaths and then goes on: 'I'd have done anything to have just a few more minutes with Dad. A few more seconds, even. And you're too stubborn to give your mum a second chance. You're willing to throw away the time you've got left with her?'

The crow pokes its beak into Ella's ribcage. *See*, it says. *See how selfish you are? How you can't think about anyone but yourself? You're just like Mum. You're worse than Mum.*

Ella steps towards him. 'I'm sorry, Sai. But it's not the same as with you and your dad. Your dad was a good person. He'd never have chosen to leave you.'

Sai steps away, holding up his hands. 'I can't be with you right now.' He puts his inhaler back in his pocket and walks out through the car park. 'Tell my mum I've gone home.'

The world is going to sleep.

It's going to sleep in the attic of Number 77 Willoughby Street, where the teenage girl tosses and turns in her bed. She thinks of the boy she loves and of his words:

I'd have given anything to have just a few more seconds with Dad.

One floor down, The Mother Who Stayed draws the father closer. *This is my last night with him,* she thinks. Once he finds out that The Mother Who Left is ill, he'll ask her to stay.

The father strokes her skin. The accident changed everything. He loves her, his true wife.

Downstairs, the little boy dreams of foxes and dogs and gardens and his two new sisters. He doesn't want to go. This feels like home.

The Mother Who Left sits beside her brother and whispers, *As soon as we can get the tickets, we'll go back to Germany.*

Have you told him? the uncle asks.

She shakes her head. *It wouldn't make a difference. He doesn't want me here. No one does, not after what happened to Willa.*

Across town, in the hospital bed, the little girl thinks of tomorrow, when they'll all be together again.

And above the hospital, above Number 77 Willoughby Street, above Holdingwell, the big dog keeps watch over the people he loves.

TUESDAY MORNING

The sun rises over Holdingwell.

In the white hospital room, the little girl stands at the window. Mummy Norah said that if she wanted Louis to come back, she had to let him go – but she's not sure: what if he feels hurt about her not talking to him any more?

She closes her eyes and sees him running down Willoughby Street. *Please . . . let me keep him a little longer . . .*

Across town, the father cycles to work. *One more day*, he told The Mother Who Left. *Then you need to go*. Once she's gone, he'll propose to Fay and their new life will begin.

On the train heading to London, the little boy sits on his uncle's lap and looks at the electricity wires whizzing past. They're going to London Zoo. *We need to give Mama time to say goodbye to everyone*, Onkel Walter explained when Mama said she was staying behind.

The Mother Who Stayed and the teenage girl sit in the front of the family car. The teenage girl is taking the day off school to collect her little sister from hospital.

Dad needs to know about Mum being sick, she says.

The Mother Who Stayed nods. *But he has to hear it from her.*

The teenage girl looks out at Holdingwell. The world's shifted.

She turns to The Mother Who Stayed:

Whatever happens, you're staying, right?

I'll always be there for you, she says. But the teenage girl knows that isn't an answer.

And in the tall red-brick house, The Mother Who Left puts on her clothes and her coat, walks through the front door and goes to find the man she walked out on six years ago.

Adam

Adam sits at his desk at the recycling plant. He'd had to get away for a while, to sort out the mess in his brain left by the last few days.

When all this is over, I'll find a way to see Nat, he thinks. *Nat will come over for holidays and long weekends. Fay will grow to love him as much as she does the girls.*

Let her sleep, Fay said when they'd found Norah curled under a blanket on the camp bed. *She's exhausted.*

We're all exhausted, he'd thrown back.

It's more than that, Adam.

He'd asked her to explain, but then Nat had come in.

The phone on Adam's desk buzzes.

'There's someone to see you,' says his secretary.

Before he has the chance to answer, the door opens.

'She wouldn't wait,' says his secretary.

His mind flashes back to Friday afternoon, when Ella burst in.

'It's fine,' Adam says and waits for his secretary to leave.

Norah stands in his office, pale, thin, deep shadows under her eyes.

Will he ever stop feeling that pull?

'I got the bus,' she said. 'I thought we should talk.'

'Yes, we should talk.'

She was right. It was time to set things straight before she left.

Norah looks around his office, just like she looked around the house on Friday morning.

'Could we go somewhere – somewhere other than here?' she asks.

He wonders whether, like him, she sees Fay everywhere.

'Sure.' He grabs his jacket from his chair and guides her to the garage at the back of the recycling plant.

They stare at the old Triumph.

'So you kept it?' she asks.

'For special occasions.' Though he can't remember the last time he took it out.

He grabs two helmets out from under the seat and hands one to Norah. They used to ride without helmets, on dirt tracks in the country, on roads where they wouldn't risk getting caught by the police. Fay had objected to it even then, though he'd always thought it was because she was worried about Norah, not Adam. Could it really be true that she'd loved him all this time?

Norah climbs on behind him and he feels her grip his waist. He'd always felt he was riding with a child rather than a grown woman, so light he could barely feel the difference from when he was riding on his own.

As he turns out of Holdingwell on to the motorway and speeds up, Norah whispers into his ear, her breath warm: 'I haven't felt this alive in ages . . .'

He thought that was why she'd left, because she needed to feel alive again – that she could only do that without him.

They take the route they always took, to the field and the oak tree. And they sit there in the long grass, leaning against the trunk and share a cigarette. For a while they look up into the branches; patches of sunlight fall across their faces.

This is Norah's kind of garden.

They look at each other for a moment and, at the same time, lean in and kiss.

'A goodbye kiss?' Norah asks, pulling away.

'Yes.'

He's glad they've come here one last time.

Norah sweeps her fingers over the exposed roots of the oak tree. 'I'd like to be buried here,' she says.

She'd always done this: made declarative statements about life and death, her vocabulary dominated by absolutes, by always and for ever. She used to scare him with her words, just like Fay's gentle, measured words made him feel safe. And yet Norah's forever had run out, hadn't it? She'd left. And Fay was the one who'd stayed.

'It's where I've been happiest,' Norah adds. 'It's where I'd like the girls to come.'

'Come on, Norah, don't do this.'

She stubs out her cigarette on a gnarled root. 'There's something I have to tell you, Adam.'

Adam feels his chest constrict. He's heard enough this weekend to last a lifetime.

'Fay's pregnant,' she says.

'She's what?'

Norah smiles at him. 'Noticing was never your strong point, was it?'

His head reels. Pregnant? Christ. Yet it made sense: the sickness, the restlessness, the fullness around her stomach and breasts.

'I didn't want to be the one to tell you – it wasn't my place. But I was worried she might . . . ' Norah rips up a bit of grass. 'After everything that's happened, I was worried . . . '

'She wouldn't, Norah.'

'No, probably not. But anyway, there it is. Now you know.'

He stands up. It doesn't feel right, him sitting here with Norah while Fay's at hospital with the girls, carrying his child.

'Why didn't she tell me?'

'The same reason why women all over the world don't tell men they're pregnant.'

'Because ...'

'Because we don't want the man we love to feel obligated. We want to be chosen, Adam, for who we are. For what we mean to you. Not for some practical reason. Especially *that* reason. And—'

'And?'

'She knows how it turned out for us ... how having kids changed us.'

Adam rubs his brow.

'Things are different now. I'm different.'

She smiles. 'Yes, I think you are.'

He stands up. He needs to go and speak to Fay.

Norah reaches for his hand. 'Wait for her to tell you.' She stands up and touches his arm. 'And stay, just a bit longer. There's something else I have to tell you before I leave.'

Fay

Fay pulls out of the hospital car park. She's got a thumping headache and her eyes keep blurring.

She glances back at Willa in the rear-view mirror. *I nearly lost her, my little girl*. Even when Fay moves out Willa will still be a bit hers, won't she?

Ella slots the *Fantastic Mr Fox* soundtrack into the CD player. Fay notices that her fingertips are pink and raw from having been bitten down so low.

You'll always be a bit mine too, Ella, she thinks.

Ella skips to the last song, 'Let Her Dance'.

As the music kicks in Willa claps her hands: 'Yay!'

'I thought you'd like it,' says Ella, reaching behind her and placing her hand in Willa's palm.

'Can we watch the film again tonight?' Willa asks. 'As it's a special occasion?'

Ella sighs and rolls her eyes, but smiles too.

'Of course,' Fay says.

'And can we get some ice-cream and popcorn and invite everyone to watch – can we have a big cinema in the lounge with Nat and Onkel Walter and Mummy Norah and the Miss Peggs and Sai and Mrs Moore.'

'That sounds nice,' Fay says.

Fay looks out at the road. The glare makes her headache worse. The sun and rain come and go in waves. Everything's shiny and lit up and dripping. She can smell the wet road. She can even smell Louis's fur from the back of the car: that damp, closed-in smell when he got wet – she used to hate it, but now it makes her miss him more than she can bear.

The sun strikes the windscreen.

Her head pounds.

In the distance, a motorbike turns into the road.

Fay blinks.

Steel fenders. *Triumph* printed across the side.

She slams on the brakes, nearly misses the red traffic light at the pedestrian crossing.

It's the Miss Peggs with their three Chihuahuas. They cross the road slowly and then stop and wave at her.

On the other side of the crossing, the motorbike pulls up.

Adam – on the bike he'd promised to get rid of.

'Look, Mummy!' Willa yells from behind. 'It's Daddy ... ' She kicks the back of Fay's seat with excitement.

Lily elbows Rose and whispers something in her ear. They look over at the motorbike and then they look back at Fay.

'He's on a motorbike! And Mummy Norah's riding on the back!'

The light turns green.

A driver behind Fay honks his horn.

Ella takes the nail of her forefinger out of her mouth, leans forward and takes in a sharp breath.

Fay puts the car into gear and pulls away.

The motorbike swerves past them and turns into Willoughby Street.

TUESDAY NIGHT

Willa

Louis? Willa whispers into the dark room. She lies in bed and wipes her tears with the back of her hand.

She's seen other people cry, but she's never cried herself. She thought that maybe it was just one of those things she couldn't do, like how Ella can't sing in tune or Daddy can't see without his contact lenses.

She licks the tears off her hand – they taste salty, like the sea's found its way into her body. Big, salty waves pushing up into her eyes and nose, waves that remind her that Louis isn't here and that he's never coming back.

Her eyes sting. More tears come out, and this time she lets them fall.

She thought that, when she came home from the hospital, everyone was going to be friends again and that they were going to be a big, happy family and that that might make her feel better about Louis not being there, but ever since Mummy saw Daddy on the motorbike with Mummy Norah, she hasn't spoken a word to him.

Without Louis, the house feels cold and echoey. Whenever she thinks of him there's a pulling feeling in her chest that makes it hard to breathe.

Willa swings her legs out from under the duvet and, feeling for the wall with the hand that's not in the cast, she walks up the stairs to Ella's room.

'Ella,' she whispers as she sits on the bed beside her. 'Ella . . . '

Ella groans but doesn't wake up.

Willa takes the Junior 10k medal that she's been wearing over her pyjamas, the one that proves that Ella can run faster than anyone her age, and puts it around Ella's neck. Ella missed the presentation because she went back to get Sai, but the organiser waited for her and when she crossed the finishing line for the second time he hung the medal round her neck and said that the mayor of Holdingwell had heard what she did, and that he was going to double her sponsorship money. And that means more money for the charity that helps people like Sai's daddy and that means that people won't die so often when their hearts don't work. Willa wishes that no one ever had to die.

She looks around Ella's room.

Earlier tonight, Daddy went on to the roof and put some more plastic over the hole in the tiles and Mummy put a bucket in the middle of Ella's floor to catch the drips. She can hear the water now, plop, plop, plopping into the bucket.

We're going to need a new roof, Daddy said. *It's got too bad for a patch-up job.*

The curtains are open and the street lamp outside the house lights up the room. Music plays softly from Ella's stereo. There's a CD case on the side that Willa's never seen before – it's got a picture of Mummy Norah playing the trumpet on the front. Willa notices that a few of the things that Ella got rid of when she emptied her room into binbags, have reappeared . . . It's a good job it was a bank holiday and that the bin men didn't come round to collect things like they usually do on a Monday. Ella's Blu-Tacked the poster of Louis Armstrong back above her desk; the corners are curled up and his face is soggy. She's placed Mummy Norah's trainers, the ones Sai rescued, at the end of her bed. Her trumpet case lies open on a chair by the music stand. And there's a photo on the windowsill of Ella

446

when she was little, littler than Willa, and she's running along-side Mummy Norah, both of them with their red hair fluttering behind them like kites. Ella's grinning so hard you can see all her teeth and her eyes are sparkling too.

Maybe she's forgiven Mummy Norah for leaving when she was little.

She lifts the edge of Ella's duvet. 'Please can I come in?'

Ella shifts over in her sleep and makes space for Willa.

Willa lies next to Ella for what feels like ages, but she still can't get to sleep. She gets up and goes back to the main landing and stands outside Mummy and Daddy's bedroom.

'We have to talk about the baby,' she hears Daddy say.

The baby? Willa's tummy does a summersault. Willa's going to have another little brother or sister, someone even smaller than Nat?

'It doesn't change anything,' Mummy answers. 'I'm going home.'

What does Mummy mean, *going home*? Willa rubs her eyes hard to make sure she's fully awake and then she continues to listen. Willa's never thought of Mummy living anywhere but with them.

'It's time to leave, Adam,' Mummy adds.

Willa's legs go wobbly. She scratches her scar – it feels like it's on fire. Thinking about Mummy not being here makes Willa think of Louis and how he's not here. Willa doesn't know what she'll do if she doesn't have Mummy or Louis around.

Why doesn't Daddy answer? He wouldn't let Mummy go – he loves her too much.

Willa goes down to the lounge. Maybe if she speaks to Mummy Norah she can convince Mummy to stay. Didn't she say that they could both be Willa's mummies?

Nat's asleep on the couch, his body nestled into Onkel Walter's side, his head pushed in under his chin.

The camp bed is empty – no Mummy Norah.

A draught sweeps against Willa's bare legs. The door leading to the garden is open. Mummy Norah stands in her T-shirt, her feet bare on the wet grass. Maybe she's come to look at the foxes. But Willa knows that Mrs Fox won't come back: she's been scared off by the accident. She'll have found another place to have her babies.

The glow from a screen lights up Mummy Norah's face. She's speaking into the phone:

'Yes, we need flight reservations for three – yes, for tomorrow morning ... I know it's late notice ... Yes, I realise it's going to be expensive, but we need to get home. A holiday? No, not quite. Two adults and a child. Heathrow to Berlin. First available flight.'

Willa scratches her scar again. When she lowers her hand she sees that there's blood under her fingernail.

They were meant to be a family. They were meant to stay together. Nat was going to be her little brother and Daddy has to get to know him so that he can love him as much as he loves Willa and Ella and Fay. And Willa was going to have two mummies – and now all of them are leaving.

She has to find a way for them not to leave. She has to get Daddy to make Mummy stay and she has to persuade Ella to be nice to Mummy Norah so that she'll want to stay too. And then Mummy will have the baby and they'll all be happy.

In the tall red-brick house, the world is going to sleep.

Or it's trying to.

In her bed, her knees hitched to her chest, the little girl closes her eyes. Even if she doesn't feel the big dog next to her any more, he must be listening.

If you help me to make everyone happy, if you help me to persuade everyone to stay, I promise I'll let you go, Louis.

In the bathroom, The Mother Who Stayed switches off her phone. She pushes her hair out of her eyes and straightens her spine and looks at herself in the mirror.

We're going to be okay, she says as she thinks of that small dark place inside her body where her baby is growing. *It'll be just the two of us, and we're going to be just fine.*

In his bedroom, the father sits on the end of the bed. Shouldn't he have got used to the thought of her disappearing? God knows he'd had enough practice. And, he was the one who'd told Norah to leave. But this was different: it changed everything. His eyes fall on the photo of him and The Mother Who Stayed. A new life inside her, a life that is part of him. That changed everything. He wants to be strong, to look after them both.

Be brave, like Foxy Fox, wasn't that what Willa was always telling him?

If only he knew how.

In the lounge, The Mother Who Left kisses her little boy and tucks him in. At least it's all said now, she thinks. She looks out at the stars and the moon and wishes, like she's wished since she was a little girl, that she could fly away, that the sky would take her up, up and away.

The teenage girl slips into her little sister's room and climbs into bed beside her and strokes her cheek.

Willa, wake up . . . she whispers. *Willa . . .*

Her little sister has been kept in the dark for too long, she deserves to know the truth – maybe more than anyone.

The little girl opens her eyes and smiles. *You're here?*

The teenage girl nods and then she tells her about The Mother Who Left, how she's not well, how she might not make it, and about The Mother Who Stayed, how she'll soon be family, proper family, because there's a new baby on the way, a baby that belongs to her and to their father – to all of them. And for once, the little girl doesn't ask questions: she just listens, as if she's always known.

WEDNESDAY MORNING

The world is waking up. Or it's trying to, anyway.

It's waking up in the small town of Holdingwell.

It's waking up on Willoughby Street.

It's waking up in Number 77, the tall red-brick house with the scaffolding that stretches up to the roof.

Ella goes back up to her room under the roof and the big dog takes her place beside Willa. He stays with her until the sun rises, and then he looks down on the world.

In front of the house, the roofers sit in their van, eating sandwiches.

We should get the job finished today, one of them says.

The man next to him looks up at the roof and shakes his head.

We'll have to fix the damage from the storm first. Draw up a new estimate.

At the top of the house, dawn tugs at Ella but she's too tired to let it interrupt her sleep.

She dreams that the boy she loves has climbed up the drainpipe and the windowsills and that he's stepped into her bedroom. She dreams that he lies beside her and wraps his arms around her and kisses her.

She opens her eyes and looks at her phone. It's nearly time for school.

She turns and pulls the duvet over her head.

Not yet ... not quite yet.

In the main bedroom, Adam reaches for Fay; he draws her warm body to his and rests his hands on her stomach. He's too tired to notice that she's only just come back to bed, that she's fully dressed, that her bags are packed and waiting.

Downstairs, Nat stands by the front door, his hair ruffled from sleep, his eyelids heavy. Onkel Walter lifts him off the ground and, together with Mama, they step out onto Willoughby Street.

The stairs creak.

The front door slams shut just as Fay comes down the stairs carrying her suitcase.

Louis has only been away for twenty-four hours but already he's learnt the rules: he can watch and he can be present and he can help in small ways, like easing Willa back to sleep, but he mustn't interfere.

Fay walks out of the house and onto Willoughby Street. She doesn't see Norah, Nat and Walter making their way to the bus stop at the other end of the street. She takes off in the opposite direction, her eyes fixed ahead. *It's time to go home,* she whispers to herself.

Louis takes a big breath and barks. And then barks again, over and over.

The barks ricochet off the walls and up the stairs and under the doors and all the way up to the top of the house, to the attic, to the broken roof.

The roofers get out of the van and climb up the scaffolding, whistling.

Ella sits up. The black wings flutter in her stomach.

Louis barks again, this time from outside the house, from

454

under the cherry tree. Tiny green buds push up from its branches. Summer will be here soon.

Through the kitchen window, Ella looks up Willoughby Street. The crow squawks, its beak pecks at her ribcage. She sees three figures heading in the direction of town. A man carrying a little boy. And a woman, her long red hair wrapped around her neck like a scarf.

Ella pushes her feet into her trainers and runs out onto the street.

The man with the rainbow jumper stands on the kerb playing his trumpet. Beside them stands the man with the dreadlocks and dark skin and wooden cross. He gets out his guitar and joins in with the rainbow man's playing ... *trees of green ... red roses too ...*

The girl dressed in black is also there.

Rose Pegg hands out slices of cake and Lily carries round a tray with cups of tea. Her Chihuahuas go up to Louis and play between his legs.

We're so glad you all came, says Lily.

Yes, we weren't sure you'd get our message, says Rose.

When they see Ella running after Norah they all clap and cheer.

Adam reaches out again to the other side of the bed. She's not there.

He puts on his glasses, grabs the box from the dresser, and runs downstairs.

At last, Louis catches up with Fay. He lies down across her feet.

She stumbles and looks back at the house.

Adam looks up Willoughby Street. Fay's there, carrying the suitcase she moved in with.

He breaks into a run.

Back in the house, Willa hears a scratching noise coming

455

from downstairs. And then a series of small yelps. She glances around her room, forgetting for a moment that Louis isn't here. Another yelp. She goes downstairs.

Pushing through the pain in her ankle, Ella runs to the bus stop at the town end of Willoughby Street. The bus that goes to the station pulls up.

The crow flaps and flaps. Ella runs faster.

'Stop!' she calls after her mum. 'Stay!'

The wind has picked up again. It swallows her voice and throws it up to the clouds.

'Mum!'

The crow flies out of her mouth.

As Ella watches the bird soar into the white clouds, she sees that it's not black, like she thought. And it's not screeching. It's twittering and buzzing, its tiny body suspended in the air. It's not a crow at all, it's a tiny hummingbird, its feathers a flash of blue and green, its wings beating so fast they disappear against the blue sky.

Norah turns round and they look at each other.

Ella holds up her hand and waves and remembers the morning when her mother left her at the school gate and thinks, *in the end, she did come back*.

Walter turns round. Nat's asleep in his arms. He whispers something to Norah and Norah leaves her bag on the pavement and runs to Ella.

At the opposite end of the street, Fay stops to catch her breath and then she turns to take one last look at the place that's been her home.

Adam runs towards her, his hand closed around a small, velvet box.

When he reaches her, he gets down on one knee.

She feels a flit in her stomach, a coming to life.

He holds open his palm. A ring.

Marry me, he says.

She takes Adam's hand and lifts him to his feet. As she does, she looks past him, and her eyes fix on Norah. They look at each other, the two mothers standing at either end of Willoughby Street.

Norah holds her hand to her chest and nods gently, and then looks back at Ella and smiles.

Fay turns to Adam and kisses him, and through her kiss she whispers:

Yes.

Back at Number 77 Willoughby Street, Willa stands in the hallway trying to work out where the scratching and the yelping are coming from. A morning breeze sweeps through the house; the back door to the garden has been left open.

A low, quiet bark comes from the den under the stairs.

Louis?

The scar under Willa's left eye feels hot and scratchy but she leaves it alone. She doesn't want it to start bleeding again.

As she gets closer to the den, she notices that the door's been pushed in and that it's lying on its side. A shuffle. The smell of earth and warm breath. A pair of big amber eyes, like warning beacons.

Willa steps closer.

Mrs Fox? She flicks on the small electric light bulb.

Nestled into Mrs Fox are four tiny bodies, eyes clamped shut, small ears in stiff peaks, wet noses, heads covered in dark, spiky fur like Ella's new haircut. Willa knows that this is how they are born: in four weeks, their fur will have turned red like an autumn leaf.

I knew you'd come, Willa whispers.

Mrs Fox gets up and stretches. The cubs tumble backwards. The Mother Who Left licks their heads and pushes them together, closing the gap she's left behind. She holds Willa's gaze for a second and then slinks past her and out into the hall.

Willa runs after her.

Mrs Fox? Willa calls.

But Mrs Fox is already in the lounge.

She darts through the back door.

Runs across the garden.

Ducks under the gooseberry bush.

And then she's gone.

FIVE MONTHS LATER

Willa

Willa looks out of her bedroom window. It's rained all morning but now the sun's setting and everything sparkles – the grass and the pavement and the cars.

They're gathering outside. Ella's sitting on the wall next to Sai; they're both wearing new trainers, white and shiny. They go running together every day. Ella's hair is growing out: long red bits hang down her shoulders; only the ends are still dark, like they've been dipped in ink.

The Miss Peggs are there with their Chihuahuas. They're wearing purple bows in their hair and they've tied purple bows to the cherry tree too.

Mummy Norah kneels under the tree, loosening the earth with a trowel. Sometimes, she looks from Mummy to Daddy with sad eyes, like she's searching for something, but it never lasts long. Most of the time, she smiles.

With his small fingers, Nat helps Mummy Norah dig the earth.

The branches of the tree are dotted with furry green buds. It'll be a few more months before it blossoms.

There are no tiles stacked up in the front garden. And the scaffolding's gone.

Daddy stands by the gate and watches Mummy's car coming down Willoughby Street. She's been working at the hospital and she collected Onkel Walter from the Animal Ark on the way. He's one of the vets there. When Mummy steps out of the car, Daddy darts forward and holds her elbow. Mummy's tummy's so big that she's not very steady on her feet. Willa can't wait for her little brother to be born. She's asked Mummy whether they can call him Louis. Mummy isn't sure yet, but Willa's working on it.

Onkel Walter comes and gives Mummy Norah and Nat a kiss, and then Mummy Norah goes over to Mummy and takes her hand and looks down at her big bump and smiles. Everyone looks at Mummy's big bump these days.

Ella jumps off the wall, runs up the front steps and comes into the hallway.

'Willa!' she calls up the stairs. 'Everyone's here!'

Willa cradles the wooden box in her arms. She's had Louis's ashes in her room for months now, and although the empty feeling hasn't gone away it's helped, knowing that a bit of him is here with her.

She stops on the landing and looks through one of the windows onto the back garden. The fox cubs are more or less grown up now. They sometimes come to say hello, but most of the time they're out having adventures. Willa sees a pair of amber eyes under the gooseberry bush. It's Mrs Fox. She always comes home.

As Willa walks past the den she smiles. When she closes her eyes and lets the pictures form behind her eyelids, she sees Louis. He'll always be here.

Sometimes, Onkel Walter brings home poorly animals from the Animal Ark and puts them in the den for Willa to look after. At first, she was worried that Louis would be upset that she's using his special den for other animals, but then she thinks about how Louis loved everyone – even the foxes in the end – and how he'd want her to be happy and to have animals to look after.

Onkel Walter says not to get too attached to the poorly

animals because some of them won't get better, and that if she lets herself get too close it will make her sad. But Willa ignores him. She knows that sometimes you only get to love someone for a while and that you'd better love them as much as you can before they go away, otherwise you'll regret it.

She walks down the hall and stops in front of a big framed picture of Mummy. She's sitting in the garden surrounded by the peonies she loves. Daddy took it and put it on the wall for everyone to see.

And then Willa goes through the front door.

Ella stands on the top step. She takes her hand and, together, they walk to the cherry tree where the others are waiting for them. Although they don't all live together (Mummy Norah and Onkel Walter and Nat have moved into a house that belonged to Mummy) they're still a family. Mummy Norah's got a silky blue scarf wrapped around her head; it makes her look mysterious, but she wears it because the treatment made all her hair fall out. Mummy explained that, when you've got cancer, the medicine you take makes you sick before it makes you better, that sometimes that's the way things go in life. Willa's decided that, no matter what happens, even if they have rows and get cross at each other, they're going to stick together.

I therefore invite you . . . to stay here with me for ever . . . That's what Foxy Fox said to all the animals. *We will make a little underground village, with streets and houses on each side . . .*

Sai comes over and gives Ella her trumpet case. She puts it on the ground, snaps open the clasps and lifts out her instrument. And then she starts to play Mummy Norah's special song. The words float through the branches of the blossom tree and up into the bright blue sky . . . *and I think to myself . . . what a wonderful world* . . . And Mummy Norah and Mummy are singing along . . . And then Daddy joins in too, and when he does, he looks straight at Mummy . . . *But what they're really saying is I love you* . . .

Mummy Norah looks over at Ella and smiles. Ella still gets cross at Mummy Norah sometimes, and shouts at her for having been away for so long, but sometimes Ella lets her come running with her and Sai, and sometimes Ella lets her give her a trumpet lesson.

Willa eases the lid off the wooden box.

The empty feeling shrinks a bit and it's like she can feel Louis a little closer: his smelly fur from having been out in the rain, his warm breath, the thump of his tail, the sloshy noise he makes when he drinks, his warm tongue licking her palm.

Mummy said that Willa didn't have to scatter his ashes if she didn't want to. Part of Willa's scared that if she empties Louis out onto the ground she'll lose him for ever and that the empty feeling will get bigger again, but then she remembers what Mummy Norah said about letting him go.

Mummy comes over and takes Willa's hand. Willa can feel the sharp bit of Mummy's ring digging into her palm. It's the ring that means that Mummy and Daddy are going to be together for ever.

It marks the start of our big adventure . . . Mummy told Willa.

But Willa's learnt something, this last year of being seven years old: adventures don't have beginnings and endings and they aren't about going away or staying in once place. They're happening all the time, every second: you just need to open your eyes to see them. Louis knew that – for him, every day was an adventure.

'You okay, my darling?' Mummy asks.

Willa nods. She walks up to the cherry tree and turns the box upside down. The ashes fall into the earth that Mummy Norah loosened around the roots. There's a gust of wind and some of the ash swirls up into the cherry tree's branches. There's a second gust, harder this time, and as they all look up, another swirl of ash shoots into the sky, past the gleaming roof tiles and up into the big, yellow sun.